I0684943

The Chess Board

Jim Reay

First published in Brisbane, Queensland in 2015 by Jim Reay

Website: www.jimreaywriter.net

Copyright © James Reay

The moral right of the author is asserted.

All rights reserved.
No part of this publication may be reproduced, stored in a retrieval system or transmitted in any form or by any means without the prior permission of the publisher, nor be otherwise circulated in any form of binding or cover other than that in which it is published.

Disclaimer

All characters and events in this publication, other than those clearly in the public domain, are fictitious and any resemblance to real persons, living or dead, is purely coincidental.

National Library of Australia Cataloguing-in-Publication entry:

Reay, Jim E. – author

The Chess Board / by Jim Reay

9780994377807 (paperback)

Detective and mystery stories
Suspense fiction
Stereotypes (Social psychology) – Fiction
Aboriginal Australians – Queensland – Fiction
Queensland – Fiction

A823.4

Edited by Patrice Shaw (www.psediting.com.au)
Typesetting and cover design by Kirsty Ogden
(www.epiphanyediting.com.au)

The poem, Empty Stock Routes, mentioned in Chapter 61 was written by Cec Fisher OAM and was published in 'Flag of Unity', ISBN 0 7242 5616 4, in 1993

Acknowledgements

Story telling is about sharing ideas, stimulating thinking and bringing enjoyment to the reader.

As I have discovered, there is a huge difference between telling a story and getting the written version to a publishable stage.

I wish to thank all those who have helped in my writing journey: The Queensland Writers' Centre, in particular Nerida Newton with 'The Year of the Novel', Dr Kim Wilkins with 'The Year of the Edit'; Marele Day at the Varuna Crime Writers' Week, Katoomba, NSW; from our writing group: Nicky Boynton-Bricknell, Katrina Bredhauer, Ian Walkley, Linda Heron and Lynette Hodgson; Uncle Albert Holt who read the early drafts of my Murri stories; Larissa 'The Tsarina' and Marg Lane for their ready support; Helena and Aleksei who helped clarify my awareness of some aspects of Russian history; Michael Dempsey for our regular lunchtime philosophising and his patient reading of my manuscripts; Sue Maytom, Aunty Heather Tobane, Aunty Peggy Tidyman, the late Bulloo Dave Tobane, Uncle Tim Kemp and other Elders who have taught me so much over the years.

While some of the story settings and happenings have been in the public domain of history, there might be occasions where not everything will match exactly. There is no intent to falsify information. This is a novel. Some artistic licence is necessary. All major characters and events are fictitious.

Thanks to Kirsty Ogden, of Epiphany Editing & Publishing, who clarified the maze of networks, protocols and requirements in the book publishing trade, as well as designing the page layout and cover. *Website*: www.epiphanyediting.com.au

If the story reads well, it is due in no small part to the wise structural and copy editing of Patrice Shaw, whose astute advice has helped make the final story much more polished. *Website*: www.psediting.com.au

My immediate family deserves considerable credit for giving me the space and encouragement to write; particularly Brenda, my wife – and to my overseas brother, Lewis, who has read all my first manuscripts and short stories.

Your backing has been invaluable in bringing my tales to the page.

Chapter 1

England. 16 December 2008

'My self-esteem is not based on anyone else's opinion of me.'

I shout with joyous defiance. I get that now. The traffic on the M4 whizzes busily past my westward-bound Mercedes, oblivious to my loud voice resonating inside the car. On this wet cold Tuesday, faint clouds of misty condensation puff above the dashing rows of vehicles, hurrying anonymously to be somewhere in the morning air, so much more fervent than on the sleepy highways of the Queensland Darling Downs, my home for the past many months.

The rented Merc is not a status statement, more a reflection of a performance requirement and availability.

I glance at my scrawled name, Spencer Avery, on the car rental agreement which I have tossed on the passenger seat. At one time, I would have been annoyed that my name and title hadn't been neatly typed – or that the document hadn't always been carefully filed in the glove box. I'm so much more relaxed now as my powerful car coasts steadily onwards past Swindon and towards Bristol. Winter has stripped every tree branch; they all stand frozen; silent mournful fingers pleading to the heavens. I sense my lips curling into a smile. My zany humour has returned – I can look at the dreariness of the scene and feel the funny side – as I visualise those trees as statued sentinels, patiently waiting to be *re-leaved* by the next change of shift; to spring.

'Don't snow,' they are saying – and I agree. I have grown to love a less chilling type of atmosphere. The meanings behind that thought maintain my grin, as the cruise control carries me along in the obedient

1

lines of vehicles; impressively conforming – zombie-like. My head tilts back in a spontaneous chortle. How different the world appears. I get it. That old social con is so transparent to me now.

The dashboard display glows on two degrees Celsius – the outside temperature. It was 32° and bright sparkling sunshine when I left the Darling Downs on Friday and a humid 35° when the big jumbo lifted off into blue skies from Brisbane on Sunday – hard to leave the perfect summer but I needed to come back to Britain. I have another type of warmth coursing through my veins – with a need to share and to move on.

The dormant fields around me flash past my speeding windows – bleak; browny-grey and grey-green, imitating the forbidding sky. I'm heading for the M5 and then down into Somerset to see my parents. I wonder what my welcome will be like. I have so much to tell them. Will they recognise the new me?

Huge signs flag the exit: Weston-Super-Mare, Bridgwater, Taunton. I'll be turning off at Taunton and along the A358 to home, nestling in the vale.

I visualise my mother, arms outstretched, hustling me 'into ki'chen' with Dad standing back as fathers do. Mum laying her plate of fresh-cooked scones on a carefully-prepared table. 'Ave one, Spencer. Special made for you. With home-made s'rawbrey jam and clo'ed cream. Your favouri'e.'

Home. It will be good to be back in the comfortable certainty of the old red-stone house; its thick walls, tiled roof and roaring hearth warding off both the cold and any threats against the family peace. I had thought I might never see this place again or feel once more the sincerity of my mother's love. My father's too – Mr Avery, 'draper to the communi'y' – less demonstrative perhaps but every bit as caring.

Will they understand what I have seen and lived through? I feel like an astronaut returning from space. How much do I want to tell them? They are happy in their simple village routine. What did Thomas Gray write?

Let not ambition mock their useful toil,
Their homely joys and destiny obscure,
Nor Grandeur hear with disdainful smile,
The short and simple annals of the poor.

Ah, there is my more recent Cambridge heritage showing through now. And that is a whole other melting pot of images that I will need to address soon enough. For the moment, I savour the language of the old Pembroke College poet, so appropriate for my home – not exactly poor but certainly a homely lifestyle. I appreciate Gray – for his way with words but also because he was one of the few professors with the perverse self-esteem to reject an offer of poet laureate.

It says something about his sense of identity.

I tune the car radio into BBC Somerset and the accent of my childhood flows out. 'Anagram of Rose Stem – one word? C'mon all you ou' there. Wha' is i'?' The words make me feel as if I have never been away and yet I have been so out of touch. 'Somerse', of course. Wha' has bin happening in the world today?'

I know I am grinning as I listen to the prattle – friendly and a bit nutty.

Apart from a sad catalogue of winter traffic accidents, the news is about people in Yeovil buying Christmas food parcels for the homeless; someone has been convicted of a terrorism attack on Glasgow Airport; the US consumer price index is falling and a bailout of American car-makers is a molar-gnashing concession as the world faces a financial crisis.

This is the local Somerset news channel but it has such a ring of familiarity. My mind is back in the Queensland bush in prescient discussions; a prophetic hint of what might now be unfolding on the world scene. What an adventure has enveloped me over these past few months – wrapped in the strands of the mysterious chain of events that had their genesis years before – and played out on the fascinating palette of Australian social priorities. But I was such a different person back then

…

Melbourne, Australia. 17 April 2008

'Dr Spencer Avery, sir?' the chauffeur enquired of me with butleresque politeness. I gave a half-smiling nod as the appropriate response.

Tullamarine airport was bustling; faces alive, alert, thirsty for the next challenge. How wise Toby had been to suggest this sabbatical opportunity.

I would show them — esteemed lecturer arriving from the old country. I felt appropriately valued and important.

How bright the colours had seemed as the plane came in to land. This was my first impression of Australia. The greens were greener and the reds redder. An optical illusion or the visual promise of a new beginning?

Young men with loose-limbed gaits, clad in orderly dark suits. A silver-haired man in pin-stripes stood easily at a baggage carousel beside a laughing family in Polynesian shirts. An electrician and his apprentice, in navy work clothes and boots, grinned as they left the area carrying their tools. Business people, workers, holidayers.

I flicked my casual shirt collar and dusted a hair from my blue jacket. Everything about my dress was quality from the brown Italian shoes to the patrician way I had learned to carry myself — lessons absorbed well.

I had arrived and it felt good.

Outside, the scent of eucalyptus. After the chilly departure from a late London winter, the balmy breeze and blue skies made for a welcoming embrace.

I was the epitome of a young English gentleman breathing the Australian air and walking elegantly to the waiting limousine. This would indeed be the start of a new chapter, a catalyst to even more promise in the years ahead, as I approached the decade of my thirties.

But alas, I didn't understand that the board on which my future would play out had been laid in place long before, not least...

Kiev, USSR. 15 October 1971

She turned again to look at the vanishing aircraft but it had disappeared into the pale Ukrainian sky.

Silently she mouthed her goodbye, 'Dosvedanya'.

What would her six-year-old know of the finality of separation? To him, he was off on a holiday to Australia with Aunt Nina — but Olga knew what it really was. Farewell.

Her Pyotr had gone — only the pain remained; even harder than the funeral of her husband. She panted gently to breathe.

No moisture left for tears. Very slowly her heartbeat steadied and the sharp sadness soothed into a dull oppressive ache.

The cold Friday breeze rolled fragile autumn leaves across the roadway as she left the terminal building.

The soldier, solemn, inscrutable, watched her lonely walk to the car. He held the door open for her. The red pennant on the bonnet fluttered lamely.

She took her seat in the back of the vehicle and, with her grief, moved off to the future she had to serve.

Chapter 2

London. 20 April 2008

Muted city lights glistened over the dark ripples of the Thames. Nocturnal traffic scuttled along famous streets and across river bridges, unaware of the clandestine conversation happening high above. Behind a fifth-floor window, three figures stared out over that peaceful nightscape.

'Sidorov is indeed dead then, confirmed by Moscow? Suicide or murder?' The first raised his dark eyebrow in question.

'My guess is murder, bullet to the head – the end result is the same. It was four months ago. Hushed up by the FSB,' the second replied.

'Mmm.' The third stroked his chin, as he absorbed the information. 'The current agents in the new Russian Federal Security are just as callous as their KGB predecessors.' He paused. 'So only one still remains. Is the plan now fully in place for Australia?'

'*Our* plan is, but possible enemy moves are less predictable,' the second affirmed.

'Any whispers that we are on to them?' The first man turned from the view, in question.

'My word is they are too sure of themselves to worry. Cocky bastards.' The second replied in a mocking tone. 'But they have the name. That's what we know at present. We are monitoring. We don't know exactly which groups are following the trail.'

'Will we warn the Aussies?' the first asked.

A sly grin framed the second's reply. 'The less they know the better, don't you think?'

'Fine, Old Fruit. Let's stay alert.' A half-chortle shook the first's shoulders.

'Agreed,' replied Old Fruit, the second. 'But we want to know of chatter from anywhere.'

They both looked toward the third man for his confirmation.

'Okay.' The third man's slow nod signalled his support. He flicked a wisp of grey hair from his forehead and absently rubbed the wrinkled brow. 'Okay. Let the Australians deal with the distracters as per normal. We can be there quietly for the coup de grâce. This is too big to let anyone get the jump on us.'

A river-ship's horn trumpeted faintly from a colourful barge of dis-coing partyers, as the three figures chinked glasses in a toast.

Chapter 3

Toowoomba, Queensland. 20 April 2008

'Poise, mate! Get that into ya, Spencer!' My newly-acquired acquaintance, Barry, plonked a hot pastry in my hand.

'Poise?' What was the man talking about? I must have looked every bit the bewildered Pom – such a derogatory term these Australians have for people from the mother country.

Despite the promising initial impressions when I had arrived at Melbourne Airport – was that only a couple of days ago? – I now harboured little doubt that my decision to come to Australia had finally ruined my life.

Where was my usual confidence? Gutted – again. I just wanted to be lost in the anonymity of the crowd.

It had only been an hour since I had arrived on the Darling Downs, following a stunning confrontation over two days in Melbourne. Barry had whisked me off to this Sunday afternoon sporting event. This couldn't be happening.

It was not a bad dream from which I would soon waken, laughing at my current emotional fragility. I was in a football crowd – a total foreigner, lost in the strange nasal-accented language of this land – and not understanding what this excited Aussie was saying.

'Carn ref. Get the bastard off im!' The woman's loud voice close by only added to my mounting confusion. Raucous sounds of passionate team supporters were rolling at counterpoint to my thought pattern.

… 'Poise?' The word hung in the air.

'Meat poise,' Barry said, grinning at me. 'Washed down by amber fluid. We'll make an Aussie of you yet, Spencer. Call me *Bazza*. All me mates do.'

Pies – meat pies and plastic beakers of cold lager.

'Offside! Get im back ten, ref! Fair go!' Bellows of advice flowed from all quarters of the ground. I watched bewildered. It seemed to me that the teams had been ten metres apart before the football gladiators ran with earth-pounding thumps towards each other. But whatever; this was clearly more about emotion, than fact. It was like some primeval force of warring tribes; bull buffaloes charging with unwavering masculinity at the threatening opposition; but it had a certain addictive charm. The baying crowds were totally absorbed; frustrated and cheering simultaneously.

Barry was a janitor at the university. Just over an hour earlier, he had helped me, the new staff member, as I arrived with my bags at my temporary apartment within the faculty grounds. With a breezy insistence, he had brought me out to see a game of local 'footy'; not the expected round ball of England nor the familiar rugby of Oxbridge but 'League, mate. The only game.'

The obligatory supporters' scarves that I associated with the English terraces were absent but they were colourful nonetheless in a motley scattering of sporting merchandise. And singing? No cacophony of sacred team songs – rather there was a rhythmic chanting; a ceaseless banter of commentary on the teams' or the referee's performance.

'Forward pass, ref. Jeezuz. Ask your seeing-eye dog?'

Somehow I could feel myself chortling. Maybe it was the sun and the beer – or the sustenance of the runny meat 'poi' – but, for the first time in the last couple of days since I had landed in Melbourne, the flow of enthusiastic jibes and laughter had actually lightened my spirit, just a shade.

I had been inhabiting a scary tunnel of darkness since the arguments of Melbourne. Even before that I'd been down – why else would I have accepted the Australian posting in the first place?

It had only been my Englishman's sense of duty that had actually seen me fulfil my commitment to arrive in this surprisingly colourful provincial town. And Barry, sorry Bazza, for all his rough exuberance, reminded me of the honest hospitality of my youth in the West Country. How long ago that all seemed now. But I guessed that had been why, despite my tiredness, I had accepted the invitation to see a game of 'footy'.

At least for an hour or so, my mood lifted slightly in the atmosphere of this sporting carnival. Tomorrow I would worry about my displeasure at this shabby professional treatment. Maybe, when I could settle down in the comfortable familiarity of helping students, I would feel some value again.

For the moment, was that *my* voice shouting an appreciative primitive 'Whaa-aay!' as the ball by-passed a decoy runner and put the most graceful of speeding athletes into a yawning gap – towards the line, and over, 'Try!!!!?'

Arms still in the air, bespattered with beer and a second poi in my hand, I could see my cheer reflected in the eyes of the ecstatic Bazza. Yes, tomorrow I would worry about being depressed. Today was about footy and sunshine.

'Knock-on, ref!' My voice echoed the chanting mob. Well, it was obviously a knock-on.

'Blind Freddie could see that, ref!' a burly man roared behind me. Who was Blind Freddie?

Another bite into the runny pie. Another gulp of the amber elixir – and I was ready to follow the next sortie into the opposition half.

I was actually laughing. I could hear myself laughing.

Good lord, what was I thinking?

Thank goodness no-one knows me here.

* * * *

The excitement of the match was over. Barry had gone. In my compact rooms, I was slowly unpacking my precious things.

The main shelf now housed three highly-respected international journals with my recently-authored contributions, as well as my leather-bound doctoral thesis: *The impact of competing ideologies on the geographical patterns of the former Soviet Union 1990-2001.*

My sturdy Colin Dexter Omnibus of *Inspector Morse* tales rested alongside Yann Martel's witty *Life of Pi* and Terayama's *Zen Brushwork* – someone had already thoughtfully placed a green-covered copy of the Concise Macquarie dictionary for my use.

As I stacked and sorted, my mp3 wafted Norah Jones' mellow voice through my soul.

The laptop work-station fitted neatly onto the left of the walnut desk top, with the precious USBs holding my back-ups, lectures and research notes in the drawer beneath. The document-case for my degree scrolls and professional references fitted into the right-hand drawer – but the central pride of place on the desk surface went to my left-handed calligraphy pens and my special-order writing paper. I couldn't wait to pen a letter; but only to Toby. No-one else would understand what my world was like, out here on the other side of the world.

I stroked the fine-grained paper as I aligned the writing pad – almost sensual, awaiting my italic script to transform the cream sheets into evocative artistic messages. I had often been regarded as different from my peers and my love of the physical act of handwriting was a case in point; despite so much of my working life being preserved in a largely paper-free status.

Above my desk, I had hung my own interpretative calligraphy based on the Venerable Bede's epigram, *Quamdiu stat Colisoeus, stat et Roma; quando cadet Colisoeus, cadet et Roma; quando cadet Roma, cadet et Mundus*, roughly meaning 'as long as the Colossus stands, so shall Rome; when the Colossus falls, Rome shall fall; when Rome falls, so falls the world'. Ah, the vulnerability of ideologies and empires – the more time passes, the more things stay the same. Fleetingly, I thought that I should craft another calligraphic ode to recognise the break-up of the old Soviet Union. What a mighty upheaval that had been since the Christmas and Boxing Day break of 1991. So fast; so dramatic, three-quarters of a century of powerful social revolution and political doctrine had just changed overnight – like the Colossus keeling over. Something had been coming; the rest of the world could see that. But, even so, it was a shock when it had actually occurred – the suddenness, the completeness. The Cold War was over – by implosion. That dangerous sparring between the Soviet Union and the United States was no more.

Finally, my eyes focused on the framed photographs: up on the shelf-top, a Somerset vale from the ridge behind the village and another of my parents standing proudly at my honours graduation. Then, adorning my desk beneath; *her* picture with me, laughing together at a late-autumn Cambridge garden party, preceding one of the best experiences of my life.

I looked wistfully at my small gestures to make the rooms comfortable and realised that I needed to be out into the fresh air, to think and catch the last rays of daylight.

* * * *

Where I sat in the empty university grounds, downstairs from my apartment, it was quiet. The shady trees with the grey-cream mottled barks seemed protective. Leopard trees, Barry had called them. I sighed in the silent air of this southern land, and pondered.

In truth, I felt banished to a penal colony, albeit devoid of the chains and the flogging. Not too dissimilar from the Soviet gulags of my research, but without the Siberian climate. The similarity was just distance, dislocation and isolation from everything familiar. But my dreamy mind could imagine the Australian trees as soul-less guards; cold, grey, scowling, dispassionate, enemies.

Then, as a welcome relief, my thoughts floated back to Cambridge, to me living a privileged dream, *her* laughing eyes, a sense of belonging, of having arrived at a destiny, contented – in a very different way from the docile acceptance of the feudal order back in my home village.

I was mystified as to how it could have gone so wrong so quickly.

Suddenly, a chattering cloud of feathered frenzy landed in the leopard tree branches above, jarring my attention upwards.

Multi-coloured parrots of some kind.

I watched them as they launched themselves noisily like a group of darts for a distant tree and – as my head turned – I caught a shadow out of the corner of my eye.

Someone watching me from a stairwell?

12

A figure had moved in the dusky light.

I peered at the spot – but it must have been my imagination. There was nothing moving now. No-one around on a late Sunday afternoon.

Just another symptom of this current torture, no doubt.

I rose and wandered, prisoner-like, on my exercise path through the grounds and back towards my accommodation.

I half-closed my eyes to shut out the reality of the surroundings and forced myself to picture again the happy smiles, of her head in my lap, feeding ducks and swans in the lake from the shade of a weeping willow, *Salix babylonica* – my carefully internalised Latin words hadn't left me, at least – and a wave of nostalgic euphoria coursed pleasantly through my veins, for a few seconds.

And then I stared back at that stairwell …

Chapter 4

Olga's eyes sparkled as her mind surfaced from deep thoughts. She had arrived in Australia a week earlier, on a visitor's visa, to meet the son she had last seen when he was just a child.

'Hi Nana.' The exuberant call jolted her attention but her expression revealed no shock.

Rather, with calm discipline, she carefully put down the china teacup, brushed a biscuit crumb from her tailored grey trousers and beamed a cheery welcome.

The happy girl, who had just rushed up the Toowoomba driveway from a night away with friends, was granddaughter Eva; lithe, blonde – a university student with sparkling eyes and a perpetual smile.

Pyotr emerged from the house, alerted by the voice. With a wave to his daughter, he said in Russian to his mother, 'How are you feeling, my dear?'

'Little tired.' She gave him a smile. 'English is fine to use.' It was the gentlest of rebukes. Olga Davidenko was nothing if not capable with understanding languages, even if she usually spoke English in her own style.

She was indeed unaccustomedly frail, despite her straight confident posture. She had fallen three days before. Just a faint, she assured her son – just the excitement of the occasion – but he had taken her to his private doctor in Toowoomba, just in case.

'What have you planned today?' she asked Eva.

'I have a class at ten o'clock, Nana, for which I must get moving or I'll be late. It's that new lecturer from England, Dad. Dr Avery from Cambridge University. Remember, I mentioned him?' Her father nodded. 'Nana, I think he is having some problems settling into our Australian ways. We must be a bit different from his Cambridge.'

'Mmm, more than little,' agreed her grandmother with a twinkle in her eye.

'He's good but. Makes you think. Pretty demanding. He'll be coming with us when my friends interview you for our dissertation practice, so you'll get to meet him.'

The elderly lady nodded encouragingly, with patience, pleased that her granddaughter thought her to be such a valuable person that she would be interviewed for her university course. There was no way she would be disappointing this girl.

Then, with the blur in which she had arrived, Eva kissed her family, jumped into the car and rolled down the driveway with a flourished wave through the open window.

'Bundle of energy, Pyotr.' The smiling grandmother basked in the warm feeling of being with family at last.

For over thirty years, her only family had really been the army. It hadn't been a bad experience; times of excitement, camaraderie, romance, even rare moments of ecstasy. Undoubtedly also, there had always been the son in Australia, living with her relative Nina; the son she had supported financially all through school and university; the teenager to whom she had sent irregular letters; the man who was always a trigger for painful guilt but a source of deep longing.

And Australia? The land that had nurtured her boy when she had not? It was a strange mixture of symbolic images in her imagination: its sun-drenched Anzac warrior tradition; expansive mining and farming on a continent nearly as vast as her homeland; and all against a shadowy ancient backdrop of kangaroos, boomerangs and Aboriginal people.

Chapter 5

Yumba, Western Queensland. February 1946

Herbie's young eyes picked out the large goanna between the gum tree and the tall Mitchell grass. It was wriggling slowly over the red-brown dirt.

'Kinny, over de la! Goanna!' The black boy stood motionless, pointing.

His brother's eyes followed the signal, nodding, soundless; shirtless body rippling with the lean muscles of a ten-year-old Aboriginal hunter. He was ready for the slow silent stalking; the prelude to the race through the grass to catch the goanna by the tail, before it could reach the shelter of the hop-bushes.

The animal lay still, eyes wary. Its best defence was camouflage – a piece of grey fallen timber to an inexperienced eye. It would be passed over, near the edge of a narrow gully – an escape route. Large coolabah trees close to scrubby bushes – the next escape route.

An elegant hawk circled through the clear blue sky, its eyes watching, but the strong graceful body gave no indication of an interest in the drama about to unfold below.

Herbie was three years younger than Kenny. He too was shirtless. They wore no shoes – just baggy shorts and flashing smiles. With practised skill, they moved gently, noiselessly, in a pincer movement to entrap the wary reptile. It would bolt soon – but the boys were fast. Goanna was food and they needed to eat.

Loud shouting broke the tense silence.

Children on the other side of the narrow gully – whitefellas.

A stone hit the dirt near Herbie. They were shouting at him. He didn't follow the words but he knew the tone. They were taunting – and the goanna was off, taking advantage of the distraction.

Three white boys about Herbie's age, flicking stones from a shanghai, a catapult. Kenny waved and whispered urgently that they should go. Herbie had rarely seen white boys; only ever in the distance; and never on their yumba; Murri country, Aboriginal land.

'C'mon, Hirbie,' whispered Kenny, a little louder this time. 'Lits git away!' As he spoke, another stone hit the ground near him and it bounced hard into his ankle, drawing a cry of pain.

Herbie could feel anger replace his puzzlement. These white boys had hit his brother with a stone. He took off towards them, through the gully, yelling menacingly, 'Whatshyoo doing?' The boys laughed. Before he had even thought, his right fist hit the smart boy with the catapult, hard on the nose. The whitefella crumpled to the ground, hands to his face, as crimson blood burst between his fingers.

'C'mon Hirbie. Lits go!' Kenny's urgent call jolted him. The other white boys looked stunned as they watched the two Murris disappear through the scrub, one limping badly.

'Why we need to go?' asked Herbie as they ran. He wanted to stay and fight. This was their land.

'Trouble,' replied Kenny. 'Whitefella trouble.'

The yumba was the blackfella camp; about half a dozen permanent buildings and quite a few temporary gunyas, cooking fires and a meeting place under an old wild cherry tree – a busy place, a safe shelter, a loving nest of laughter and care. It was their home, where they belonged, where they learned the ways of their people.

The boys told their mother about the meeting with whitefellas. Her eyes widened with fear. 'Go bush! Hide. Watch yumba from distance. Government man come. Go!'

'The government man' was a bad man who took children away. All the people understood, even the young ones. They always hid if some new whitefella came to the yumba.

The boys took off.

From an old box tree, they watched.

The police arrived on horses and talked to the men, asking for the boys from the gully. There were lots of head shakes and pointing in several different directions into the bush. No-one argued. They nodded and said little. The breeze blew some of the words towards Kenny and Herbie. Something about 'causing trouble ... bulldoze the whole bloody place ... how can you people live like this?'

At night, the boys returned to the yumba, hungry with no goanna for the fire. Their father was sitting listening to his curly-haired friend, Husk, who was telling his young daughter, Edna, an old droving story – but the story stopped and all attention was directed to the boys on their return. Herbie's father told them all again what they had heard before. The government man could take any of them away whenever he chose. That was whitefella law.

'Where they take em?' asked Herbie.

'Woorabinda, Cherbourg, Toomelah, Palm,' was the reply.

Herbie shivered with dread.

His father stressed again that people were allowed to stay in the yumba as long as they were working for the whitefella; labouring – cutting timber, railway gangs, cattle mustering, domestic work. But, there must be no trouble with whitefellas. That was the way things were.

'Why we like this?' asked Herbie. He had been learning some at the camp school and a preacher had been telling them about the Bible; about Moses, the Egyptians, the pyramids and the exodus to Israel – but they were slaves in another man's land. Herbie was in the land of his ancestors – *his* land. He wasn't a slave. He didn't understand at all.

His father just replied, 'That's way things are.' But he talked about the Murri way, the rules of culture, the stories of the Dreamtime, the sacred places, men's business and women's business – and of a happy time ahead.

Chapter 6

'Damn this weakness,' Olga muttered as she straightened her short grey ponytail and returned to sipping her morning tea in the autumn sunshine.

The verandah view reminded her somehow of the Ukrainian steppes of her youth – and yet, the Darling Downs would never be mistaken for the Russian plains.

Her fall was worrying. Perhaps more serious than faint, she thought. They should hear the test results today. But the tea was refreshing and the view peaceful. From the map on her knee she guessed that through the gap in the hills would be Cambooya, then on towards Leyburn and the flood plain of what looked to be a life-blood artery, the Condamine River.

Pyotr's wife, Anna, interrupted her thoughts. 'Are you okay, Olga?' She had brought a fresh teapot from the house.

Olga smiled at her daughter-in-law. 'Was thinking black-soil fields reminded me of chernozems in Russia. But Ukraine doesn't have quite same sweep like that open valley to south. Don't these flat-topped plateaux look solemn yet beautiful watching over chequer-board of fields? I feel like poet.'

Anna's grin seemed to reflect her admiration for Olga's command of elegant English words but she chose to ask, 'Do you think of the Ukraine as home? Peter said you were born in Turkey.'

Olga jolted internally at the anglicising of her son's name. But she smiled politely. She was Russian, yet she herself carried the Ukrainian surname of her late husband. Live and let live.

Despite the flash of thought, she answered without missing a beat. 'I was. 1945. Area was Cappadocia, in central Anatolia. My grandparents' families had fled Russian Revolution. Is where I learned Turkish *and* Russian.'

'So when did you go to Russia?'

'After Stalin's death in early 1953. My parents moved into Ukraine; they worked in Donbas coalfields. In 1954, my father joined Red Army and moved to East Germany for large parts of every year, leaving me behind with mother. My father was good with languages. He encouraged me to learn some English as well. At eighteen when I followed him into army, I could understand four languages reasonably, with German included. But I was and am Russian.'

Anna frowned in thought. 'The world has moved on, hasn't it? My grandparents in Latvia didn't like Russians. The Red Army were the persecutors following on from the Germans – yet my parents were happy to allow me to marry the son of a Russian out here in Australia, even while their own parents' homeland was still occupied. I think we see places differently when we are outside looking in.'

Olga's tiredness was unusual – a contrast to the warm assurance she had been feeling when she had stepped off the plane at Brisbane Airport, just a week before. Her polite expression read, I don't need argument as guest in my son's house.

'We are not all same, Anna – no matter what Soviet state did. Not all Latvians fit mould either.' She looked at her daughter-in-law's blonde hair, blue eyes and fair complexion. 'You don't fit Muscovite caricature of Latvians as mushroom-eating thieves. And we Russians are not all brutal ogres with no sense of humour.' Her smile seemed to ease the tension. 'You are right to be proud of your parents.'

'But you were Red Army.'

'*Konechno!*' She lapsed into her Russian language by reflex. 'Of course, you are right. Different world. Different values; mistakes, changed attitudes, we were what we knew – but within every country we are each individual people. Countries create fear of others. You are fine wife, mother and daughter-in-law. Let's not carry on narrow views of past. We are better than that.'

Olga sensed her daughter-in-law's struggle to believe her words.

She watched as Anna said, 'You are not how I imagined you – from Peter's photos and my perception of what a Soviet soldier would be like.' She grinned. 'You are just like a grandmother.'

'Is what I am – and happy to be here with you all at last.' She held Anna's hand and squeezed gently. 'I am just grandmother who is not good patient. I don't like not being … strong. Military background perhaps.' She shrugged her shoulders into her accustomed straight-back, and cast quick eyes over her neat lemon blouse topping the tailored pants. 'Has taken long time to get to this place – good to fill in missing years. I think your parents are right, Anna. World is not living in past.'

A shadow of regret flitted over her smile as she reflected that perhaps they *should* have met much earlier. But, she thought, they wouldn't have understood world she knew, and know. Perhaps she needed to describe it as pretty story; as adventure … without all danger, trauma and evil.

She rose to her feet as Pyotr rejoined them on the verandah. Repenting reflections still cascaded behind her mask of politeness.

'Today *is* day we get test results, yes?' She was beginning to doubt even her memory. Why was she so shaken by fainting?

'Yes. Do you feel able to be driven into town?'

'Of course!' concealing her mild disappointment that her physical strength was being queried. 'I was just saying to Anna I'm grateful to have managed to get here at last. We have lot of catching up to do. Do you think my six-month visa will be long enough?'

'We have a lifetime, Mama.' He had a familiar smile – warm, seemingly strong yet with a hint of fragility above the cheeks. 'You don't know how long I have dreamed this time would happen – and here you are at last.'

'My dream too, my son,' she whispered, rare moisture glowing in her eyes. 'Was hardest decision to let you come out here with your aunt. But, was right decision – for you. Would have been no life having to live in world I was about to enter; no mother or father to look after you.' She looked at Anna. 'We are all people, no matter, eh?' Olga embraced them both, her intense grip suggesting a need for their reassurance, as she wondered whether she actually deserved their understanding after all this time.

* * * *

An hour later, Olga and Peter walked together to the car and set out to see the doctor.

'I was telling Anna that view over valley here reminded me of Ukraine,' Olga said, taking in the panorama as the car travelled down the driveway. 'Is scale of place — black-soil fields with huge blue sky overhead; big birds soaring. You have done well, my son, from humble beginnings.'

He smiled in acknowledgement. 'Peter Grushko, electrical engineer, designer and installer of programmable logic controllers, at your service. We've been lucky with the mining industry expansion across Queensland but the demand is booming even into South East Asia. Business is going well. We are comfortable. Eva is nearly through her degree. She has good friends and is happy. What more can we ask of life?'

'Good, *Peter*. No more called Pyotr, eh? Except, sometimes from me, your Mama.' Her smiling eyes reflected her son's proud sense of achievement although her thoughts cast back to a vision of his handsome father, Oleg, taken from her in tragic circumstances back in 1967 — to that terrible day near Berlin ...

Chapter 7

Outside Berlin, East Germany. 28 August 1967

The side of his face was squashed against the weathered wood of the barn loft and his head hung motionless through the high hatchway. Pungent fumes of wood-tar oil from the door-framing stung his nostrils and slowly brought the soldier back to consciousness.

His right shoulder and hip were deadened from the shock of the bullets hitting. A Kalashnikov automatic rifle lay just beyond his grasp on the loft's wooden floor. With his head lolling through the high exposed opening and blood soaking his grey-olive uniform, he knew he would look lifeless to the Americans down below. He grew increasingly aware of the wind whistling like a choir of owls through leafy, summer branches.

As the soldier's right eye opened partly, grey shadows scudded in front of the waning full moon and stars, lighting the courtyard below in pulsating waves. The scene flickered frustratingly like an old black-and-white movie; but this was real, very real.

He could see Oleg on the ground of the courtyard below, his hands restrained behind his back, wincing in pain from the gory wound in his left thigh. The soldier listened to the voices from below.

'What's your name?' There was a cold menace in the American's tone.

'Oleg Davidenko,' came the reply; the Russian officer's eyes watched his inquisitor carefully. There was no way to avoid the gun which pointed towards Oleg. The two Americans whispered urgently to each other.

In the loft, spasms of agony were now spearing through the hip of the soldier as the numbing shock started to wear off. The mists of confusion were clearing. The acrid smell of the treated wood stirred his thinking back to the memory of the intruders as they had moved into and through this camouflaged security facility, a listening base for tracking Western communications; then the gun flashes, the dulling paralysis as his body would not respond, the realisation that he had been hit by bullets … He must stay still, not draw any attention to himself.

He knew his friend Oleg would be thinking of his wife, Olga, and baby son Pyotr. They had often talked of families. They each had young children. This was a diabolical situation. The American agents were in control – but they would have trouble getting away from East Germany.

His eye opened wider as the gun fired again and again and again. He could hear the moan from Oleg and then, mercifully, it was over. He forced himself to memorise the faces of the murderers. This crime would be remembered. He must stay alive. He must be the witness to what he had just observed.

The Americans had gone. Oleg lay lifeless.

The soldier replayed in his mind what he had seen and heard. He knew he would be found. He must stay alive.

Chapter 8

The sign on the medical specialist's door simply read *Charles McBride*. Inside, Peter had heard that the test results were inconclusive.

Dr McBride had arranged for more to be done while Olga was visiting the hospital. As that process was being carried out, he talked quietly to Peter on his suppositions. 'I've consulted with colleagues in Brisbane and Sydney and there are two likely scenarios. Neither is good.'

Peter waited. They were old friends. They played weekly squash fixtures together; but the doctor was choosing his words with care.

'My suggestions are, and I'd be happy to be proved wrong and to apologise to you if I am.' McBride's hesitancy was surprising Peter. 'Your mother has a swelling in the brain. It is abnormal and has caused her to fall. I thought she might have had a minor stroke but it doesn't appear to be that. We are running more tests now.

'In addition, we have discovered an unusual anomaly in the heart. It is rare in my experience, possibly caused by Chagas disease, almost unknown in Australia, picked up from a parasite, often in places like Colombia and Venezuela. She tells me she has been there. Chagas disease would certainly have affected the functioning of her heart.'

Peter's expression was frozen in confusion. Venezuela? Colombia? It didn't make sense – but McBride was still talking ...

'I am trying to prepare you for the possible news your mother may not have a good prognosis from these tests. Both the scenarios I have suggested to you, Peter, have the possibility of shortening your mother's time to months or a very few years at best.' He let the information slowly sink in.

'The treatment?' asked Peter.

'It depends on what we find and how advanced the situations are. There are treatments but, in the worst case scenarios, it is as I have described to you.'

'When will we know for sure?'

'Within a fortnight. What would you like your mother to know?'

'Tell her we will know in a fortnight, without mentioning all the worst case scenarios, but thank you for telling me, for preparing me. It's a shock. We have just met up again after over thirty-five years.'

* * * *

'I must be sick, eh?' said Olga to Peter in the car, driving home. 'What did doctor say to you?'

'That they won't know anything for a couple of weeks.'

'Whatever is meant to be will happen.' Her eyes had a dreamy calmness. 'Let's just enjoy every day, my son.'

Her thoughts had already moved to the interview which she had promised to give to Eva and her friends. Would be something about her past, she knew. She wondered what she would be prepared to tell. Years of programmed deceit? Was that what she was going to say to her precious granddaughter? She hadn't even had a chance to tell her son. The real story would be too much for Eva, along with university friends she hadn't even met yet.

'You know, Peter,' she announced after some thought. 'My memory is not what it once was. I used to be showcase of retentive memory. Now, I have difficulty recalling important names of people I have known for years. Blank periods of time where I don't know what I have been doing – like micro-sleep, but in my case, more like macro-sleep. You know what I mean?' She laughed wryly.

'You are getting older, Mama. That's all.' His voice sounded more relaxed than he felt.

'You don't think I might have Alzheimers or something creeping up on me?' She grinned at him.

'I think you're looking for problems. Leave it to the doctors and we will enjoy our time together before you forget why you came over here.'

They both laughed. She was getting used to Peter. He was her flesh and blood but also… a stranger. She could see glimpses of Oleg in occasional expressions but her son was more serious than his father had been.

She could see a reflective man – maybe even a lonely man, despite his confident outer appearance. Perhaps it was her fault if he had found it easier to bottle up emotions rather than share them. He had a dry sense of humour. She was pleased he had turned out to be a good person who cared about family. So different from his mother! A pang of a long-suppressed guilt fluttered through her – and then it settled again, as it had been trained to do over the years.

She lost herself in her thoughts. Standard story would be fine for students. If they probed into her army experiences, she would just gently fob them off with practised skill of decades – although, maybe not.

Some things would have to stay confidential because lives would still be at risk but, as for her views on that world and how it had all worked, she was past the flag-waving patriotism and fearful respect for the politburo.

Now, she actually yearned for people to understand why things had happened as they had. It had been a mind shift since her retirement – but it had been growing for many years. The world had changed. She had lived in many lands, with different cultures, attitudes and questions. She had watched, listened and merged with other social customs.

Policies that she had defended so strictly for decades were in many cases no longer even the policies of the current Russian government.

And, for all the mistakes of the past, they were nothing compared to the abyss that Western countries seemed to be blindly heading towards.

Chapter 9

Dr Spencer Avery
Toowoomba
Queensland
Australia

25 April 2008

Dr Tobias Stanley-Smythe
University of Cambridge

My dear Toby (or G'day as they seem to say out here)

What have I done?

Why am I in this Philistinian colony of my mother land? How could I have left the hallowed cloisters of Cambridge to come here?

As you know, I agreed with the university to come out to Australia for eight months of extended teaching on the clear understanding that I would go to, at least, a university in Melbourne or Sydney. I did expect that adjunct-professor would not be out of the question for a Cambridge Fellow.

Where am I? Toowoomba. On a misty range beyond even the sight of the sea to the east and with thousands of kilometres of flat searing plains to the west.

Understand my plight. Yesterday, I took a group of undergraduates in a mini-bus to do some pre-arranged interviews about the environmental impact of a proposed water pipeline. While travelling to a village to the north, the radio was crackling away with weather forecasts and local news. The reporter's voice was chirping along about rises in the Macintyre and Weir Rivers near Goondiwindi and Millmerran. We have had some rain recently. 'Water across the road,' she advised. Then, deadpan, she announced, 'Anyone passing water on the roads near Goondiwindi should exercise extreme caution.' Well, I imagine they might.

I looked at my undergrads to see if any of them had the same mirthful reaction I had to the statement. Like a fast bowl whizzing through to the keeper.

That is what I am up against. It's such a different culture here, Toby.

Today is Anzac Day – a laudable national holiday to commemorate the fallen, but with a special emphasis on the first Australian independent military force at Gallipoli. They retreated after about nine months, albeit having shown valiant stoicism. I like that. There is a certain sense of heroic rebellion in celebrating a retreat as a symbolic national day. We should have a similar day in England – we've had a few glorious retreats in our time, don't you think?

I did expect that Australia would be more like England. On Tuesday, scarcely arrived in the country, I had to travel out to a tiny settlement, which has an exploratory mine and an airstrip, to assist a post-graduate with his thesis. I flew, in a tiny plane shaped like a box underneath a single wing, west over endless plains of huge fields and 'bush'. Now, there's a concept.

'Bush' is an Australian term that covers everything not settled nor ploughed. That is a lot of western Queensland, I can tell you. It is generally woodland; dry, olive-green and stretching for ever.

I'm told that one of the high points in this term's social activities will be a '*bush* dance'. I know that you are envisaging something like a Shakespearean movement of Dunsinane Woods from *Macbeth*.

Not so, dear Toby. A bush dance is a gathering of locals; in a farm shed, where a live band plays Celtic jigs and reels on improvised and traditional instruments. There is a 'lager-phone' for rhythm – a broomstick with beer-bottle tops screwed on, shaken and bounced to give the beat for dancing. I know you're getting the feel for this already. Throw in a banjo – for the pig-skin effect; a bit of bass; an accordion to fill out the Celtic sound; a penny whistle or a flute, maybe a fiddle or a mandolin; and a guitar – and you have a bush band.

Whoop-ee!

I asked my students what kind of dances one might attempt to these Celtic rhythms. They replied with such old favourites as *The Drongo, The Waves of Bondi, The Pride of Erin* and *The Heel and Toe Polka*. How could I contain my anticipation?

But wait, there's more!

When we go to this bush dance, we will be camping out at a place near Goomburra. Where do they get these names from? I am told that they are Murri names. No, I have spelt that correctly – not one of the Scottish spellings. It is a Queensland term which the descendants of the Aboriginal people use to describe themselves. There is a host of different tribal groups from before white colonisation – a bit like the highland clans, I suppose – and 'Murri' covers them all. I'm told they use another term, 'Koori', to describe the Aboriginal people of New South Wales. Are you still with me?

Now you know my attitude to camping – a four-star hotel, nothing less. I am not one of those geographers who will blithely sleep the night away in a peat bog, excited by the prospect of identifying multiple varieties of sphagnum moss in the morning. Can you imagine me lying under the vast Australian sky, with the rivers potentially in flood, in eager anticipation of dancing *The Drongo* – whatever that will turn out to be?

I'm told that Murri Elders will be on the camp. Not some jolly sing-a-long, I hope.

Toby, my friend, I am a specialist in the political geography of Eastern Europe. Surely I am above doing surveys of local residents' opinions on the environmental merits or otherwise of recycled-water pipelines. I don't want to seem ungrateful – it is just that there is a huge cultural gulf between the Australian, and my appreciation of the world and its importance.

And, in what passes for humour here.

I did remonstrate when I arrived in Melbourne that I felt I had been shabbily treated in being allocated to a provincial university. I told my hosts about the papers that I have presented to the Royal Society and the international demand for my opinions on the geopolitical scene. Do you know what the reply was?

'It's not far to Toowoomba, mate.'

'How far?' said I, fully aware of the likely distance from Melbourne to Toowoomba in kilometres.

'Walking distance,' was the reply.

Aghast, I gave him my most ferocious querulous expression.

'Well, Leichhardt did it!' came the response, with that impish Aussie grin and nasal twang, bearing reference to an early explorer from the 1840s.

Toby, my friend, this is a far cry from cocktails at dusk, a punt on the River Cam and some philosophical debate before taking in a choral performance pre vespers. How will I survive?

Do write back. Tell me of the world I have left behind. I trust you to respect the confidence of this letter, lest I be thought a total fool for having come here. I hope to write again before too long but I will await your reply to lift my spirits. The end of the year seems a long way away.

Your friend in colonial service,
Spencer Avery

Chapter 10

'I thought you should be informed, Sir.' The police inspector's voice in the earpiece was clear and controlled.

The phone had rung early in the Canberra morning. Superintendent Jeff Fowler of the Australian Federal Police was used to interruptions at strange hours. The hour signified the importance. His wife scarcely moved her position in the bed as he spoke quietly into the handset. The call was from an inspector in Western Australia. It would still be dark in the west.

'We have detained a man at Perth airport. He came in on the last flight from Singapore but he was originally from Pakistan, via India.

'He was carrying a photograph of a Major Olga Davidenko of the Russian GRU – their military intelligence unit. Not very forthcoming, Sir, on his reasons for carrying such information but we have established that an Olga Davidenko did indeed arrive at Brisbane Airport two weeks ago on a six-month visitor's visa. Her disembarking details gave her place of residence as being with her son in Toowoomba.'

'Do we know anything about this Major Davidenko?'

'Not a lot, Sir. A background brief came up on a security note against her name but she *has* been recently cleared for entry. No more explanatory details. We weren't aware of her arrival. We are checking further with our security intelligence contacts at ASIO now. Initial inquiries tell us she's sixty-three-years old and has been GRU for most of her military service. Her Russian passport showed her to be well travelled, but never before to Australia. She's a *retired* major, Sir, which makes this all the more puzzling.'

'Mmm,' pondered Fowler. 'Thanks for giving me the heads-up. Appreciated. Please file your report, marked for my urgent attention.'

'Good, Sir.' There was a tone of satisfied relief in the inspector's voice. 'It might be nothing – but I thought you should know. Good night, Sir.'

Fowler lowered the phone and smiled at his patient sleeping wife – a policewoman herself in the early days. How would he have coped without her unfailing support? He padded through to the kitchen to pour a glass of water.

Jeff Fowler had a responsibility for anti-terrorist defences in Australia. A lot of those defences revolved around getting accurate and early information about possible threats. He scoured his memory for other pieces which might bring sense to the puzzle, then made some notes.

* * * *

Canberra was hardly awake when Fowler summarised the situation to his senior team at the AFP. There were regular weekly briefings of his key people but he had called this meeting specially. A Pakistani entering Australia with a photograph of a retired GRU major had put all of his senses on alert.

'I need some background on Major Olga Davidenko,' he said. 'Some background on the son in Toowoomba, too. Go over the Western Australian interviews with this Pakistani, detained at Perth Airport. Check other reports over the past two weeks for anything that might match with a suspicion around this woman. She may be retired but do they ever actually retire?'

Fowler could feel the buzz in the room.

The Russian GRU was a huge section of the Red Army which dealt in international espionage. The FSB, the state security successor to the old communist regime's KGB, handled threats largely within Russia while their intelligence arm, SVR, gathered counter-espionage information internally and around the world. But the GRU's work was espionage, to infiltrate foreign countries and acquire military information. It was an outreach facility of the Russian state – and just the acronym produced a very healthy professional respect from anyone in state security or indeed, as Jeff Fowler was, in anti-terrorism.

The GRU were not terrorists. Undoubtedly, they had formidable undercover enforcement units within their ranks – legendary even – but they were primarily listeners, spies. Their job was to keep the Russian Army well informed about their competitors and enemies. If they were newly active in the country, they could well be associating with people of interest to Fowler and his team.

'She has been given a visitor's visa so the immigration people must have verified the tourist status. Liaise with ASIO on anything they might have on a GRU link.' And why had he not been advised that a retired GRU major had been issued with a visa to enter Australia? Who had approved that, and where, without passing the intel on? Something was odd.

'Alert the Toowoomba police. Where is she going? Who is she meeting? I want discreet surveillance on this retired Russian operative, until the situation is clarified. I'll get the clearances approved.'

This was all routine police work; all in a normal day's work for the AFP but somehow the adrenalin was flowing with this puzzle for the anti-terrorism unit.

Chapter 11

Toowoomba. 28 April 2008

'Consider this as an alternative.' My Cambridge tone had enough assertiveness to demonstrate my very strong professional recommendation. These Australians students didn't quite respond like their British counterparts.

I looked intently at my final-year group, Steve McGrady, Eva Grushko, Melanie Bell and Warren Davis; relishing at least the opportunity to work with such a small class. Enrolments in my other year levels had huge numbers of general degree students but this was the group choosing to specialise in their final year; like private tutoring – luxury. They appeared keen; thoughts prepared. It was Monday. We were getting ready to visit two Darling Downs residents to test our research skills for a wider dissertation on social geography.

Academically, they seemed capable but, frankly, I had been disappointed with their interview strategy; every question laid out – routine boring questions, no space for the person to take the interviewer into new territory. They might just as well have asked for Yes/No answers.

I needed to take them rapidly back to first principles if they were going to realise any potential they might have. Time would tell when they interviewed Olga Davidenko, Eva's grandmother. It was sad really – colonial disadvantage, no doubt.

'Essentially, the skill is *to listen*.' I ignored their puzzled expressions. 'Open-ended questions. Let the person being interviewed speak with as few interruptions as possible.'

'Is that it?' Warren looked at me in askance. 'That's all?'

'So keep it simple.' Melanie's eyes searched each of her classmates. 'Simple is good,' I verified.

Did they not understand the importance of ears? Why did they think they needed to have a battery of smart questions?

'You are social scientists. You are not seeking an endorsement of your own views. You want to hear what the interviewee might volunteer, and then you can build more of your hypotheses to test,' I emphasised.

They were being very patient with me – a polite tolerance; waiting for a complex pearl of wisdom and being confused with simplicity. I said nothing more as I waited for a realisation to dawn.

As they tried to make sense of the situation, I grudgingly accepted that it was actually a therapeutic process for me. My sense of being needed was gently soothing the dark dejection which had been gripping me with a fiendish ferocity.

My bubble of professional pride had undoubtedly been deflated after being advised in Melbourne that I was not to be lauded as a visiting 'professor' from the 'old country'; and then being posted at lecturer level to Toowoomba. How bad could it get? Working with learners was at least reaffirming my sense of worth. This was familiar territory, even if they were slow at the moment.

'So, we ask a simple question and just let them talk? That's all we do? Are we following you correctly?' Eva's questioning expression suggested she was sure she had missed the point. Tolerance, I told myself.

'Simple on the surface but, I assure you, it is much more sophisticated behind.' I was getting a cruel enjoyment watching their mild torment as they strained to grasp my intent. 'Patience. Trust me. You will understand when we use this.'

Melanie's eyes reflected her mental effort. At least they were not just accepting what I said, like mindless sheep. There was a wonder in her look as she struggled to catch some, as yet unseen, vision but Steve and Warren were quietly waiting for the punch-line to appear.

There was a shy mannerly way about them – respectfully polite; not brash nor uncouth as I had dreaded. I knew they were impressed by the mystique of Cambridge while I was trying hard just to be factual about my previous workplace; neither to add fuel to their fascination nor to denigrate their belief.

Routinely careful about social interaction with students and their families – my in-built sense of probity – I had surprised myself by agreeing to their invitation to a camp-out and a bush dance with community members at Goomburra. It had been their initiative that impressed me. Or maybe it was a measure of my temporarily fragile ego needing to be stroked. Goomburra was to be the site of one of their research studies and they had it all organised for me anyway. More than the people in Melbourne ever offered – but I hoped I wouldn't grow to regret my impetuous acceptance.

Both events were loosely linked to their assignments and would give me an opportunity to see the Queensland way of life. I probably needed to make some effort, now that I was here; and they certainly seemed to be without any ulterior motivation. Parents had been involved to smooth the path into local circles. It would have been more flattering had I actually wanted to be in this forlorn place. Yet, there was a benign innocence about it all, so different from my recent experiences.

My Englishness appeared to captivate them too – as if they were charmed by its quaintness. Queenslanders should look to themselves with their peculiar phrases and laid-back ways. More as a disparaging anecdote than to build a bond, I had told them of my 'adventure' with pies, beer and language at the footy within hours of arriving. They had hooted with laughter. I could only assume that they were enthralled by my description of the vulgarity of the experience. Perhaps they had felt complimented that I was prepared to make an effort to understand such a crass cultural occasion in their part of the world.

'The essence of the interview is to listen.' All eyes were on me. 'Get the person talking and then focus actively on what is being said, not what you think should be said. You might be surprised if you give people the chance to tell you.'

Nods all round. They were trying hard.

'What is it we want to know, Steve?' I recapped.

'How did they come to be here on the Darling Downs? What is it that they do? Why are they here?'

'And more,' Warren added. 'Where did they come from to be at this place now?'

'And when you are asked what you will *do* with this information?' I continued.

'We want to map the movements,' said Melanie, 'in space and time so we can analyse the reasons behind particular patterns that might unfold.'

'Correct,' I agreed. 'And these two short interviews are to sort out any problems in our technique. We may well use them in the main study.

Chapter 12

The students seemed to fill the room, at Eva's parents' house, with the bustling excitement of youthful anticipation.

Olga watched Anna greet the four youngsters; and there was a slim man with them – dark wavy hair, intense expression, casual cream slacks and shirt, set off against his navy-blue jacket, early thirties perhaps.

Could be going to a rowing regatta at Henley in England. Must be Cambridge lecturer, Dr Spencer Avery, she thought.

She gave them an encouraging smile.

This interview might be fun. Oh, what happy faces they have.

Olga listened intently; taking in the process of the introduction.

Melanie was slim and about the same height as Eva, but with dark hair and eyes. She said she came from cotton-growing property just over state border in New South Wales.

And Steve; similar in height to the girls but whippet-thin with dark curly hair and darker tone to his skin; came from out Mitchell way.

Perhaps is farther west from Toowoomba, thought Olga.

Getting used to the relaxed language and accent of the Downs, she accepted Warren's respectful bow. He was tall and tanned with an easy manner and flashing white teeth. Olga gathered his family were dairy farmers 'just down the range' near a place called Goomburra.

Then there was the interesting Dr Avery.

'Please call me Spencer, Ma'am.' Avery bowed graciously, too.

His voice would not have been out of place at any regal gathering. He thanked his host for the welcome, 'This is very kind of you, Mrs Grushko, letting us use your home for this interview.'

Olga was pleased to hear the gushingly polite words of English society through the language of Dr Avery. It had been a while since she had heard that speaking style – and Olga always liked to understand nuances of dialect; as a listener rather than speaker of languages.

She settled down, with a cup of unsweetened unmilked tea, to be questioned by her interrogators. She had been told that it was to be a very quick interview, where they would try not to interrupt very often; but rather, they would just listen to what was being said.

Olga was intrigued.

* * * *

Conscious of my role as the university lecturer, I looked around the room.

The Russian grandmother and Mrs Grushko were waiting patiently. My seniors were watching me for a cue. Time was a priority. I needed them to learn this technique, albeit only one of many examples of good interview practice.

I nodded for them to start.

'Nana,' Eva started, and looked at me. 'Too informal?'

'*Nana* is fine from any of you,' Olga encouraged while I totally ignored the query.

'Nana, could you tell us please who you are, why you are in Toowoomba and how you came to be here?' She activated the recording machine.

'I am here to see my son and his family, especially my granddaughter.' She gave a special smile to acknowledge her blonde relative. 'I am Russian, brought up in eastern Ukraine, which used to be part of Soviet Union, and is now independent. You are geographers. You understand, I'm sure.

'I worked most of my life for Russian army, mainly based in Moscow but also serving in Western Europe, Americas; and what you would call Middle East. I have retired now.

'I was separated from my son when he was small child.' She paused. 'Life was not as easy then as seems now. He came to live with family members here in Australia, and our only communication was by letter and photograph over years.'

She stopped as if to invite comment but there was silence. I watched her puzzling to see the students straining to ask a question; but they caught my stare quite clearly. None of them spoke.

Good. Discipline.

'I am here on visitor's visa, so I have six months to spend time with family and to see this part of world. And I am enjoying.'

My interest was growing as the lady talked. Her grey-blue eyes sparkled as she spoke commanding attention, yet with a gentleness. I have visited Russia several times and I can understand the written language at a competent research level – my spoken skills have only ever been at the level of politeness in addressing people. Frankly, I'd always been wary – indeed, ultra careful on all my visits. I'd used interpreters on every occasion to conceal my level of understanding. For all my interest in their ways, I resented, even feared, the restrictions of their state censorship – an inherent disquiet at being vulnerable to their compromising traps, being given the party line, even in my academic circles; and my trepidation at a real sense of danger. Yet here I was sitting next to a lady who was 'living history'. She had been part of the 'Russian army' during a significant part of world history. I was quite fascinated to hear anything this lady had to say.

I caught Melanie's eye and nodded. She could now ask a question.

'You have lived through the dismantling of the old Soviet Union into lots of independent nations,' Melanie said. 'Could you give us a feel for what those changes meant to you please, Nana?'

Good question. Surprise, surprise!

Olga smiled as she seemed to search for words which would make sense to the students. 'Was working in what you might call … *communications*. Was always need for different parts of service to have information and means to deliver it. That part of my work didn't change – but culture of organisation did.

'Under communist regime, discipline was tight, really tight. We were engaged in *Cold War* with NATO forces, the North Atlantic Treaty Organisation of Europe and America. Had been build-up of nuclear weapons and neither side wanted to set off cataclysm which would end everything – so cold relations rather than active conflict. We didn't like each other. We had small skirmishes, to let off steam, you understand

– not big battles. That's different story to your question, Melanie, but you need to understand context.'

She collected her thoughts again and continued with a sudden passion glinting in her eyes. I could see the change registering in the jut of her jaw. It was as if she was thinking: Tell it as it was.

'From my perspective,' she said, 'West saturated world news channels, movies and books with *evil Russian empire*. To me, was most insidious propaganda campaign. They painted themselves with white hats; suave James Bond types saving world; super heroes from the US Central Intelligence Agency who conquered nasty growling Russkies.' There was steel in the voice, yet it was pitched low.

I watched Eva's jaw drop. Steve and Warren shared stifled grins; devotees of the very movies to which Nana Olga was referring, perhaps? I was surprised at the emotion in her comments and her command of complex words – if not the syntax. But mainly at her boldness in even talking like this. Was that her honest considered view of the Western world or just programmed vitriol? But then I had met very few Russian soldiers. My interest was the effect of politics on geographical patterns, so my meetings were always with academics and apparatchiks, the communist party members.

'And is while Americans dropped pattern bombs on Vietnam...' There was a definite underlying feeling in her tone. '...invading Grenada in West Indies, funding movements like Sandonistas in Central America, Mujihadeen in Afghanistan and Saddam Hussein in Iraq. And they demonise *us*?'

She paused with an enigmatic smile.

I was quietly puzzled to interpret her expression and statements – such an impressive English vocabulary range; and no really heavy Russian accent. She could be from any non-English-speaking European background.

It was as if she sensed a freedom to express opinions – or was I being patronising? She was clearly confident and had her own views. Why should I assume that she would be trotting out a party line? Wouldn't I expect a Western soldier to be staunchly patriotic – surely an asset in a military sense, not a flaw? Maybe her frankness was more a reflection of her stage in life when jingoism no longer mattered?

The students had said nothing, intently watching with quiet amazement. Hardly a restrained talk from an old grandmother. My eagle-eye continued to instil the silence.

'Sorry, back to question, Melanie. *Glasnost* and *perestroika*, you appreciate meaning of terms: safe open discussion without official politburo control and freeing up economic system from central planning' – she paused to register the students' understanding – 'they were means to break control of old communist machine. Had become power-crazy, although in smarter way than viciousness of Stalin's time.

'President Gorbachev is hated by many in Russia because he dismantled power structure but he deserves enormous credit for courageous leadership. If you asked me what his chances of living through that period would be, I would have said, zero. Yet he lives successfully; and new Russian Federation and independent states are flourishing to greater or lesser degree. Was, in my considered view, greatest statesmanship of twentieth century.

'However, we had to protect against political vacuum created by changes. Gangsters replaced centralised control. We guarded against army being compromised. Even so, Americans took advantage trying to destabilise our countries to increase their own profit and power. That grates with me – you understand – saviour knights in shining armour? Pah!' She stopped to draw breath. The four students were looking at her, even more wide-eyed. 'Does all make sense to you?'

I had landed in academic paradise. If I had to be marooned in this barbarian outpost, Hollywood could not have scripted it better. For one who has read every significant research paper in English or Russian about Cold War politics, here, in this colonial backwater of Toowoomba of all places, so far from Cambridge that any farther and I would be heading back, I was sitting with a retired Russian soldier who had lived through it all and was apparently comfortable to talk. And, she was so very different from the guarded restraint I had experienced from the procession of officials served up by the Russian state. Nana from heaven!

I took in the expressions of my students and wondered if her views and prejudices had been too full-on for young minds.

43

Or were they just hearing a story that didn't fit with what they believed or had been taught?

The student presence was keeping my questioning urges in check but whole catalogues of research thoughts were cascading through my mind. Suddenly realising that my look must have appeared impressed, I consciously adopted my academic lecturer face. I could see something in Olga's eye. Had she noticed my change in expression?

Steve McGrady interrupted the thought patterns with, 'Nana, I think we have the key information we need for this first part of our study technique. Will it be alright if we talk to you again later, to explore these ideas further?'

'Will be fine, Steve,' she said. 'Was quicker than I expected.'

I felt the need to clarify; just to speak actually.

'The students are practising their core technique to get information for mapping purposes at this time – with family. This is intended to be a very quick technical practice for reflection. We will go away and consider what we have learned. Then they can delve further into explaining the processes that allowed those patterns to develop. I'm sure that they, *we*, would love to listen to more of your story at a later date.'

'Thanks so much, Nana.' Eva's tone was appreciative. 'You are such a good sport to help us like this. I'm really looking forward to hearing more. It's fascinating.'

'Fascinating indeed,' I agreed, hoping my expression wasn't too obvious. 'I look forward to catching up with you again before long.'

'We'll all be at the bush dance this weekend, won't we?' asked Melanie.

'Bush dance?' I queried. Surely she had it wrong. 'That's not until we go to the camp-out at Goomburra, isn't it?'

I had it clear in my mind from my diary – or was that the camp-out? Damn! They all sounded the same, these Goomburra experiences.

'No, Dr Avery,' corrected Eva, respectfully. 'The bush dance is at Goomburra *this* weekend. It's to get to know the locals before we go camping and doing our research exercise there later. We're all going, my folks ... and Nana; Steve's folks and hopefully his uncle and aunt; all of us and the locals – Warren *is* a local.'

Nana? Well then. I would get the chance to chat casually with Olga. The prospect of the bush dance was no longer quite so unappealing. So many questions. What a blessing to have had this fount of information just land in my lap like this.

'Thanks for that, Eva,' I said, and then to Olga. 'I look forward to catching up with you on the weekend then, Ma'am.'

She smiled encouragingly, appearing more at ease with my accustomed polite enthusiasm than my students had seemed. Everyone said kind farewells as we moved on to interview Steve's Uncle Herbie. And that promised to be a very different experience.

Steve was of Aboriginal descent and the gist of what he had told me about his Uncle Herbie was that he was an Elder, a custodian of traditional knowledge; and he and his wife, Edna, worked with homeless young people in the Toowoomba area.

Chapter 13

Toowoomba. 8 March, 2007

Henry caught the tall thin girl as she came flying through the open door into the night. She had a large lump forming on her eyebrow, not helped at all by the pierced silver stud already skewering the flesh.

'That bastard! Shit! He's off his face!' the girl shouted back towards the sound of crashing inside the dimly-lit weatherboard house.

The rough walls were suddenly brightened by the reflection of the red and blue flashing lights from the police car that had arrived silently in the sleepy street.

Two men in light-blue uniforms moved past Henry, who was standing with a thin, dark-clothed man and the now crumpled girl. A following policewoman said, 'How many inside?' but the girl, dazed, said nothing. Henry and his companion just shrugged.

As the police moved through the door, the girl fluttered like a frightened bird. Appreciating her distress, Henry gently moved her out of the red and blue strobe into the welcoming protective darkness beyond.

The noise of crashing from inside had ceased but the torrent of screaming male language continued – and then it stopped suddenly too.

'I'm Henry.' He nodded towards his companion. 'This is Tooki.'

The girl looked at the two faces through her good eye, while the other was swelling painfully, tearing, as it tugged at the decorative staple.

She processed what she was seeing. Henry was clearly Murri. Fit looking. Very calm. Tooki was paler and had long blue-rinsed hair. Thin as a rake. Tallish. Older. Sharp eyes. Both in dark clothes. They would fit easily into 'the people of the street'. Her people. The displaced. The angry. The deprived.

'He's mad,' she said eventually. 'High as a kite, punching walls and then me. The lousy bastard.' She looked at them again. 'Who are you? What you doing here?'

From the shelter of their dark cocoon, the three of them could see a tall handcuffed man being bundled out of the deserted house to the police car.

'We got a call from the network.' Tooki spoke quietly. 'Trouble happening in a squat. Saturday night; we try to be out and about. Henry came to see if he could help.'

The girl looked confused. The network? 'What are you? Do-gooders?'

'Just people who have been there.' Henry spoke quietly.

The policewoman was looking around for the missing girl.

'I'm outta here,' the girl said quietly, fear in her voice.

'You need help for that eye.' Tooki's voice was almost in a whisper. No smile – just matter-of-fact. 'We'll take you to Aunty Edna's.'

The girl just looked. Two strangers. Blokes. She was wearing a shiner from a bloke.

'Who is shitting Aunty what's-her-name?'

'A friend,' said Tooki. 'Henry will take you there. No shit. I'll speak with the police.'

They didn't flap. Very calm. They could just walk away. So could she. They were both skinny people. Not pushy – just there. She could handle herself if she needed to but she didn't have many options. Stay. Go. Or go with Henry … to some Aunty. What else could go wrong on a night like this?

She nodded thoughtfully and followed Henry into the darkness for a short drive.

* * * *

The old Toyota Corolla rolled up to a high-set weatherboard. The girl climbed the steps with Henry to be met by a wrinkled Murri smile, 'I'm Edna. Come in.'

With an icepack placed carefully on the girl's swollen eye, the old lady asked, 'Could you handle a bowl of my vegetable broth, hot on the stove?'

47

She nodded.

The woman didn't follow with any more questions and Henry just stood in the background.

The girl took the bowl of broth carefully in both hands, while Edna held the icepack in place for her. After a few seconds of warming her shaking palms, she slowly started to spoon the tasty soup.

Eventually, the older woman asked, 'Hard night, eh?'

The young woman tilted her head in response and looked more closely towards the Murri lady standing at her side, seeing the strength and depth of experience in those bright eyes and that creased dark face.

The empty soup bowl was a testament to her need for sustenance. 'Izzy. I'm Izzy.'

Edna nodded. Her smile was more an expression of: I know. I've seen it all before.

'Aunty,' Henry said. 'She got thumped by a druggo in a squat. The police have taken him. They saw Izzy there.'

Edna's response was a twitch of an eyebrow. 'Izzy,' she said gently, 'You can't stay here just now. The police will be here soon. It's their routine. Henry will take you to our refuge for women. Not flash, but safe and better than the street. I'll come to see you tomorrow. There's one other girl there. Ellie's her name. She'd be about your age.'

Izzy looked dazed but nodded slowly, thought about saying, Thank you, but in the end said nothing.

She took the offered bag of biscuits, bread and cheese from Edna's hand, then followed Henry's lead back to the Corolla.

Chapter 14

Peter sat alone on a verandah chair, thinking through the possibility of losing his mother so soon after this joyous reunion.

She was justifiably proud of his achievements; just what he had hoped for. Yes, he had done well. His mother was right. He had retained much of his Russian language, living with migrants in Queensland. There were memories of his early days growing up in the Donbas industrial area of the eastern Ukraine. His grandmother had worked in the coal industry offices – cleaning, his mother was in the army and his father was 'away in GDR', the German Democratic Republic.

It had seemed like a real adventure for a six-year-old to travel out to Australia to live with his extended family, Uncle Ivan and Aunt Nina. He remembered his mother's tears at the airport. He was just going on a holiday with his aunt. He hadn't understood till much later what had been so upsetting. His mother had always been away a lot. It had been his grandmother who had been caring for him most of the time – and she was grumpy, forever uptight and complaining.

The scent of that hug with his mother in Kiev had remained clear in his memory – the last time he had been in her arms. He had that image of her waving goodbye as he boarded the plane, the tears – and then the adventure had taken over.

Woolloongabba in Brisbane, his first home in Australia, housed many Russian immigrants. He had settled into the local schools, played soccer well, was good at maths and could speak two languages capably by the time he reached high school.

Ivan and Nina weren't really his uncle and aunt. Nina was Olga's cousin but in the extended Russian family, that was the way it worked. They had two older children of their own and Nina was descended from grandparents who had fled the Russian Revolution in 1917. They told the story of refugees crossing Siberia to Manchuria in northern China and escaping the Japanese invasion in the 1930s to start a new life in Queensland. So Pyotr, known to friends and family as Peter, grew up as a third-generation migrant with his two much older cousins. He took on the surname, Grushko, from his adoptive parents. It was easier than explaining all the time. He was lucky. Uncle Ivan and Aunt Nina were good people.

He did well – with a childhood as happy as any adopted migrant in a strange new land – but he missed his natural mother. She came to his thoughts at night, this Olga Davidenko, this mysterious lady who wrote to him; who was there in his memory bank; whose voice and scents he remembered as a son would always remember a mother – but she was never actually there to touch.

She sent him letters and photographs of her in uniform. Her writing was about Russia or the countries she was visiting; about family news, people who were just names. He had no real faces to associate with the names. His mother was the only important person in his memory from that era. She had been the one who had told him eventually, in a letter, that his father had been killed in a battle in Germany when Peter was only two; the father about whom he had no memory, no stories.

Had he been a good man? How would he know? His mother usually avoided writing about him. She had written that it caused her great pain but he had never fully understood. Loss he could appreciate – but there was something missing.

Even his mother had gently morphed over time from a person to a subliminal powerful scent and an image in a photo. Nina and Ivan were the 'parents' he spoke with on a daily basis – and they had both passed away now.

Milestones of his life had come and gone; the sense of loss was always nagging away – when he graduated from school, then from university; when he married Anna; when Eva was born. There was always a reason why his mother couldn't come. She was on active duty. She couldn't be released.

He knew she was in the army – and he did get told once by Ivan that it was something more than just army. It would be unlikely she would ever be able to come to Australia. She wasn't available to be visited in Russia either, apparently. He had tried. As a family, they had been to Russia, Latvia and Ukraine. They were all prepared to fly anywhere to see her. But, no – that wasn't possible.

Why was she being so controlled? Was that just the way the Soviet, and later Russian, state operated? Or was there something more?

No reasons were given – just a cold denial of his requests from the authorities and veiled apologies from his mother later, by letter. He had felt anger, betrayal, loss, rejection; as well as a resigned numbness in realisation at what could not be.

That was why this visit was such a bonus. The impossible had happened. Her scent was just as he recalled from the airport in Kiev all those years ago. His memory had not failed him.

As the Toowoomba breeze fluttered over his verandah chair, his recollecting smile was laced by very private tears, rolling unchecked.

Chapter 15

'Hi, Uncle and Aunty!' The visitors greeted each other with the customary Murri greeting and a hug.

Uncle Herbie lived in a white-painted high-set weatherboard home on the north side of Toowoomba. Edna had the teapot brewing as Steve walked in with his fellow students and me. It was a bright sunny Tuesday. Somehow, I felt a spring in my step. Could it have been yesterday's meeting with the Russian grandmother, Olga Davidenko?

As I breathed in the floating aromas of home cooking, fond memories awakened of my mother's fluffy scones back in Somerset – straight from a warm oven, begging to be covered with melting cream and blackcurrant or strawberry jam. Was that really only a dozen years back? It seemed like a lifetime ago. How that time had flown into the mists of memory as a twang of guilty regret jolted me.

Edna presented home-made iced cup cakes to go with the tea. No serious talk took place until everyone had a sip and had tasted one of the house-speciality treats.

Steve explained that we were seeking some simple information by way of practising our interview techniques for a mapping project. Herbie nodded for Steve to start asking his questions. I was happy just to take a back seat. They had learned.

'Uncle, can you tell us who you are; where you are from, why you are in Toowoomba and how you came to be here?' The red light on the recorder flashed on, activated by the sound of the voice.

Uncle Herbie spoke confidently. 'I have lived here since I worked on the railways. Edna and I brought up most of our kids in this house

– and now we are retired. Mind you, I've never been so busy, so *retired* might not be the best word. We do a lot of work with the community; with Native Title and with cultural teaching. Now what did you want to know? Oh, yes! How did I come to be here?'

The students and I sat silent, gently refusing to fill in any gap in the conversation. I watched the effort as the young ones resisted their automatic reaction to assist his memory.

'I was born a Gunggari man out west near the Maranoa in the yumba and I have Kamileroi on my father's side. The yumba was our Murri camp outside the whitefellas' town, just out of sight of the main highway. We had the river and it was a great place to be a kid. True, no electricity or water laid on; water carted in twice a week and we had hurricane lamps for the evening. A few permanent cottages there and anyone could move in when they was empty. The rest lived in humpies they built nearby. A big bush shelter in the middle where the older ones could gamble – cards, you know. Drinking was never a problem in them days. We played rounders, footy and cricket. We was really happy there, even if we didn't have proper houses or anything. We swam, fished and explored for ripe bumbles, a kind of bush orange, or sweet mistletoe from the wilga tree; hunted goanna and porcupine.

'I suppose life was hard but it was what it was. We stayed away from whitefellas; collected wood, hunted and learned bush skills along with our traditions from the Elders. We never had to pay for rent, electricity and water like now. We was happy enough, you see, in a way; left alone to live like we wanted.'

I watched Herbie look across at his wife as he recalled the old days. Her lined face had a look of strength; resilient, positive. She had a lighter colouring than her husband. Steve had told me that Aunty's father had been called 'Husk' because of his wild appearance and the way he talked – he had been an older man; dark-bearded, curly-headed. Some had said he had come from overseas and worked as a drover on the stock routes, down to Mungindi and along the NSW border.

I sensed Steve had wanted to save me from embarrassing myself in a strange social situation. As if I couldn't ask my own questions to find out? Yet, how genuinely protective these students seemed to be. Maybe there were cultural protocols that I didn't appreciate. I couldn't profess to understand their care. It wouldn't have happened in England. Here, it seemed to be well intentioned.

Edna smiled back at the memories. Perhaps she was quietly pleased we weren't talking about those precious thoughts at this time. I was a stranger to them; yet, despite that, Herbie was still sharing lots of personal observations – really quite trusting.

'In 1967, the very year that white Australians decided to give Aboriginal people the vote in all elections, they ordered the bulldozers into the yumba; and, by the next year, it was demolished.

'We was forcibly resettled in town where we felt neither welcome nor comfortable. This was difficult for everyone, black and white. I was thirty by then. Edna and I had our first two children.' He smiled at his wife again. I could see the memories in his expression, floating back to those days with little ones running around the home. She returned the grin.

'Suddenly, I needed money to survive. Bush skills was no use when you had to pay for everything. Kids had to have things for school so that they didn't feel any worse than their black skins would already have them marked.

'I had worked regularly for a white contractor as a tree feller, but when the yumba was gone, I went off on the droving routes. Then on the railway gangs, laying and maintaining tracks – hard physical work in all weathers but I did it for the family – and, while I worked, I listened and watched.

'It was really important to Edna and me that our Gunggari and Kamileroi culture was maintained and taught, as we had learned in the bush from the old ones. We'd been given the vote but there was still a lot of resentment and discrimination in the community. None of our culture was respected or taught in schools. We was never consulted about our traditions or sacred places. We carried on our old trusted ways through stories, corroborees and ceremonies led by the Elders, all done very quietly within our people.

'When I was working on the railways and whitefellas asked me if I could speak language, meaning Gunggari, I just replied I was only a dumb Murri and that spared me from more questions or tampering with our traditions. It was all just passed on amongst our mob, word of mouth.' He rose to his feet, moved over to the window and gazed out to the trees for a few seconds before continuing.

'In the late 1980s, respect for our Aboriginal culture was starting to grow. We got this house here in Toowoomba. My older brother, Kenny, was already living here so that made it easier. He was Steve's granddad. He's passed away now.

'I was still working on the railways, an experienced foreman by then. I also did a roster of night patrols in Toowoomba looking out for our young ones who might be getting themselves into trouble, you know drinking and fighting. Aunty Edna here did a lot of work – still does – helping the teenagers who could see no hope, who couldn't keep jobs, who didn't like the comments they heard; sometimes dressed up to sound smart, mainly just vicious. We tried to get them back on track by teaching them to be proud of their culture, their traditions.'

He paused again, his eyes fixed on something outside. 'Edna, someone is watching the house. Were you expecting anyone?'

'One of ours? Or police?'

'Naw. Looks foreign. Uncomfortable, like. He's moving away now. He was definitely watching the house though. Mmm.'

The students glanced at each other, eyes widening; while I had a cascading ripple of dread pass through me – my sense of being followed. Here it was again.

'No worries, though.' Herbie shrugged dismissively and smiled back into the room. 'Where was I now? As yes, helping the lost ones on the street. Well, it comes back to showing them another way. Education for our mob, for sure. Helping them understand the world around them … and the values that was part of our tradition. So that they can fit in … and move on. But not just for Murris. The white kids too; they didn't understand either … but they wanted to, see? Kids question the world. They ask really clever questions. Not just about boomerangs but more like, what does it mean to be Aboriginal today? They had mates who were Murris, see? Edna and I got invited into the schools, to talk about our lives and experience. It opened all our eyes, I think … and started to build a trust.

'Slowly, we became part of more education programs in the classrooms and on their learning camps in the bush. Out there, they wanted to know about bush tucker and tracking. How to catch a goanna. What does a witchety grub taste like. How it was that we have survived for tens of thousands of years, living off the bush.

'We was lucky that I met Warren's grandfather back then, when I was visiting the Goomburra school for a culture talk – that's years ago now. We hit it off straight away – timber fellas from way back – and that is how the camps started on his property. We just got to yarning, sharing stories. Then when the old man passed on, Warren's dad and I carried on a similar friendship.

'We work with the local Elders. This is *their* country. The traditional owners here are Barunggam and Jarowair with some Waka Waka and Yuggera, depending on how far you go from Toowoomba. We are visitors – but still accepted as community Elders working to help people.'

Herbie stopped. His eyes came back from visualising the story he was telling, to looking at the faces of his visitors. I was captivated by his description of a world that I scarcely understood. An appreciative silence enveloped us as we took in the story he had just shared.

'I don't know if I have been answering your questions, Steve, but that's why we are here in Toowoomba and how we came to be here.'

It was Melanie who spoke, her voice quivering a little. 'Uncle Herbie, that's real good. You've put a face to some history for me; how some of the pieces of the jigsaw fit – and I grew up in this country.' She shook her head slowly.

Steve's face was impassive. I could guess this story was all part of his normal life but perhaps kept hidden even from friends – because it was easier; no fights, no explanations. I could empathise with the hidden secrets and I could relate to feeling different – not like Uncle Herbie, but still being tagged as not the same as the mass of others. I had conformed too, to fit in – just to survive.

Edna passed round some more cup cakes.

'Thank you, Uncle Herbie,' my voice broke the quietness, 'for sharing such a personal story with us.' But I winced to myself. My accent sounded so affectedly precise. The smell of the home cooking had reminded me of my real West Country dialect – not my current diction. A rare twinge of remorse jagged my conscience. 'I come from England. I certainly didn't appreciate you had grown up in a world like this. I feel very honoured that you have shared your memories with us.' I paused, reflecting on this tale. 'Well students, do you have enough information for this part of the research?'

Warren nodded patiently. I realised from his look that he would have heard Uncle Herbie talk on camps on his property before. But I was guessing. He'd said nothing. Perhaps he felt he had to be very careful with the stories. He wasn't Murri. Any knowledge would have been given in trusted confidence. My opinion of him just raised a couple of notches. Or maybe it was just I who didn't understand.

Eva lightened the mood, 'Will you both be coming to the bush dance on the weekend at Goomburra?'

'Would you want an old couple like us there?' asked Aunty Edna with a grin. 'We might not be able to swirl around the dance floor like we once did.'

'Oh, yes,' endorsed Melanie. 'It would be really good if you could come. Eva's Nana is coming too. She hasn't been well so she might not dance. It's a chance to meet the locals and to listen, before we go to our camp-out there later in the term – and I've heard that the band is brilliant; lots of fun. You'll love it.'

'Then I think Herbie and I should be there,' said Edna with a smile. 'What a nice invitation.'

'What will you do with the story I have given you?' Uncle Herbie asked.

Warren replied, 'We are just practising Dr Avery's technique of interviewing where you don't interrupt the interviewee.'

He said the last part with a big grin to me. Maybe these students were astute after all.

'Uncle,' added Steve. 'All we'll do is map where you live and where you came from. Then we will be interested in why you came to live here. You have told us some of that already. We're tuning our techniques to get the information to map the geographical patterns. We'll have more questions as we try to analyse and explain the processes that caused those patterns to develop.'

I needed to come to the rescue. 'As geographers, we have to be skilled in getting basic information quickly to map patterns. It is usually easiest if the questioner doesn't interrupt the flow of thought all the time. It is about listening rather than dominating a conversation. You have been most helpful, Uncle Herbie.'

With thanks and pledges to catch up at the bush dance on the weekend, we departed.

Chapter 16

1 May 2008

Email: spenceravery@bigpond.com.au

From: tobystanleysmythe@cam.ac.uk

Spencer old boy

Pretty though your handwriting always is, your snail mail of 25 April took nearly a week to get here. You may be out in the colonial sticks but we do have email and texts, you know. Glad to hear you have arrived and are keeping up the stereotype of the whinging Pom. Enjoy the experience.

Use email old chap.

Toby

PS Love the Aussie humour
PPS Mary sends her regards.

Mary! Well, thanks for adding that postscript, Toby.

Mary. The main reason for leaving Cambridge. My thoughts were tumbling in the fluttering adrenalin that Mary's name had evoked. I had almost managed not to think of her.

Mary Johnston. Daughter of a professor. No, more than that, daughter of the Dean of the Faculty. Beautiful. Intelligent. Great company. My constant companion for many weeks as we punted on the river, attended classical concerts and even went hunting grouse in Scotland.

It had all looked so perfect. The up-and-coming doctor of philosophy, specialising in geo-politics; touted as a potential professor in a very few years. Matched with the Dean's attractive daughter; a prized guest at Cambridge society parties; skilled in the ways of the better English gatherings; graduate with promising prospects.

It went pear-shaped when Mary's mother made it abundantly clear that one Spencer Avery was not 'a good fit' for her daughter. 'There is breeding to consider,' she had said. In her view, I was one of the 'new academics' – those who tried to sound as if they fitted, produced a battery of research work and dabbled in the world of contemporary politics – but I was the son of a draper from a small Somerset town, after all.

Mary, on the other hand, could have her ancestry traced back by her mother to dukes from the time of Henry VII. The difference would be stark to those who value such differences.

To cut the long sad tale short; despite the genuine strong feelings Mary and I clearly felt we had for one another, there was the matter of societal fit and, even with the egalitarian values of the 21st century, some still saw the world through the prism of the heraldic crest.

I didn't accord with Mary's mother's view of an appropriate suitor for her daughter. Mary did not have the steel to stand up to her mother. So, desolate, I confided in my good friend and fellow lecturer, Toby Stanley-Smythe.

It was Toby who had told me about the opportunity to gain international experience, with a suitable salary, in Australia – only for a few months, less than a year – some space and time to see if there really was a future for me with Mary.

The initial contact with Australia had seduced me into believing that I may be a visiting adjunct professor at a prestigious university which, coupled to my status at Cambridge, might just make me acceptable to my lovable Mary and her demanding mother.

The reality had sadly dawned soon after I had landed in Australia; when I had been posted to a university in Toowoomba. I was told forcefully and repeatedly that my vision of a high-calibre Melbourne option did not exist, even though I had been flown into Tullamarine airport in Melbourne, initially. It didn't compute with common sense but there was no reasoning with any of them. They pointed to the fine print in the contract that I had signed in Britain with scarcely a glance at the time.

I just had to live with it or flee back to Britain – and that wasn't a realistic or even possible option either, given the shameful situation I had left behind.

Toowoomba was to be my position for the next few months – that was final – and I couldn't see how that experience would be useful on my Curriculum Vitae of worthiness for a future mother-in-law.

Then, again, if I had been accepted into the House of Windsor, I still probably wouldn't have met the prospective mother-in-law's high standards.

Anyway, Mary had sent her regards. 'Be grateful for all mercies, Spencer,' I muttered to myself.

Email: tobystanleysmythe@cam.ac.uk

From: spenceravery@bigpond.com.au

Toby old son

Thanks for your email. Take your point. I was just feeling a nostalgic need for the handwritten word. My therapy. You know me. Over it now, old chap.

You'll never believe what has happened. On some interview practice for the undergrads, we spoke to a very interesting retired lady who worked for the Russian army in communications. Haven't established what branch yet but seems willing to give her perspective.

Perhaps this won't be a lost sojourn in the wilderness after all.

Thanks for passing on Mary's regards. Please return the sentiment. Is there anything else to report on that front – a mother contracting bubonic plague perhaps?

Bush dance this weekend. I will report on the 'knees-up' after the event.

Yours ever
Spencer

The students certainly seemed to be impressed by what they were calling the 'Avery interview technique'. I was mildly amused. It was only routinely good practice, after all – hardly a revolution in method.

Nevertheless, Nana Olga had given them her perspective with a surprising passion – as had Uncle Herbie. That might have opened their eyes to something new and stimulating.

My confidence was coming back. Thank goodness for the interaction of teaching.

And the upcoming bush dance promised to be different. I could bet they were all anticipating my reaction to what they call *The Stockyards* or *Strip the Willow*.

It would be interesting.

Chapter 17

The Saturday night bush dance scene intrigued me as my gaze wandered round this distinctive social occasion – quite unlike anything I had attended in Britain. Groups of people, in a dress version of farm attire, had mustered in the main hall.

Laughter and smiles graced every face – a sense of anticipation. The students and I were apparently very welcome guests. Warren was a local. No formal introductions; just confident relaxed people catching up with friends.

The Goomburra hall appeared very small to my eyes to be catering for dancing couples. Serried tables lined the sides of the main floor. The band was setting up on the stage. People had deposited 'a plate' in a side hall, a quaint Australian custom – a platter of food – savouries, sandwiches, sweets. Melanie had offered to bring my plate as well as her own; delicious home-made pumpkin scones, the culinary fare for bush dances apparently.

'Thank you, Melanie. You have been very kind.' I was rewarded with the most radiant of smiles – an attractive young woman.

The band was called 'The Fair Dinkum Bush Band'. True to form there was a lager-phone, a banjo, a guitar, a mandolin, a piano accordion and a bass guitar – quite an ensemble, with the guitarist alternating between the flute and penny whistle.

As the band struck up an apparent Australian classic, Slim Dusty's *G'day G'day*, I knew I was out of my comfort zone. The locals seemed to know every word of the songs and had an in-built understanding of the social mores of these country occasions.

Despite feeling out of place, I was damned if I would let it show. I sidled over to where Olga had found a seat; talking quietly to Herbie and Edna. They seemed to be getting on famously, sharing interview stories. It was flattering listening to the comments. 'University' seemed to have a hallowed impact on them all. I just listened, on the edge of the group, waiting for my opportunity to engage Olga in some conversation.

The first dance was the *Heel and Toe Polka*. I had heard the opening tune somewhere before – *Little Brown Jug*, perhaps. Eva corralled me onto the floor with the claim, 'It's really easy. You'll love it.'

True to her word, the dance was within my skill level and she was a good partner. Her infectious smile helped me relax as she carefully explained the steps. I appreciated that. I didn't want to appear to be a total goose on the floor although I noticed a few others who were all left feet – and no-one seemed to care.

My comfort lasted only until the band said, 'Now we snowball!' and everyone scattered. She explained that I had to get another partner and soon there would be twice as many people on the floor. 'Ask Nana. The first dance is always the gentlest.'

I wasn't feeling much confidence at these strange routines; but I definitely wanted the opportunity to talk with the Russian lady on her own. Emboldened by ulterior motive, I bowed and asked Olga graciously for the dance.

She accepted, advising she couldn't do anything too strenuous. Before Peter or Anna had time to intervene, I, with the experience of five minutes training, walked her through the steps.

The band struck up again. We moved with a grace that seemed to surprise those who watched, judging by their pleased expressions. We were light on our feet; chatting and laughing.

At the dance's end, Tony, the lager-phone player, suggested everyone go and get a drink. 'Are you going to shout, Gary?' he called out to the mandolin player.

Receiving a muttered smiling, though negative, response, Tony added, 'Gary Tate, folks. I'm afraid Gary wouldn't shout if bitten by a shark!'

The crowd all laughed.

'Shout?' I asked.

'It means you buy a round of drinks at the bar,' explained Steve.

I smiled as I thought: perhaps the Tates of some famous Scottish glen.

As I had discovered quickly, bush dancing was hard work. Olga didn't dance any more but she was clearly happy watching everyone else learning new dances, making mistakes and generally having fun.

Herbie and Edna need not have feared being strangers. Warren's parents already knew them well and a constant flow of locals engaged them in conversations. By the time everyone had danced *The Stockyards* and *Strip the Willow*, with expert tuition from the band members, there would have been few people in the hall that our group hadn't met. Such was bush dancing.

The Drongo, I discovered, was actually a bird with an erratic flight pattern and the namesake dance was a variation of musical chairs with the stranded person having to dance in the silliest manner. There were plenty doing their best to emulate nature.

The band had a seemingly endless variety of progressive dances which forced partners to change and people to meet. By the end of the night, even the most energetic was exhausted. There were no strangers in the hall and I was left pondering how successful this spontaneously happy event had been for mixing.

* * * *

Email: tobystanleysmythe@cam.ac.uk
From: spenceravery@bigpond.com.au

Topic: The bush dance

Toby, old son

I have never been to a better social occasion in my life.

You would swear it was going to be appallingly kitsch but it turned out to be really the most genuine way to meet new people. Everyone had a laugh and joke.

The nearest equivalent might be a Scottish ceilidh, but I don't remember a dance with such an opportunity to make new friends, with so much laughter. At one point, a fairly inebriated gentleman asked the band if they would play Elvis Presley's 'Blue Suede Shoes'. After a look to his band members, the lager-phone player knew it wasn't in their repertoire so, in the blink of an eye, he said, 'We will play you this song. It has a lot of the same notes as Blue Suede Shoes, just not in the same order.' The band promptly played the Irish tune, 'Black Velvet Band' and the inebriated man smiled happily. Incredible!

As the night went on, the Aussie accents caused me to miss a lot of meanings. I heard a person at the next table talking about 'the harpist'. I like the harp, so I wondered whether it would be a classical harp or an Irish harp. I couldn't see a harp on stage, so I asked him about the harpist. In fact, what he had said was that one of his friends was 'half pissed'.

Clearly, I need to attune my English ear to this Aussie twang.

But Toby, it was brilliant. I take back all my earlier comments about bush dances. I am actually almost looking forward to camping at Goomburra later in the term – with suitable comforts, of course. The people are very friendly. There is an uninhibited manner about them. As they say here, 'No bullshit!'

When I come back to Cambridge, I'll have to see if we can put together a scratch band to replicate this happy atmosphere.

All is well.

Cheers
Spencer

* * * *

Olga understood what she had missed – just seeing Eva dancing away all night.

'So much happiness around.' She hugged her granddaughter as they all left the hall. 'Had good talk with Herbie and Edna, such amazing strong culture.'

'Did they ask much about your life?' Peter queried.

'Oh, my life has been drab by comparison.'

Her son looked faintly puzzled as he took her arm and announced, 'Early tomorrow, Anna and I have some catching up to do at work but in the afternoon, we can start filling in all the missing years. Then the day after tomorrow, it is the May Day holiday. We can have most of the day to talk.'

'Will be fine.'

She was smiling as they moved towards Peter's Toyota Land Cruiser.

It was a pleasant evening with stars twinkling away high up in the huge clear dome of the darkened sky. The smells of the grass and the country life permeated the air – a clean wet earth scent billowing gently on the light breezes.

The car park was full, mostly farm-style four-wheel drives and utilities. Maybe that was why Olga's attention was drawn to two in particular.

Ping. One was a four-wheel drive with a city look about it, despite the mud-spatters.

It was more its position, just out of line with the others. She had years of looking for anomalies in patterns. That one didn't fit.

Ping. The other car that caught her glance was a dark Holden Commodore. She had been observing car types in Toowoomba – definitely a Commodore – all part of the routine discipline from her former life.

Olga's steady walk never faltered; her antennae alert. Over forty years of watching one's tail created a sixth sense. Were they here to follow *her* or for someone else?

'Good you have work to catch up tomorrow morning. I invited Spencer out to home for cup of tea tomorrow at ten.' She quietly advised her arrangement to the family as they reached their vehicle. 'Will that still be alright? Just quick chance to catch up. I spent time in Cambridge, years ago. Perhaps we have mutual experiences?'

Peter and Anna nodded happily. Dr Avery was Eva's lecturer after all.

Olga smiled her appreciation at their flexibility. 'Tomorrow afternoon – and the day after tomorrow, as you said, Peter, you and I will talk; for as long as you like. You too, Anna and Eva. So many years...' She patted her son's hand as her eyes went distant for an instant.

But she was interested in Dr Spencer Avery. He had all the affectations of an aloof intellectual. Yet, she could see through the cultivated mask. He was not all he appeared to be. Why was an academic from Cambridge cooling his heels in a provincial university on the other side of the world?

As the Grushkos neared Toowoomba, both of the suspicious vehicles from Goomburra were in the queue behind. Not necessarily unusual. It was the main road. What *would* be unusual would be if Olga could still see them when she got out at the top of the driveway at home.

As she emerged from Peter's Toyota, she noted the four-wheel drive on the main road.

'I just want to watch stars for few minutes,' she said to Peter. 'Beautiful sky tonight. I'll just stand under tree and come in shortly.'

Peter nodded as he and the others went into the house.

In the quietness of the evening, she watched the Holden Commodore cruise slowly by at the bottom of the driveway. It had taken a few minutes for it to appear but there was no mistaking that she had two vehicles following her.

In a previous time, she might have felt flattered but now, who would be interested in a retired army officer? When all that part of her life was over and all she wanted was some quiet time with her family, someone was apparently still after her.

She turned to enter the house quietly but was startled by a loud rustling of something big in the branches of a large tree.

Fluttering.

Big.

She saw the dark bat wings of flying foxes cutting silently across the night sky – crashing loudly as they landed en masse to roost in the high branches of the trees. Raucous chattering and squeaking from their communication. No silent radar with these big beasts.

An omen? she thought. Probably bad if you choose to believe omens.

Chapter 18

'Was there anything particular you wanted to know?' Olga had just the slightest of smiles on her face, but it was the flickering laughter in the eyes which rattled me. I had the sense she was trying to unsettle my accustomed confident façade.

The timing had been perfect. Ten o'clock on a Sunday – so peaceful. I had arrived in the Grushko family driveway just as Peter and Anna were leaving, apparently to deal with some contracts at work. I could always be relied upon to be punctual – my father's shop-keeper diligence absorbed by osmosis.

I gathered that Olga had planned to spend the afternoon and the Monday holiday with her son and his wife; talking through some of their long separate family histories. Eva had mentioned to me earlier that her parents had met at university and now, together, they ran the family business, AA Electrical. I wondered why these students always wanted to prepare me for meeting their families. Did they doubt that I could be tactful enough to find out for myself? So genuine in their sharing.

'I have kettle on for pot of tea.' Olga smiled with the offer.

'That will be fine, Ma'am,' I replied through force of habit.

'Now, if I have to call you Spencer,' she said, mimicking my voice, 'you have to call me, Olga. Agreed?'

My polite smile hid my disappointment at my opening gaffe. I had been so looking forward to this meeting. I was amazed that I was nervous. I hadn't been myself with all the upheavals of the move to Australia.

'Do you play chess?' she asked suddenly.

'A little,' I ventured. 'Yes!' Suddenly, boldly, with confidence. 'Yes, I can play chess.'

'Good!' She was grinning. 'Let's have game of chess with our tea – on verandah, so we can take in view and have good chat. What you say?'

'That sounds very good, *Olga*.'

The Russian lady smiled a little in response.

It didn't take long to set up the chess set and tea on two adjoining tables on the wide verandah. The view over the wide agricultural valley to the south looked serene; the blue sky with scarcely a cloud, crowning bright green and brown fields.

'I would be pleased if you be white and start.' She invited me as the guest to take the honour in the game. I nodded acknowledgement and moved my king's pawn forward two spaces.

The first few moves were played quietly until she asked, 'Did Boris Spassky teach you that move?'

I was stunned. Boris Spassky was a Russian chess grandmaster and a former world champion. The best I could do was to give a silent questioning glance.

'Boris used that opening in his match against Bent Larsen in 1970.' She smiled. 'I watched that game.'

I gulped. I wasn't even born in 1970. 'I'm just a social chess player, Olga.' What was going on?

'No matter,' she said. 'You are playing well. Now what did you want to talk to me about?'

I struggled to collect my composure. Her Spassky comment had quite thrown me. How good a chess player was she to have watched grandmasters in action?

I rambled briefly about my university research into Cold War Russia and Eastern Europe. 'I thought you might be able to help me understand what it was like for you to live through that time. Why not start with what you did in the army?'

I moved my knight into an attacking position.

'I was in communications. Languages, really,' moving a bishop to cover the aggressive knight move.

'So you would have been an officer?' I queried innocently.

'I held rank of major.' She watched me for my reaction.

I was impressed. And she was toying with me. I knew it but she was in control.

'Major?' I mulled over the idea. This was no old granny. But she didn't fit any of my mental images of a Russian army major – not at all like a hard-faced disciplinarian who could toss a discus out of a stadium. I was conscious that, even with all my studies into Cold War matters, I had really only operated at the geo-political level. Despite my best intention, I was probably falling into the trap that she had flagged at her interview with the students. I did have a stereotyped view of what a female Russian officer would be like. 'That is impressive.' I continued as casually as I could manage, moving my queen forward to pre-empt a disguised attack. 'You would have a lot of high level knowledge, and time in other countries?'

I watched as she quietly registered the direction of my probing. 'Well, I spent time in Cambridge.' The comment was so offhand that my guard was thrown again. Damn!

She laughed aloud as my eyes must have widened. 'I accompanied Master of Clare to Chancellor's Ball.'

I could sense that I would be looking impressed and incredulous, simultaneously. 'Wow!' was all I could manage initially. I struggled to stay in control. 'Why were you at the Ball?'

'Was embassy attaché in London.' She grinned. 'Important person who was charmed to be invited to such occasion.' The mystery sparkled in her eyes again.

I was having real difficulty, blown away by this lady who had both watched Boris Spassky play chess and had attended the Chancellor's Ball at Cambridge – and all the time she was teasing me; almost flirting. Goodness! This lady would have to be in her sixties, more than twice my age and here she was confusing me with smiles and laughs. What was going on?

I settled. I could see she was having great fun. She knew exactly what sort of information I was angling for and she was flustering me.

Perhaps it was a test and she was judging if this was just an innocent conversation or whether I was some form of threat. I knew the theory but I was being swept along like a cork in a stream.

She changed tack. 'Wasn't bush dance fun, down at Goomburra?' She took a pawn in a threatening move. 'Everyone was so happy – lots of smiles.'

'You're absolutely right, Olga.' I silently told myself to be careful. 'I was wondering if it was just I who enjoyed it so much. I think I met everyone in the hall. Don't know all their names but I would have had a laugh with each of them. And the band was just brilliant.'

'Mandolin player so impressive,' she enthused. 'His speed at playing those jigs. He could keep company with best balalaika players in Russia.'

I could only agree. 'Great way to meet people. I had no idea what to expect. Yet it was so down-to-earth, no airs and graces – not quite like you would find at the Chancellor's Ball, for example.' I grinned with implication at her privileged past. She scarcely reacted at first.

'Oh,' she parried with that mysterious smile. 'You need wide range of experiences to appreciate what is important in life.' There was the twinkling grin again. 'I'm sure you have danced at many formal balls. You had lightness in your step. You have danced before.'

I was not sure I was getting all the intended meanings. Discretion suggested a quiet nod might be safer than exposing my ignorance.

'Tell me, Spencer.' The innocent question fluttered in her eyes again. 'Why are you lecturing in Toowoomba? Did you strangle Cambridge professor's cat or something?'

She watched for my reaction from behind her veil of charm. Despite my best efforts, I felt myself react, ever so slightly. How could she know?

Could I share something so close and painful to me? Uncle Herbie and Olga had shared personal experiences. Not everyone was deceitful in this world. I had been living the expected façade for too long.

She watched my struggle quietly. I took my time to reply. 'I felt I needed a change from the claustrophobia of the Cambridge academic life and Australia seemed to be as far away from that as I could find.'

I could tell from her glance that my Russian interrogator had recognised the lie as soon as it was spoken. Her questioning smile challenged me but she said nothing. It was a long pause. She shifted her gaze back to the chess board as if planning her next move, while I thought, *Speak. Damn you.*

'Doesn't that answer satisfy you?' I asked at length. Why did I feel like she was seeing through me on every move?

Very carefully she said, 'I think either you have strangled professor's cat or you are fleeing from something else. Would there be love interest?'

I felt totally exposed – and yet, I could sense in her ... a genuineness. Not at all like a member of the regime. And she was retired from all that. Her manner; a lady who had lived – worldly experience – yet one who cared; and she was a charmer. What did I know? I was out of my depth – and I held no state secrets anyway.

'Well, you are partially right,' I admitted eventually. 'It is the Dean's daughter as it happens. I suppose I am here to see if the relationship can survive the separation.'

She nodded, while moving a bishop forward to attack.

'Separation is always hard,' she agreed quietly.

I could have bet she was thinking that I was just a lonely academic. Not too far from the truth, I suppose. Not lonely really, certainly not normally – just hurt. Wounded pride. Needing to recuperate.

She watched me. What were her instincts telling her? Perhaps, I gave an impression of emotional confusion behind my fragile formality. And she was like a calm counsellor, a psych with whom I could share my pain – and I needed that. I was definitely lonely for someone to trust.

'Have you experienced separation, Olga?' What was she prepared to share? I watched *her* now. I could see the cogs turning. Whoopee! Got her.

'Peter is my son,' she said quietly, stating the obvious. 'I had to send him away to be brought up by relatives in Australia when he was six years old. We have just reunited; now, after all these years. Yes, I understand separation, Spencer. Was my choice – was no other way I could see at time.'

Looking silently into each other's eyes, I could feel some kind of shared experience. Perhaps we had each passed a preliminary test – a spark which we both sensed simultaneously. Or she was a damned good actress.

The game of chess continued with me conceding to avoid the inevitable check-mate. The conversation was light; about the Darling Downs, about granddaughter Eva and her studies; about my research topics and my papers on the changing political patterns in Eastern Europe.

Olga showed interest and acknowledgement of my general academic prowess. She offered no alternative opinions although I knew she would have held them. I had tasted that in the earlier interview with the students. But, for the moment, it was innocuous, no arguments, no corrections, no strong views.

I relaxed. I felt that a kindred spirit of sorts had been struck with the Russian grandmother. We both had pain in our pasts, although I was only twenty-nine. What had this lady lived through in twice my lifetime – and more? And, in common, we both seemed to laugh at similar quirks in life. We had loved the bush dance and we were each getting used to the peculiarities of the Australian way of life – the humour and the language in particular.

As I rose to take my leave, I had a sense of anticipation for the next time we would meet.

I noticed Olga's eyes move down to the end of the driveway.

I followed her gaze. A dark Holden Commodore cruised slowly past. There were three occupants – one in the back seat. We both caught the pale flash of faces briefly looking up the drive.

I sensed an unknown danger. Fleetingly, I recalled my sense of someone watching me.

I glanced at her. Was it co-incidence that I had this sensation in another place – and that Olga had noticed too? But I said nothing.

She ignored my polite offer that I should wait until Peter and Anna returned. We parted with smiles and a polite hug. I felt we had become friends, in a way that I was not sure I fully understood. She was so unlike any Russian I had met before – although I recalled some representatives of the regime who had that quirky suggestion of mischief but they always quickly brought it back under control.

As I left the driveway, a dark four-wheel drive vehicle approached on my side of the road. I tooted the horn and it swung back to its own side as I took evasive action. The driver must have been concentrating on something else.

Chapter 19

The reports were coming in, being analysed and relayed to Superintendent Jeff Fowler.

- *A man picked up at Darwin Airport, just yesterday, with a Syrian passport. His bag inspection revealed a photograph of a Major Olga Davidenko. Contact details for the major were on a note indicating her presence in Toowoomba in Queensland. Checks are being carried out into the Syrian's background.*

- *The background check into the man from Pakistan (alerting details phoned in earlier) revealed association with known terrorist-training groups in the northern part of that country. Suspect is saying nothing about the major or why he has her photograph in his possession.*

The stakes were rising. It was time to be ready for more direct action.

The challenge in policing against international terrorism was that the terrorists only need to get it right once. Timing was everything.

Fowler picked up the phone to speak to the office of the Queensland Commissioner of Police. Some approvals now needed to be cleared with a minimum of fuss.

While waiting for the call to be answered, he typed an email note to his executive secretary to book him a flight to Brisbane and accommodation in Toowoomba.

* * * *

Eva, Melanie, Warren and Steve were with me in the Arts/Business building.

'Are you comfortable you can get the information you need, using this technique?' I asked.

We had been analysing the interview recordings; distilling the essence of their needs for the mapping project.

The students nodded agreement.

'Now you have chosen Goomburra as your sample group. Why?'

'Yeh, no, I suggested a twelve per cent random sample of the population of Toowoomba,' explained Warren with a grin. 'But the wise Eva pointed out that the 2006 census of Toowoomba gave the population as 96,226. Twelve per cent would be about eleven and half thousand interviews. That would have been just a shade too many, I reckon.'

There were stifled chuckles at the recollection of the enormity of Warren's suggestion. I was just beginning to appreciate the quiet irreverence of the students but they were 'mates'; a precious self-effacing honesty.

Melanie laughed towards Eva. 'So I suggested: What about doing Cambooya then? It's not too big; when Miss Statistics announced that Cambooya has over six thousand people, so we would still be interviewing several hundred. Smaller. We needed to go much, much smaller. So it fell to wise Steve to suggest Goomburra which has only three hundred people. We would only need about thirty interviews if it were done randomly.'

The quiet Murri lad took his bow with due solemnity.

'And we know many of the people already,' added Eva, 'from the bush dance; and Warren is already a local.'

'And we'll be doing some learning on the camp-out too.' Melanie was enthusiastic.

I checked with them all by glance. 'Okay? Goomburra? Eight interviews each? Manageable?'

Nods all round.

'But,' Steve hesitated. 'We don't want to lose the start that Nana Olga and Uncle Herbie gave us with their stories. Can we add them as an additional study, perhaps to contrast with what we find at Goomburra?'

Melanie was getting keener by the minute. 'They're coming on the camp-out? Can't we listen to their conversations there and build the profile of their stories?'

'Good.' Warren nodded thoughtfully. 'But we have a ways to go yet to appreciate the potential of the open-ended approach and I think it could link into a bigger research project which could involve Toowoomba.' He seemed determined to take on something more substantial than eight interviews each.

'Agreed,' I interjected, 'At least for listening to their stories.' Their confidence just needed to be tempered with some common sense. The bigger picture was to complete all the final year degree tasks, not just one assignment. 'But Warren, that project is massive, to do it authentically. Our little dissertation could well be the catalyst to encourage someone to invest in the longer research.'

They seemed to be satisfied with their roles in the task ahead. Work to be done.

'Till tomorrow, then,' I said by way of dismissing them all. The group dispersed but Melanie held back as I packed up.

'Did you enjoy the bush dance, Spencer?' she asked cheerily. 'I can call you Spencer, can't I? I mean, here, in the university? Not just at the dance?'

'Yes.' I smiled. 'Of course.' That was progress sitting easily with me. And how typical of her to ask. 'Yes, to both, Melanie. Lots of laughs at Goomburra. Goodness, though, it's hard work – all that dancing. How about you?'

'Oh, I thought it was great. The Fair Dinkum Bush Band is pretty well-known on the Downs. They've been out near home in Goondiwindi and even in Moree,' she added, 'although I hadn't been to their dances before, out there.'

'And thanks for saving my embarrassment by providing the plate.' I added, 'I liked your pumpkin scones.'

She gave a happy smile.

'Do you have everything?' I asked as I switched off the lights

We moved out to our separate cars and waved goodbye.

It had been an interesting day. My thoughts were about Olga. It was hard to imagine her as a Red Army officer, and a major at that. She was so ... human; so full of laughter. Those smiling eyes did not fit the caricature of the grim Russian soldier, spitting out 'Nyet' to any pleasurable activity.

She had been teasing me this morning, actually telling me next to nothing – and beating me at chess. Well, she would, wouldn't she, if she had moved in the company of chess grandmasters? She seemed more like an understanding grandmother actually – which indeed she was.

I did ponder some of life's mysteries. Why couldn't the charming Olga have been Mary Johnston's mother instead of that unbearable snob who saw no genealogical merit in one Spencer Avery?

My thoughts were on a roll.

Then a salutary idea occurred to me. I had danced the night away at Goomburra – probably danced with every woman in the hall, with scarcely a thought of missing Mary. Interesting. Was I starting to question this untenable infatuation?

Even more interesting was that I'd had such a happy laughter-filled dance experience. It really was a ball – much better than my memory of other much-vaunted society functions, where we were all dolled up in the best finery available but we didn't laugh, make dance mistakes, sing along with the band, swap partners naturally and innocently in every progressive barn dance or reel. Goomburra had been spontaneous happiness.

The language of the bush dance had been earthy but not rude nor offensive – more homely. Some people drank more than they should, but there always seemed to be family members and friends to handle it all with banter and understanding.

It was about having fun, not worrying about 'the proper way' to do things – and yet, even the most 'tired and emotional' stayed within the limits.

The band exhausted everyone. The dancers went away, knowing that it had been a good evening; and they would still all be friends in the morning.

Amazing, I thought as I drove out of the car park.

* * * *

Fowler ran his eye over the most recent reports.

- *The detectives in Toowoomba note three men in a dark maroon Holden Commodore who had followed Olga Davidenko to a bush dance at Goomburra. They have then kept up a regular patrol, in the hire car, on her son's home on the south side of Toowoomba.*

- *The identities of the men in the car have not yet been established. Local police are tracing.*

- *Interpol has established that the Syrian in custody in Darwin is associated with a Lebanese terrorist group, which has been suspected of bombing raid involvement into Israel and some western European cities.*

Chapter 20

The phone rang at AA Electrical and the receptionist announced the call to Peter Grushko.

'It's the doctor, Sir.' She always addressed him as 'sir'. He had never asked her to speak to him in any other way.

The familiar voice of the specialist Dr Charles McBride said, 'G'day Peter. We have your mother's test results. Would you be able to bring her in to see me? Today, preferably?'

'What do they show, Charles?' He trembled with his need to know.

'Peter, with all of these things, we need to talk through what they mean. Not over the phone, my friend.'

'A clue?' he persisted.

'I gave you a possible prognosis a couple of weeks ago. We have more detail now. You need to come in with your mother. We need to talk this through.'

'We'll be in this afternoon. Two pm?'

'I'll get that time cleared for you,' replied the doctor. 'See you both then.'

Peter's secretary freed the time in his schedule for him to take his mother to the doctor at 2pm.

'Have we got our management system fixed yet?' he asked as an aside. It niggled him that expensive computer software didn't always work as it should, when it should. That management package had been very pricey.

'Yes, Sir. A clever young man came here this morning. He works for Fuzzy Electronics, the computer maintenance firm for the university.

He fixed the problem. He has been the first one to identify the difficulty correctly.'

'Good. Fuzzy Electronics, eh? Be sure you have his name in case the thing goes askew again.'

'I have noted it, Sir.'

He focused his attention back on his mother. He had things to do.

* * * *

Peter thought Olga was surprisingly calm as they drove into the car park at the consulting rooms. She had hardly reacted when told the test results were back.

In his room, Dr Charles McBride made them comfortable with a pot of tea.

'Olga, the results are back,' he started. 'They are very detailed. Let me cut to the chase.'

The Russian lady waited, straight-backed yet relaxed; calm eyes looking gently at the doctor.

'The tests show a swelling in the brain which is being caused by a tumor. In the opinion of my specialist colleagues, it is most likely to be a malignant tumor.' McBride let the words sink in. Peter looked anxiously at his mother whose demeanour had never changed. No reaction – just the same serene expression. 'Where it is positioned, it is inoperable!'

She leaned forward slightly, paused, then asked, 'If you can't operate, are there treatments?' Her eyes watched the doctor's expression.

'Yes, there is chemotherapy or radiotherapy. Chemotherapy involves injecting chemicals into your body at just a strong enough level to kill the tumor. Radiotherapy would be the preferred method for this type of growth, though. It can target the tumor more directly. You would be positioned on a bed and slid into a machine which can beam radio rays to the point of the tumor to try to kill it.'

'I see.' She glanced across to her son who looked very pale. 'If I don't have treatment, what will happen?'

'The tumor is likely to continue to grow, with potentially fatal consequences.'

'How long would that take?' she probed.

'Months. Probably not years.'

'How many months?'

'Well, it is always hard to put times on such things ...'

'Doctor, I have learned Queensland term recently. Is *No bullshit*, tell as is.' Her mouth curled in a weak cheeky grin.

The doctor looked across at his friend, Peter, and said, 'Six months at most. Quite possibly, three to four.'

'*Spasibo*. Thank you,' she said, peacefully.

Six months? The shock hit Peter hard as he listened to the conversation. After all the years of separation – reduced to six months or less.

'If I have treatments, Doctor, what are chances of cure or prolonging life?'

'Well,' started the doctor before being interrupted by Olga.

'On scale of one to one hundred, are chances of success ... more or less than one?'

She hadn't needed to demonstrate her mastery of the Queensland vernacular again. 'In my opinion, and that of my more expert colleagues, less than one. But there is always hope.'

Peter shuffled. He could feel his face drain of colour.

'Glass of water for Peter, please,' said Olga, completely in control of the discussion. 'I don't deal in hope, Doctor.'

McBride poured a glass for each of them.

'Pain?' she asked. 'Side effects? What will next months be like?'

'In the later stages, there will be severe headaches. Perhaps memory loss along the way; dizziness, perhaps loss of some other bodily functions. We can treat any pain you might get with drugs, but that may limit your ability to interact with people.'

She nodded and reached out to squeeze her son's hand.

'We have lot to talk about in not too long ahead,' she said with a wan smile. 'Do tests show anything else?'

'Yes.' The doctor seemed keen to give all the information that this inquisitive lady required. 'The tests on your heart show that the effects of the Chagas' disease are not as bad as first anticipated. Indeed, it is likely these will not give you any real problems in the meantime.'

Olga smiled, which broke into an unexpected chortle and then into a laugh.

'Do you tell me bad news is I will die from brain tumor within six months but good news is heart condition is getting better?'

Both Charles McBride and Peter followed Olga's lead, shedding the shock of the test revelations into bemused smiles.

'Music-hall joke, no?' she asked.

McBride refrained from correcting her amendment of his medical opinion. It was clear, even to Peter's numbed brain that he had not said that the heart problem was improving, just not getting any worse. But why ruin the moment with the truth? It had brought some levity into a difficult situation.

The bemused Peter watched the interplay. He assumed that Charles had dealt with many such conversations in his time – but, judging by his reaction, never one with a reaction quite like this.

Olga's dignity didn't falter. 'Thank you, Doctor. I appreciate your honesty.' She paused. 'Tell me, again with frankness; you say 'six months'? How long before I cease to function properly?'

The doctor looked across again to her son. Peter was vaguely aware that his mouth was open and his eyes must be staring blankly at the other two in the room. He and Charles had been in service clubs together and played sport in the town fixtures. They were friends. But this information …? He shook his head slightly to focus his attention back to the reality of the present and the doctor speaking.

'Maybe four months. These things are hard to predict.'

'*Ya ponimayu*,' she said. 'I understand.'

Peter watched the doctor looking surprised as he watched the Russian grandmother showing about as much emotion as if she had been told that a grocer's shop was out of bread.

The room was silent – waiting.

'I think, Doctor,' she said, after some reflection, 'no chemotherapy or radiotherapy. I will take offer of pain killers, when stage arrives. In meantime, I am going to live these last months – fit in all quality time I can. I have had full life. Not everyone gets to know they have particular time to live. Some just get cut off in prime, with no time to say goodbye.'

Peter had heard the story of his father in the previous days. Perhaps his mother's thoughts had drifted back to the love of her life, her husband – the apparently handsome Red Army and KGB officer, Oleg

Davidenko. He did not get a chance to say *Dosvedanya* to his wife and son; cut down by a American bullets in a manner that had never left her consciousness.

'At least,' Olga was speaking again, 'will give time to share missing stories with Peter, Anna and Eva. At least, will be closure. Respectful. They will know their family history – good parts and painful parts.

'Tell me, Doctor. I am aware I have had some memory loss. I can't recall some things that have happened, while other passages are really clear in my mind. Are those memory gaps gone forever?'

'Possibly not. You have pressure within your head and the tumor is growing within the brain – but you may well find those memory gaps come back to you, like a sudden flash-back, maybe like a still photograph in your mind. They might be triggered by a scent or a sound or a situation. Yes, be prepared to have strange recollections of things you might think you have forgotten.'

'Thank you, Doctor. Is there anything else?'

Charles McBride shook his head.

She gave him an encouraging smile. 'At least you gave me comic line. Laughter is important. Don't you agree?'

At the doctor's nod, she added, 'Was at bush dance a couple of weeks ago; the sounds, the scents, the feelings.' She looked at the other two as she collected the right words. 'Easy giggles, sweaty warmth of dancers; fresh-baked scones, cake and tea; mesmerizing finger-work of the mandolin player – they just merged with happiness of piano accordion. Yes, laughter is important.' She paused before, 'Peter, will you be able to drive me home now?'

She had her answer without a word needing to be spoken. Peter looked pale and clammy.

His mother continued to take over. 'I'll call Anna. She can come in taxi and drive us home from here.'

Dr McBride interjected. 'No, I will drive you over to Anna and she can take you both home from there.'

Peter attempted a confused smile and a nod as the doctor encouraged another sip of water. Words took time to form. 'Thank you ... Charles. It's been a shock.'

* * * *

Anna had consoled herself that they both appeared alright but it wasn't an easy ride home. Mother and son sat in the back seat holding comforting hands together. Charles McBride had told Anna that it was better for her to drive and for them to have a restful cup of tea when they got home.

The tea was being served on the verandah just as Eva drove in with her usual ebullient wave. Olga returned the greeting with a big smile, squeezing her son's hand. 'Probably best we tell everyone together, eh Pyotr?' she said quietly.

He replied with a slow nod, ignoring the worried look from Anna.

Settled with tea, Olga was in control … and appeared comfortable to be so.

'We had test results today.' She smiled as she spoke. 'The doctor gave me good news and bad news. The good news is my heart condition is improving – well, not getting worse. The bad news is I have brain tumor for which there is no cure.'

She paused only for a couple of seconds before continuing. 'Not to worry though. It is bonus at least we know what time we have. We can use it really well together.'

There was comfort in her smile as she held the proffered hands in support. The Grushkos gradually digested what their mother and grandmother had said.

Peter spoke haltingly. 'Charles said it would be six months at the most.'

Eva's eyes widened and moistened but she said nothing. A sympathetic tear beaded in the corner of Anna's eye.

Olga quickly added with a smile, 'Which is quite convenient since my visitor's visa is only for six months.' Wry grins appeared but none of the family could quite muster a laugh. Then the tears flowed. The family hugged.

With more cups of tea and support from the Russian grandmother, they slowly came to terms with six, maybe only four months, of time to share the stories, the missing pieces of the family history; time to take the photographs, to make the videos, to preserve the memories.

Olga encouraged, 'People die in plane crashes, car accidents or just have strokes from brain tumors – and are gone in instant. We are lucky. We have time – time to plan, to talk, to reminisce. This is good thing. Be happy!'

The next few hours were taken up with who should be told; how people should be told; what priorities should be listed. It was also a time for Olga to advise the family to keep things as normal as possible.

No, they should not put the business on hold. No, Eva should not give up her studies. By all means, take time off as necessary – but keep life as normal as possible.

Chapter 21

The policeman at the random breath-testing site waved the dark maroon Holden Commodore over to the side of the road. It was one of several cars in a queue.

He walked to the driver's door and explained it was a random breath-test. The driver passed over his licence with an international permit, issued in the Russian Federation.

'Hire car, Sir?' The policeman looked casually at the two other occupants. 'Have you been drinking today, Sir?'

The driver shook his head.

'I will need you to blow into this tube, Sir, when I tell you. Deep breath and keep blowing till I tell you to stop.'

A pause while that was carried out.

'Thank you, Sir.'

The driver sat quietly while carefully watching another policeman take an examining walk round the car.

'That's all good, Sir.' The policeman indicated a clear result. 'Enjoy your day.'

He waved the car through and the Commodore moved slowly back into the traffic; carrying the tracking bug under the back mudguard.

* * * *

Email: spenceravery@bigpond.com.au
From: tobystanleysmythe@cam.ac.uk

Spencer old boy

You are not going native on me are you?

You seemed to have been really taken by the local dancing. It sounds so unlike you. I can't really picture you doing a ho-down; arms folded in front and a piece of straw hanging out of your mouth.

Life is pretty routine here – exam paper proof readings, budget committee, strategic planning meetings, ethics committee – you get the drift. I hope you aren't subjected to that bureaucratic treadmill in the sunny colony.

Any more on the Russian army woman? Do tell!

It is warming up here at last. We must be reaching degree exam time, eh?

Had a lovely weekend of shooting on Penelope's father's estate last weekend. You may not know Penelope. She's just come down from London. The estate is not far north of here. There were a few lords and ladies gracing the event. Quite a coup for the pater, I fancy.

No gossip really.

Keep in touch

Toodle pip

Toby

I read the email from Toby with a strange sense of detachment. This had been my world, my chosen path, my aspirational lifestyle only a few weeks ago – and yet the mention of college meetings and shooting on the estates of the gentry didn't seem to impress me as it once had.

Maybe, Mary's mother's vicious criticism of my breeding had been absorbed and I didn't want to be part of that societal circus any more.

Using the Latin 'pater' now seemed strangely archaic. 'Bullshit' was the word that came into my mind. Now where had that term come from? I laughed as I recalled the banter at Goomburra. Normally, I would not have been seen dead at such a function. Then, maybe I had just been a poseur before, putting on airs to impress Mary – well, not Mary at all; to impress her unimpressable mother.

Mary and I had just clicked from the start. I had been totally absorbed by her and the novelty of her social swirl; pressing the flesh, making insignificant prattle about horses – or who was allegedly playing around with whom. A strange world for me, and I was never very relaxed in that side of it.

Maybe 'mater' Johnston was absolutely correct. Maybe Dr Spencer Avery would never have the breeding to mix and relax 'in good company'.

Chapter 22

A knock at my office door – and there was Melanie Bell.

'Hello Dr Avery,' she looked to see if I was on my own before changing to, 'Spencer, I was just passing by and I thought you might be needing a break.' She paused for my querulous reaction and continued. 'Have you seen the art gallery in town? You might enjoy some of the local art work.' She alternated between apologetic and enthusiastic. 'You won't find Matisse or Van Gogh there, but you might be surprised at the quality of the local artists. Would you like to join me?'

'That sounds very nice, Melanie. Just give me a couple of minutes to tidy up here. My car or yours? Mine is only a Japanese car, I'm afraid, but it does have a sunroof.'

'Japanese cars are very good. We have nothing else on our property. I'm sure your car would be much more luxurious than my early 90s model.'

I smiled as we left to take in the sights of the local gallery.

* * * *

The displays were impressive, with artists showcasing their landscape scenes of eucalypts, tropical flowers, mining town scenes, sheep shearing – the whole gamut of country Australia interpreted in pastel shades; reflecting the impact of the huge sunny country with its vast plains, flooding rivers, bushfires and drought.

There were even two Japanese calligraphy-art pieces sent from a sister city on Honshu. I admired the skill of the artists. My writing usually settled for Roman Italic. That's hard enough for a left-hander in a world set up for right-handers. But I like what I write. No hoops to jump through for anyone else's approval.

Melanie was good company. Having grown up on a cotton farm in northern New South Wales, she was a fount of information about laser-leveled fields, irrigation pumps, table-drain siphons, cotton-picking machines, crop-dusting planes, cotton gins and the impact of the global markets. Coupled with her stories of spotlighting for kangaroos and pigs in night-time hunting; racing around the field bunds on trail-bikes and four-wheelers; B & S balls – bachelors and spinsters, no wonder they abbreviate to letters; picnic races; and the country shows. I was absorbing the flavour of the country life.

My mobile rang, echoing through the library-like gallery.

It was Eva. She didn't sound her usual breezy self. She was phoning to say that Nana Olga would like to meet with me tomorrow. Would ten o'clock be possible?

My morning was clear. She probably wanted to humble me again in a game of chess. Nevertheless, tomorrow at ten would be fine especially as it would give me the chance to find out more about this tantalising lady's life. She was unsettling; yet I really did like being in her company. She had moved in circles beyond my understanding – and I wanted to know more.

I assured Eva that I would visit her grandmother at ten tomorrow and hung up, wondering why Olga hadn't rung herself. She didn't have my mobile number, I rationalised

Eva had sounded strange. No cheery chat as usual.

Odd!

* * * *

I thanked Melanie for suggesting the art gallery trip. I had learned so much about farm life and how young people grew up on the properties. It had been good to be the student for a change.

I was starting to appreciate the genuine friendliness of the Australian people – and so respectful to a visitor from overseas; it was there in their manner, their polite speech, even to students instinctively calling me 'Sir' or 'Doctor'. I had never asked them to do that – but I hadn't specifically told them not to, either. It just seemed to be their way of acknowledging me as different; but in a nice way. I had thrown out a generic, 'Call me, Spencer,' at the dance and at the interviews. Gradually, they seemed to be coming round; being more comfortable with a more relaxed style around me, especially Melanie. She was a confident young woman.

But they were all tolerant; not trying to score points. I felt able to be myself. It had taken *me* some time too; and I certainly appreciated that it was alright for their lecturer not to know things. It was okay to have a laugh. There appeared to be so few norms or protocols to break compared to the strictures of the circles of home.

The darkness which had characterised my thinking over the past weeks was fast becoming just an unpleasant memory. I silently pledged to catch up.

Chapter 23

Olga watched Spencer Avery alight from his car in the driveway. She could have set her clock by him. Ten o'clock to the second.

The Grushkos had all gone out – trying to keep to the normal routine as much as possible, as Olga had suggested; and also to give her some space to tell Spencer her story in the way she wanted it told.

The Englishman had been good company at the dance, with a sense of fun. Certainly behind the urbane intellectual polish, there was a genuine person bursting to get out, and he was interested in the politics of her homeland.

'Tea, Spencer?' she called from the verandah. He smiled and nodded back, letting her catch his expression.

'Chess?' he queried.

She pointed to the chess set already set out. Whose move would he think she was copying this time? Gary Kasparov?

* * * *

I sat at the table, my eyes sweeping again over the view of the valley to the south. It was a pretty scene, yet so different from my Somerset vales or the closely-settled antiquity of the Cambridge area.

I watched her as she poured the tea – a most infectious smile; never quite letting me know whether she was laughing with me, at me or whether she was just genuinely happy. I hoped it was the last option. There were enough challenges on the male ego, without having a retired Russian major having a joke at my expense.

We sipped our tea and Olga insisted that I should have the honour of starting the chess game again, since I had lost last time. Wince.

The Evans gambit was my opening in the hope that a Russian would be less familiar with a nineteenth-century Welshman's move.

She seemed relaxed. 'We didn't get to talking about what you wanted to hear about Russia.'

Directness to rattle but I would not be unsettled today.

'I was interested in your passion when you answered the students' questions.'

She gave me a quizzical 'Tell me more' expression. True to form, however, she used no words – just a look.

But I was in control. 'You know the parts where you spoke about the West behaving like knights in shining armour while they portrayed the Russians as the evil empire. And then there was the part where you were protecting the nation from gangsters after *perestroika*.'

'Spencer, I think I will be happy to talk about that but is something I must tell you first. Put down tea cup, please.' She was composed, almost prim.

I did as I was requested. I was really growing to like her company.

'Yesterday, I visited medical consultant. He advised I only have few months to live. I have inoperable brain tumor.'

I knew my jaw had dropped and my eyes widened. Damn her! Why did she shock me so?

'That's why I told you to put down tea cup.' She smiled. 'Is not matter for sadness. Am grateful I know time, and probably place, where it will end. And it also has given me different perspective on secrets I have been trained to protect. So, let me tell you some of my story and we'll see how we go, as you would say. You are allowed to pick up tea cup now and play your next move.'

Goddamit! She laughed. After dropping a bombshell like that, she laughed.

I could feel my gulp and stammered out, 'I'm so terribly sorry, Olga.'

Which she dismissed with, 'I told you not to be sad. Don't disappoint me now, Spencer.' Then she gave me another of those confusing smiles.

'Spencer, I was major in GRU,' she started deliberately, and let it sink in.

A chill flowed through my veins at the mention of that acronym, surging down through my body and up into my brain.

My mind had immediately filled with images of highly-trained special agents, killers, torturers for the cause; people who could make James Bond's adversaries pale into insignificance.

I forced myself to be calm, to concentrate and listen. Perhaps not all GRU were the same. It was a huge organisation. There must be many roles for officers apart from my worst-case scenario.

'Don't forget to play move now,' she advised. 'Was more rank for my qualifications and expertise rather than for commanding in battle – but I did lead number of teams in many countries.'

I could hear my gulp again as my Adam's apple bounced. But her gentle voice encouraged me … slowly, carefully, 'Obviously I was based at Khodynka Airfield in Moscow. You would know that. Just tell me if is anything you don't understand. I worked initially in signals intelligence.

'In Soviet era, we were very secret which is significant benefit in foreign intelligence gathering. All eyes were on KGB who did *death or glory* stuff. Yet we are six times size of SVR, intelligence successor of KGB. Even now, we have tens of thousands of people gathering information in overseas countries. In spite of our reputation in West, work of my teams was primarily about listening – not fighting. You understand?'

It was rhetorical. She continued her story while she fixed me with her peaceful gaze.

'My working knowledge of several languages was strength. I was in Germany initially, with my husband, who was KGB.' She paused. 'He was killed in 1967 in botched operation near Berlin, shot by American CIA.'

Was that just the slightest tremor in her voice – a chink in the polished protective barrier?

'You asked why I feel so strongly, especially way we Russians are always portrayed as passionless killers while NATO are suave saviours of freedom. Many operatives died on both sides but, in my experience, should be no pretence of *the knights in shining armour*, if I may your English *epithet*,' she grinned fleetingly at her use of the term for the figure of speech, 'were chivalrous or gallant. Were nothing other than cold assassins.'

Fire glowed in her eyes. You could never accuse her of being cold. I would ask her later about her husband.

She resumed her tale. 'I told about being in England. My job as embassy attaché was to make my way into circles of information and set up networks for future.'

She went on. 'I moved to Washington in similar role and then to Lourdes in Cuba.' She chortled at a thought. 'Was before my time – Lourdes is closed down now – but I laugh at posturing between Kennedy and Khrushchev in Cuban missile crisis. I'm afraid Chairman Khrushchev gave impression of being your *no bullshit* politician.'

I was warming to her story. 'Perhaps, often misquoted, Olga,' I offered seriously. 'Like his *History is on our side. We will bury you* speech in Moscow to Polish diplomats in 1956 which populist commentators frequently attribute to his UN speech in the 60s.'

'*Ochen khorosho*, well done, Spencer,' she laughed. 'You are indeed astute analyst – and, as you know, it wasn't about *bury* in literal sense. Opponents underestimated him. He sorted out U2 spy planes. Made unpopular stand with Berlin Wall. Scared daylights out of Americans by sending missile ships towards Cuba but, is often not realised, was also first Soviet leader to start work towards peaceful co-existence with NATO. Was just that he wanted to negotiate from position of strength. It was all about politics – making a diplomatic statement.

'You see, Americans are ferocious opponents, motivated by power and money; using one to get other. Usually smart operators. Seldom will US government agency be caught manipulating sovereign country. Instead, will use CIA to engage contractors to tamper with economies, to acquire valuable resources, to supply weapons to insurrectionist movements.'

I bit my tongue.

Her eyes were distant. She could have been delivering a lesson on political history to one of her teams. 'I don't pretend we in Soviet system didn't do this too. Just we didn't pass ourselves off as saviours of world.'

I chose not to argue. There were plenty of anecdotal reports of regime destabilisation and terrible suffering under the oppression of the very saviour-like ideological expansionist doctrine that Olga was so gently glossing over. And I continued to struggle with the mismatch of the gentle grandmother I was watching in front of me and my mental image of the dangerous Soviet and Russian GRU.

She was talking. 'Warfare after World War II ceased to be about pitched battles. Took on more subtle approach; guerilla movements, coups, resistance groups, economic warfare – all relied on accurate timely information. Was my business. Foreign intelligence. Where countries got drawn into pitched battles, they generally lost. Americans in Vietnam. We lost in Afghanistan. Your *Coalition of Willing* may be following same mistake there – probably is.'

She stopped; the raw passion slowly subsided from her face. Then, like flicking a switch, she returned to the charming smile. 'Is your move or mine?'

'Yours.' I was absorbing her words and assimilating them into my framework of academic research. 'Even if you were poorly represented in the propaganda war, you were still running gulags for political prisoners, all through Siberia in particular. You were still ruthlessly crushing dissent and opposition in the Union and Warsaw Pact countries. You can't claim the high moral ground.'

The controlled fire returned to her eyes and her tone. 'Gulags were penal system of NKVD, secret police, which eventually became KGB. It is undoubted that atrocities were carried out, particularly during Stalin's time. No sensible person would deny. Were not good times.

'We didn't live in Soviet Union in those years. My grandparents and parents had fled revolution in 1917. They chose to live in Turkey. But as soon as Stalin was gone, my father yearned to return. Was land of his roots. He and my mother always considered themselves Russian. Although Turkey had made us welcome, we weren't Turks. We didn't really belong there.

'In 1950s, my father joined KGB.' Her voice softened as she spoke with pride of her father. 'His work was to counter oppressive American subversion of our country and allies. He was in intelligence gathering, particularly with regular deployments in hot-spot of Berlin. Our family table discussions, when he was home, were often about politics and philosophy. It was natural I would want to follow him into army – we had always talked about world affairs. He educated me in how the world worked; about power and deception.

'But, yes, was not pretty era, Spencer. We had country which needed discipline if was not going to collapse into anarchy. Political suppression was necessary. You have to understand we were under significant attack from forces that would undermine whole philosophy of *Soyuz*, Soviet Union. We had to be strong – with ourselves as well as enemies. Now your question was? Ah yes, gulags,' she reminded herself.

'Their significance,' resuming her story, 'really finished with death of Stalin in early 1953. Were officially liquidated in 1960. Is quite erroneous to talk of gulags today.'

'My research would suggest that many of the gulags weren't emptied until President Gorbachev's time.'

She shrugged acceptance. 'Are still prison camps in our country, today, of course, even on old gulag sites. Would you pretend Americans don't have them too? Do you need to look further than Guantanamo – or do you want to speak of torture rendition?'

She went quiet.

Even more so when I took her queen and triumphantly said, 'Check!' The Evans gambit had set me up well. Gotchya!

She laughed. 'You clever devil! You got me fired up and hit me while I was distracted. Well done!'

I took the compliment with English grace but returned her to the conversation. This was too good to lose. 'You mentioned Cuba made you laugh?'

'Yes.' She was smiling at some thought. 'Don't you think it strange that in Cuba, where Castro's communist regime has existed untroubled since 1960s, where *our* sophisticated Russian listening base at Lourdes was under constant American observation on main Cuban island until 2001, that US has *its* super-sophisticated military base at Guantanamo Bay on the same island under our watchful monitoring? Don't you ask why no-one did anything about that? Well, don't you?'

I watched, asking her to continue with my expression. I felt back in control. Talk on, dear lady.

She said, 'Clearly, it suited major powers and Cuba for status quo to be maintained. Was stalemate – which is probably where this chess game is heading, Spencer.'

There was that laugh again. 'Enough of politics for now,' she said. 'Now you know some of my story. Thank you for listening. Usually nobody from NATO would bother. Too busy with own agendas – to their cost, I would add. Now tell me about your Dean's daughter.'

It was a gentle request but it hit me with a wallop.

'What do you want to know?' My defensive hackles were up.

'You have told me you are here to see if relationship can survive separation, but is not logical choice for intelligent male like you to make. You have been pushed.'

'Am I so transparent?' I knew I was speaking very quietly. She was making me nervous.

'Not you,' she replied. 'Is human nature. Who hurt you, Spencer? Wasn't girl or you would not even be considering continuing relationship.'

I looked at her. For all our differences in political philosophy, Olga was a strangely attractive lady – intellectually and emotionally. I could easily understand her success at enchanting people in many lands.

'She is Mary Johnston. We began our relationship last year. We really enjoyed each other's company. We had a lot of fun together. We came from different worlds and I think that was part of the attraction. I took her into my world and she gave me access into a privileged circle that I had only really read about.

'I was already an established lecturer at Cambridge. Mary is five years younger; with a first class honours degree; clever – in an academic way; maybe not so aware in other ways. She is writing now, creative works but with an intellectual feel.

'She is the daughter of the Dean. He's a good man. Professor Byron Johnston. Her mother is different. Her name is Prunella. The name sticks in my mind as well as my craw. She has a deterministic view of the world. Your family tree determines your potential success in society. I come from humble honest roots in the West Country. Mary's mother can trace her ancestry back to Henry VII.'

I paused with a forlorn look, checking that Olga understood my meaning. Her earnest expression for me to continue told me that she was following the story.

'At the start of this year, the mother confronted me with a diatribe of my genealogical shortcomings. There is not much I can do about my ancestry. Then it went on to a total vilification of my person – the shallowness of my academic prowess, my lack of social polish. In short, I didn't fit and I wouldn't ever be a suitable partner for her daughter.'

Olga gave a sympathetic frown. 'And Mary's reaction?'

'Interesting. Sympathetic. Apologetic for her mother's behaviour. When I asked about our future, she could only see the obstacles her mother would put in the way of any happiness we might share together. I suppose she had to live in that environment. She didn't see how she could leave the social and financial benefits of her family to take up with a young lecturer who might well have an ostracised future.'

'And you think Russian system is vindictive?' she said with a wry smile.

'Mind you, I suppose I didn't help when I returned a dig her mother made.'

Olga smiled her question, without words.

'Her mother was on her harangue, looking down her pompous nose at me, and she said, in the most condescending way, *Oh, I suppose you have more than average intelligence for a person of your background.*

'To which I replied, *If I hadn't promised my mother to always tell the truth, I would return the compliment!* I shouldn't have said it, I know – burning bridges. But at least the sow had enough brains to get the insult.'

'Touché, Spencer!' said Olga.

I was feeling strangely more relaxed in her company. 'Anyway, my friend Toby had seen an advert for visiting lecturer posts in Australia, eight months only at a number of universities, and I was so dejected that I applied, thinking I would be coming here as some highly-prized adjunct professor perhaps across a number of universities, but based in Melbourne – a valued visitor from a premier British university. As it happens, while I have skills to contribute, the colonies have been an eye-opener.' I paused to look at her. 'I don't mind self-deprecation – it's just that I'm not very good at it.'

I allowed myself an inner chortle. It was probably lost in translation. She didn't react. 'And I have met you!' I was actually horrified to be baring my soul like this. What was wrong with me?

She looked at me with gentle eyes. I could tell she knew where this was heading. I must have looked quite bereft.

'And now you tell me you have only months to live. I find that so sad – although you are being very brave about it all. We shall just have to make sure you have the best few months we can muster.'

'You are good man, Spencer Avery,' she said quietly. 'I can't understand why Mary Johnston could let you go. Pressures of upbringings can be very powerful.'

I managed a smile at the compliment. 'Olga, you are so unlike my expectation of a major in the GRU. My studies suggested someone so much ... harsher, more inflexible, cold.'

'My point exactly, Spencer. Egocentricity of the Westerners who think they know everything. Present company excepted, they don't listen or watch or respect – from basis of understanding.' She paused and then laughed. 'But then you don't fit my perception of a Cambridge Fellow.'

I raised my eyebrows to encourage a response.

'Veneer is not very thick,' she explained. 'You care more than you would like me to believe. Maybe you are too nice for competitive academic world.'

I kept my face impassive.

'Tell me,' she said with scarcely a pause. 'This Toby. What is his surname?'

'Stanley-Smythe. Why? Do you know him?'

'No, No!' She laughed. 'Just interested in surname someone with first name, Toby, might have. I am not disappointed.'

I chuckled – very therapeutic, distracting from my recent exposure of my vulnerability.

'I'm afraid my heart is not in this chess game,' I said. 'Can we agree on a stalemate and just enjoy another cup of tea?'

'Good idea. Then let us talk about plans. Time ahead is precious. I want to use it well – to have fun.' And she paused. 'Do you feel anything strange, Spencer?'

'Like what?'

'Like something happening in parallel with us?' She screwed up her face momentarily. 'No, I'm talking rubbish, Spencer. Must just be this ill brain of mine at the moment.'

Spencer smiled in agreement ... but he did have such a sense. That he was being followed; that something larger than him was moving just out of sight; like puppeteers pulling strings.

Chapter 24

Superintendent Fowler arrived at Brisbane Airport and was quickly whisked into a private meeting room with his AFP officers.

- *The Queensland Police have located the Holden Commodore and its three passengers. The driver of the hired car is from the Russian Federation. Probably the two passengers are from a similar background.*

- *A tracking bug has been placed on the car. It seems to be maintaining its vigil close to the Grushko home, with the three men taking rotations of surveillance.*

- *Olga Davidenko has visited a medical specialist, Dr Charles McBride, yesterday. He is a well-known physician. The police will follow that up.*

- *No more information has been forthcoming about the Syrian and Pakistani people who are still being held in Darwin and Perth under the anti-terrorism legislation.*

Fowler accepted a USB memory stick from the local AFP officer and settled at his laptop to pore through the background information which had been collected so far on the Russian major.

* * * *

The airport meeting room smelled of fresh caffeine. The bubbling percolator and platter of gourmet sandwiches scarcely distracted Fowler from his analysis. He scanned the ASIO background brief quickly, needing to understand the context. Something wasn't fitting for the AFP superintendent:

Major Olga Davidenko. Born Olga Popova in Turkey to Russian parents in 1945. Grandparents were White Russians who fled the 1917 revolution, south through the Ukraine and over the Black Sea to Turkey where they settled to the south-east of the capital, Ankara, in an area known as Cappadocia.

The file noted as an addendum:

Cappadocia in historical times was the centre of the Hittite culture, a focal point on the famous Silk Roads between China and Europe. It was a refuge for religious minorities over generations, who sought the protection in the enormous maze of tunnels and caves, going down many levels underground. The complex was hundreds of kilometres in length and included churches, hospitals, animal stalls, granaries, living areas and a complex series of cleverly designed defensive traps and secret places.

Like the Viet Cong all over again, Fowler thought as he continued reading:

In early 1953, after the death of the dictator, Josef Stalin, the Popov family moved to the Ukraine where the parents gained work in the Donbas coalfields.

In early 1954, Olga's father joined the Red Army and was recruited almost immediately into the KGB to work primarily in East Germany. No reasons are on file for his move into the Red Army or the KGB but it is known that he was fluent in several languages. His work was in counter-intelligence and disinformation. Olga's mother remained working in the coalmine offices.

Olga followed her father, Sergei Popov, into the Red Army at age eighteen; later selected into the training program of the GRU for her language skills. She married Oleg Davidenko in the Ukraine in 1964 and had one son, Pyotr, in 1965. Oleg worked for the KGB. Despite the intense rivalry between the two Soviet agencies, they remained happily married until Oleg's death in 1967.

Fowler lifted his eyes from the laptop screen to let the information roll around in his mind.

The major had been a mother and widow at twenty-two; a linguist perhaps, working for the GRU. Those were hardly reasons for terrorists to be tracking her after she had retired unless she had heard something very sensitive.

Deep in thought, he looked at his AFP officers. They had done well amassing the brief. Their eyes were looking at him expectantly but he remained expressionless as he silently gestured to them to eat the delicacies provided.

After a minute of matching Olga Davidenko's past with the current situation, he scrolled down again through more of the file material:

Oleg worked with his father-in-law in Berlin, assisting Stasi information gathering. Olga was in Berlin intermittently during this time.

Sergei has been credited with a significant role in compromising the CIA/SIS Berlin wire-tapping exercise where the Russian/East German spy network fed disinformation to NATO for many months.

Oleg Davidenko was killed in a shoot-out with CIA agents outside Berlin in 1967. Notation on file from a senior supervisor: Olga's passion for her GRU work took on a new intensity.

In 1971, after several years of having her mother caring for her son, Olga sent Pyotr to live permanently with relatives in Brisbane, Australia. She moved to Moscow to take up a position at GRU headquarters at Khodynka.

Fowler stroked his chin as he read. The reference framework was building but he could distill no tangible meaning to provide a link with the current situation – a retired Russian major ostensibly being pursued to Toowoomba by foreign nationals. Clearly she had reason not to like Americans or NATO operatives. Perhaps it was mutual? But that couldn't be the answer.

Toowoomba as a location was understandable – the connection with her son – but why were they tracking her in the first place? What had she done? What did she have? What did she know that was so important?

His finger tapped the mouse pad to scroll on:

Extended sessions working as an embassy attaché in England, USA, Belgium, Cuba, Colombia, Venezuela, Lebanon and Syria. Her forté was intelligence gathering from spy satellites (SIGINT – signals intelligence) agent interviews and recruitment; as well as dealing with certain special forces' support resources.

Ah ha! Fowler thought. Could that be a missing link? But there was no detail on the file about who she had interviewed or what 'support resources' might actually mean.

'Why can't ASIO be specific instead of this jargon-speak, which can mean anything or nothing?' he said to his men as a rhetorical line.

They looked up with non-commital shrugs and continued quietly eating, patiently waiting for their 'super' to finish his reading:

Retired from active duty in 2006.

Application to visit her son and his family (all Australian citizens) approved after vetting clearances –2007. Visa application endorsed by UK agencies.

'Now that is very interesting. Britain approved the Major's visitor visa.' He floated more potential rhetoricals at his troops. 'What might Britain have to do with vetting a Russian citizen applying to enter Australia? Why would they even get involved? Was there some obstruction to a visa being issued? And, if so, why? Did she apply in Britain? We are not still a bloody colony – we have our own checking processes.' He smiled to take the annoyance out of his tone. 'Another question for ASIO, eh?'

Arrived in Australia in April 2008 from Paris on a six month visitor's visa.

'There's the same question,' he continued. 'She has come from France. So where did she apply for the visa? In Paris? Why was Britain even involved?'

His men continued eating – smiling in sympathy – but shrugging at the valid queries which, as yet, had no answers:

Currently living with her son, Peter Grushko, in Toowoomba, Queensland.

Background check on Peter Grushko. Son of Olga Davidenko. Has been in Australia since 1971. Electrical engineer. Took on the surname of his adoptive parents, Ivan and Nina Grushko (both deceased). Runs own company in Toowoomba, mainly mining contracts. Wife Anna; daughter Eva.

No political affiliations. No security concerns.

Clearly Olga Davidenko was a long-term Russian operative. Was she really out of that role? On the other hand, she might very genuinely be in Australia to see her son and his family. She had been given clearance for a visa – UK endorsed, no less.

If she really was an innocent retiree quietly visiting her son in Queensland, should he reasonably expect a Pakistani and a Syrian to enter the country a week or so later – each with her details in their possession?

Even more troubling than the Pakistani and the Syrian were the ones that hadn't been caught. Who else was out there looking for Olga Davidenko and what was it that was so valuable to them?

A car was waiting to drive him to Toowoomba. He needed to meet this retired Russian major – to see her for himself. He was already forming an impression of who he expected this lady to be.

Chapter 25

The local radio news chattered away in the car as the Grushkos drove home. There was a story about detonator caps being stolen from a local quarry.

'What possible use could detonator caps be to thieves?' asked Anna.

'It will be gangs of kids breaking in. They just steal. No understanding,' said her husband in a flat tone. 'Some of the deadbeats you can see roaming the Toowoomba streets just now. Homeless, I suppose. The great unwashed. People who don't want to conform or hold down a job.'

'Don't be so judgmental, Dad,' said Eva. 'There's a lot of hopelessness out there just now.'

'Hopelessness, Eva?' Her father shuddered as he spoke. 'They are drop-outs. Who would want to give them hope? They could start by having a haircut and getting a job.'

'It's not always that simple, Dad.'

She wondered whether she really wanted to get into an argument with her father.

Peter just humphed.

Eva was glad he had let it drop. She knew how hard her father worked, self-made and proud of it. He could be pig-headed but, at other times, so soft.

His moods had been swinging from irritable to emotional very quickly in the past few days. She knew there were more important things on his mind than the marginalised members of society. He was the head of the household, who had just been told his precious mother had only a few months left.

That was serious stuff, given his history of separation from that Russian family world. And her father always took his responsibilities very seriously.

The car was nearing the house.

The Grushkos could see Olga and Spencer sitting on the verandah, drinking tea; waving and smiling at them.

Peter seemed pleased they both looked so cheery.

'Spencer and I have had lovely chat,' said a grinning Olga.

Eva smiled her appreciation at her lecturer.

Chapter 26

Inspector Ian Reid of the Queensland Police in Toowoomba, had made contact with Peter Grushko at work – a request for the inspector and one of his colleagues to meet with him and his mother, Olga, in the privacy of Peter's office.

Olga was intrigued but said little as she waited with her son in his office.

Two men were shown in.

She gave a gracious smile to the Toowoomba Inspector of Police and a plain-clothes Superintendent Jeff Fowler of the Australian Federal Police, as she and Peter received their business cards.

'I wonder how we can be of help,' she queried after the brief introductions.

There were some very routine murmurings about her intentions while in Australia on her visitor's visa.

'Gentlemen,' her voice had a quiet confidence. 'I am here on approved visa for six months to visit family. You know that. You know who I am. Is not why you are here.'

Fowler nodded; appearing comfortable that the courtesies were over. 'Major, may I speak simply and to the point?'

'I'd prefer,' she replied.

'We believe you are being followed. Have you had any suspicions?'

Her gentle smile preceded, 'Perhaps three men in dark red sedan and couple more in dark SUV – four-wheel drive, you might call it?'

Inspector Reid's eyes widened. 'Yes, the three in the sedan appear to have come from the Russian Federation. The four-wheel drive, we know about.'

Olga nodded.

Peter sat amazed.

Fowler then added, 'We also have suspicions of others who might have an interest in you; from Pakistan and the Middle East.' He waited for a reaction and there was none. 'Would you have any idea why these people might be interested in you?'

'None,' she replied. 'As former army officer, I have had access to information which some might see as valuable but I am not active. I don't have any knowledge about what they might be seeking.'

She looked at her son – clearly well outside his normal sphere of comfort. Her family had been given essentially the same information that she had shared with Spencer. To the straight-forward law-abiding Peter, this was clearly new territory.

'Am I in danger?' asked Olga, her eyebrow raised slightly over a quizzically curled lip.

'Yes,' Fowler replied. 'The people from the Middle East and Pakistan have terrorist associations. They each have your photograph.'

'Interesting,' was all she said, but the smile had faded.

'Major, I need you to help us help you,' continued the superintendent. 'What is it that terrorists or the Russian state would be seeking from you?'

She thought for a moment; looked at Peter once more and said, 'Gentlemen, I have recently been advised I have inoperable malignant brain tumor. My life expectancy is but few months.'

She watched the policemen carefully as they took in the information. 'One of side effects of tumor is I have gaps in memory – complete blanks.'

Another pause to let that message be processed.

'I used to pride myself on memory, keeping everything catalogued in my head. Now, sadly, I tell you genuinely and honestly I don't know what these people could be after. I can't tell what I don't know – or can't remember.'

The policemen looked mildly perplexed but said nothing.

'I *can* tell you,' she said on reflection, 'three men in red sedan are not from official Russian state. Anyone from government channels would know how to contact me and would not be secretive. More likely, people are Russian underworld – criminals. Since collapse of Soviet Union, free enterprise and capitalism have created opportunities for gangsters to control market and to make fortunes.' Her nose flared slightly with distaste as she spoke.

Fowler was thoughtful. 'These memory gaps? Are they permanent?'

'Perhaps; perhaps not,' she suggested. 'Specialist doctor thought I could expect recollections to flash back into my consciousness – but they need to happen soon. I probably have about four months, realistically.'

Inspector Reid said, 'That specialist is Dr Charles McBride, isn't it?' After a nod from Olga, 'Will you give us your written permission to speak with him, please?'

She nodded but Peter said, 'Why?'

'Routine police work, sir. Dotting 't's and crossing 'i's. Sometimes the most innocuous bits of information provide the key to a mystery.'

Peter nodded vague understanding as Olga signed a pre-prepared permission note for the inspector.

Fowler returned to his questions. 'Do you have visits or trips planned while you are here?'

'We have planned camp-out on private land near Goomburra with family and young people, university students. We may go to community events. We were at dance recently. I don't want to be imprisoned inside security cordon, if you are implying. Enough restriction with death sentence hanging over.'

Fowler continued. 'I understand that. Appreciate my situation though. I have people associated with terrorist or criminal groups trying to enter our country to make some sort of contact with a retired GRU major.

'Now I find that the Major has memory loss, limited time to live and has no idea what they are looking for. Somehow, I have to establish what this security threat is and prevent it from happening. I also have to protect you and those who are close to you.' He looked pointedly at Peter, who was not enjoying the scenario being painted.

Reid interjected. 'We would like you to wear a tracking bug, please. That would enable us to know where you are – and to provide a degree of protection.'

Olga wore a polite smile as she considered this compromise to her privacy. 'I have nothing to hide. If will give peace of mind and less restrictive presence around my family, then I will wear device. I won't wear voice recorder. I need space to share personal stories with family.'

The superintendent was matter-of-fact. 'It is a discreet bug, not a listening device. You place in your undergarments. It sends out a homing signal. Just remember to transfer it when you change your clothes.'

Olga smiled tolerantly. She was thinking of her involvement in the development of a whole range of special operations gadgets in her later roles with GRU. She could remember that. Exploding pens, concealed guns, umbrellas with poisoned tips, ear pieces which could amplify a whispered sound up to twenty metres away. This tracking bug seemed almost prehistoric by comparison.

'I'll do that, Superintendent,' she agreed, to indulge the request. 'I wouldn't want your men following tracking device through pulsations of washing machine.' They all grinned at her perspective and her command of vocabulary.

Olga and Peter both agreed to contact Inspector Reid if she remembered anything significant. Superintendent Fowler pledged to keep them informed of any emerging threats beyond what they already shared with each other.

After the police had left, Olga hugged her son. Time was running out. So much to help him to understand.

* * * *

As Fowler prepared to board his flight back to Canberra, he received a call from his contact in ASIO.

'Jeff, the Brits have a serious interest in your Major Davidenko. There's not much detail yet. All we know is that their intelligence agencies are aware she is in Australia and they say she is involved with them in some way. You know what they're like. Layers and layers of security; and no-one speaks to the others about what is going on. We'll keep at it. Just thought you should know.'

Fowler hung up and pondered. This was no ordinary situation and she was quite a lady, this Major Olga Davidenko – not at all what he had expected.

Something was poised to break soon.

* * * *

I was not normally slack in my organisation, but I had not been across the arrangements for this weekend's event.

'So, tell me again who will be on the camp-out?'

Eva's voice was patient. 'The original list had us five, our parents if they wished to come, Uncle Herbie and Aunty Edna, and some of the Goomburra locals – but that has changed a fair bit since.'

'Yes,' Melanie added. 'Eva's parents can come and Warren's folks will be there. It's their property. My parents are in China on a cotton marketing trip. Steve's parents can't get away from commitments out west, this week-end.'

Steve said, 'Aunty Edna wanted to invite some of the kids she works with around Toowoomba; kids who have had problems. It is a chance for them to get out bush and listen to Uncle's stories in the right environment. She has taken young people to the property before.'

I was surprised but Warren looked unfazed and it was his parents' property. 'How many of those people will come along?'

'Maybe four or five,' Steve replied. I looked again at the faces to see that it was alright. They didn't seem to be bothered in the least. 'She's had homeless people out there before,' he encouraged.

'Oh!' added Eva, 'and Nana Olga will be coming too.'

Somehow that comment had just lifted my spirits – a purpose beyond the routine of work and social engagement.

'And the planning for the camp-site?' I asked.

'All taken care of,' said Warren. 'Our Goomburra people will prepare the site. There are enough tents and tarps. The food is organised. Uncle Herbie will tell his bush tales and show us the country.'

'Where will we sleep?' I asked.

Steve laughed. 'Oh, Uncle said to tell you he had organised five-star accommodation for you.'

I smiled cheerily. Why did I feel suspicious? I said nothing lest my cultural naivety be exposed. 'And the learning for us, as geographers, will be?' I questioned instead.

'We will do some ground work for our dissertation based on Goomburra,' Melanie replied, 'as well as develop an understanding for the native bush in that part of the range, the traditional lifestyle and the current land use practices – and, I imagine, we will learn a lot from the stories round the camp-fire. There will be no television or radio or computers there. Most mobiles don't even work there.'

'Well, you seem to have organised everything quite effectively,' I said. 'I'll look forward to your company on the weekend.'

* * * *

Darkness was descending quickly as I stared from my apartment window towards the leopard trees on the lonely campus ground. My mind was struggling with the mismatch of conflicting images; Olga, the charming grandmother compared against my long-held sense of danger around the concept of GRU.

Was I being conned? It didn't feel like it.

But then what did I really know about the people from that world? Only the scare stories, the alarm bells of my British perspective.

That was when I sensed, rather than saw, the figure again.

There, beyond the far leopard tree, watching my window. It was just a shadow, moving, merging into the gloom.

Once could have been my mistaken imagination. This was twice.

Chapter 27

My bed felt safe. The door was locked and the curtains drawn. It made a comfortable haven for thoughts to swirl – for mental demons to be ignored, for ideas to form and be discarded; and future plans to be formulated.

I had come a long way from the red stone and brick buildings in my little Somerset home village; and what a strange world I had arrived in now – weirdly contradictory and strangely challenging.

From Barry, 'Bazza' to his friends, giving me the good oil on the finer points of footy through to the enigmatic Olga, it had been a bizarre journey – a huge jump, physically and emotionally, for the son of a West Country draper.

Draper. What an antiquated word. Who uses that language today?

I had known from my early years that I was not the same as others. My name was the start – my father's bright idea. But I didn't quite fit in other ways. I would not be following him into the fabric and clothing business; haberdasher, curtain maker or men's outfitter, whatever pre-historic terminology was used. He sold textiles and clothes. It was too mundane, so tiresomely tedious.

I was good at school work. Only once had I not topped the class – and then I had come second. I could mix well enough as part of the group in my teens; it was an act, but I could do it. It was obvious I would be going off to university sooner rather than later, leaving this rural world behind. I was different – scholarly, artistic. Not a rebel, more its antithesis actually in using the social ladder to aspire to something else.

West Country people are tolerant. There is an honesty about Somerset which accepts the order of things – as long as no-one gets uppity; no lording it over others. I would leave the village and the others would remain. It was as simple as that. Even my father eventually overcame his paternal disappointment that I didn't want to follow him into the business. It was a significant mind shift for him but he found ways to justify it to others in the town – and then somehow it was alright. As he put it without any sense of irony, 'Ya-ar unique, son, jus' like every-wan else.' My distinctness had passed a social test.

So, off to Bristol University and a first-class honours; and to King's in London for the PhD in political geography, in accelerated time. The natural progression was to Cambridge to lecture. Clearly I, the humble draper's son, was headed for greatness. The talk back in the village, to my mother, was 'Alert lad, your son, Mrs Aivery; attractive in an arty way' – though I bet that wasn't what was said quietly in the pubs – 'a fresh thinker and poloite – always a good soign, Mrs Aivery'. Politeness was a prized virtue in my home and the village. Even if I pushed the boundaries in other areas, my parents would die happy as long as people thought their only son was well-mannered.

As a lecturer, I emphasised the importance of the evidence dictating the generating of hypotheses and subsequent investigations. I railed against those who channeled researchers to look for supporting evidence – fashionable, sensational, but lacking in honest intellectual rigour. I had been respected as a clear thinker and an eloquent speaker – and socially polite with it. I was rapidly assuming the status of a young man to be groomed as a senior lecturer and future professor.

But it was at a price.

Gone was that soft West Sarmersit accent, although I could revoive it in seconds when visiting my poirents' home.

No! Now the urbane polish of academia littered my conversation, my articulation and probably even my attitudes. I was trying to fit in. Copying the accents and vocabulary certainly helped me merge.

It wasn't easy. I was a 'migrant' living with native speakers; but the balls, cocktail parties, soirees, receptions and grand openings provided the ideal platforms for me to be noticed beyond my lecture theatres. I was slowly becoming practised in the ways of the upwardly mobile.

My good friend, Toby Stanley-Smythe, was a great asset.

Toby was casually elegant. Seemingly disorganised, routinely in a rush and fashionably late; but he always appeared to have time for me. Life was a sport to him, a pastime befitting his status as an absent-minded academic. What an admirable role model for me. I am the non-sporting type. I suppose people would regard me as 'serious'. Toby was my tutor in learning the skills of good society.

He claimed to have been descended from landed gentry. He assured me that the ways of those born into leadership roles were in his genes; 'Nothing to be learned; part of the breeding, what ho! Happy to show you the path, Avery, old boy. Let me introduce you to the circuit.'

And so began a beautiful friendship.

We were both lecturers, both successful, both looking the part. I brought a grass roots perspective to the partnership, I suppose; the way the ordinary people might think, the masses; while Toby opened my West Country eyes to horses, hunting, polo, skiing, yachting, croquet and the pastimes of the more socially privileged.

He was a butterfly was Toby; incessant energy, visiting every part of his social domain and never resting very long in one place – the net-worker extraordinaire.

Then I met Mary; several years my junior but part of the social set in which I was by then moving.

She was 'a lady', academically well-read yet insulated in a naïve way from the world that I could share with her. She seemed intrigued by my insights. I discovered that you apparently acquired a lot more worldly awareness, if you had done your schooling in normal schools; 'a micro-cosm of the real world', as she called it.

She looked so refined, almost untouchable and yet – she was the most passionate vixen in our private moments. Such a contrast. Behind the cool demure propriety of the public image, she and I shared an ecstasy beyond my dreams; completely consuming my conscious thinking.

Presumably this was love. I was no sexual novice. I had been a dater of girls since my early teens; some I introduced to my mother and most that I didn't. They were all fantastic pleasurable learning experiences but nothing to the times I shared with Mary.

I had to grin inside as we walked through the cloisters in the mornings, as sedate as the personae of serious academics might suggest, while our bodies ached sweetly from the night before. All that appeared on the surface were enigmatic smiles, reminiscent of the Cheshire cat.

Life was euphoric and the world was good. I had moved so far beyond my almost forgotten childhood into realms only dreamed about. I had thrown off the vestiges of the old life and embraced the new with an arrogance befitting my need to deny my humble past.

Mary and I seemed an admirable match; each of us an asset to the other; both madly intoxicated by the romance of our lives; a valued part of an active social scene; successful careers in the offing when THWACK! With the force of a lump of two by four between the eyes, Mary's mother had tipped the proverbial bucket on the whole beauteous affair. So unexpected.

If she had been harbouring such destructive thoughts she had kept them well hidden until the delivery of the bombshell.

In the couple of days after, as I realised that Mary could not withstand the tide of her mother's will, it was like being washed out to sea in a cruel cold tempestuous storm. Thank goodness that just at that time Toby came to the rescue – ever reliable Toby.

'No big deal, old chap. Plenty of fish in the sea …' the platitudes rolled easily off his tongue until I watched him take in the expression on my face. Then the message registered. He could at last see that his friend, Spencer, had been seriously wounded – confidence shattered, place in society in jeopardy, unable to remain, nowhere to retreat, only desolation appearing in front.

No doubt my expression would have shown the depression I had entered – the freefall from the highest ecstasy to the pits of despair.

That was when Toby produced the opportunity to go to Australia – a sabbatical, old boy. See a bit of the colony. Only a few months. Help the disadvantaged along the way. Bit of space from mater-in-law. Could be a real tonic for you in these troubling times.

He was so upbeat. He led such a carefree existence that I was sure he must have dealt with such dramas as a matter of course. And so the deal was signed; bags packed; plane flight to Melbourne – and then my already disastrous few weeks went pear-shaped all over again.

Not the blue-chip university of Australia not even visiting expert across several institutions. No! Toowoomba. On the Darling Downs. Where? I was so much in shock that I had to get out the map to re-check my memory.

That was when all my insecurities were revealed. Those that had been so carefully disguised on my rapid elevation through the academic ranks; that was when they all came tumbling down in my mind – a dark hole from which I could see no exit; nor did I even have the desire to escape. I just wanted to be swirled away into the vortex.

I had overreached. There would be knowing winks in the old village if they had heard back there. Even in the egalitarian society of twenty-first century England, a chap could move too far and too fast. Social mobility was one thing; aspiration above one's status was a nice encourager to work harder; but there was a sense of order ingrained in the psyche of English society and you flaunted that sanctified system at your peril.

The feudal structure might have gone, apart from a few heraldic relics and property inheritances, but there was an in-built barometer which allocated some to understand the meaning of service – their station in life – and others to understand leadership, the responsibility that came with entitlement.

Toby understood leadership. It flowed through his being; while I had learned from my draper father that the customer must always be served, always be right. That was the order of life.

And so my expression would have resembled shambling shell-shock as Barry had carried my bags to my room in Toowoomba.

How wise he had been to insist I accompany him to the footy on that arrival day. A few cool ales, a meat pie, the rolling tumult of the baying crowd and the rough-and-tumble Aussie's impish irreverent humour got me laughing again. What a saviour he had been!

And now? Where to?

Chapter 28

'We must be near the edge of the range now,' Peter declared, as he carefully guided the four-wheel drive along the route of blue and white signposts.

Aged three-bar wooden fences spoke of the length of time this Goomburra country had been farmed. It was dairy cattle country.

'These are Illawarra Shorthorns,' Eva announced, pointing at the cattle in the field; with the surety of a university student educating her parents.

Peter's big Land Cruiser slowly crossed the field of curious animals, en route to the camp-out.

They had passed the cattle grids nearer to the civilization of the homestead and dairy. Now they were negotiating the occasional obstacles of old field gates, each to be opened and closed as they followed the markers.

'They were right,' said Anna, navigating from the front seat. 'This place would be very hard to find if Warren's people hadn't put up all these signs for us.'

Peter concentrated on the faint track through the grassy paddock. He had Nana Olga, Eva and Anna with him in the powerful vehicle. The big tolerant eyes of the reddish-brown and white cattle tracked the progress, with detached cud-chewing interest, through the field and up to the next gate.

Eva leapt out and opened it. She was getting practised and patient, as she sniffed in the moist dung-filled air.

The vehicle passed through.

With the gate closed, they progressed on along a narrow track through the woods.

'That marker says, *Nearly there!*' Eva pointed and, sure enough, they emerged into a grassy clearing with vehicles, tarpaulins and brightly-coloured tents at the far side. Smoke from a camp-fire circled lazily into the sky.

'There's Steve with Uncle Herbie and Aunty Edna,' said Eva, pointing to a group sitting in camp chairs, watching four people in dark clothes, organising a billy-can for water over the fire.

Peter's eyes zoned in on the four figures – long hair, black tee-shirts, scruffy jeans with patches and tears in the legs. He was hard pressed to identify whether the shapes were male or female.

'Who are *they?*' He spat the words out, his nose wrinkling.

'Tolerance, Dad,' said Eva. 'I told you Aunty Edna was bringing some of the people she works with, to give them a chance to be in the bush; to get a different experience.'

'Do you *know* who they are?' persisted her father.

'No. Aunty Edna and Uncle Herbie help young people who are homeless. They give them a fresh start; rules and order in their lives.'

'Not many rules with clothes, apparently,' replied her father gruffly. He was clearly not at all happy to be bringing his precious family into this company – but they were there now. He swerved his vehicle away towards where the Goomburra farmers appeared to have erected their tents.

'No sign of Dr Avery and the others yet,' observed Eva as she scanned the groups.

A Goomburra local, with a wide-brimmed hat topping a grinning, tanned face, came up to welcome them. 'G'day, I'm Ron. My wife, Shelley,' he said, introducing a cheery lady in a checked shirt, jeans, boots and farmer's hat.

Olga, Anna and Eva disembarked as the welcomes were made.

Peter, still fuming quietly, nodded to Uncle Herbie's group, about ten metres away. 'They don't look like farmers.'

'Yes, I know. A bit different,' said Shelley, referring particularly to the four in dark clothes, 'but they'll be fine.' She sounded reassuring.

'We know Edna. We've had her street-kids out here before. Gets them back on the rails, eh?'

Peter's frown suggested he wasn't convinced. They were introduced to two other couples: Graham and Jenny; Bill and Dot – from local farms; taking the opportunity to meet up with the visitors and to listen to Uncle Herbie.

Graham and Bill chatted away. Indeed it seemed to Peter, from the way Graham spoke and carried himself, that the camp-site might actually be on his property.

Uncle Herbie was apparently well-known in this country. Graham talked about how the old Murri helped the community understand the traditional culture, and the consensus of locals who had met him thought he was pretty good with bush medicine and history.

'Saw you all at the dance,' said Shelley with a big grin, to distract the 'men talk'. Anna remembered the faces and soon they were chatting.

'C'mon,' Jenny said. 'I'll introduce you to the others.'

She accepted no resistance as she walked them all, even the hesitant Peter, over the short distance to the camp-fire.

'I'm Warren's Mum,' she added to the Grushkos, as if that was the explanation needed.

But, Peter was not feeling in the least relaxed and her comment didn't register with him. Really he didn't know Eva's classmates at all. Not unless they had visited the house when he was there – usually he was at work. He'd never enjoyed being gregarious unless it was required for the business. On those occasions, he had his well-practised acting skills to be quite the life of a party – but otherwise, he liked to keep to his own.

'Uncle Herbie, Aunty Edna, Steve – Peter, Anna, Olga and Eva,' Jenny said. 'Oh, you have already met.'

Then she turned to the group of four around the billy.

'And this is Tooki,' introducing a thin young man with very long hair, with a pale blue tinge through it; 'Henry,' smiling at a young Murri lad wearing a faded dark shirt with the red, yellow and black of the Aboriginal flag across the chest. 'Ellie.' Her welcoming palm indicated a slim teenager with big eyes and frizzy hair. 'And Izzy' she added finally, greeting the fourth person – a taller pale-skinned girl also with bushy hair and with some studs in her nose and eyebrows. Izzy gave a weak smile back.

'These young ones are all friends of Aunty Edna and Uncle Herbie,' Jenny announced as if confirming their valid right to be part of the group.

Peter's unease was palpable as was his effort to do the right thing – protocols, order and a work ethic; that was what had brought him success in life.

The group of Tooki, Izzy, Ellie and Henry went back to organising the metal stands over the fire for the billies.

Olga was already engaging with Uncle Herbie, Aunty Edna and Anna.

'Have you been interviewed any more by students from university?' she asked Uncle Herbie, carrying on their discussions from the dance – and the groups continued sharing their chat.

'No sign of Dr Avery and the others?' Eva asked Steve, as an aside. She watched her stern-faced father starting to unload the tents from his vehicle.

'Coming through the gate as you speak.' Steve pointed over her shoulder.

* * * *

'Do you want a hand?' asked Tooki with Henry standing behind him.

Peter was taken aback but managed, 'Yes, thanks,' aware that the rest of his family were immersed in chat with others. 'Yeah,' he continued, 'Appreciated.'

They didn't say much as they unfolded two tents, unravelled guy ropes and sorted pegs.

'Do you want them put up here?' asked Henry, pointing approximately to where the canvas was placed on the ground.

'Yes. That'll be fine.'

'I'll give you a hand with that one.' Henry moved to assist Peter while calling, 'Izzy!' in the direction of the two girls, 'Can you help Tooki with this tent, please?'

Peter hesitated but went with the flow, as the three assisted him erect the tents. They seemed to know what they were doing. 'Down from Toowoomba?' he asked Henry.

'Yes. We help Aunty Edna with young people who are in trouble or who have no-one to turn to.'

Peter glanced at the slim Murri man. He could sense an assured air which perhaps could inspire trust in angry or frightened teenagers.

He humphed. 'Are there many like that?'

'Yes! More and more. Some gravitate to the gangs. Others have been thrown out of home or school. Some are on the juice. But all of them need someone to care. We can't help them all. Some don't want it. We have to wait until they're ready. All we can do is to try to keep them safe.'

'From what?' A self-made man never expected help or a hand-out.

'Themselves mainly.' Henry had a matter-of-fact tone. 'Self harm. Drugs. Getting in trouble with the police. Getting beaten up or worse. Topping themselves.'

Peter looked at the relaxed man; that quiet unflappable manner.

The last comment was clearly not intended to surprise – it had just been a statement of the distress that apparently existed.

Peter had never really given the matter much thought, other than to wonder why society had to put up with, and pay for, dead-beats who couldn't do a decent day's work. But, he decided that it wasn't the time to express his views, since the three had just helped him put up the two tents.

'Thanks for your help,' trying not to sound grudging.

'No worries, mate,' replied Tooki, as they returned to the camp-fire.

* * * *

I looked around the clearing in amazement.

'What a beautiful spot. I thought we were never going to get here. We really are in the middle of a wilderness.' My gasp of genuine English wonder at the scale of the Australian bush drew grins as Warren and Melanie emerged from my car.

Two local women arrived right beside us. 'I'm Jenny. This is Dot. Welcome. You must be Doctor Avery. The boys have your accommodation fixed up. Warren, welcome home.' Dot followed Jenny to give her neighbour's son a hug. 'Melanie? Welcome to Goomburra. I remember you from the dance.'

It took no time at all for lots of friendly hand-shakes and smiles. Melanie stifled a grin when I said, 'Please call me Spencer,' to everybody. We caught up with Ron, Bill, Shelley, Graham, Peter, Anna, Nana Olga, Eva, Uncle Herbie and Aunty Edna. We were introduced to Tookie, Izzy, Ellie and Henry. The group was all there.

I watched the 'busyness' as the camp was prepared. Air beds were inflated. I didn't ask about my sleeping arrangements. I assumed, without really thinking, that I must be staying in the farmhouse we had passed. I had wondered why the others all seemed to have tents and then I considered it no more, as two sulphur-crested white cockatoos interrupted my thoughts, flying overhead with their blaring sequence of raucous calls.

'Did you see that?' I said with an amazement that embarrassed me a little. I grinned with realisation as Melanie gave me an indulgent smile. 'Of course, you have all grown up with this.'

We settled round the camp-fire on the big tree trunks which Ron and Bill had pulled over behind their powerful farm utes. Billy-tea was poured for all.

'Well, it's good to have you on the property.' Graham was in charge. 'Let me give you all an official warm welcome.'

I watched Peter. He had a self-satisfied smile on his face. What was that all about? I had him picked as a detached serious fellow, above most mundane trivia – not a smirker. I wondered how he was handling this news of his mother's illness. The smile was gone suddenly. He was looking at the street-kids. I could tell he didn't like what he was seeing.

Frankly, I found the whole scene a bit bewildering; too used to being in control, the organiser. But this camp-out was largely conceived and planned by my students – as a welcoming gesture for me. I understood that and was trying hard to adjust to their ways.

Graham was speaking. 'This camp-site adjoins the Main Range National Park which is part of the Great Dividing Range,' he looked at me – the foreigner, 'that runs right down the east coast of the continent from the far north of Queensland to the high Alps in Victoria. Here, near Goomburra, the range forms a huge escarpment, nearly a thousand metres above sea level at its high points. The little watercourse over there flows into Dalrymple Creek, and then over the cliff, down into the Lockyer valley.'

I nodded my appreciation for the explanation. I was supposed to be the geographer but I hadn't done my homework on this place.

Graham continued, 'We thought Uncle might walk us through the forest this afternoon. Then we would take you to see the cows being milked before we settle down to some yarns by the fire. Does that sound alright to you all?'

I watched Peter look across to his mother. She smiled back as if to say it was okay.

Herbie added, 'We might leave in about three-quarters of an hour – gives everyone a chance to get the camp organised for the evening. Remember to zip your tents when you leave or you'll come back to a big goanna or two burrowing through your gear.' He laughed, along with the farmers. We city people looked more earnestly at each other. I didn't have to worry. I didn't have a tent.

Olga approached me. 'Good to see you again,' she said, taking my arm. 'Walk me to tree-line, please.'

'Certainly, Olga,' I replied. 'It's exhilarating to be out in the countryside, isn't it?'

She laughed. 'They won't know what you are talking, 'countryside'. We are in 'bush'. I have learned already in short time here.'

We reached the tree line and found a log to sit on.

'Spencer. Thank you for listening, other day. I wonder if we could meet regularly over next few weeks. Are things I would like to talk through with you.'

'Good.' This was a prayer being answered.

She continued slowly, 'This illness is playing havoc with my memory.' I could only nod as she spoke. 'Are things I need to remember but can't. I think if I can talk my story with you, you might be interested in experiences I have had – and maybe help my memory be jogged into recalling blank areas.'

'I would be very interested.' Truly. This was a lady, quite unlike anyone I had met before. She shook my cultivated coolness.

'I never told you how I met Mikhail Baryshnikov at Kirov Ballet in Leningrad, did I?' she said with a teasing smile.

I gasped in amazement. 'Is there no end to your name dropping?'

'I just thought you might be interested,' she responded, with a pretended pout.

She was toying with me and I was loving it.

'You might talk to me about Cambridge,' she continued, smirking again. 'I had happy times overseas, including Britain. Will be good to renew memories. Maybe, we could talk about what you will do when you return.'

If there was anyone with whom I might talk through my dilemma with Mary, perhaps it would be the experienced Olga. She didn't seem to sit in judgment.

'Walk me back to group before Peter starts worrying. Look at that bird,' she said suddenly. It was a glistening blue-purple bird about the size of a large pigeon and it had a plastic straw in its beak. 'What spectacular creature! Do you know what it is?'

I shook my head but it was the first question I asked of Ron on our return.

'He'll be a satin bowerbird,' said Ron as the other Goomburra people nodded. 'Beautiful plumage. Collects anything blue in colour, decorates his nest with it all – his bower.'

It was a good lead-in to Uncle Herbie's walk. They were all ready, tents dutifully zipped. Peter fussed over his mother while she patiently acquiesced. Melanie and Eva jointly took responsibility to look after me. I wasn't complaining. Aunty Edna made sure that her charges stayed up near the front to listen to Uncle's words.

The old Murri man stopped as we entered the forest and held up his hand for silence. He spoke in his native language. The guttural words seemed to soar up into the high branches. I watched two kookaburras sitting on a branch, listening carefully with their curious eyes peering beyond their long beaks.

When Herbie stopped, everyone stayed silent. It was as if a prayer had been wrapped round the whole group.

Uncle explained that he was not an Elder of this area. Indeed, he was not of this particular land. It was Aboriginal custom, when entering new country, for the senior Elder to make a greeting in language, to let the ancestors know there were people entering and that they came in peace.

He watched our puzzling to understand. 'In my culture, we believe the ancestors are not just on the land; they are part of everything. Their spirit is in the plants, the animals, the birds, the rocks, the earth and even the wind as it blows through the leaves. When an Aboriginal person is in the bush, he is at one with his ancestors. He is part of the land, never alone.'

I looked again at the kookaburras on the branch. Their expressions had taken on a new meaning. Were they indeed the spirits of the ancestors of this area, watching, monitoring, listening to the words of Uncle Herbie? Suddenly, their presence was imbued with a whole new significance – and we had scarcely entered the forest.

Uncle's gentle stroll led us past the creek and stately trees. He pointed out medicine trees, weapon trees and a range of bush foods, as if he was outlining the wares on supermarket shelves.

He deferred to the locals for the trees that had been used in the area's century-old timber industry. Together they showed us red cedar, hoop pine, tulip oak, carabeen and purple laurel as they spoke of Herbie and Graham's father striking up their friendship through their mutual interest in timber trees, years before.

Before leaving the forest, Uncle sat everyone in a rough clearing and quietly asked them to feel the sacred spirit of the forest.

I couldn't help but notice Peter watching Tooki, Henry, Ellie and Izzy while they listened to the knowledgeable Murri. They seemed to be taking in the peace and majesty from the trees.

I was guessing that Peter didn't approve of them; their clothes, their demeanour or indeed that they were even there. I hoped I was interpreting him wrongly.

Uncle described the ochre and shell trade routes which followed the ridges down the length of the continent. He talked of corroborees where the travellers met, danced, sang and shared their customs. The gap through the range to the south was named after a nineteenth century explorer called Allan Cunningham; yet, he said, it was a trade route for Murri peoples for tens of thousands of years.

The enormity of the history of the place was sinking in as the crimson rosellas darted noisily overhead, making for their evening roosts.

It was time to head for the milking sheds; the modern use of this part of Queensland – grazing cattle to supply the insatiable milk product markets of Toowoomba, Brisbane and the coastal cities.

As we emerged from the rainforest, Graham, Bill and Ron loaded us into the utes and cruisers to take us a few kilometres back down the track. The cattle were already there, following their well-practised routine in the evening.

We city-folk watched in fascination at the process of moving the animals onto rotary milking stalls – a very sophisticated operation in the middle of a forest area. The care taken over keeping the milk sterile and the animals healthy was an eye-opener.

'Illawarra Shorthorns,' Graham answered to my question. 'The whole herd is that breed. Superb milkers, they are.'

We took in the sweet warm grassy smell of the cattle mixed with the antiseptic scent of disinfectant. It was a busy operation.

Graham introduced our group to his two pre-teen children, who were assisting with the milking process. They were Darren and John, Warren's younger brothers. Jenny's sister was there too. She was acting as baby-sitter for the several young children from the three farming families.

As I noticed the big gap in years between Warren and these young-sters, he whispered that his sister had been lost in a farm accident and another at birth. They always needed to explain things to me. Why was that? It was up there with always wanting to address me as *Sir* or *Doctor Avery*, despite my general offer for people to call me Spencer – certainly away from the work environment. I got it – it was a kind of respect, perhaps it was more country manners than city – but quite flattering really.

Nevertheless, it was a shock to understand what Warren had just told me – even the casual frankness as he spoke of such tragic events. There was a frontier toughness just beneath the surface in these people who chose to live close to nature. Quiet people – a strength behind the eyes as they dealt with life's challenges.

'The kids could have been on the camp out with us,' said Anna, gesturing inclusively with her arm.

Dot replied, 'Oh, they get lots of chances to camp here. This camp is adult time.'

I watched Anna nod, faintly surprised.

Perhaps this was just the sharing rural way. It dawned on me, as I studied the never-ending workload in milking and the temporary supervision arrangements which had been put in place, just how much effort these families had made just to make us welcome on this weekend; the importance of visitors, perhaps.

I hoped this wasn't just because I was from an English university. I had never been comfortable with the deference to a mystique. I just wanted to be seen as an ordinary bloke from England. This wasn't my lecture theatre – and this antipodean experience was gently challenging my views.

The dairy hands calmly moved the cows through the milking shed so that there would be enough for the road tankers when they arrived in the morning. It was an impressive operation which needed to be carried out every day. No holidays on dairy farms. Cattle needed to be milked no matter what.

Chapter 29

The Thames sparkled in the midday sunshine as it flowed under the bridges.

They were just two men lost amongst the many out for a brisk Saturday lunch-time walk – Albert Embankment, Lambeth Bridge, Millbank and back over Vauxhall Bridge.

With scarcely a glance at the Houses of Parliament on the far bank, they crossed the river, slower than all the other strollers.

'The Australians are asking questions,' the younger said. 'A chap called Fowler seems to be in charge. Federal Police. Superintendent.'

'What do they have?'

'One from Lebanon, another from Pakistan, a couple of Russians under observation. Things are certainly moving.'

'As we expected. Good for the Aussies. They'll keep the pressure up. What are they asking for?'

'Just general. What is going on. What do we know about the business. Who endorsed the visa. It's all classified. They'll get nothing important. But they'll keep pushing, especially if it hots up more.'

The older man gave the frown of experience. 'One way or the other it will hot up. Hold back as long as we reasonably can but we don't want to lose it all through playing too hard. Drip feed them. Move the pieces on the board as required. Keep them involved. And our man?'

'The reports are positive.'

'Good. Old Fruit was right. Good. And we want these trackers when the Aussies have finished with them. Too much to lose if we miss something small. The Yank cousins will want them too.'

'I'll see that it's done.'

The younger man dropped off at the old Tate Gallery. The other sauntered even slower, glancing at the young lady walkers, as he continued the route back to base.

He had been fit once. Now, he had nothing physical to prove. It was his knowledgeable brain which was in demand today.

As he crossed the Vauxhall Bridge, he sniffed the familiar Thames, rolling on through the heart of the national capital, as it always had; silently ignoring the intrigue afoot.

The man lifted his eyes to his fifth-floor office on the far bank. Impressive building. Such comfort after all his years in the field.

His pace quickened in the home stretch. Once a competitor always a competitor. No time for complacency. The Australian strategy had to work.

Chapter 30

The camp-fire crackled. We were all gathered around; seated on fallen tree trunks and camp chairs. Herbie's descriptions held us spellbound, his words creating such clear images in our minds; we could almost smell and hear the lowing cattle mobs being moved down wide stock routes and across the Channel Country. His words sounded almost poetic.

It was a world of horses, hobbled at night; men and their cattle dogs; friendships; teams working in harmony; rogues bending the rules as they killed an unbranded beast over the fence to provide fresh and salted beef for the trip.

'It sounds so romantic,' said Melanie wistfully. 'D'you know, I've never been on a muster. Seen them occasionally when we've travelled but we don't run cattle. Yet the old tracks still pass through our property. That's my bush heritage in northern New South Wales and along the Macintyre.'

I remembered her at the art gallery pointing out the paintings of an Australia now largely past. She had sounded nostalgic then too. In her lifetime, cattle were transported by road-train, not on the hoof. Herbie's stories brought history to life for us all.

'Yes,' acknowledged Herbie. 'They's all empty stock routes now – but we mustn't forget the history ... and the people who made it happen.'

He talked of Aunty Edna's father, droving right down into New South Wales. They'd called him 'Husk'. Edna had a dreamy looked as she listened, no doubt picturing her dad droving a steaming mob over the Warrego or the Balonne or the Macintyre.

Melanie sat close. 'It's good to be able to call you Spencer, out here,' she said.

Progress? Perhaps, I was starting to be accepted as more than a visiting curiosity.

She followed her comment with, 'A bit different from the hallowed halls of Cambridge, eh?'

Damn! That misplaced cultural cringe.

'Your Australian *forest of learning* has its own very valuable forms of knowledge.' I hoped my tactful response would hit its mark.

She gave me a warm smile in response. 'Are you happy?'

'Yes. Very. Fascinating stories – and good company.' She had a refreshing innocence about her – disarmingly easy to be with. No doubt, she was very popular with her peers.

Uncle Herbie talked of his early life under the Aboriginal Protection Act – about feeling like a second-class citizen when he came into the presence of white people. He was fine, he said, out on the yumba where they were family, his own mob – but in town in particular; the pubs, the shops – Murri people took second place to whitefellas, if they were served at all. A sad time, fast going into history, but still lingering on in some attitudes, he said.

I watched Olga listening carefully. I imagined her translating Uncle's experience through the lens of her own upbringing – a Russian migrant in Turkey; resident but different.

'Herbie,' she said, and I felt a satisfaction that I could read her better at last. 'Is very interesting if sad observation. As Russian in Turkey, I always knew I was different but was all about sense of belonging. I think I had gentler acceptance than your people though. My family returned to USSR when I was eight. I had to adapt to Russian ways. But even having successfully achieved transition into southern Russia, I soon realised I was now Ukrainian, not Muscovite. Not right fit, yet.'

She gave a quick glance to me as she continued:

'You see, was pecking order even in classless communist world, even in Soviet Union; not pronounced as in English system – but it existed. Had to prove myself again having merit to belong to Moscow set.'

She looked across at Tooki, Henry, Ellie and Izzy, her expression questioning. Was she wondering about their feelings? What was their sense of belonging? Or were they just comfortable to be part of their own space and group? No doubt they felt tagged as 'those street-people'.

Could they see a way out, forward? Perhaps that was Edna's plan with this camp.

The evening was quiet, except for the crackling fire and insect sounds in the trees. People with their own thoughts. Uncle had told his story, a personal history. Olga had opened a tiny window into her past.

Aunty Edna was a peaceful presence, the calm yet strong lady. '*Belonging* is an interesting way to put it.' She wore a positive smile. 'Things are much better now for us Murris in 2008, since the Prime Minister apologised to Aboriginal people in February on behalf of the parliament for all the injustices in the past.

'It's not possible now for anyone in Australia to say they didn't know that Aboriginal children had been taken forcibly from families; or that my people had no vote until 1967. They know we were treated like slaves in our own land – second-class citizens in our ancestors' country.' Her soft eyes panned around the group. 'It's very hard when you are branded as *no good* – I mean not just as an individual but as a whole group, a race – difficult to have hope that it could get better, when blackfellas are the butt of anyone's jokes and prejudices.'

Shelley frowned and nodded. 'That isn't a proud part of my history. We didn't know about any of it when we were growing up. It wasn't taught in schools. There were hardly any Aboriginal people around here.'

Edna raised her hand in agreement. 'That was what made it easy for people to be in denial. The only Aboriginal people white folks saw were sitting under a tree in a park, usually having a drink, and I bet you thought *What a mob of no-hopers they all are.*'

'Yep, suppose so,' admitted Shelley with a faint grin. 'There was no-one giving the other side of the story – not till Uncle started coming out here with Graham's father. That is part of why I'm really glad we could come to this camp-out – to hear some more.'

Herbie responded gently to the quiet compliment. 'It was institutionalised racism that brought up a whole population to believe that what was happening was right. Even today, there's an older generation that believes their White Australia policy was good for Aboriginal people.'

'But they were well-intentioned,' said Dot. Her furrowed brow framed a focused stare. 'My parents were good people – helpful people. I don't think they meant or did harm. I remember listening to my grandparents' talking about looking after their black workers. They cared, but they were strict.' She was like a woodpecker tapping at a tree. 'That's not a bad thing. No doubt about it. They were looking after people worse off than themselves. They were trying to do good. It was a different world. It was all they knew. I won't have them criticised.'

'Exactly.' Uncle Herbie spoke patiently. 'None of us has had a choice about the world we was born into or who our parents was. We all just had to make the best of what we found back then, what we was told and in terms of the people who made the rules.'

I thought he could easily have taken offence at 'their black workers' but he just let it pass, with a patient peace in his expression. As if he understood that was the way it was back then – and in the mind of Dot today.

'So, pigeon-holing people is the real problem?' asked Warren. 'Is that the duck's guts of all this issue?' Another new term for me.

'I'd say.' Herbie answered. 'Especially if the people have distinctive looks or ways of speaking. People are never all the same. There's good, bad and different in any group. You know that as well as I do. It's just like branding a mob of beasts – suddenly they're all just anonymous cattle, no longer individual animals with characters, like pets. No personal attachment on the way to the abattoir.' He batted his dusty hat against his knee and replaced it hard on his lowered head.

I looked at the faces. Thoughtful, puzzled, annoyed.

Eva broke the quiet. 'So if you were a Muslim in today's Australia?'

'Spot on,' agreed Melanie. 'I was just thinking the same. Jazzy! You know her, Eva. Jasmine. In our softball squad – and Muslim. Just like you're saying, Uncle; since 9/11, feeling unwelcome in the land of her birth. And her brother has left because of the terrorist hysteria – all the suspicion.'

Her comment raised a polite smile from Herbie.

But Steve spoke, 'Mel, just like it was against us Murris. I've never understood why people do the *I'm alright* bit and pick on anyone different.'

'Maybe because you wasn't one of the *I'm alright* mob, Steve. You was in the other groups,' Herbie added with a cynical grin.

I watched Izzy and Ellie – one interested and attentive, the other picking her nose with attitude. I wondered what the farmers' wives thought of the scowling Ellie.

Tooki spoke for the first time. He had a strong voice, educated yet with an edge. 'It's all about manipulating through fear. If you get everyone frightened, they'll jump at shadows. If someone is on the margin, being picked on, then *you're* not the target. You're safe.'

'Yes, we appreciate that,' Bill interjected. 'Divide and conquer – been used for generations but terrorism *is* real now. Surely there's enough evidence around to show the seriousness?'

The insects seemed to have gone quiet. I watched the reactions in the flickering firelight.

'When did we last have a terrorist on the Darling Downs?' asked Tooki, pausing … but not waiting for an answer. 'Yet, whether or not we have them here, we're all subjected to the same restrictive rules and whipped-up panic. It's just to build a story.'

'D'you really believe that?' asked Shelley incredulously.

'Absolutely. What's not to believe?' Tooki had an audience. 'Most news broadcasts are never news. Who decides what's *news*, anyway?' He paused before answering his second rhetorical question. 'Editors filling an entertainment slot with local car crashes or video footage of *celebrities* or non-news happening in America where every sensation can be guaranteed to happen on any given day. It would be news if there were *no* car crashes.'

The group watched Tooki quietly. Some flickers of condescension appeared and disappeared quickly. Olga had the slightest of grins curling her mouth.

'We like to hear views, Tooki,' said Graham, ever the diplomat. 'An interesting thought. Healthy stuff.' I watched the genial host looking around his Goomburra farmers, catching each by eye, cleverly giving a reminder of accepted social norms on his property. 'This is a good chance for us to think beyond farming.'

'Buddha said, *Find yourself,*' mused Tooki though his intense expression never changed.

'Before SatNav, though,' chirped Steve to an unappreciative audience. He shrugged dismissively. I tried to catch his eye to tell him I liked it, but he was looking away.

Ron chimed in to the debate. 'You're defeating your own argument surely, Tooki. You say ignorance is the problem and then you criticise the people who are trying to inform us all. Everybody watches the television and reads the papers. How else would we know what is happening out there?'

'Perhaps in your generation,' volunteered Izzy, adjusting the stud in her eyebrow. Her quietly-assured voice was hardly a fit for her appearance. 'No-one in my circle watches television rubbish and even fewer read newspapers.'

'So how do you get your information?' asked Jenny.

Ellie replied for her, head slowly lifting as her aggression pitched higher. 'On-line, right. Like Facebook, email or just texting. TV and papers are peddling their lil own fucking fantasy world.' She frowned as she watched eyebrows rise at her language. After a quick look at Edna, 'Yeh, right, okay ... making up sensations. I'm not scared at the world – just disappointed. I agree with Tooki. It's bullshit. We prefer hearing what is happening from the mob we can trust.'

I'd been watching Peter. It appeared to me he had contained himself as long as he could. His reddening pressure-cooker look suggested this flippant disregard had gone far enough.

'With due respect, Ellie, Izzy and Tooki,' the tone was almost derisive, 'but it is this farming community which is producing the milk for you to drink. It is the working population like me who are paying our taxes so that you can access all this electronic communication amongst yourselves. Then you criticise the communication of mainstream Australia. You need to get a job and contribute.'

Silence!

Tooki looked at him nonchalantly and shrugged, 'Nobody's listening to what you think is mainstream Australia. It's all driven by greed, voting for whichever politician will protect their precious lifestyle. The rich get richer and the poor get marginalised.'

'Like I said,' responded Peter Grushko forcefully. 'Get out and get a job. Then you are entitled to criticise on behalf of any marginalised group. Otherwise, fit in and obey the rules. Get a haircut while you are at it. Then it'll be easier to fit in.'

Silence.

I looked at Olga. Her expression was calm, interested.

Peter ignored Graham's pointed stare. A night bird's call whipped through the darkness.

Edna quietly asked, 'Are you judging Tooki because of his long hair?'

'All I am suggesting is that they get jobs before having a go at the rest of us who are working hard to get ahead.'

Maybe it was the camp-fire atmosphere. Everything was peaceful. Dot was nodding seriously in support. Did Peter feel he was the spokesman for the silent majority – those whose roving wondering eyes belied tongues held silent by Graham's controlling looks?

Edna's measured voice continued, 'Despite Tooki looking different and spending his time helping those in trouble; he *does* have a serious job – and a degree in information technologies. He *does* fix broken computer systems for the university and others. He works very hard.'

'Really?' Peter turned towards the object of his derision. 'Who do you work for?'

'Fuzzy Electronics.' Tooki's voice scarcely broke the silence.

It seemed to me that a slow realisation started to wash through Peter's expression. I could see the cogs turning. Anna placed her hand on his leg, but I couldn't read her meaning; support perhaps ... or 'Stop this ranting'.

From his lip-pursing movement, I was betting Fuzzy Electronics was known to him – just not the name, Tooki.

The only sound was the crackling of the camp-fire.

I was reading his expressions better now. He had dug a hole – and in front of his family and friends.

Ellie picked her nose pointedly. She looked ready to have a go.

'Fuzzy Electronics?' Peter said quietly. 'Do you know AA Electrics?'

'Fixed their system this week.'

I could add the connections as quickly as Peter was doing. The others were making querying eye-contact.

He looked at Anna; then at Eva, his face impassive.

140

Henry had a confident air about him. Maybe he was employed as well. Poor Peter! Suckered by their unconventional dress.

Peter gulped and said, 'Yes, right, I believe you did. Well. Okay. It appears I was wrong in your case, Tooki.' After a reflective pause, 'I'm sorry.'

Dot wore a disappointed, confused expression. She shook her lowered head.

'To all of you,' he added on further reflection. 'I haven't been myself for a few days.' Anna's hand gently squeezed his thigh. His serious face accompanied the apology. It was as if he had just been swatted down like a fly. All his assertiveness … gone. Clearly, he was much more fragile than his earlier brusque image would have had us believe.

The tense quietness was only broken by the crackling fire till Ellie humphed and scratched, while poking a stick into the glowing coals. 'Yeh, right,' she mumbled.

Tooki gave an encouraging look. 'Hey! No offence taken.'

The older man nodded with what appeared as grateful thanks.

What a strange mixture of bluster and contriteness he was – like a struck match extinguished – a complex man.

I jumped in to defuse any further tension, 'The issue is surely, as Warren pointed out, the natural tendency to stereotype.'

But Olga cut in with a comment. 'You know, I think young ones could be right.'

There was a resonance in her tone which made everyone stare with interest.

She continued, 'Is fear of unknown which targets any group as enemy, whether because of looks, speech, ideology or lifestyle they are identified. Fear helps ruling group maintain control. Young ones could *well* be right.'

The eyes of Izzy, Ellie, Henry and Tooki were suddenly all looking intently at the Russian lady.

'Right,' muttered Ellie, surprised even confused.

I watched Peter looking at his mother; suddenly very attentive – stoically handling his embarrassment. As I listened to the discreet power in Olga's voice, I wanted to know more about this ethereal world of espionage that had given her this calm self-assurance.

No doubt, to Peter, she had always just been his mother – now an old lady with limited time to live; an old lady whom he hadn't seen since he had been six years old, until a few weeks ago. Now, it appeared to be dawning on him that there was subtle authority in his mother's quiet speech. She was not just the greying granny sitting quietly by the camp-fire with a rug over her knees. She was the lady in uniform from the faded photographs of his childhood. She had been a commander of army personnel.

I must confess I had been taken by surprise that Olga had even commented. As I glanced at her with the unsaid question, a flutter of squawking birds split the darkness with their calls at the far end of the clearing.

Chapter 31

Damn these birds!

The man whispered a curse at the noise. He had jumped at a sound coming at him through the bush. Damn this alien forest. Snake? Wild pig? His startled backward roll had shaken the bush behind him and sent up a cloud of caterwauling birds.

The powerful binoculars he had been using to study the camp-fire group swung from his neck as he quickly flicked his night-vision goggles down from his forehead.

In the seconds it took for his eyes to adjust to the green thermal images, the birds were settling into distant trees.

He could see no dangerous shapes. There was no movement from the camp-site but his cover was compromised. Like the shadow he was supposed to be, he carefully retreated through the trees towards the plaintive calling of cattle near the farmstead.

* * * *

'Must have been a fox,' suggested Dot calmly, as a loud lowing of the dairy herd formed a brief background noise.

'Mmm, or a dingo,' added Graham. 'I've seen a couple around only this week, before I could get a shot at them. But it's quietened down now. Sorry Olga, you were saying.'

Olga continued with a theme I had heard before – but it was new to the others. 'All through 1950s, through to 1970s – during Cold War, if you like – Russia was portrayed by West as evil empire. At same time, United States and Britain were always good guys, always heroes – white hats. We were villains. Don't you agree, Spencer?'

I gulped. She had interpreted my look and was dropping the conversation onto my lap.

'Well, you were running a pretty tough regime as the USSR, were you not?' I hoped my voice had the impartiality of an academic scholar. I had a mental catalogue of research documentation on the civil rights breaches of the old Soviet Union, in case it might be needed.

'But I am *Russian*, Spencer. I am *not* USSR. Should I be apologising for who I am?' she asked with a quiet vehemence. 'I worked for Russian state, patriot, but do I have to take guilt for every mistake made in name of state?

'We had different view of world from other countries but I don't think we were all nasty people – any more than Muslims are all terrorists or Aboriginal people all drink under trees. Is my point. Stereotyping. You can't brand all Russians, or any group, as evil. Do you carry blame and responsibility for all ills and bad decisions of England? It would be long list.'

I nodded. 'Fair point.'

I watched the others. What were they thinking of this charming Russian? How easy, perhaps, to accept a portrayal of the unknown – and assume it must be dangerous. Indeed, Olga was giving out all the signals of a warm, if assertive, lady who was not going to let any small-mindedness hold sway in a discussion round the camp-fire.

She was on a roll. 'And follow-up point made by young ones is older generation probably have little idea how younger generation communicate. Don't we tend to steer away from anything with new technology, or young people jargon? Would be deluded if we thought majority of Generation Y is really influenced by television news or daily newspapers.'

Ellie's eyes were wide. She had stopped poking the fire. There were questioning gazes from the farmers.

Olga was not finished. 'If you follow on logic of Tooki's argument, take it to discussion of terrorism Warren and Melanie mentioned; do we really understand what makes terrorist take own life for cause? Isn't one person's terrorist, another person's freedom fighter? Do we understand why American way of life is so hated in parts of world? I would be certain only small percentage of Americans would understand – and so they react, in ignorance, to dehumanise the enemy and attack. Then, hatred is compounded.'

She stopped fleetingly for emphasis. She certainly had everyone's attention.

Her low, almost hypnotic, voice continued, 'Was Russians who were selected demons of 50s and 60s. After collapse of USSR, title of *evil enemy* moved to Arab countries in Middle East. After 9/11, attention has focused on Muslims generally – most are absolutely peaceful – just misunderstood by West.'

She paused again and then addressed her next comment to the young people.

'Ever been picked on, girls?'

Izzy grinned, 'My apathy causes me problems but I don't care.' She stifled a snigger while Dot's expression screwed into puzzlement. 'You're kidding, eh? We lived on the street. There is no-one beneath us to pick on. We're just a notch below the garbage.'

I was loving this. No need to be the facilitator – others happy to take that role. This wasn't a chat about the prices of milk or local sporting success.

Ellie shook a cloud of red embers from a large gum log in the fire. 'There's Muslims on the street too, right. Like Mel said about her softball mate. They're around.' She scanned her eyes round the group and nodded to Edna. The fire glow reflected in each of the faces. Frizzy-haired Ellie's expression pleaded for understanding and yet with a strong dash of *up yours* as she said, 'No names; but on the street, even here in Toowoomba.' She nodded emphatically at everyone. 'They used to be at the bottom of Ruthven Street, right, but nobody goes there anymore – too crowded.' She turned back to poking the fire for a second or two, almost concealing her smirk. I watched with interest.

Izzy grinned across at her friend. Private joke?

Ellie continued. 'Look Arab, y'know. Jumpy at this mad f ... frenzy about terrorists. Even thick beards no disguise. Make it worse, maybe.'

Izzy took up the cue. 'Most people in Australia would have trouble knowing the difference between a Muslim, a Sikh, a Hindu or a Buddhist, unless the Sikh wore a turban. Anyone who looks vaguely

Arabic, Pakistani or Indian gets added to the *suspicious* group. These people Ellie mentioned, most were born here.'

Steve checked the reactions in the firelight. 'That's Uncle Herbie's point. Murris were easily identified. And not just us – other minority groups copped similar when they arrived; Chinese, Italians, Germans, Greeks and now the Middle East is fair game.' He looked over to catch Eva's eye.

I watched Peter scanning the group. He was quiet, very quiet; listening carefully. Was he seeking redemption or just to understand? There seemed to be no malice lingering in the air.

Izzy ruffled both hands through her thick hair in resigned frustration and sighed, 'Yaaa … ah! Somebody else is writing the script and expecting us to follow. Pawns on a chessboard. We won't cop that any more. We're pariahs; but at least we're honest. That's just the way it is. Shit happens.' A stunned silence followed her pronouncement. She wasn't fitting the image of a down-and-out no-hoper. Despite her different appearance, she was using mature words and even more mature ideas. Where would she have learned words like 'pariah'?

It clicked for me. This was a smart young woman. Izzy was educated in her own way – not just in the rules of the street – perhaps, she was well-read; she certainly had her own moral understanding of how society actually functioned. She just didn't look the part. She was supposed to be helpless.

Dot rose to the occasion. 'Just slow down though. What about all those extremist views, including those from religious leaders – Imams, is that it? – splashed across the TV news. They're stirring people to commit serious crimes. That's not Australian.' She pursed her lips.

Ellie shrugged. 'Whatever,' and went back to poking the fire.

Tooki replied, 'Extremist views are just that. There are fundamentalists in other religions too – most of them, if truth is told. The responsibility is with the broadcaster to show some conscience, control the bullshit instead of whipping up sensation.'

Olga gave a questioning look. 'You want to censor media, Tooki? You want controlled information?' She grinned. 'We certainly need discipline. I believe firmly society cannot let everyone follow their whims. We are on finite planet. Need to live together. But people need freedom of thought – but educated critical thought, not brainwash control. Otherwise, are no checks on corrupt dictators – Stalins of world – nor indeed that mindless capitalist notion of infinite growth.'

She looked pointedly around to emphasise her last point, and continued,

'Somewhere, sometime, world society will have to manage expansion or nature will do it for us, no? Seems not palatable in democratic societies to have discussions about restricting personal freedoms.' She threw her hands open in a frustrated gesture. 'Ordinary people will have own thoughts. Will find ways to communicate – just as Uncle and Aunty have by preserving culture through oppression. Perhaps same is true for your group, Tooki. But bans and censorship? Counter-productive in my experience. Need educated understanding – not controlling what we should think; not prohibiting, not fear.'

Dot shook her head, eyes glazing as she struggled with her thoughts. Tooki said nothing immediately.

'Ethics!' he said eventually. 'Surely, we can expect integrity of reporting.'

'Transparency,' Shelley asserted with inspiration.

'No, no, Jeez,' Izzy challenged. 'Transparency is another fraud – a different disguise, butt-covering manipulation to appease the crazies and to lose any common sense in endless arguments. I don't trust anyone to be transparent. Transparency is not the same as honesty.' She looked slowly around the group. 'Why should we have to check that people in power are telling the truth? Transparency is a three-card trick. Just a con; flicking the responsibility back to us. If we miss it, these supposed leaders are left grinning at our stupidity. I don't trust any of the lines they feed us.'

I was impressed again – a street philosopher.

'Right on, Izzy. Can't we expect honesty then, rather than rhetoric?' asked Tooki quietly. His open hands were pleading. 'Reporting shouldn't have to degenerate into mindless sound bites. It's the new opiate of the masses. I don't want state regulation but there has to be some integrity left in journalism to ensure that the information is accurate, without the hype.'

The Russian lady smiled. 'Lovely ideals. Forgetting profit? Unregulated market will have greater influence than ethics. But keep your ideals. I have lived in many lands with different cultures. Young people challenging ways of the past was always healthy for society – revolutionary even. All countries need revolutions throughout their histories.' She gave a quiet laugh which merged into a supportive smile. 'I wouldn't always have said this in my life but don't stop challenging. Otherwise things will stay as are – not as can be or should be.'

I watched Izzy and Ellie who seemed only to have eyes for Olga. She had spoken up, for them, and she had the authority to be believed – a different perspective, another view of the world from another country. Not a scary brain-washed demon at all and not putting them down.

To all external appearances, she came across as this charming grandmother – refusing to rise to the bait of expressing the strong communist or socialist views that she must have held to have survived so long as a major in the GRU. What was she up to or had she really changed her views?

The Goomburra farmers sipped their tea, as always the good hosts.

'This is not easy,' said Melanie after a few seconds of silence.

'There is nothing simple about power and the politics of nations, that is true,' I agreed while quietly appreciating the subtle game that Olga appeared to be playing. 'If a visitor could be permitted an observation on your discussion, I am hearing a lot of confusion about who Australians really are: the Aboriginal peoples, the early colonists, the waves of migrants since the immigration policy was relaxed. Do you have a national story or are you all too self-conscious to join together?'

I looked around their questioning eyes and continued, 'It seems to me, in a geo-political sense, that Australia puts a lot of its cultural energy into overseas aid activities and international sport, aiming for global recognition. The world forms views of who they think Australians are. Why is Australia not ready to address the internal dilemmas we have been discussing here? You are all intelligent people with valid viewpoints but … are you also part of a nation? What is the culture of Australia in 2008?'

Ron spoke up, 'I think you could be on the money there, Spencer. Sometimes things are too hard to get your head around. Lots of bottled-up feelings.'

Jenny had been quiet, processing her thoughts.

'Taking Olga's points with yours Spencer,' she said, 'then white Australia shouldn't be feeling guilty for what happened to Aboriginal people before our time, should they?'

'It's not about guilt.' Herbie's voice had a resonance. 'It was *never* about guilt in my view. I don't speak for all Aboriginal people. We can't change the past, but I think it is about recognising these things happened. It's about reconciliation – matching past pain with hope for the future – and working in the present to build understanding.

'Part of that is facing it – not just glossing over an invasion as if it was some welcome settlement in an empty land or pretending that atrocities didn't happen in the resistance. They did happen. But this generation is not at fault for that; as long as we all move forward in mutual respect – not prolonging the ignorant prejudices of the past. That's what I think reconciliation is all about.'

Jenny nodded. 'That's what Spencer is saying. We need a national story that includes all groups.'

'Perhaps it is time for another cup of tea for supper,' suggested Graham. 'Maybe there's no simple answer, but there's one truth; that we need to hear each other – especially when we disagree. Tooki, somebody will be listening from now on.' His eyes roamed round the thoughtful group.

Izzy quietly moved over to Olga in the darkness of the flickering camp-fire, and she squeezed the Russian lady's shoulder gently.

Olga looked up into a smile, topped by studs glistening in the orange glow from the dancing flames. She had touched a soul needing to be heard and she had made a friend.

* * * *

The group was readying themselves for bed. I asked Uncle Herbie, in a whisper, where my accommodation would be. I didn't want to be getting privileged treatment – not in the midst of all this equality discussion.

Herbie's face broke out into the happiest of smiles. 'Come with me,' he said, in a conspiratorial tone. We walked over to a tent, clearly not the farmhouse.

'Steve said you had arranged accommodation for me.' I spoke very quietly, as the realisation of a set-up was fast dawning on me.

'Humour me, Spencer,' said Herbie. 'Lie on your back on that air mattress.'

What else could I have done? Lying on my back on the mattress, with my head jutting outside the tent flap, Herbie asked, 'See up there? That is the most famous constellation in the Southern Hemisphere – the Southern Cross. D'you see it? How many stars? Five stars – for your accommodation.' Herbie was in pain controlling his mirth.

I looked around as the others all chortled with him. Australian humour. Bad? It even brought tired smiles to the faces of Ellie and Izzy.

'Good one, Herbie.' Perhaps I was becoming more Aussie than I had realised. A few weeks ago, I would have been mortified to have been the butt of tonight's practical joke. Now it was almost a badge of honour, even acceptance.

It had been quite a day. The Murri history. The dairy farm. The debate about stereotypes and the challenge to accepted culture. And none of these people seemed to fit my preconceived images of what they should be – none of them.

Chapter 32

Jeff Fowler glanced through his office window onto a chilly Canberra morning before concentrating on his daily briefing about the Olga Davidenko business.

- *Inspector Ian Reid reports that the three Russian suspects have left the country through Brisbane Airport, having returned the hire car. The tracking bug has been recovered by the police.*

- *Being unable to hold the Pakistani and Syrian suspects any longer under the anti-terrorism laws, they have each been deported to an airport on the Indian sub-continent, where US and British agents are waiting to interview them.*

- *Olga Davidenko has gone camping with family, some university people, Murri Elders and Goomburra farmers. No issues. She is still wearing the tracking device.*

- *British Intelligence flags a period between 1990 and 1995 when Major Davidenko was on special GRU duties with four others. Their job is loosely described as protecting the GRU secret weapons during the period of instability as the Soviet Union re-organised itself into a range of capitalist federations and independent nations. British Intelligence reports that each of the other four GRU officers is now dead. Major Davidenko may either be on a death list or be in possession of information which others want.*

Fowler contemplated the briefing.

While on the surface, having the five pursuers of Olga Davidenko out of the country might seem to have solved a problem; it had created another – he no longer had information about who any current pursuers might be. He had no doubt that others would have replaced those detained.

The British Intelligence angle was important in that it might give a clue to the general area of interest in the major. If it was true that she really couldn't remember, perhaps a suggestion of this brief might jog a lost memory.

Chapter 33

A chorus of chattering bird life heralded the dawn and, before long, sleepy human shapes started stumbling from the tents.

I was aware from the sounds that Uncle Herbie had been the first up, stoking last night's coals into this morning's warming camp-fire. Henry and Steve were there assisting, getting the billy on the boil. Two barbecue plates were readied. The crackling sounds, with smells of sausages and bacon, had people sleepily shuffling round the camp-fire warmth as Aunty Edna pressed an enamel mug of billy tea into each hand.

I emerged from my tent after the best night's sleep I'd had in weeks – such an unusual sensation for me. Usually on mandatory field trips, I'd had to be a very good actor – never letting anyone see me suffering. Something was changing.

The Goomburra farmers looked almost brushed and polished for the day. I watched them admiringly – surely a special breed that the dawn makes them so chirpy, at such an unsociably early hour.

I noted Peter and Tooki, busy relieving the early cooks. It was good to see them working so well together after last night's moment. It seemed to have been forgotten.

Onions and eggs followed the sizzling meat on the hot plate and soon all the group were eating their fill.

* * * *

With the breakfast eaten and everyone settled with a second mug of tea, Graham commented to the group generally, 'That was real good last night. I like hearing all the views. We tend to be a bit sheltered from different ideas, here on the range.'

'Yes, I thought it was good too,' his wife added. 'I'd often wondered why Americans seemed to generate such bad reactions in Muslim countries – I mean apart from the fighting areas – but when you hear it from a different viewpoint, you can understand it better.'

'Yeh, snap on that, Jenny,' Bill added. 'I tell you, I never realised that the young ones had such a totally different communication network from us. Mind you, mobiles don't work real well out here on the range.'

Dot was the quiet ponderer. 'I've been thinking,' she said. 'If we are being fed only one viewpoint about international affairs like Olga was mentioning, are there other areas too where we might be missing the point?'

Despite my changing sense of self, I couldn't resist the clarifying teacher role. 'What we were hearing last night was a difference of opinion on ideology, Russian, Australian and American, and then how that is reported in the mainstream media.'

Dot's eyes widened in bewilderment at my words. I must have been losing my touch. Hadn't I been clear?

'And,' added Aunty Edna, 'that a sizable chunk of our society has little faith in much of that reporting. They have their own way of getting information, from a whole lot of sources.'

'So what is this?' asked Dot simply, furrowing her brow. 'The mainstream chunk watches TV and reads papers. Those who feel left out are using computers and mobiles? Is that what you're telling me?'

Tooki's voice now held a welcome familiarity for us all – a gentle if serious persuader. 'I don't think it's about a social structure. I don't really think there is much of a mainstream Australia any more. I don't think it's simply about money or generation either. People older than us have more computers and mobiles than we do. I think it is more about your view of the world – a bit like Spencer is saying, your ideology. Oppressed people have always had their own grapevines for passing information.'

He had an audience again. Dot's gaze was glued on him.

He continued, 'If you think you're being fed a line, then you find other sources of information to check against. Additional frames of reference. It is about being well informed rather than following the herd, if you'll pardon my dairying example.'

Knowing grins came from the farmers and I was feeling quietly pleased at Tooki's endorsement of my earlier comment. This discussion was gently exhilarating for me, especially out in the Australian bush.

'You're right, again, Tooki.' Olga seemed happy to keep in the conversation. 'Powerful politicians using brainwashing to justify fighting. Believe me, I understand how armies use information. I think we are fed economic rubbish too about wealth or access to it.'

She had everyone's attention again. 'In many societies, people's status is judged by wealth, position in community – business person compared to someone who doesn't do paid work, like housewife or even homeless person. Do we agree?'

'Ah hah, not necessarily,' I interjected with a smile. 'Even as far back as the Romans, Cicero was saying that there was more to politics than bargaining about maximising wealth. He said it was about getting agreement on what was for the common good. And that a civic bond needs people to be well informed. That's not just status or wealth in society.'

'Need shared story, yes,' Olga continued. 'I'm pleased Romans talked about it but was hardly equal discussion with their whole society based on keeping slaves. Given what I see around me here, perhaps Australia might be less discriminating than many places.' She gestured with open palms. 'Nevertheless is human tendency to respect wealthy people more than poor. No?'

The question was to the group. I grinned and left it to others. Listening is always more important than talking, or winning an argument.

Peter was busying himself putting more logs on the fire.

Izzy had her admiring expression on again. Even Ellie was alert, if not watching directly. This Nana Olga was striking notes with these girls.

A couple of tentative nods.

Olga seemed comfortable expounding her views. 'Trouble is people tend to see wealth equating to power; so put massive energy into acquiring money at expense of other things – and perhaps ethics.' She inclined her head with a knowing look towards the attentive Tooki. 'At national level, countries judge themselves on growing Gross National Product. Have you considered what would happen if economic growth stopped?'

She paused to let her question register.

'What if no more resources to plunder from poor countries? World is finite after all. What if businesses no longer make fantastic profits? Basis of capitalism. What if bottom were to fall out of gambling side of banking and stock-market industries?

'Paper-value of wealth would fall fast. Maybe it's starting to happen. Properties and businesses worth less than money owed. Public lose life savings. Would be outcry against greed and obscene payouts. But skills of people who can live self-sustaining would suddenly be most valuable commodities on planet. Now there's thought for you all.'

Her eyes held her audience spell-bound as she weaved her own world views in so delicately. The quiet revolutionary. And not a mention of communism, anywhere.

'And who are those people?' She was the story-teller about to deliver the punch-line. 'Farmers who produce food. People who live in harmony with nature. Your Uncle Herbies and Aunty Ednas. What if?'

'Well,' Ron gave an easy grin. 'I feel a bit more important about being a dairy farmer now.'

'I think us Murris got a gong too,' said Aunty Edna chirpily. 'Maybe our homeless ones will find they have survival skills that would be useful too,' she added.

'Now there's the sensation for your news broadcasts,' Tooki asserted. He looked and sounded vindicated. 'No power generation. No running water, no flushing toilets, no trucks bringing food to shops – and having money would make no difference. Then indeed, it would be a whole new world order – not necessarily a pretty one. Few people actually choose to live on the streets. I wouldn't recommend it.'

Quiet. Almost imperceptible nods from Ellie, Izzy and Henry – an understanding.

'C'mon,' Shelley chuckled encouragingly. 'Let's leave aside all the doom and gloom. No-one is going to let the world markets collapse. All we are saying, surely, is that we need to be hearing each other and not be snobbish about what information is out there.'

'Agreed; but more than that,' I added, as I told myself to stop needing to comment and clarify. This was not a tutorial. 'If I am hearing the discussion correctly, it's about being aware where there is manipulation of the truth. Taking Olga's and Tooki's points, we observe for ourselves and listen with educated ears.'

My Russian friend was carefully avoiding all the contentious issues around the savage oppression and suppression which were integral parts of the regimes she worked for and with. I vowed to test that notion at a later more appropriate time.

Shelley had been watching Ellie and Izzy closely. 'Isn't it boring on the street?'

I could see Henry burr at the comment, his shoulders tensing. Izzy's lip curled. Angry, disappointed, disinterested? But she surprised me again.

'Being bored keeps me busy,' Izzy said, with a grin.

These girls were not taking a backward step. They were so much sharper than I had realised. Scruffy they might be but these ones at least were far from stupid.

'Look, if there was a better choice don't you think we would have taken it?' Izzy shrugged, then raised both upturned palms. 'You haven't lived our lives. You don't know us. We're not asking for sympathy. It can be hard but you learn.'

She looked straight at Dot and said, 'I used to think I was indecisive but now I'm not so sure.' Her glinting jewellery masked the sly grin. She was taking the mickey. These digs were going over Dot's head, but Ellie was on her wavelength. I noted Melanie's suppressed smirk.

'And being aware,' said Dot, with a growing self assurance but oblivious to Izzy's words, 'that there are other means of communication apart from radio, television and newspapers. And watching what the big players in the world are getting up to. I'll be paying more attention to the Internet. But I think all these other Spacebooks or whatever are a bit beyond this old farm girl,' she added laughing.

'Facebook,' said Ellie with a condescending indulgence. Perhaps that wide-eyed expression was her sense of feeling valued or maybe she just didn't care. But she was not going to be put down, by anyone. She'd have the last word – a grunted word, at least.

The morning passed quietly as the groups broke camp.

Some were promising all sorts of faux resolutions around being more alert. Ellie, just in earshot, was clearly unimpressed by platitudes. She curled her nose and lip with a quietly muttered, 'Yeh, yeh, fff … f … yeh.' She rubbed the fire ash off her solitary soft bag and tossed it in the back of Herbie's truck.

Izzy and Edna bobbed like emus around the campsite picking up remnant pegs and litter. Henry and Steve did the heavy lifting. The clearing was returning to nature. Over the fence came the plaintive lowing of what I now assumed would be an Illawarra Shorthorn.

It had been an interesting experience, so gently controlled by Graham's eagle-eye; the land-owner quietly asserting his leadership role. Even out here under the trees and the wide clear sky, social behaviour conformed to its own accepted sense of convention.

Izzy and Ellie gave a hug and a smile to 'Nana Olga', as they were calling her now. 'She's alright,' they had said to Eva, which appeared to be a compliment – up there with knighthoods in their terms.

The Goomburra farmers and I promised to stay in touch. I would long for billy-tea back in town. And, for their parts, the farmers said they felt honoured to have had such a prestigious academic in their midst – that genuflecting again or maybe I should just learn to take a compliment. I actually felt I had fitted in okay.

Graham mentioned that Uncle Herbie and the boys would be coming out during the week to split wood for the old people's fires. Maybe I would be able to come out too? It would be another chance to join them in the bush. It even sounded quite attractive.

Peter had been quiet after his rant at the evening camp-fire. I had watched him share some quiet words with Tooki. They had even managed shaking hands before leaving.

Edna and Herbie looked serene. It seemed to me that Murri people needed 'country' to be at peace. And their street guests? It wasn't just Peter who was looking at them through new eyes.

And I was feeling more genuinely relaxed than I had been in weeks, but ... so unprepared for the danger building like a silent storm cloud, hidden just over the horizon.

Chapter 34

Email: tobystanleysmythe@cam.ac.uk

From: spenceravery@bigpond.com.au

Toby

Just had the most fascinating camp-out. I don't think I am going native because the Australian humour is still different but I am growing to appreciate a certain straight-forwardness about how they live.

I wasn't aware of the intensity of the Aboriginal Act which governed the way Australia operated for most of the 20ᵗʰ century and I have been learning a lot about how the traditional people saw all sorts of bounty in this often harsh landscape.

You asked about the Russian lady. She is a retired GRU major called Olga Davidenko. Absolutely charming person, old chap. Such a valuable source of Russian perspectives. I'm having to reassess some of my academic views. She has some different theories.

Anyway, I'll have to be quick as she has a terminal illness. Very sad. Only a few months to go.

What news of Mary? You mentioned she sent her regards. Have you no more information to pass on to this lovesick fool?

Yours

Spencer

* * * *

Melanie Bell knocked on my office door.

'Are you busy, Dr Avery; Spencer?'

'Please come in, Melanie. I was just putting the finishing touches to a lecture for my second-year students.'

'Did you enjoy the camp-out?'

'Loved it. I think I might slowly be starting to understand you Australians and your ways.' I was still smiling at the memory of Herbie and the five-star accommodation. 'I really liked the camp fire discussion. Tooki and his friends certainly made some fair points. And didn't you like the way Olga jumped in with all those global perspectives?'

Melanie's eyes were admiring. I took it at face value. It was easier than reading anything else into it.

'You are helping open up a whole new world for me,' she said, 'for us, in this course. We didn't really get involved much in those sorts of thoughts until you arrived.'

I didn't mind the praise. If a Cambridge Fellow could contribute anything to a provincial university, it should be in the area of academic rigour. So I was pleased with the compliment.

'Spencer,' she continued, 'by way of increasing your awareness of Aussie culture, I thought you might like to know of another opportunity coming up.'

'Tell me more.'

'Well, in a few weekends' time in Goondiwindi ...' Her eyes sparkled. Another pause for dramatic effect. 'There will be a phantom picnic races event-cum bush dance, at the showground – and The Fair Dinkum Bush Band will be playing to the crowd. It could be very good.'

I knew I was wearing a bewildered smile. I looked forward to the time when I wouldn't be surprised by Australians. Normally, I thought I was quite quick in taking on new information. But here, it was always different.

'Just when I thought I was starting to get a handle on Aussie culture, you come up with a new one. What is a phantom picnic races event?'

A smiling Melanie gushed her explanation, 'We had an outbreak of equine influenza not long ago and there was a ban on moving horses anywhere. It has slackened off now but most people are too edgy to move horses to races, so we invent horse races and people bet on them.'

'You invent horse races? And people gather for these imaginary races?'

I watched her savouring every moment of my baffled expression.

'Nothing about this land would surprise me,' I said in amazement. 'I think you are a nation of inveterate gamblers. You would bet on two cockroaches running up a wall or indeed phantoms at a horse race. Don't tell me how it will work. I'd rather find out on the day.'

'Does that mean that you will come?' asked Melanie with rising excitement.

'Well, I think it could be very interesting. I think Nana Olga might jump at the chance to see the bush band again. The others in the group might well like to come too. Do you think we could all travel out there? That would be six of us. We wouldn't all fit in my car. I could take the mini-bus. How long does it take to get to Goondiwindi in a mini-bus?'

'A little over two hours, if the road is okay.' Her enthusiasm was infectious. She continued, 'Another thought is that on the Sunday, we could all visit the lagoon at home. It is really just a large billabong but *lagoon* sounds much more exotic. You could see the real Australia of a cotton farm, formerly a cattle and sheep property. My folks will be back by then. I'm sure we could all be put up in the farm buildings. We have the main house and the quarters for seasonal workers.'

For the first time looking seriously at her impish smile, I felt a trace of worry. 'I'm quite happy to stay in a motel in town.'

'It's no problem,' she persisted. 'I'm sure we will have space.'

'I'm also thinking of you, Melanie, and not compromising you.'

She looked puzzled.

'You are a final year student,' I said seriously, 'and I am your supervisor. It is important I don't put you in a position where anyone can say your results were affected by your kindness to me. And you have been very kind. I would have to record your generosity as a gift.'

She looked bewildered, perhaps even insulted at my suggestion. I watched her struggle with what I had said. I guessed she was alternating between feeling offended that her integrity was being questioned, to being miffed that her motives for being generous were being probed. But she didn't tell me where I could stick her kind offer, if that was all I thought of her.

'Register it as a gift if it is important,' she said finally. 'If we all attend, you can't be advantaging me above others, can you?'

I was pleased she had decided not to take offence. Those were the rules. It was an ethical stance. She was an attractive young lady and I had been without amorous company since Mary and I parted – not the easiest of situations. I needed to be super-careful that my actions around Melanie, and indeed the others, could not be misinterpreted.

I clearly remembered an innocent colleague in England being drummed out of the university by innuendo. Perhaps people were less vindictive in the more casual Australia. I hoped so.

'Melanie, I would like to come – with the others too. Do you mind if I ask them? I would really like Olga to come as well.'

I wasn't sure if the students were aware that Olga was on borrowed time. It wasn't my place to inform them – but she was really well-accepted anyway, something about the way she challenged dogmatic perceptions that made young people forget she was old enough to be their grandmother. Sometimes it even surprised me to think that she *was* Eva's grandmother.

'That's super!' Apparently she had forgotten any offence she may have felt earlier. 'I'll talk to my parents.'

Chapter 35

'Major, I have some information for you but I am in Canberra, do you mind if we talk about it over the phone?' Fowler sounded business-like.

'With respect, Superintendent, while sounds like you, how do I know you are person I have met?'

Fowler pictured a careful smile on Olga's face and she had just risen up another notch. 'Do you have the business card I gave you in your son's office?'

'Allow me to get,' she replied.

He listened as she walked over to her purse.

'I have card in my hand now.'

'If you turn it over, you will see four hand-written numbers in the bottom left corner. I will tell you those numbers as confirmation of my identity.'

'Go ahead,' she said and, on receipt of the correct four digits in the correct order, she said, 'Please ask questions, Superintendent.'

'Information first. The three Russians who were following you have left the country. We are tracking them overseas. Also, the two men with terrorist affiliations have been deported and they will no doubt be interviewed by other agents where they have gone.'

Olga said nothing.

Fowler continued, 'I have little doubt that others will replace those people and, now, we don't know who they are. I would ask you to be very vigilant and to keep me informed of any suspicions.'

It was a vain hope, he knew, for her to override years of training and conditioning to confide in a policeman from another country. She was a sharp operator, but also dying.

'Have you had any other thoughts about why people might be following you?'

'No. I can think of nothing specific or current which would interest anyone.'

Fowler had already decided to take a chance by precipitating some answers. If she needed a memory jolt, it may come if he shared some of the British briefing with her.

'Major, I have been advised that in the early 90s, you and four others were taken onto special duties to protect some secret special weapons. Would that information be correct?'

'Is possibly correct, Superintendent,' she said slowly. 'Is era where I have memory gaps. But if there was anything from then, other four would have same information surely?'

'Major, they are all dead,' he said simply.

Olga broke the few seconds of silence on the end of the phone. 'So do you suspect terrorists are coming to kill me? They had better hurry or nature will beat them.'

'No, I don't think that. They would have made an attempt by now if that was their goal. No, I think you have information that they want – and you are now the only one still alive who has that knowledge.'

She was silent again.

'You can get me day or night on the phone number on that card,' he encouraged. 'If you get any recollections, even vague ones, please call me.'

There was a long pause.

'I will, Superintendent. Thank you.'

* * * *

Olga Davidenko sat quietly, the dead phone still held loosely in her hand. A dull ache pulsed behind her eyes as she thought about the policeman's call.

Who were these pursuers?

Her lip curled as she thought of the deported people with terrorist connections being interviewed by agents in another country. If those other agents were American, then the men would by now be in some less-than-pleasant facility in a neutral country. She had no regard for US agents. They had caused her too much pain.

* * * *

I pulled up at the Grushko home as arranged from the camp-out. Olga was there to greet me. The other family members were at work or study.

'How are you feeling?' I didn't want to ask a dying woman superfluous questions but I did want her to know that I cared.

She was smiling. 'Quite good. Come in. Tea is brewing.'

We settled on the verandah and sipped the Earl Grey.

'Tell me, Spencer. Have you written to your Mary since you have been here?'

'No. That was our arrangement. I would let the time pass without writing. It was to be less emotionally draining.'

'And has she written to you?'

'No. I have had only her regards passed through an intermediary.'

'Regards? Is all? And intermediary would be your Toby Smythe?'

'Yes.' I was surprised that she could remember.

'Don't you think, if passion was still flying, either or both of you would have been in touch?' There was no reply I wished to make, as she continued, 'Some romances, even most passionate ones, only last one summer.'

Ignoring her question I said, 'You were going to tell me about Mikhail Baryshnikov.'

She smiled at the change of topic and went with the flow. 'Was 1973. I was in fleeting relationship with most attractive ballet dancer at Kirov – not Baryshnikov, but we met him regularly at rehearsals and performances. Was amazing dancer and athlete. My ballet dancer was example of romance only lasts one summer.' A warm grin sparkled across her face at some memory.

I remembered how light she had been on her feet when we danced the *Heel and Toe Polka*.

'I wanted to talk about my husband, Oleg.' She scrunched her eyes and the grin became a wince before relaxing into a gentle stare. 'Was most handsome man; and charismatic too. I was eighteen when I fell for him. Had just followed my father to army, better than coal mining. When army realised I could understand four languages, I was channelled to start training for GRU.

'Oleg was Red Army but moved into KGB. They looked after state security, my work was foreign information gathering. You know anyway. Sorry, I'm insulting your obvious intelligence.'

I dismissed the apology with a flick of my hand.

'Oleg was sent to East Germany. I was happy because my father was in Berlin. He was protecting sector from infiltration, not long after the Berlin Wall had been built. Everything went well. I was posted to Germany after we were married. GDR, or DDR as Germans said, was joyless country on frontier with NATO – very poor, grey and unhappy – but being with Oleg made posting blissful for me. Pyotr was born in 1965 when I was twenty.

'I moved back to Ukraine. That was very painful – really upsetting – but couldn't bring up my son in GDR and fulfill my duties to army. World was very different to today. You had to be in it to understand; split loyalties, and both very powerful. We lived in state-controlled environment but, Spencer, I was still mother. Personal freedom took second place. GDR was no fun for any Russian child, no sense of belonging. Was very aware of problems of not feeling belonging, when small. Oleg understood – such good man. We made decision together. We had long-term plans. Anyway, my own mother helped me with rearing my son, especially when I was away on exercises – including returning to Germany for short times.

'Back to Oleg. NATO forces in West Berlin had set up listening post in old Nazi facility that had not been commissioned when World War II ended. We knew about it. We supplied information and disinformation, knowing they were listening. Confused them well for several months. Had our own listening facility just outside Berlin, in East Germany – disguised as farm complex on our own territory. American agents staged covert raid on that post. Oleg was one of defenders.

'Something went wrong. In fighting, Oleg was wounded. Apparently they believed all other defenders had been killed but one was hiding in loft with full view of what was happening below.

'Americans tied Oleg up and ... I didn't find out at time what had actually happened because my father would not let me near information. But years later, I accessed file which held eye-witness report.'

She was sounding more and more Russian as she spoke. Her eyes glazed as the emotion took her back.

'Agent names were Carter and Mayfield. They decided to leave no witnesses. Carter is reported saying to Oleg, *What is your name?* When he replied, Carter shot him several times in painful places, last one between eyes. Was 28 August, 1967. Date is etched in my mind.'

She gulped and carried on.

'Had lost love of my life with two-year-old son to raise while serving on active duty. I tried to maintain living in Ukraine with my mother looking after Pyotr while I was away. Then my father died in 1970 – natural causes, heart condition, but was profound loss; such strong sensible man.

'Was clear I couldn't continue to serve and stay at home bringing up Pyotr. My mother wasn't coping, from own hard life. So I made decision to give up my son – he was six years old – to send him to my cousin, Nina and her husband in Australia'

Her distant eyes focused back and she clasped her hands tightly, 'Selfish? I didn't think so. I thought I was being responsible and very *selfless*! Giving him a better chance at life. You see, Pyotr was effectively being raised by my mother. Couldn't carry on like that; for his sake. She too passed away year later – legacy of poor nutrition and overwork. Was mess waiting to happen. I couldn't know about that but sensed that I needed to look after my son ... by giving him up.

'I definitely thought my very hard decision was in my son's best interests – but, I don't know now. Was very painful, much much more than I realised when I made arrangement. I steeled myself not to be soft. But was grief-stricken then and for long time after. I make no excuses now. I passed mothering duties on to Nina. I've lived with that all these years – and even Nina and Ivan are gone now. We don't seem to have long lives in our family, do we, Spencer?'

I controlled my expression with an effort.

'Was officer in army and they became main emotional support. I had career mapped out and obligation to country. Were different times, Spencer; such different values and priorities. Given those years again perhaps I might have battled on or left the army – but, back then, didn't seem right choice to make; and seeing Pyotr's success today, he has done well, hasn't he? Hasn't he?' Her eyes pleaded for endorsement. 'Better than I could ever have offered, back then? Is easy to be judge looking into past with today's eyes, isn't it?'

I sat silently with what I hoped was an understanding look … and nodded, slightly. There was no sensible comment to make.

Seeming satisfied with my response, she continued, 'So, I decided; and agreed Pyotr would take Grushko name and be brought up as their family. I would support him and them financially until he was adult or whenever. I forced myself to sit back, out of it – for too long, I think, looking back. Didn't believe I would be able to handle being half and half. I chose to stand right back. Made myself cold inside, isolated, unavailable, as defence against pain. Torture seemed somehow less if didn't think about being with Pyotr again. Forced myself to move on – but never lost feelings of mother. Am still mother, not monster. Strong soldier, *da*, but weak in dealing with such deep personal feelings.' She paused as she pulled her shoulders straight and jutted her jaw. 'Seeing them now, I should have been available sooner. Is past now. I can't change it.'

I could see that she wanted me to ask something. I read into her eyes a plea not to pillory her for her choices so long ago. But, I wasn't thinking that way at all.

'Why Australia? Why that cousin? It seems strange to me.'

She breathed a sigh of relief, yet seemed to ignore my questions. 'Really was most agonising decision of my life. Only mother could understand. Hardest moment was bidding him *Dosvedanya*, emotionally and physically painful. Was 15 October 1971. He didn't know how final it was, but I did. I'm not heartless, Spencer. Have trained myself to be tough – to wash things from thinking. Eats you otherwise. But dates, I still remember.'

I patted the back of hand to give her some comfort. She was clearly suffering and needing some form of redemption.

Her face was suddenly calm, eyes far away for a few seconds as my earlier question registered. 'Why Australia? My father's uncle had gone to Australia in 1919. His name was Nicholas. Had travelled with my grandparents and my father to Cappadocia but couldn't settle. So worked his way through Middle East and linked up with steam ships taking Australian troops home from World War I. Got passage as stoker on ship to Sydney and headed to outback. Never liked crowds.

'Family got occasional letters through 20s and 30s and even into next war. I remember my parents talking about Uncle Nicholas living in Australia when I was growing up so perhaps was why I felt familiar when it came to give up Pyotr. I did have other cousins. You are right. But somehow, Nina seemed to be most appropriate at time – and she was willing.'

'What happened to Uncle Nicholas in the end?'

'Was wartime. Letters stopped. My father never explained that. Only talked of pre-war travels in outback. Who knows? Millions had lost their lives. The living had to move on.'

'So after Oleg was killed and Pyotr came to Australia?'

'Was very angry person; angry at losing my beloved husband – not even Baryshnikov would be replacement for Oleg.' She tried a smile but it formed a lop-sided shape. 'Was angry at losing my father and desolate at giving up my son. I knew others had done it. Many children went as refugees to Britain in wartime. Indeed, listening to Herbie, state took away Aboriginal children here in Australia. Would have been more devastating having them taken from you.

'Went hunting for information on what had happened to my Oleg and found file. Then went looking for Carter and Mayfield. Mayfield had died in action in Africa and my father had avenged my husband by tracking down Carter in West Germany and killing him. No details, but I can imagine vengeance would have been appropriate. My father knew my pain.

'Had no object for anger then. Was frustrated at way Russians were being portrayed in world. Was mobile and could speak several languages. My role with GRU evolved naturally into working in many overseas locations.'

Rapt in her story, I listened with minimal comment, allowing Olga to keep unloading. I knew she was only telling me what she wanted me to know – but even that was gold.

'Bonus job was to charm into official circles and recruit new agents for future. Routine work overseas was to monitor signals on foreign military intelligence.' Her jaw firmed and her body leaned forward. 'I worked hard to ensure Soviet Union would have best information to protect from invasion or attacks such as killed my Oleg. I believe in philosophy of communal society, despite abuses and faults I saw happening. I believed it then and believe it still.'

I felt her stressed use of the personal pronoun that she usually omitted from her speech. She was hurting badly.

I steered away from argument. I needed her to keep talking. 'And that was how you came to be in Cambridge, Cuba and Washington and all the others?'

She nodded.

'And when the Soviet Union was disbanded at the start of the 1990s, did your work change?'

'Yes, my role was to protect our intelligence assets from internal forces, criminal gangs and old powerbrokers, as well as outside influences. Americans were always dangerous. They undermined and infiltrated; in Russia, in new federations, in independent countries and in our interests overseas. Was very difficult time. Old politburo controls had gone. We resorted to our wits. But is period I can't remember clearly.'

'Did you travel much in that period?'

Her eyes screwed up almost as she heard the words, trying to squeeze a thought from her brain. She had her hand held up and was moving it from side to side to give me a silent message not to interrupt.

'Remember *suitcases*,' she said. 'Suitcases.' Slowly her eyes opened. 'Is gone. Was remembering something. Something to do with suitcases. Don't forget, please. Has gone – like catching ghosts. Thought I had it and it just melted away.'

I nodded. 'It is encouraging though. At least it shows it is there in your memory.'

'I'll be ready when it returns. Knew talking with you would help, Spencer. Thank you.'

'The pleasure is all mine.' An Englishman should always be gallant, although I knew I paled beside Mikhail Baryshnikov, let alone Oleg.

'Olga, Melanie came up with a good idea. See if you are interested. She tells me that in a few weekend's time, there is to be a phantom picnic race meeting at Goondiwindi. Don't ask me what that is – but it will be good.

171

'She also said that The Fair Dinkum Bush Band would be playing. It might be a very different set-up to the Goomburra dance because this is on a race-course. Are you interested?'

Her eyes lit up. 'Oh yes, Spencer. Sounds good. Would like to see mandolinist – Is that proper English word? – with his fingers flying again to play Irish Washerwoman.'

'There's more. Melanie said we could go to her property on the Sunday after the races. It's a cotton farm; used to be a cattle and sheep place long ago. There's a lagoon, a billabong, and probably some stories to go with it. I thought the senior class might go along, with you. What say you?'

'And I thought you were inviting me specially.' She pouted in mock seriousness. 'Of course, would be happy to go. Will be good to have Eva along with others. Might stop Peter and Anna from worrying. Say 'Yes!' Spencer, please.'

I was suddenly struck by emotion. This lady had shared a lot of very personal information and she was a good confidante for me at this difficult time. I could feel moisture in my eyes. It was involuntary.

'You are a special person, Olga. Thank you for your advice about Mary. I'll think about what you said. And I'll tell Melanie, *Yes!*'

Then I bit my tongue because I was about to mention how sad it was that we had only limited time left to spend together. She must have been reading my mind, always with that ability to rattle me.

'You will be careful around these young girls, Spencer. You are teacher and they are innocent in so many ways.'

'What do you mean?' I asked in a mild confusion. I wasn't used to being chipped. I had shown my ethical credentials in all my dealings.

'Eva and Melanie are smitten by urbane lecturer from Cambridge,' she said, with an almost maternal smile, 'who thinks profound thoughts, has had worldly experiences and yet is strangely naïve in Australian bush. Heady mix for young ladies – even older ladies.' There was the enigmatic smile again. 'Don't tell me you hadn't noticed.'

She laughed.

How easily she could defuse and disarm situations with her mysterious chortle or smile.

Chapter 36

'Brother, would you like to go to Goomburra on Friday – chopping firewood for our community?' Uncle Herbie could have been talking to one of his own mob. I was flattered that he had phoned, let alone that he might call me 'Brother'.

I remembered some chat from the camp-out of catching up with Goomburra farmers again. The chopping part was not overly appealing but the chance to go back out to the forest, to my pleasant surprise, sounded quite enticing.

'There'll be a good crew to help; me, Henry and my grand-son, William, along with Warren and Steve – all going down from Toowoomba.'

Neither of my students had said a word about this. Maybe they had thought their lecturer was too soft to be out chopping wood. I hoped, rather, that they would have thought me to be too busy to have been considered.

Out at Goomburra there would be Graham and Ron with their wives Jenny and Shelley – and Graham's young son, Darren. The group had apparently been working away intermittently over the past weeks, splitting timber in the old-fashioned way, then sawing it into manage-able lengths to bring back in a truck to Toowoomba.

'Happy to be part of it, Uncle,' I replied. 'It will be good to be with you all again. Who gets the firewood?'

'Edna's network distributes it to needy old folks and homeless people. It gets pretty chilly in Toowoomba in winter. The timber's a godsend for the stoves, or even in open fires for those who have no homes.' His voice resounded with pride about this service. 'The farmers are pleased too. We are volunteers clearing their fallen trees away.'

'Yes.' I could see the wisdom. 'Otherwise farm workers would have to clear it, I suppose – time, waste. It makes sense.'

Herbie gave his throaty chortle. 'You're right, Spence. But these cow cockies really just want a few visitors to break up their routine. The milking cycle never stops. Everyone's a winner.'

I offered my car to take Warren and Steve out. Uncle Herbie, Henry and William would be in the truck.

Friday. It was a day with no lectures for me or the senior students. Other routine appointments could be postponed.

* * * *

I loved the scents of the Australian forest. As we emerged from my car in the Goomburra clearing, the truck was already there with Henry helping two primary-school-age lads to load the cut timber. I sniffed the eucalyptus in the wind, coupled with a more general smell of moist vegetation – earthy and welcoming.

'Not at school today?' I asked the young ones, William and Darren. 'Helping Dad.'

Graham smiled. 'There's more to education than schooling, Spencer, eh?' the farmer grinned.

I could only nod diplomatically.

'A bit of physical work,' Herbie added. 'Toughen them up a bit.'

'All part of the business of farming,' Ron explained. 'They're old enough to be starting to think like adults on the land. This is how we learned.'

A small camp-fire glowed with coals. The billy was boiling for a quick brew. They all took the opportunity to stop work and gathered round, wiping sweat from their brows.

I noticed a huge dark bird circling high above the trees.

'Wedge-tailed eagle,' said Graham, seeing my interest. 'They catch the thermals off the range. Terrific eyes. They'll see small creatures moving on the ground, even from that height.'

I tilted my head in silent thanks, my eyes never leaving the graceful freedom of the soaring flight.

Uncle Herbie brought me back to ground as he explained the traditional way to break up huge tree trunks. 'Split them by putting a steel wedge into a crack in the trunk and then hit with the sledge-hammer to drive it deeper, widening the weak point.'

Henry gave a demonstration, placing two metal rams into a huge old log. Within a minute, his accurate sledge-hammer blows had broken the trunk apart easily.

'That's the way it's been done for decades,' explained Ron. 'This was all timber country in the early days. Once the logs were split, the big bush saws and axes chopped them into lengths. No chain-saws back then.'

I was intrigued. 'I thought you would use a big axe to split the timber.'

'Believe me,' said Ron. 'It's an awful lot easier to use the natural weaknesses already in the timber and just widen the split with the wedges.'

'Amazing.' I watched in wonder at how simply Henry was able to break up the huge trunks.

'D'you wanna try?' Herbie was the great encourager.

It looked so easy. I might like my comforts but I was relatively fit and strong. Here was a chance to show these Aussies that I was not a desk-bound academic all the time. 'Yes,' I said, gamely. 'I'll give it a go.'

Uncle led me to a large fallen trunk. 'Try this log over here. It will give you a fresh start.' He swung a two-handed axe to make a split in the timber and placed a wedge in the gap. Herbie's strength and skill were impressive. He would have to be around seventy, yet he swung the two-handed axe like a twenty-year old – a legacy of years of practice.

Just fleetingly, I was reminded of the life this dignified man had led, from the yumba to the timber cutting to the stock routes to the railway gangs. There would have been a lot of very hard physical work in this Murri's life.

'There you go, Spencer,' he said cheerily. 'Here's your hammer. Give it a few belts. See if you can keep pace with Henry there.'

With a grin, I gave a few lusty blows and made scarcely an impression on the depth that the wedge had penetrated. I took a quick look across to Henry who had just split another log with only a dozen blows.

Not to be out-done, I laid into the wedge again – with a similar result. I was tiring fast. The hammer was heavy and I was having difficulty directing the blows onto the metal block each time. After a few more blows which missed the target entirely, I was aware of the laughter from the men, and Henry had stopped after splitting yet another log.

'We'll have to nickname you … Lightning,' said Graham, laughing.

A fair compliment to the speed of my hammering – although I was making no difference to the log. 'Am I that impressive?' The sweat was pouring off my brow. 'As fast as lightning?'

'Oh no!' Herbie was in peals of laughter. 'More like, *never strikes twice in the same place.*'

They were all hooting together, holding their sides.

'Sorry, Spencer,' said Ron. 'We've been having a joke at your expense. That's the first lesson in splitting logs, I'm afraid.' He stopped as another fit of laughter grabbed him. 'I'm in pain.'

I shared in the frivolity, more through bewildered exhaustion than understanding. I could handle being the butt of their humour … again. My self-esteem could manage that – although this personal confidence was a recent phenomenon; something about the atmosphere, the supportive camaraderie – these weird Australians.

Practical jokes seemed to be a rite of passage. For some reason, it didn't feel demeaning. It was more like being welcomed as a member of a club.

'And what is the first lesson in splitting logs?' I asked, grinning that I had been 'had' again.

Graham was the helpful one. 'Choose an old dried-out log – one with a lot of nature's cracks already in it. Do you notice that Henry is splitting these old dry gum logs that have been lying here for months?'

Uncle was still chortling away. 'I'm afraid we tricked you, Spencer. I'm sorry. See how I had to take an axe to make a split in this log? You've been trying to split a green ironbark. You could be hammering away for a month and make hardly any impression. It's full of sap, too hard to split – a good lesson for new chums and you have fairly earned the title, *Lightning.*'

In most other company, I might have taken offence. But out here in the Goomburra forest, even with my students and young children around, it was just shared humour and another traditional skill of the Australian bush learned the hard way.

Graham explained the different timbers to me. 'When you know what to look for, it's obvious.' His enthusiasm for the feel of the wood was rubbing off onto me. This son of the timber man was as much a teacher in his familiar world as any lecturer in a university auditorium.

Savouring the physical tiredness from my efforts, I lay back. I recalled my father sending apprentices down to the store for elbow grease or a long weight. You'd think I would have seen these jokes coming, from miles away.

The wedge-tailed eagle flew over again, soaring much lower now.

Had he been watching too? Coming in for a laugh as well? Was there no end to Aussies having a joke at the poor clean skin on the block?

After the initial prank, I was protected for the bulk of the later work. Indeed, it was impressive how hard even the young boys could labour with their sledgehammers, axes and bow-saws. They really were good people, albeit with a zany sense of humour.

* * * *

The splitting work of the morning was completed quickly. The main task was loading the wood onto the truck by a human chain. After a couple of hours of muscle-cracking effort, the interruption of a farm ute was most welcome.

Jenny and Shelley emerged with baskets of freshly-made pumpkin scones, in moist tea-towel wrappings. They melted in the mouth with home-made butter and honey from the farm hives. Could it get any fresher than that?

It wasn't long before the conversation had gone back to the camp-out. Olga had certainly made an impression on these people.

Shelley'd been busy on the web setting up her Facebook site – only family members but a start. 'I'm just amazed that so many of these kids who are battling to get by in life are on-line or sending text messages. It's a different world but it sucks you in. Blogging is the new word I've just learned – some new type of electronic to and fro-ing.'

She continued, looking at me. 'I can see we're going to have to learn if we are to keep up with young Darren and William here. Y'know,

Spencer, only a few years ago, no-one had even heard of the Web or emails or texting. We'd meet people for a yarn when we went into town or there'd be an occasional phone call. That was it; unless a visitor dropped by with news. No wonder we rely on television, radio and the newspapers.'

I could only smile.

'The technology is one thing,' agreed Graham. 'But I was impressed that Olga was across all of that. She's not a new model. Maybe she's had a different exposure from us farmers, eh? But, I reckon the real message was about how we're always trying to see where people fit into the scheme of things. We do it without thinking. That Izzy and Ellie were smarter than I expected them to be.'

I watched him roll his thoughts out. Yes, those street-kids were two steps ahead with their in-jokes. Good on Graham for picking it. Whatever he read in my expression seemed to encourage him to continue. 'Not all farmers think the same, believe me. We have some ding-dong blues at meetings. I think we get stuck with what we've been used to. I never got past compulsory school. Couldn't get away fast enough. Suppose that's what university's like, Spencer? Thrashing out different points of view?'

'Indeed,' I agreed. 'That's a lot of what we do in universities and there are university gatherings who would be happy with the interchange of ideas we've had out here. I must confess I didn't expect it. I'm learning too.'

As Jenny smiled at the affirmation, I grinned ruefully at my fanciful mission to bring education to the colony.

'You know when Olga was talking about a terrorist being another person's freedom fighter?' asked Warren as the others munched into their scones. 'Guerrilla action will go on forever – one side or another. It's never going to be resolved until they all sit down and talk. Too simplistic?'

'Naw, Warren, you're right,' said Ron. 'Wasn't that what Olga was saying too? The challenge is to make it happen. Break the pay-back cycle. Sabre-rattling doesn't solve anything. Like your Dad says, if *we* get problems out here with neighbours, we all sit down and work out the solution. Everyone's involved. No-one gets everything they want but we find a way forward. You agree, Shelley?'

'That's the country way,' she agreed. 'Bush solutions.'

'You'll have to bring Olga out here again, Spencer,' Jenny said quietly. 'She's certainly got everyone thinking.'

I don't think Jenny had missed too many subtleties from the chat at the camp-fire either. I gave her a cheery reply that I would see what could be done.

But my mind had already been jolted into thinking about the shortened time my new-found friend would have with us all.

My eyes lifted to the sky and the wedge-tailed eagle had gone. Had he found his prey?

The sky seemed strangely empty without that imposing presence.

I thought of Olga. An omen?

* * * *

The powerful motorbike roared easily past the early-morning semi-trailers, up the steep winding highway on the face of the Toowoomba range.

Two lanes up and two lanes down, cut right into the side of the huge escarpment. It was the only highway from the plains of the Lockyer Valley up to the city of Toowoomba sitting regally on top of the range, glistening; an imperial army guarding the battlements of a castle wall.

The bike took the climb with ease.

The gleaming monster pulled in to a petrol station, with the huge engine growling gently as its slow cadence came to a stop.

One of the dark-clad bikers filled the tank while the other stepped well away from the fuel pumps, his mobile to his ear for a brief message.

'We have a place, on the north side,' was all he said on his return.

The other nodded, face concealed behind the dark visor of his helmet.

A few minutes later, the two were back on the bike as it swung onto the road, heading north into the sleepy city. The last wisps of mist were dispersing with the rise of the eastern sun as it crossed the plain from Brisbane.

The riders idled the machine through empty streets. No need to draw attention.

They had left the areas of expensive houses, with their tailored gardens at the edge of the range and cruised into a poorer area.

Wheelie-bins at the side of the road sat unloved after the last garbage collection. Straggly grass adorned their wheels. Little appeared to have moved in the street for a day or so.

The gentle air of decay hung like a pall.

The bike wheeled off the road onto a short, steep driveway. One side of a large double garage opened briefly to accommodate the growling machine and closed quickly to swallow it into anonymity.

As the big engine was quickly stifled, the street returned to quietness. Only a few black and white birds chirped from tree to wintery tree, causing the remnant leaves to flutter to the carpet of moist foliage on the cold street below.

Chapter 37

Uncle's truck rolled into the flat backyard to a cheery wave from Aunty Edna.

'Tea's on, Herbie!' My car pulled in behind. 'You too, Spencer. Come on up. Fresh batch of johnnycakes – just made.'

Uncle passed me a steel wedge to put in my car. 'A memento, Lightning. It'll hold down papers or something.'

I held the bush tool in my hand – the object of my furious hammering. What provenance. It was a touching gesture delivered with a wink.

'Thank you, Herbie. It will have pride of place on my desk.'

Warren had stayed behind with his family but Uncle, William, Henry, Steve and I climbed the stairs to the cosy verandah with its wooden table, adorned with newly-baked damper biscuits and jam.

'Tuck in,' Edna encouraged. I was feeding well.

'Tea?' as Edna filled the cups. Sore muscles relaxed. We had a truck load of wood to be distributed but Uncle would look after that later.

'Just like old times, Edna,' Herbie gave that earthy chortle of his. 'The smell of wood. Old Spencer did himself proud, too.' He smiled. No mention was made of Lightning. Men's business. I grinned my quiet appreciation to the reminiscing Murri man. 'The old yumba over again. Those were the days, eh Edna?'

'Were you from the yumba too?' I asked in surprise. Had I been told that before? It certainly hadn't registered properly, if I had.

'That was where Herbie and I met.' She laughed at her husband's expression. 'He chased me till I would marry him.'

'I could run fast then.' He grinned. 'Edna was the best-looking girl in the yumba and in the world, to me. Still is! We had a lot of fun. She was a bit different from the others. We always got on well.

'Her Dad was a drover, away a lot. He wasn't Murri but he travelled all the stock routes back to my relatives' country, Kamileroi land over near Toomelah, on the Macintyre in northern New South Wales.'

'And he wasn't a Murri person?' I was surprised, not following – the yumba was a Murri camp

'No,' said Edna. 'He claimed to be Russian. They called him *Husk*. I don't know if he was or not. A husky is a Russian dog, isn't it, Spencer?'

'Can be,' I acknowledged without commitment.

She carried on, 'Quite a few non-Murris lived with Aboriginal families, especially in the early days. Scots, Irish – Duncans, Andersons, McGradys, McIntoshes and the like.'

Another lesson. I'd been at it again – assuming.

'My Dad's name was Pope. Doesn't sound very Russian, I know, but there you are. I was Edna Pope – and not even a Catholic.'

'Well, I'll be,' I said in astonishment. 'And your Dad lived on the yumba?'

'Yep, when he wasn't away droving. He died when I was quite young. I have happy memories of him but – his stories, his shaggy black beard. He *was* like a big husky dog.' She laughed at a fond memory. 'He yarned to us about the droving. Looked after Mum real well. Brought back salt meat for us all – a change from the rabbit and porcupine we trapped round the camp.'

'He was a good man, old Husky Nick,' added Herbie. 'Real strong accent till the day he died; and always showed respect to the Elders and the traditional ways. People liked him for that. He was one of us.' He nodded warmly. 'He's buried somewhere on the stock route, somewhere beyond Mungindi. A couple of our people was on that stock drive. They gave him a respectful Murri funeral on the edge of a creek. We never knew exactly where.'

Edna smiled thoughtfully. 'Yes, well, it's all a long time ago – but some happy times back then and happier times ahead. How's your tea, Spencer?'

'Just a treat, Aunty. I don't think I could ever have been a timber cutter. It's hard work.'

'We all have our place in the scheme of things, Spencer,' she said. 'Your job is to get Steve through his university course and on to greater things. We wouldn't have believed these advances back in our young day.'

I was still a bit bewildered at being so readily accepted. 'Thank you so much for sharing your story with me again, both of you. You're very kind.' What had I done to have such an honour bestowed upon me? 'You won't believe what an eye-opener this is for me – and all this voluntary work you do for the community, helping kids who are having a hard time ... and distributing wood. It's just marvellous.'

Chapter 38

Olga leant forward with a conspiratorial grin.

'Was *Hartley Star* in Caribbean. I was working with Venezuelan businessman called Diego; super-rich chairman and chief executive of a massive oil company. Diego could afford to hire this luxury ship and its entire crew for two months out of petty cash.'

No trouble remembering this part of her life. How ironic.

It was an all girls' affair. Anna, Eva, Melanie and Olga; gathered at the Grushko home to spend some time together. The camp-out had been great, as had been the bush dance – but men had tended to influence the conversation.

Anna had wanted to know about the exotic places where Olga had visited. Eva and Melanie were keen to hear about anything beyond the Darling Downs. They were both twenty, soon to graduate from university. The world awaited.

'Where is the most exciting place you have been?' Eva had asked. 'The place where you just went *Wow*.'

'Caribbean,' she had replied without hesitation. 'Spent several years there. Was based in Cuba, then in Venezuela. Had many trips, cruising around Windward and Leeward Islands. Just as romantic and exotic as you could imagine. Large isles and tiny coral cays, with greeny-blue waters lapping against white sand beaches, palm trees drooping over at crazy angles.

'As place to snorkel or scuba, it probably has no equal. Reefs teem with spectacular fish – fast fish, big fish, right down to tiny specks of life which glow in filtered sunlight. Absolutely wonderful.

'And exciting people; colourful, different languages, music, rhythm, dance; bright clothes like plumage of parrots. And yet, can still drop anchor in secluded bays and imagine you were like old pirate ships.'

Everyone's eyes were popping with interest at the image of this tropical paradise.

'What sorts of boats were you on?' Melanie said.

'Some sailing boats. Yachts. Others – luxury cruisers.'

* * * *

This was how the conversation had come round to the *Hartley Star*, a multi-million-dollar ship registered in Nassau in the Bahamas.

'Was named after some billionaire. We toured islands for two months on it.'

'More!' Eva was enthralled. 'What were you doing on it?'

Olga could have been telling a bedtime story to mesmerised children. 'Will seem like I'm telling stories, but part of my role with army was to work *undercover*, civilian identity.'

The girls were agog.

'Was about fifty metres long with four levels of deck. Many boats in West Indies were bigger but *Hartley Star* was luxury from bow to stern. Jade green; twin diesel engines; glided effortlessly through sheltered islands.

'And girls, all furnishings were in pale-cream leather and mahogany wood, which always smelled as if bouquets of blossoms had been washed across just that morning. Rich curtains ranged from turquoise to deep reds in each of entertaining rooms.'

Olga ignored the gasps of wonder. Her eyes were distant, picturing the memory. 'And quality? – even down to gold taps in spa. Ship's tender was bigger than most boats in any marina – was hauled up inside mother boat.

'Diego used boat to entertain – cocktail parties almost every night. We would pull into new island and invite local politicians and businessmen, with wives. Networking – with champagne, caviar, canapés – even small jazz group travelled with us. They provided background music – for atmosphere – as if tropical island settings were not enough.'

'How did you keep up with the clothes?' asked Anna in amazement.

Olga laughed. 'Money was no object to Diego. We had advantage being on move, so dresses could be used again in next location. Had range of Gucci, Dior, Yves Saint Laurent. Nearly all made from silk. Absolutely fantastic.

'And accessories?' she continued to her awe-struck companions. 'Earrings, necklaces. And shoes? Half walk-in wardrobe for shoes.'

'What happened to all of that gear?' gasped Eva.

'Oh, some still in storage back in Russia,' she replied. Her face creased with a quick worried frown before resuming its former confidence. 'Haven't had cause to wear recently. Some I gave away. Diego was very wealthy man and whole purpose of hiring *Hartley Star* was to make favourable impression on as many local communities in islands as possible. This was work, you understand. Was like an actress playing a role. It wasn't lifestyle that I was used to, nor one that I was comfortable with. But to achieve mission that was job; and good clothes, good food, good entertainment and good conversation that Diego provided, they were keys.'

'I'm just about your size,' hinted Eva earnestly.

'So you are.' Olga laughed. 'Would you have occasion to wear those clothes here? Would go over well at bush dance?'

'We could start a new trend,' encouraged Melanie. 'I'm about your size too.'

The flutter of unease rippled through Olga. She hoped her laugh was hiding her wash of guilt. All those luxuries and never shared. Thoughtless? Selfish? There had been reasons – state security, anonymity. She had washed the sense of revulsion from her mind years ago. Such extravagance had been absolutely against her socialist principles back then, but was what the army had required her to do.

Now, looking at family and friends in the unquestioning honesty of Queensland, she felt again the compounded hurt from all those years ago.

'So is that what you did for two months?' asked an incredulous Anna. 'Just hopped from island to island, swimming and partying.'

'Networking,' corrected Olga. 'My work was to meet people, to listen to what was being said. I recruited supporters ... for trade.' She smiled and changed away from dangerous territory. 'You asked me about time when it was most *Wow*. Well, days on *Hartley Star* were pinnacle – all paid by very wealthy Venezuelan businessman.'

'But he must have gained from this arrangement?' asked Eva, guilelessly.

Olga smiled as she thought what to say to a granddaughter about that world. What luxury to be able to grow up, safely sheltered from the clandestine realities of life. She doubted that Izzy and Ellie would share such rosy naïveté. They would have understood the noxiousness.

'Apart from my company,' she continued, tactfully, 'Diego and I were working with Venezuelan government for over year to protect against foreign business take-overs, either obvious kind or more subtle. That was Diego's motivation. But money involved was more than some countries would dream of spending in whole budgets.'

Melanie said laughingly, 'I can see now why you would like the Caribbean. It's like a movie story. It's not real.' She smiled across at Eva whose cheeks had reddened as she realised of the question she had just asked her grandmother.

'Oh, real alright,' insisted Olga, 'but agree was like fantasy. Growing up in Turkey and Ukraine, we were more concerned about getting any food on table in post-war era. Would never have dreamed there were people who could live this way – and in such beautiful surroundings.

'Now remember, that was pinnacle – my normal reality was very different. Most of my work was spent in cold, damp boring assignments, some of them dangerous. We were trying to collect information to keep our country safe. Was what I did for all of those years.

'You know money being splashed around on *Hartley Star* back then was probably small change compared to deals being done openly in the corporate world today. All legal, declared to shareholders. Is world of present-day capitalism. Madness! I can't believe people don't see that.'

'I wouldn't mind just a little slice of that madness,' said Melanie, with some feeling. 'I'm getting tired of being the frugal student watching every cent.'

'Nice to have enough not to worry,' said Olga, 'but, for too many rich people, is only reason for living. Whole lives are spent working out how to make another profit.'

'Nothing wrong with profit,' asserted Eva. 'Profit and service are what small business is all about. Like Dad's.'

'Not always. If built on belief you can borrow money to buy cheaply and sell fast in growing market for profit, there will be losers.' Olga marvelled at the trusting eyes. 'No service is provided – not like AA Electrics. Is just gambling. Nothing is being produced. No benefit for common good. Is craziness.' She changed away from controversy. 'What I have seen on Downs is refreshing. Luxury is not as important as simple things. Take my word.'

Eva was unconvinced. 'I still wouldn't mind a little bit of spoiling though.'

'Olga, your time in the Caribbean sounds just idyllic,' Anna said dreamily. 'I know there'd have been hard times too – but I'm with Eva, I could be pampered like that and feel no pain about it at all.'

Excited laughter at the exclusive images was cut short by Olga's question. 'So, next year, when you finish university? Where are you going?'

The girls looked at each other.

'Hard to decide,' said Melanie.

'Me too,' agreed Eva. 'We are just trying to make sure that we pass, before making too many plans.'

'You'll both pass alright,' assured Anna, her gasp illustrating a mother's frustration that the girls didn't believe in their obvious abilities.

Melanie ignored the compliment. 'You know since Dr Avery, Spencer, arrived, I've been really taken with the idea of studying in England.'

The elderly lady looked at her granddaughter for her response.

'Yes, he's really interesting,' Eva acknowledged. 'No chance of nodding off in his lectures. He's always pushing us but ... to think in a more complex way.'

'Well, I'm glad,' said Anna, relief in her tone. 'A good lecturer to guide you is so important, especially in your final year. What makes him so good?'

'That's what's odd, Mum. When he's lecturing, you know he's read everything but he's funny too. It's the way he speaks. I'm forever doing a double-take, thinking *What'd he just say?* Don't you agree, Mel?'

'Yeh. Like he talked about an Englishman's home being his castle, in a *manor* of speaking. That sort of thing. But he just moves on. Doesn't wait to see whether you got it or not. No smile, maybe just a look … to check.'

'Then when we go to tutorials,' agreed Eva, 'and he will ask us questions – and you know he's going to say, *And why is that the case?* And he will say, *Now, is that an opinion or do you have evidence to back that up?*'

She threw her hands up to emphasise her point and Melanie added, 'When I presented him a beautifully logical argument for the development of the Warsaw Pact, he said, *And the evidence is?* So I quoted my sources and he said in his funny English way, *Are you not quoting someone else's opinion as evidence? Did that person have evidence or proof or is it just his opinion, being given credibility by your repeating it?* and away we go again discussing what is the evidence, as against quoted books that only give someone's viewpoint.'

Olga laughed. She could just see Spencer toying with his students, challenging their assumptions, being the devil's advocate. 'Isn't that what Tooki was saying on camp-out, in his own sweet way, about understanding the motivation of who is feeding you news – rather than just swallowing all, as fact?'

'I think that was you too, Nana,' Eva whispered with a grin.

Her grandmother winked.

'And yet,' Melanie added, 'for all Spencer's confidence with world geography, our Queensland ways seem to bewilder him.'

Olga understood immediately – part of his attraction. The contrast between the witty expert on geo-politics and the *little boy lost* who needed to be helped.

Was Spencer putting on innocent look to draw girls in, spider-like, funnelling curious people to web? Or was he really the ingenuous soul abroad – making him even more enticing to help – not just for young ones? Even elderly lady was finding him marvellous company – that undemanding gallant behind appearance of confident aspiring professor.

'He talks about Cambridge, Nana,' said Eva, 'and I can't help thinking about all these great minds who have studied in the same buildings. You know, the trail-blazers – Isaac Newton, Charles Darwin, Milton and Coleridge – it's like a fairy land of intellectual history; wonderful, untouchable.' Her eyes were dreamy.

'It's not beyond your reach, Eva,' insisted her mother. 'You can study at Cambridge too. Students can apply from overseas to study there. Lots have done it from Australia – well maybe not lots, but it can be done.'

Melanie and Eva sat looking at Anna as if a dawning light of understanding was passing through the mists of their awareness.

Olga smiled gently as if to say, *C'mon girls, anything is possible. Look at me.*

Melanie broke the silence, almost to change the topic. 'My Dad often talks about the *Light Blues* playing rugby over there. I think maybe Cambridge sporting teams play in light-blue and Oxford University must use dark-blue. Would that be right? He likes his rugby union. I think some All Blacks and Wallabies must have gone over there to study and then they play for the universities. They must be mighty teams with internationals like that in their line-up.'

'Yes,' said Olga. 'They finish degrees in home countries and go across to Cambridge and Oxford for post-graduate study, often on scholarships. Can be done. When do you girls graduate?'

The rhetorical question ignited the spark of awareness which was slowly opening up into a full morning of realisation.

'Well, what are you waiting for?' laughed Olga. 'Are you going to take opinion or are you going to find some evidence?' She smiled wistfully at her parody of Dr Spencer Avery.

* * * *

Olga had savoured the excitement of the girls growing up. She felt uplifted, valued and happy – until her mind rolled to her present predicament.

Who were these people hunting her?

What was it that she couldn't remember?

That it should have come to this, when all joys of family and lost years were returning.

Chapter 39

Withered leaves blew in rolls across the paved square. Locals were talking about a brutal westerly chill in the air. It was the sub-tropical winter, bringing out the best in the blossoms of the famed gardens of Toowoomba; still a month or more away from the Carnival of Flowers – the advertising for the annual festival was ever-present on the television and around the town.

No northern European would have considered these blue-skied days to be winter but I humoured the natives by agreeing that there might just be a touch of the Antarctic in those south-westerly winds.

Walking across the sunlit, wintery, university campus at Toowoomba, I saw the strange familiar figure of Tooki, deep in thought, leaning against a pole. The dyed-blue hair and the hippy-like clothes made him hard to miss. He looked derelict; although on closer inspection the clothes were clean and not nearly as threadbare as first appearances would suggest.

'G'day Tooki,' I called out, surprising him from his deep contemplation.

He took a second to recognise me in my regulation cream slacks and blue blazer – one of an Englishman's idiosyncrasies around the university to combat the Aussie humour. If I had to be the butt of Pommie jokes, I could at least dress like someone from Cambridge, who still respected standards of professional attire. I grinned at the thought. It usually got a laugh and created a talking point.

'Ah Spencer. Didn't recognise you. Sorry, mate. You look a bit different from out bush.'

I smiled at his confused expression. 'That was a super camp, Tooki. Good to meet your friends and hear you debate your views. Not too many were on your wavelength when you told them nobody was listening.'

'Ah, they're all well-meaning,' he said dismissively, 'but deaf. They don't want to hear. I thought the Russian lady spoke well. Izzy, Ellie and Henry were impressed that she spoke up for us. Especially since it was her own son who was having the chop.'

'She's a remarkable lady is Olga.' I was happy to take pride by association. 'Quite an amazing life she has led.'

'She *is* Russian, isn't she? She's not what I expected. Sharp thinker, knows lots of big words; but a gentle speaker. Her accent doesn't sound too different from heaps of overseas people. Just the way she uses words, I suppose.'

'Yes, she's Russian,' I confirmed, 'but she has lived in many countries. That'll be why her accent isn't like the stereotype.'

'Ah! The stereotype,' mused Tooki. 'She was big on that. And on the money with hearing the younger generation. They're in *la la land* if they think we watch TV news or are sucked in by pompous opinions in the papers.'

'Do you really have a texting network amongst the street-kids?' I was still not sure if I was being *had* again by the Aussie humour.

'Yeh. Our grapevine is up there with the Murri network. The word goes out fast – and we're informed about things that are important to us. Our texting would put your news agencies to shame. Even homeless ones are right with on-line and the new Twitter which is growing in the States – but our network is on mobiles cos everyone is close to somebody with one. There's more coming, Spence. Tiny smart phones that can do anything a computer can – translate any language while you're travelling, link to any communication system in the world. There's no limit.'

I took it in. 'I'm impressed that street-people are across this technology – indeed that they even have phones and computer access.'

'We get mobiles to those who don't – pre-paids, funded through the Fuzzy Electronics business; what goes around, comes around. Everyone who has been helped understands what that means – even after they get back on their feet. Keeping in touch is vital for survival and safety. It's a very hard life if you don't know what is going on. The network is the key. That's what it's all about, really.'

'Impressive. I would have thought that the homeless would be the absolute down-trodden battlers in the cut-throat commercialised world.'

'That's the point, Spencer. A lot of the displaced aren't stupid. It's just circumstances. And the commercialised world is all bullshit. No sense of reality at all.' He spoke quietly, flicking his blue hair from his face. 'When the whole financial system crashes down; and it will someday, all their fortress exclusiveness will come tumbling down with it. They live in a fantasy.

'Spence, their wealth is an illusion – shares are just bits of paper that people gamble over. You can't eat shares. Until someone pays you, you don't know what they're worth. Rich people's games. They criticise our generation for being *All about me* but we are really all about networking and friendships; society rather than ourselves. It's not our generation that has stuffed the environment with greed and throw-away goods. We don't worship money. We just refuse to be manipulated by power-crazy idiots.'

He was on a roll and I was happy to listen to his fascinating world-view.

'You don't see us installing security systems to keep others out. We aren't creating laws to protect the wealthy rather than community good. It's all bullshit, Spencer, and you know it too.'

He drew breath. Some emotion there. Vehement. A flood gate letting it all rush out.

'I tell you.' Tooki's voice was now an animated whisper. 'I fix computer management systems and I guarantee you most of these businesses are right on the edge, so far in on borrowed money they'll be gone if someone calls the debt. And most are so easy to hack. If I were them, I'd be out learning the technology that Izzy can already master rather than ridiculing people because they're different.'

Maybe the serenity of the bush had relaxed me because I felt so peaceful as the tirade flowed. 'Well, you persuaded the people on the camp-out, even Peter.'

'Ah, yeh, at least he apologised.' He had a strange dreamy expression. 'Yeh, you're right. Maybe we did strike a chord.'

193

I wasn't sure I'd understood the comment about Izzy mastering technology. A homeless girl? Presumably, no resources?

'Izzy is an interesting young lady. She's good with technology?'

'Bright girl, Spence. Settling down. Henry and Edna are looking after her.'

'How did she end up on the streets?'

'The old story. Had enough of home. Copped a flogging for being out on the drink. I think that had been normal for her for a long time. She took off. Too many restrictions – busy professional parents; too much image, not enough love. Henry and I found her with a black eye from an addict in a squat. We got her to Aunty Edna and slowly she's got her life in order.'

He looked at me with passion, maybe pride, glinting in his eyes. 'She's one of the lucky ones. But bright – she'll get her certificate soon and then onto uni – you watch. Hey, I gotta move. Aunty has some people Henry is trying to help. They want me to listen in. Where are you off to?'

'I'm just preparing lectures just now. Routine stuff.' But I added, for interest, 'We're going out to Goondiwindi on the weekend. To some phantom races and then we'll have time on Melanie's farm near the river. We'll take Olga out too.'

'Cool,' he said. 'Give my best to the Russian lady. Tell her that Took and the girls said she's alright.'

'Will do,' I replied, in as *hip* a manner as I could manage.

He disappeared with a wave, mobile going to his ear in his other hand. I needed to be a chameleon to belong in this new world.

* * * *

Eva came running up to me as I reached the Arts building.

'How are you, Spencer?' A happy smile lit her face and her cheery look had the same effect on me. She didn't have any tutorials with me so the meeting was a surprise.

'I'm well,' I said. 'And you?'

'Just catching up on some reading. I thought I'd see if I could talk to the careers counsellor. I graduate this year and I don't really have a plan. Do you think I'm good enough to do post-grad?'

'You really need to know what you want to specialise in. But, yes.'

She pondered for a few seconds. 'You're friends with Nana. Can I ask you something?' I think she took my patient pause as agreement. 'She really likes you. Been talking to me about her life and I'm very interested in studying the types of work she used to do – it brings me closer to her. Not the army so much as the global ideas. Her dealings with corporations and governments are part of my heritage; and it seems important work. Does that sound snobbish? It's just that I want to study something useful, meaningful to the world. I don't think I could get absorbed in counting the rings on trees.'

I could identify with that. 'Well, Russian geo-politics is my particular area of study,' I agreed. 'I've found it interesting. Indeed, I thought I knew a lot about it but I have learned some new perspectives from your Nana. Subtle things. Impressions. Your idea has promise.'

We had been walking as we talked. Reaching my office, I opened the door to reveal my desk, computer and bookshelf.

'Is your office like this in Cambridge?'

'An office is an office. But no, it doesn't look like this. It's in an old part of the university, where students walk through the cloisters. It has a high ceiling, old ornate plaster work; an oriel window in Tudor style juts outwards, and my desk is set in the window. I can see in three directions – and out over the gardens. It's an old desk, wooden, dating from the nineteenth century. There's a heavy sheet of glass over the surface so that I can work without damaging it.'

I stopped, suddenly realising that she was wide-eyed. I had been waxing on about my Cambridge office, painting a picture so academically romantic, that she was almost in a trance. A captivating expression. Stunning. Artistic.

I startled myself back to reality, shocked at my eloquent description – it was just an office – and even more stunned at my reaction to Eva's look. *Don't tell me you hadn't noticed,* Olga had said. Well, I had noticed now.

'Eva, it's not all that romantic. I didn't tell you about the dry rot and the cockroaches and the heating that never works and how the oriel window actually leaks in a storm.'

She wasn't hearing. My description had transported her to a dream world, couched in academic history and spiced, perhaps, with just a touch of privilege.

'Eva!' I repeated to get her attention. 'If you are thinking about post-graduate study in Australia or overseas, have a long talk with your parents. They might not be too keen on their only daughter leaving for the cold, damp winters of England.'

Had I managed to temper her enthusiasm with some reality? Probably not.

I needed to talk with Olga. The Grushko family didn't need any more hassles. I had no desire to be a catalyst in enticing Eva to go overseas.

'I was thinking of dropping over to see Olga this afternoon,' I announced. 'Is she home?'

Still distracted, she said, 'Oh, yes. She's showing Mum how to make some traditional Russian dessert. I'm sure you'll be very welcome.'

'Fine. I'll give her a ring. Have a good day with the counsellor.'

I waved as she headed off to get some career advice – and then I breathed out a large sigh. I didn't remember relationships with my students at Cambridge causing me this angst. Then, of course, I was besotted with Mary.

Ah Mary! Maybe Olga was right. Maybe I should test the water.

I knew the Email.address by heart.

Email: maryj@googlenet.com

From: spenceravery@bigpond.com.au

Hello Mary

You have been in my mind a lot, so I thought I would just drop you a line.

I hope you and yours are well. Toby passed on your regards to me in a previous email. I do hope he passed on my best to you in return.

It seems like a long time ago that we were together. I do miss you. I suppose you have been busy with the usual round of parties and functions.

How is the writing coming along? Any publishers interested? It is a pretty hard-nosed business getting a start in that market. I'm sure some wise entrepreneur will see the merit of your creative work in time.

I've been busy with a good teaching load in most year levels. I am finding my small group of four final-year undergraduates to be my stars. They're quite capable, really – a pleasant surprise. One has even floated the idea of post-grad study at Cambridge. I think she could make a fist of it.

The social activities here are very different to our usual fare in Cambridge, dearest. I've been to a bush dance and a camp-out on a farm. I've had Aboriginal Elders and farmers explain their their deep understanding of the land. I'll be going to a phantom race meeting at Goondiwindi this weekend. That's right. That's the name of the place and people are apparently going to gather in large numbers to gamble on horses that aren't even there. I know it beggars belief – but that is the interesting world I am trying to understand.

Well, enough of me. Please reply soon.

I know we said that we wouldn't correspond while I was away but, you have been in my thoughts and I hope I have been in yours.

All my love
Spencer

Chapter 40

The phone-call to the Grushko home had resulted in Olga sounding most enthusiastic about me visiting her. I had arranged to go out for only an hour.

Anna made me very welcome and showed off her traditional sweet called Mikado, a layered honey cake, which she and Olga had just made. The small sample tasted good but the rest was to be kept for when Peter and Eva came home.

Olga and I retreated to the verandah. I noticed she was looking more drained, despite her cheery enthusiasm.

Seeing the concern in my eyes, she said quietly, 'We both know time is not far off, Spencer. Be strong for me, please. I have medication now to help with headaches. Let us spend our precious hour talking about my past. Maybe will spark memory. Did I tell you about when I was courted by Venezuelan oil millionaire?'

The cheeky teasing expression was back in her face.

'Nothing about you would surprise me,' I said, laughing. 'Tell me about this exotic handsome businessman.' I assumed the South American would have been at least a match for Baryshnikov.

'Was 1976,' she said. 'His name was Diego. Ruggedly good-looking in Latin way and extraordinarily rich. Venezuela's oil fields are substantial and had been exploited by exploration companies for decades. But in 1976, nation took control of all oil production. Intent was to revitalise whole country, get rid of poverty. Lofty ideals.

'Was in Venezuela, honoured guest of Diego, to ensure no foreign capitalist company could slyly engineer social unrest and pocket resources. My role was foreign intelligence; to build network of listeners who could infiltrate local syndicates as well as corporate boardrooms. I think we were very successful.'

I listened in wide-eyed amazement to another saga far beyond any of my experience.

'Diego was my discreet link into government and we were able to share information. I think we possibly stopped dozen attempts to undermine one of most successful oil industries in world and we, in our own right, sold Russian technology into that market.'

I gasped. 'What? Do you mean you were in this for capital gain? Where was the integrity of your political philosophy?'

She laughed. 'By stopping others getting foothold, we were preventing Americans getting stronger. That was philosophy. You can only stop world domination if you prevent others from getting too powerful. You can only have détente if you are strong enough to stand up to others. We call that process *razryadka,* in Russian – relaxing pressure from position of strength, just like Khrushchev did in 60s.

'Anyway, Diego wined and dined me for nearly year. I solved his oil problems and he gave me lots of information in new oil technologies; and gadgets. He was gadget freak. Was when I first got involved with special forces' aids. You would think of them as James Bond type gadgets – but were mainly listening tools back then; spy tools.'

I was amazed. I had no real concept of the behind-the-scenes operations that countries engaged in as part of the strategic chess game of world power.

She continued. 'Even back in 70s, Diego was dreaming about computer applications which didn't become reality until end of century. It seemed science fiction to me at time but he was talking about financial transactions occurring in nano-seconds with linked computers speaking to one another across countries. Then he would devise gadget to hack into system, record information and replace vital components. Are worms and viruses of today.

'He couldn't produce them back then but he dreamed the dreams. He lived in billionaire's world of fantasy and was very generous to me. I now have more than enough money in Swiss bank account thanks to Diego.'

Her thoughts were drifting in tune with that happy mystical smile. I could only watch in wonder.

'What happened to Diego?' I asked eventually. 'I haven't heard of him.'

'Sadly, lost in fighting between drug cartels. Colombian and Venezuelan gangs were very powerful. Still are. Diego was sad loss – and I fell ill while I was there. Some tropical fever. Lots of bugs and bitie creatures over there. Is probably where my heart condition started. All academic now. That part of me is not getting any worse.' There was the grin again.

'What a fascinating set of adventures you have had in your life.' I shook my head in admiration. 'You are helping me with your insight into the machinery behind the public face of international politics.'

She gave a disbelieving look. 'Are you suggesting you only lecture about superficial to your students, Spencer?'

'I'm not qualified to talk about the world of espionage.' I laughed at her jibe.

She had gone suddenly quiet, eyes closed; concentrating. Her expression was a grimace as she seemed to be fighting the pain of a headache; hand raised as if to say that it was alright.

She was remembering something.

'Five of us.' Her voice was quiet as if describing some recalled wraith. 'Secret project to shield special weapons from gangs, during perestroika. Suitcases! Was responsible for suitcases. Had to get them out of country and hide somewhere safe.'

I was bursting to ask a question but could not interrupt. What was in the suitcases? Where had they been taken from and to? Who gave the orders? Where were the other people in her team?

'Has gone again,' a sense of disappointment in her tone as her eyes popped open.

'You said there were five of you. Could the others help you remember?'

She looked at me strangely. 'Oh, you don't know about my conversations with Superintendent Fowler of AFP, Australian Federal Police.'

I must have looked totally bemused. We had been supporting each other intellectually and emotionally now for some time – lots of things said in trust – but not about the AFP.

'Spencer, have talked to you about some of my life. I think you can hear from less personal side – things in GRU,' she said. 'Did many hard things for my country – some bring me shame today as I mellow, but we were soldiers for survival and war is not pretty.'

She paused to collect her thoughts.

'You ask about others protecting special forces' gear. Spencer, they are dead! I would presume that they have been murdered, maybe made to look like accident. Had superintendent from AFP contact me. I am only one left who had knowledge and I can't remember. Superintendent said were people in Australia tracking me, perhaps to get information. Maybe, I am dangerous person to be around.'

She smiled unconvincingly.

'Don't know if anyone is in any direct danger. Is best you are aware. Peter has been informed. No-one else knows.'

I took in the information. I didn't feel frightened – perhaps just more in awe of Olga than I had been before. She was so calm in the face of adversity – so confident; and that was rubbing off on me. This was a lady facing death within weeks and here she was trying to remember something, presumably to help others.

No-one else knew the secret she was trying to recall, so I guessed she would be needed alive to be of use to anyone seeking the information.

But what was it? Suitcases? Taken from somewhere to somewhere to keep them away from criminal gangs? Out of the country? Where would they be safe?

Was something from my own memory starting to click into place?

* * * *

As I walked to my apartment from the car park, my mind was rolling with all the ideas that Olga had shared with me. Suitcases, undercover work, Diego the Venezuelan billionaire, Olga's GRU team all dead . . . what a bizarre world it all seemed.

And then, as I was passing the leopard trees, I was conscious of being watched again – a presence; I could feel it.

I'd thought I had been aware before – seeing someone looking at me – but I wasn't sure.

I glanced quickly over my shoulder ... to see a shadow disappear.

Chapter 41

The preparations were in place for the trip to Goondiwindi. I had the mini-bus organised. The overnight bags were packed. I would be picking up the others in about an hour. Time to do a last check of the emails.

One new message in the inbox.

Email: spenceravery@bigpond.com.au

From: maryj@googlenet.com

Dear Spencer

What a surprise to get your email.

Thank you for all your news about life in the land down under. I'm glad you are well and learning to enjoy all the strange customs. They certainly sound different.

I'm well. You are right. The merry wheel of social engagements continues to turn. Most of the same faces appear as usual.

Spencer, I'm surprised Toby didn't tell you when you have both been apparently emailing. Toby and I have been attending the dances and parties together. We have become good friends.

Even my mother seems to like him. He appears to be descended from the Smythes of Lincolnshire – propertied people going back to the seventeenth century. That impressed my mother.

I had been thinking of writing to you and explaining what was happening but you didn't want correspondence while you were away, lest it made you homesick. I did think Toby might have hinted. I asked him to send you my regards.

You are a lovely person, Spencer. It is just that I think it is time to move on.

I hope you are meeting lots of nice people out there in Australia. I know we will catch up when you return next year. I would like us to continue to be friends. We did have some special times together. I will always be grateful for that.

Best regards

Mary

I blanched. I could sense the draining sensation. Blank emotions flowed through me like colourless sludge.

Shock!

That I should find out in such an impersonal way. If Mary's email was her attempt to let me down gently, that hadn't been the effect.

And Toby – the bastard! I could handle a break-up. It had been on the cards, potentially. But the treachery; that was something else. I should have seen it coming – but I hadn't. I had trusted him; my friend, my confidant. My saviour in a time of black depression.

How totally naïve had I been? Behind my back, while I was away … and it had been his idea for me to come to Australia in the first place – nearly made all the bloody arrangements for me. The bastard!

Cuckolded. That was how I felt. Toby had known my feelings for Mary. He knew how close we were. The rat! To manoeuvre himself into such a position of trust and then betray me. Where was his moral fibre? And descended from the Smythes of Lincolnshire too. What a cad!

How was he expecting to tell me that he had run off with my girl? Would they just be away on holiday together when I returned from Australia – or was he planning to front up like a man?

Silent numbness.

I sensed that time was passing but I couldn't move.

My angry pulse slowly started to settle.

As the thoughts rolled incessantly but more slowly through my mind, my involuntary reasoning surprised me with its logical clarity, unexpected under the circumstances.

Perhaps it had all been inevitable. Toby would have been trying to comfort Mary, with me being overseas. Of course, he would accompany her to dances and parties. It was the decent thing for a chap to do – look after a friend's girl. And she couldn't have gone to any proper society function without a suitable partner. Yes, it probably happened almost by accident. Damn it all.

And then Toby had clearly passed the genealogical test of the delightful mother, Prunella. How appropriate that name had always seemed to me. I had tried to see merit in the woman, just in case; but really, I could never see a redeeming feature in that jumped-up snob who lived in an imaginary world. She probably did believe in knights in shining armour.

Olga was right. Some romances seem destined only to last a summer, or a winter.

Strangely, I was feeling no pain – only numbness. It had been a shock.

I was bloody angry at Toby for deceiving me but I didn't feel the pangs of loss that I thought I should be feeling. I was bloody disappointed in Mary too.

We'd had some really good times together; better than good in all honesty – so, for her to go off with my best friend, without even a note till I wrote to her, was disillusioning at the very least.

Cold logic told me it would never have worked anyway. The critical mother would always be the foul harpy in the background. I may well have been saved from a much greater hassle further down the track.

But who needs logic? I just felt bloody dudded.

My mind snapped back to the present. There was no time for pining. I was the bus driver. I had people to collect. The phantom races and Goondiwindi awaited. Now was not the time to pen a response either to Mary or Toby.

I decided to not even reply – just to let them sweat about my lack of reaction. That appealed to my slightly deflated ego.

Let them stew!

I closed down the computer and stepped out into my new world.

Chapter 42

The trip to Goondiwindi was uneventful; endless fields, infrequent villages and farm buildings.

Brightly-coloured agricultural Millmerran broke the trip; and then more bush and wide fields – an occasional kangaroo still awake and grazing in the lush grass of the table-drain beside the road. My now experienced eye could pick up the distinctive shape of a high-flying eagle so far above all the lower hawks. How majestic was that feat of soaring.

I had not yet gained the sense of comfort that Uncle Herbie had talked about when he said that no Murri person was ever alone in the Australian bush. I would need much more familiarity with the subtleties of this huge land before I could feel that sense of belonging – a few more lessons from Elders like Herbie. Then, there were lots of farmers, graziers more correctly, who lived out here with their own bond of peace with the bush.

Olga peered at me, from under raised eyebrows. Could she read my mind, even now?

She was putting on a great show of strength – chatting, laughing, being interested in every new scene as the journey continued. I knew she was increasing her intake of pain-killers. I tried not to think of her suffering – she would just tell me not to be soppy.

Eva and Melanie were swapping stories with Steve and Warren. The chat was about friends and even lecturers. They were careful not to comment on me.

I was grateful. I wasn't in the mood to make any witty ripostes.

* * * *

Men in jeans, moleskins, riding boots, big cowboy hats and distinctive checked shirts; women dressed in pretty much the same gear – just with different shapes and a more tailored look.

The showgrounds were already bustling in the busy picturesque river-town of Goondiwindi.

I had taken Melanie's advice and bought my bush-show clothes a week before. She had told me to roll them in the dirt. Wash them at least twice so that I didn't look like a 'blow in'. Well, I'd had them dry cleaned … some concession at least.

It was the afternoon. I parked the vehicle and we wandered round the dusty grounds. There was plenty of grass on the racetrack and out in the centre. But, elsewhere, a fine dust covered the shoes and gave a tan tinge to the legs below the knee – especially on cream-coloured moleskins.

Olga took my arm for support as we moved slowly past the fairground attractions for the children, bars for the men and farming displays for the captive market. There were tractors, harvesters, utilities and the status vehicles of the top-of-the-range four-wheel drives. A fashion show leaked its distinctive music from one of the big sheds. Cotton clothes were on the catwalk as we passed – and the sign said that woollen fashions would come on at 6pm.

Something for everyone.

Punters gazed up at a huge screen in front of the grandstand. Under a sea of hats, they waited for the first novelty event. It was to be a camel race, a real race, while there was still daylight. The animals pranced around while jockeys in silk bibs tried hard to stay mounted.

The massive electronic screen flagged the event timings so that punters could plan their breaks to the bar. There was to be a cockroach race beamed by video-link up onto the feature display – I wasn't off the money at all; followed by lizard and frog races. Interspersed between the weird events were a whip-cracking contest and a dingo-trap throwing challenge to meet the needs of the strong men and women, in from the stock routes. Then the serious list of races would begin, using video of phantom horses on the big screen.

Men and women placed betting-odds on boards.

Melanie shouted over. 'They're from the service clubs. All the money goes to local charities and to supporting people through hard times.'

Laudable. At least it was not some shady entrepreneur making a dollar at the expense of well-oiled locals.

I was glad I had Olga on my arm. She looked elegant and happy, taking in the sights, sounds and scents of the country.

'You seem distracted,' she said.

'I emailed Mary yesterday,' I said quietly. 'I got a reply today.'

She looked at me as I paused.

'It seems she has taken up with my friend Toby and our romance has moved into history.'

'I *am* sorry.' She gave my arm an encouraging squeeze. 'And you?'

'Shocked initially.' I was surprisingly comfortable sharing my feelings with her. That wouldn't have happened previously. Too much face to be lost, too many insecurities, imaginary walls protecting a cultivated image. But there was a bond growing between the two of us. 'I had no indication this was happening; from either of them. I suppose it's the way of the world but I do feel a breach of loyalty.'

She said nothing. We just kept walking slowly.

'Yet, I don't feel totally dejected, or rejected for that matter,' I continued. 'Clearly, it wasn't meant to be... and I won't have to deal with her oppressive repugnant mother.' I grinned at the thought as my companion gave another supportive arm-squeeze.

'Well, looks like you'll just have to take this old grandmother to phantom race ball.' As she gave me the most radiant smile, I realised the challenge that Diego and the others would have had in withstanding the charm of this lady. If she could produce such a captivating presence when she was near death's door, she must have been irresistible in her youth.

The band was setting up their stage on the back of a huge farm trailer. Huge lights hung from tall poles all round the area. In an hour, the whole area would be floodlit presumably. The bar and the catering venues were already serving flat-out; another country gathering moving into full swing.

An impressive number of people had turned up. Melanie explained that the properties were far apart. People came to town occasionally for produce but there were few actual times where everyone in the community could gather for a social event. That might be at the district show or a charity ball or an occasion like this. So, when an event was organised for a good cause, everyone made the effort to support and socialise.

'Melanie is right,' Olga commented. 'Whole families are here. All ages. Ladies have own activities and places for cup of tea, or stronger drink. Children have show rides and chance to parade baby animals.'

The men generally just hung over the racetrack rail or the bar with a cool amber fluid in hand, chatting about animal prices, the weather or politics.

And everyone had a smile.

What was it about bush people that they were so invariably happy – a lack of pretence? Was it part of trying to make a living off the land while being at the mercy of the vagaries of nature?

No doubt they were very independent on spread-out properties but they would still rely on each other when times were tough. Perhaps that was it; a curious blend of social linking and personal resourcefulness which had forged the irreverent innovative toughness of the Aussie bush larrikin.

The Fair Dinkum Bush Band started up its first number, while still checking sound levels. The lager-phone player's patter flowed, as usual, with his introduction of the band. He introduced the man on the mandolin, as Gary Tate.

'You'd know his family,' said Tony. 'They're all over the Downs. You know Dick Tate from Warwick who wants to control everyone and his sister, Agi Tate, who stirs up trouble.'

The crowd got the message. The ripple of polite chortle swelled into a mixture of groans and belly laughs as the banter came in from all the band members, 'Oh, related to Row Tate who tries to turn things around.'

'She's a cousin to Hesi Tate who is always putting off jobs.'

'Is she related to Imi Tate? I can't stand the way he copies what I do!'

'Well, his cousin Irri Tate is even worse!'

The band was introduced. The tone was set for the dance and the *Heel and Toe Polka* was the first number as usual. Olga and I did our own quiet toe-tap back from the main dance, in deference to her health.

Olga smiled with approval. 'They *are* good.'

'Yep,' I agreed, getting into the rural chat. 'Love the patter and they can play.'

At the end of the dance set, the couples stood gathering their breath and one woman shouted out to the band, 'I'd like *The Drongo* for my husband!'

Quick as flash Tony replied, 'Sorry, we don't do swaps!'

Gary, the mandolinist disappeared at the back of the trailer, while the others sang the melodious *Clancy of the Overflow*, to give the dancers a rest.

The mandolin player returned, apparently just having replaced a broken string.

'Where have you been, Gary?' asked Tony.

'Just been killing some flies,' replied the curly-haired Gary. 'Got three males and two females.'

'How could you tell them apart?'

'Three were on a beer can and two were on the mobile phone,' came Gary's reply, to the rapturous guffaws from the crowd.

To which Tony said, 'If bullshit was bitumen, you'd be the Bruce Highway.'

Strip the Willow was the next dance. Tony remained on stage calling the couples into sets, while the other band members demonstrated the moves to the dancers on the floor.

As the band returned to the stage, the banter from Tony gently mocked and encouraged the dancers until the mandolin and accordion launched into *The Irish Washerwoman*, alternating with *Fred's Delight*.

The laughter flowed as the fit young country people twirled and pranced through the dance routines.

'You danced really well at Goomburra.' I looked at Olga with her happy smile. 'Really light on your feet.'

She laughed. 'I had practice with some handsome men at Kirov, remember. You danced well yourself – must have been that promenading at university balls.'

We grinned at our own happy memories as the dance set finished.

Then, Tony was beamed up on the large screen to explain the races. He sounded like a showground ring master, encouraging and informing.

'Roll up! Roll up! The phantom races are about to start! Roll up! Roll up! Today, for your enjoyment, we have *the little horses*, crafted from wood, ten of them, side by side facing a ten-metre track. They might be only twenty-five centimetres long but they will pack a gallop from the jockeys selected from you, the crowd.'

Tony was the circus clown demonstrating with exaggerated movements how the mechanical horses were pulled along the course by a string on a pulley attached to the far end.

'The propulsion comes from the ten jockeys each turning a handle to control the speed of the pull. So place your bets, ladies and gentlemen!

'Or wait, because there's more.

'Hidden from your very gaze, near the handle for each jockey, is a variable gear. A low gear takes many more handle turns than the high gear which would need more strength.

'Now you have more choices! Place your bets!!'

Just as the punters were rushing to the service-club bookmakers, Tony's voice came on again.

'But wait, there's more!'

The laughing crowd skidded to a halt, awaiting the next instruction.

'Tantalising Tom, our chief steward of the course, secretly and randomly adjusts the hidden gears before each race so that you don't know whether the strong jockey has a good gear selection or not.

'So my advice is; since all the money goes to local community causes, back them all! You might not make a buck but Tantalising Tom will make a fortune to distribute around. Place your bets!'

The jockeys were chosen at random from the audience; a blend of gender and age. Tony adorned them in the racing silks. The gamblers had invested their flutter.

Melanie helped Olga and me through the maze of gambling odds.

'How much would you like to bet, Spencer?'

'Melanie, the man who bets is a fool and the man who doesn't bet is no better.'

Her eyes widened in instant awareness and she burst into spontaneous laughter. Brilliant. She was on my wavelength. I shared her happiness. I was actually laughing – not just my accustomed professional chortle – and I was suddenly glad I had insisted on a group approach to probity around this trip.

I bet my meagre dollars on a fit-looking girl with horse number eight. All to a good cause ... and I hadn't even had a drink. Then Melanie was off helping Olga with her decision-making.

The jockey's job was to turn the handles as fast as possible to move the wooden horses down the track and the young girl impressed everyone with her twirling speed, just to be nudged out by an elderly lady with a superior gear on horse number two.

The crowd cheered. The bookies paid up. Punters sighed with their losses. The entertainment echoed around the showgrounds and my money disappeared in the process.

There were ten races during the evening. The band stopped playing for each one. Everyone watched the event unfold as the video camera beamed live coverage up onto the big screen. Tony's patter was the entertainment feature in the jockey selection and race call.

The night unfolded with hilarity, race competition, dances and a lot of people just catching up with friends; such a pleasant, happy atmosphere in the cool of the winter evening.

Not that the dancers were cool. Bush dancing generated some heat and every dance was fully patronised. They weren't game to lay themselves open to Tony's wit if they didn't get up to dance. And the patter seldom stopped.

The mandolin player said with exaggerated concern, 'Tony, you've got a newt on your shoulder?'

'I know. His name is Tiny.'

'Why Tiny?'

'Because he's My Newt,' replied the deadpan Tony to more rapturous groans from the laughing dancers and punters.

I shook my head. It couldn't be an accident that everyone again seemed to be laughing and having fun at another bush dance with The Fair Dinkum Bush Band. They were quite a combination and the painful one-liners just kept pouring out.

I watched the uncoordinated movements of stockmen and their dancing partners getting confused with the progressive dance movements and dissolving into peals of laughter. I realised that was half the fun. If everyone had danced every step perfectly, then Tony would have needed a whole new line of jokes to keep the humour flowing.

But no, he had more than enough ammunition for his quick banter as the happy dancers struggled to replicate the 'over and under' ocean movements in the Waves of Bondi dance:

'Extra tuition for the remedial group,' he called. 'No, not over and over, over and under. You are a wave not a surfer. Poetry to watch this group near the front – like a zephyr through wheat fields. That's a wind, Gary, not a car.'

Olga could hardly contain herself. She thought it was an absolute hoot. And when the evening came to an end under the starry winter skies of the western Downs, a whole community wended its way home, knowing they'd had a lot of fun.

I was growing to like these quirky Queensland ways – a warmth of familiarity, of acceptance, of belonging.

Olga had a colour and joy in her face which belied her deteriorating health. It had been a super evening and she spent most of the trip to Melanie's property, thanking everyone for such a wonderful time.

And she said that the mandolin player could be an honorary Russian balalaika player any time.

Chapter 43

Jeff Fowler was being briefed by his ASIO liaison. They had received an update from British Intelligence.

- *Information gained from a Russian military intelligence defector indicates that America has been significantly penetrated by the Russian spy network; to the extent that there are apparently hundreds of listeners at all levels in the US military and that intelligence was being passed back on a regular basis.*

- *Further, the defector advised that there are arms caches hidden across the US waiting for use by Russian special forces. Perhaps the major knows those locations.*

- *The informer implied that Britain is similarly infiltrated.*

The superintendent considered the new information. No doubt, Major Davidenko would know the names of key people in their networks in a range of foreign countries. While that would be useful intelligence for Allied security agencies, would the same information be worth criminal or terrorist gangs sending their operatives to Australia in pursuit?

'It has to be something more significant than just knowing some names of agents.' He looked at the ASIO contact, who shrugged his shoulders.

'We pass on the information. Its relevance is your call.'

Fowler persisted. 'Knowing the location of arms and explosive caches in America or Britain would be useful, but it doesn't fit the bill for this level of interest. This group of five was doing something very important back in the early 90s; something that Major Davidenko can no longer remember and the other four can no longer tell us.'

The ASIO man gave a non-committal grin.

Fowler turned away after a nod of frustrated appreciation. He still had little to work with.

His smart-phone showed the tracking device in place on the Major's person. She had travelled to Goondiwindi for a weekend away with her university friends.

Chapter 44

Olga settled into her comfortable room at the farm house.

I was next door. Probably Melanie had told her parents about 'the five-star accommodation' prank. The Bells were treating their daughter's lecturer to the best available and I appreciated the gesture – never knock back the comforts of life. The students were all over in the quarters where the seasonal workers stay.

Olga knocked on my door to thank me for a wonderful evening.

'You are good company, Spencer. I like talking with you because you listen – and you hear interesting things in what I say, which stimulates more conversation. I like that. Have been worrying about not being able to remember what we were doing in early 90s. Keep getting these suitcase pictures.'

I listened silently. No point in ruining a good perception.

'When AFP man spoke with me last, was urging me to tell him anything that might help solve mystery. He said I could phone day or night. Was wondering if I should bother him with something as trivial as that.'

'Only one way to find out,' I suggested. 'Phone him and see if he really wants to be disturbed at any hour. Here. Use my mobile.'

She smiled her appreciation. 'You are thinking straight. Am getting confused. Maybe this illness is creeping up faster than I expected. You are calm ... and logical.' Compliments were nice. My smile remained in place.

She took the phone and extracted the superintendent's phone number from her purse. 'Please stay here.' Maybe she had thought I was going to leave her to speak in private. 'How do I put this on speaker, so that you can listen too? You might hear something to help my memory.'

She called and pressed the speaker button.

'Fowler.' I could hear the tone of the policeman answering a number he didn't recognise.

'Olga Davidenko, Superintendent. Sorry to trouble; you did say to phone any time.'

'It's no problem,' assured the superintendent. 'Do you have something for me?'

'Not lot, I'm afraid, but I thought I should tell I have been having flashbacks. Don't last long and I don't know what they mean – but you might be able to piece together. Am not thinking as well as I once did.'

'Go on.'

'Flashback has to do with suitcases. Am moving suitcases – big suitcases. Image goes before I can identify what is in them or where I am taking them. Suitcases. Big black suitcases. Am afraid is all I have but it might be piece of puzzle.'

'You are in Goondiwindi just now?' verified Fowler.

'Yes. Tracking bug must be working.' She grinned at some thought. 'You can get me on this mobile. Belongs to Dr Spencer Avery, university lecturer from Toowoomba. We will be close to each other until return to Toowoomba tomorrow afternoon.'

'Thank you,' said Fowler. 'I'll be in touch.'

* * * *

The superintendent immediately rang his ASIO contact.

'Suitcases. Big black suitcases. Does that mean anything to you? Major Davidenko has had flashbacks which she thinks may be connected.'

'It means nothing at the moment,' the contact replied. 'I'll check and get back.'

* * * *

Within an hour, Jeff Fowler's phone rang. It was ASIO.

'British Intelligence think that Major Davidenko may have information about suitcase bombs,' the contact said.

'Tell me more,' said Fowler. 'Tell me everything you know. Why the hell didn't British Intelligence think to share this thought a bit earlier?'

'They don't talk to each other over there,' said the ASIO man dismissively.

He continued, 'We believe there was a very secret program in the late 1980s to develop small-scale nuclear bombs. Bombs which could fit in a large suitcase – such as the one you described.

'British Intelligence is now joining the dots because the group of five agents, including Major Davidenko, were definitely charged with the responsibility of protecting certain secret weapons from the Russian mafia or freelance terrorist groups. It would appear, based on your most recent information, that hiding and protecting suitcase bombs could have been part of Major Davidenko's brief in the early 90s.'

'How do you hide a nuclear bomb?' asked Fowler.

'Oh,' replied the agent, pleased to be able to explain some detail. 'These are very small nuclear bombs. They are not like the ones dropped on Hiroshima and Nagasaki at the end of World War II. No, no! These bombs might only take out a city block. Two at most,' he added with a single-minded jollity, as if the difference was insignificant.

'But aren't nuclear bombs radioactive?' asked Fowler. 'Wouldn't they show up on even the most primitive detectors?'

'Ah! Well. They are radioactive to an extent,' enthused the ASIO agent, 'and the suitcase would have been lined with lead and maybe some other insulators so that only minimal radioactivity would be emitted. Quite effective really. And, you see, they wouldn't be armed in their normal safe state in the suitcase. Oh no!

'But you are right in a way. Even in their dormant state, you'd pick them up on the post 9/11 state-of-the-art machines. They can even pick up someone who has just had radiotherapy but how many of these hi-tech devices do we have in Australia, eh? So, no, Jeffrey, they probably wouldn't register on routine Geiger counters. And back in the 90s, the security was nothing like today.

'Now,' his excitement rose again, 'if they were armed, that would be different. Oh yes. They would be easily detectable if they were armed – and ready to explode. If they went off, as I said, there wouldn't be much left in a city block; or maybe even a bit more.'

Fowler shook his head. The ASIO boffin was in raptures at having an audience to hear his expertise on the subject.

'But it is the radioactive fall-out which would spread on the wind; that would be the main problem. That would be a bit like the Chernobyl malfunction. Probably cause masses of health problems to an awful lot of people but, even more importantly, the problem would be *the threat* of health problems. The threat alone would spread panic. Yes, yes. Definitely. Panic would be the major effect of a bomb like that going off. Could you imagine what the press would make of that; let alone the propaganda machines of the terrorist groups on YouTube? They would have a field day.'

'This is sounding more promising,' Fowler said quietly. 'Terrorists – and nuclear panic could be what they are after.'

'Indeed, Jeffrey. Indeed.' The ASIO man's enthusiasm waxed earnestly. 'I think you could be right on the money now. I agree. Suitcase bombs would certainly be of interest to terrorists. Nasty business, eh?'

Fowler thanked his contact. If, indeed, Major Davidenko had been in charge of hiding suitcase nuclear bombs, then that could explain Syrian, Pakistani and Russian interest in her – especially if she was the last one alive to know where they were hidden.

There was a nagging worry however.

Helpful though this information was, he still didn't have any knowledge about where these bombs might be. They could be anywhere in the world – and the clock was ticking down on Olga Davidenko.

Chapter 45

Another dawn chorus of birdsong woke Olga as the rays of the eastern sun poured in the farmhouse window.

She remembered that she was on Melanie's property in northern New South Wales – and what an experience they'd had last night. If she had to slough off this mortal coil, she was glad she'd experienced the phantom races, as well as the bush dance, and the camp-out – this was a good land for her son and granddaughter to be growing up in.

Her head was hurting, badly.

She couldn't remember dreaming last night and she had slept well, but the splitting headache wasn't good. She popped a couple of Dr McBride's painkillers and lay back till they could take effect.

She heard a phone ring.

'Ignore it,' she thought. 'Enjoy rest.'

A gentle knock came at the door. 'Olga?' It was Spencer's quiet voice.

* * * *

I listened to her quiet, 'Yes.'

'Phone for you. Our friend from last night. Can I come in?'

'Of course,' she said. 'This old lady is decent.'

I handed her the phone. She pressed the speaker key and I could hear Jeff Fowler's apology for the early hour.

'I have Dr Avery with me, Superintendent – you remember, university lecturer. Is that alright? He is helping me with my memory.'

'If you trust him, that is fine by me. I have information for you.' He paused for acceptance. 'A defector has told us about nuclear bombs in suitcases. Could they have been your suitcases in your flashbacks?'

Olga's face remained calm. 'Possibly, Superintendent. Possibly. Thank you for memory jog.'

If Fowler had been expecting her to gush out all the information from a newly-opened memory, he would have been very disappointed ... but she was quite upbeat nevertheless.

'Superintendent, I find ... if I relax ... and talk with my friend Spencer, my brain sometimes goes into flashback. Will be on cotton property near Goondiwindi today. We are going to sit by billabong and see what I can make this old brain recall.' She smiled benignly to me.

'Ring me any time, Major,' said Fowler. 'I have no other information for you at present. Good luck.'

She closed the phone and glanced at me quizzically, to check that I had picked up most of the drift. 'Remind me to talk about nuclear suitcase bombs when we get to billabong, Spencer. You might be one to make me remember where we hid them. Oh, I hate this memory loss. Can handle prospect of dying but not of losing my functions.'

I gave her a sympathetic smile. What could I say? Just that I was there for her.

I was struggling to take in what it might mean to be talking about nuclear bombs in suitcases. A fleeting strange thought of immense impending danger crossed my mind – that I might never again see my parents in their Somerset home, and suddenly that priority was very important to me.

A guilty tingle sparked through me like an electric current at the realisation that I had effectively and selfishly disowned my family and their heritage in my rush to be someone important, someone valued in society. I knew that I didn't deserve to be welcomed back by them but I desperately wanted to right the wrong I felt I had committed.

'C'mon.' My voice had a new nervous urgency. 'Breakfast; and we'll see what the young ones have planned for us.'

She gave me a quiet reflective smile. Hard for a chap to compete with Baryshnikov but I liked being in her company.

And still I had a sense of a danger, quite apart from Olga Davidenko.

Chapter 46

We had done the early morning tour of the cotton property in the big farm four-wheel drives and tried our hands at using the black-pipe siphons – a timing of hand, eye and pipe that I couldn't get to work. Yet Eva and Melanie accomplished the same feat with ease. Warren and Steve had no trouble either. Must be a cultural thing. We had seen the cotton plants, the laser-leveled paddocks, the picking-machines and how the cotton modules are transported to the gin for processing.

I made a mental note to come back here. Melanie's father, Alan, was clearly right across the commercial aspects of cotton production and the geographer in me wanted to know more.

It was still early morning.

Our group had settled beside 'the lagoon', the billabong. Steve and Warren were planning to go with Melanie's father in about half an hour to see if there were any wild pigs out on the far paddocks beyond the cotton fields. The women and I decided we would be happy enough just to stay at the quiet lagoon.

The peaceful water reflected blue, contrasting with the pale gums along the banks. The winter sun made it very pleasant to sit on a grassy area. A couple of white cattle egrets were wading near the water's edge and a flock of pink-breasted grey galahs chattered as they flew from tree to tree.

Alan Bell explained that the lagoon was an old billabong. Now it was filled by rainwater … and never seemed to dry up.

Steve said chirpily, 'Maybe that's because you don't know the Murri explanation for the lagoon.'

'And what is that?' asked Melanie with a laughing grin.

'My Dad and Uncle Herbie have Kamileroi roots. This is Kamileroi country. Well almost. It is really Bigambil country but the people who live here now are Kamilaroi.'

'Now, I'm confused,' said Olga.

'No, it's more of the black history of Australia,' Steve explained insistently. 'As my Dad told it to me, most of the people who live here now originally came from near Walgett, Kamilaroi country, and they were transported under the Act to the present site of Toomelah on the bend in the Macintyre.'

'I see.' A thoughtful Olga nodded her understanding..

'So how was the lagoon formed?' reminded Melanie.

'Our stories speak of the rainbow serpent, Moondagarra.' Steve had adopted a serious tone. 'Moondagarra moved through the river, then underground. Eventually, he broke through onto the surface and, where he emerged, he formed these waterholes to bring life to the land for the birds, animals and the people.

'The waterholes are part of the spirit of the land. They are part of Moondagarra and they will never run dry. Our people are charged with the responsibility to look after the land, to protect the heritage of the ancestors and the spirits.'

We could appreciate that he was sharing part of a sacred story, a respected ancient belief.

Alan nodded slowly. 'I've heard that story. We have Elders out here from time to time. They check historical sites and help us understand the significance to their culture. What do you think, Dr Avery? Do you like Steve's explanation or do you have a more geographical story to tell?'

I deferred. 'I'm the clean skin out here. I am listening and learning. I would like to think that Moondagarra is watching over us and this lagoon. Steve's Uncle Herbie talked to us about how a Murri person is never lonely in the bush because he is surrounded by the spirits of the ancestors.'

'He could well be right.' Alan Bell had a cheery accommodating approach. 'As long as it stays as beautiful as it is, I'm happy.'

We all sat quietly absorbing the peace of the boundless sky framing the blue lagoon. I was thinking back to the tens of thousands of years of habitation in this area. What a tale this land could tell. A wonderful place.

* * * *

The boys left for the far paddocks, leaving the girls, Olga and me to enjoy the tranquillity.

'Swim, Eva?' asked Melanie.

'Looks good, Mel,' as they stripped to their togs. With a few squeals as they entered the chilly water, they swam quietly out to the centre.

'It's beautiful, Spencer – refreshing, once you get adjusted to it,' called Eva. 'You should come in.'

'Am I excluded?' asked Olga. 'Can't I come in for swim? Come on, Spencer.'

'I didn't bring swimmers,' I said, recovering from my surprise.

'Neither did I,' she replied. 'Come on, live dangerously. Look away if you are embarrassed.' She removed her skirt and blouse and waded into the cool water. In no time, she had stroked gently out to the girls near the centre.

'They're right, Spencer,' shouted Olga. 'This is living. Don't miss out.'

I wasn't sure if it was my prudish English ways or that I had been shamed by this elderly Russian lady but I didn't want to leave her swimming in the middle of a billabong in case she felt unwell. I removed my shorts and shirt, shuddered with the initial shock of the cool water; and then stroked easily out to join the ladies.

'Now, wasn't too hard?' she laughed.

We paddled around laughing and joking for a few minutes before Olga headed back in to the bank. 'Enough for moment,' she advised happily.

'We have no towels,' I said as we landed on the side.

'The girls have towels. We will share. Go on. Be rascal.' She was chuckling at my discomfort.

We dabbed most of the water away and lay on the wide fallen gum trunks to absorb the gentle morning sun. Neither of us actually now seemed in the least self-conscious.

The girls continued swimming gently over to the far side where they emerged, waved and lay down on the bank to bask in the warmth. I was pleased they were sunning themselves at such a distance, for more reasons than one.

'Can we talk some more about past?' asked Olga. 'Am keen to stir my memory about suitcases.'

Ever trying to be the helpful memory-jogger, I said, 'Do you remember when you were on the camp-out, you were suggesting that people didn't understand the terrorist mind? Could you talk to me some more about that?'

'You're right. Am amazed people can't see situation for what it is. Is United States' influence.'

'You *really* don't like the United States, do you?' My tolerant grin was accompanied by a tired shake of the head. 'You wouldn't be stereotyping all Americans now, would you?'

'Point taken, Spencer.' She smiled quickly and then became serious again. 'No, what I mean is cultural immersion, espoused through education system and media – just political rhetoric. Is strong protest movement in States. I know that … but powerful institutions ride rough-shod over any alternative views. Brainwashing the masses beyond their intelligence level, under guise of being educated and informed. They think their land of the free is just that. They don't realise how manipulated their thinking is.'

'And that didn't happen in the Soviet Union?'

She was struggling and she knew it. 'At risk of same blind patriotism I accuse them, problem is underlying values. So many ill-informed Americans chant same convinced righteousness of their spokespeople.' She gave a wry humph. 'Spencer, you have trapped me in my own argument.'

I laughed. 'Let it pass, Olga!' Spassky might have been impressed at my figurative checkmate.

But she wasn't finished. 'Do you know only twenty per cent of them have passports? Never leave own country. Wouldn't that be major part of problem? Only understand what they are told through media – and American media are, with only few exceptions, woefully sensationalist and partisan.'

My grin was fixed. This was my payback for the chess defeats. So sweet. She was lining herself up for another checkmate.

'How many Russians would have passports?' The idea was intriguing me as I mentally tried to calculate the level of state-controlled media manipulation in the old Soviet Union.

'Is mirror image,' she replied. 'Eighty per cent have passports – but there are lots of neighbouring countries for people in Europe to cross into. More languages to learn too.'

Such a blinkered view. Almost disappointing. 'So, is the issue that they don't travel or that they don't understand?'

'First would contribute to second, wouldn't you think?' She looked in askance. 'To me, is conceit in way American agencies deal with anyone in their sights. At moment, is War on Terror. Was us in Cold War. Pattern is same. Demonise any view different from current US administration and attack. Sometimes with troops – and they have more soldiers than any other nation on the planet. Sometimes through controlling economies; and more often through setting up rebel groups to cause instability which American agents use to advantage.'

'You *really* really don't like them. But at least you have changed from criticising all Americans to targeting their agents. How does causing instability work to their advantage?' I had my own views but I needed her to explain her thinking.

She smiled at my gentle chiding. 'Lots of levels. First they have huge defence force. US marine corps on its own is bigger than entire British army. Did you realise? Is just *one* section of vast American army, not even including navy or airforce. Can't have all these troops sitting idle. They need fight otherwise Congress will not approve massive defence budget – so unrest and insurrection creates valid reason to have fight.'

Such logical deviousness.

'A follow-on is so much of US economy relies on defence contracts – from people who feed troops, through to equipment makers and on to super-expensive strategic weapons, most of which are never even used.

Imagine waste. But if those programs stopped, American economy would collapse and legions of jobs with it.'

I was working on my patience. 'Would that not be just like the Soviet system collapse at the end of the 1980s?'

'Indeed,' agreed Olga. 'Every regime has its time. The Soviet experiment fell apart through greed and corruption – but there were, and are, lots of people who believed in those social ideals in the USSR. And, I admit, many who didn't like state control.'

'Didn't like state control!' I gasped in astonishment. 'The understatement of the year. The state oppression of dissenters would have to be considered horrific. How could you justify that?'

Her face was calm but the eyes were sparkling. 'Spencer, you have naïve notion that democracy based on capitalism would necessarily be more successful than participative communism. In both, people have say and are simultaneously manipulated. In both, is need for discipline. Let me explain.

'Capitalism's success is based on consumption growth. But, Spencer, there is definite limit on growth. Only communist China has bitten bullet and introduced one-child policy to reduce expansion of population. Takes discipline rather than self-interest to put society before rights and pleasures of individuals, does it not?'

I sighed. 'You can't ignore the brutality of oppressive communist regimes, can you? Admit it! Since the Berlin Wall came down and the USSR disbanded, a dozen of the former communist states have gone over to the Western style, your staunchest allies. That is the people saying, *No more of the austerity and pain of those regimes.*'

She gave a tolerant smile and then a hardness set in her jaw. 'Undoubtedly leaders of former regimes were ruthless malusers of information ... and of people. But don't preach, Spencer! Don't feign innocence, my friend. Can you pretend current Western polices of rendition are not ruthless abusers of their captives? You are well aware CIA sends prisoners to countries who will torture by proxy. You know about these. You can find even on Internet from last twenty years – long after fall of USSR.

'Society certainly needs safe mechanisms for views to be heard. But is recipe for disaster to have individuals being more powerful than common good. You even quoted Cicero saying that back in Roman times.

'Naysayers always point to disasters. You are doing that now, Spencer – and Soviet Union has clearly failed like other empires before. Is always easier to give in to noisy individual than is to move system or society forward.' She was fired up. Just a glimpse of the old GRU officer flitted through me in an electric spark of danger. 'Okay. Be critic. Just give time for those states that moved to European Union to see generous subsidies start to be removed. Growth has to be self-sustaining. Capitalism is based on infinite expansion. World is not infinite!'

I shook my head as my pulse subsided. I was on firm ground.

'But they are free, Olga. They can travel and work and live where they choose. It's about freedom.'

'No argument, Spencer. Looks like being given huge present. People will take present now rather than delay gratification.'

'That's my point too, Olga. The only actual examples of world communism have been oppressive regimes – not the rosy ideologies; dreams of some future utopia.'

'Spencer, don't disappoint me. Are many totalitarian regimes which are not communist. Are just as oppressive as my old country that you condemn – and have nothing to do with communism.'

'But,' I replied. 'They are all about total control.'

She lay back and sighed. 'Spencer, we need to agree to differ. In end, ideologies are like religions; you either believe in promise or you don't. Time will tell, as planet gets more crowded and more depleted. Jury is out, as you say. You're right, of course, for present at least. I don't think we will achieve much pursuing this debate just now, eh?'

I liked hearing her concession. But she couldn't let it go.

'Ruins of many empires litter the Earth,' she continued. 'Go and wonder at Angkor Wat or Machu Picchu. British have just been through painful denial at loss of their empire – and, in my view, US is about to start its great decline, if it is not already.'

'Interesting,' I said.

'And if that is so,' she added astutely, 'American people are not ready to be part of world where their view, or culture, is not dominant.'

'We never really got past the US Defence Force,' I said patiently. 'Come back to people not listening.'

She beamed. 'I like the way you steer conversation. So silken, so diplomatic and yet – so unconvinced. Will explain. Guerrilla resistance and terror campaigns are really only weapons small causes can use to fight big empires.'

She continued, 'Ho Chi Minh proved it in Vietnam and Al Qaeda is using same now. You don't leave big country's army anything to hit at. So becomes *hearts and minds*. The resistance movements create terror because they want somebody to hear their voice. If call is ignored, climate is created for terrorists to fight and die for cause.'

As if wondering whether to say more, she paused and looked at me. 'But is only part of the problem, because criminals come in behind zealots and use resistance platform to escalate terror to new levels. For some, there are idealistic goals. For rest, follow money trail.'

'How do you mean?'

'Is fighting in eastern Congo,' she said. 'Look for money. Is world's main source of coltan, to make mobile phones. Is fighting in Iraq; major supplier of easily-accessible oil. On other hand, is no *big power fighting* in Somalia or Sudan or Chad. No resources found there yet. Just my view.' Her tone was matter-of-fact. 'But based on years of listening to intelligence chatter across world. You are geographer, Spencer. Do you see pattern?'

'So, where will the next targets be?'

'Follow money. Look to places which would cause outrage, cause wealthy people to sit up and take notice. 9/11, Bali, London and Madrid gave template but were lots of others before them and attempts since. Country with showpiece building or economic icon would feel quite vulnerable.'

'Or a city where terrorists could place a nuclear suitcase bomb?' I barely muttered the words. The significance was registering now.

'Exactly! And don't rule out agitators who would set scenario to look like another group set off bomb.'

I watched her, willing her to continue.

'If I wanted US to invade particular country, would attack US. Agreed?' she asked, hands spread to emphasise her simple logic. 'They would retaliate, wouldn't they?'

At my slow nod, she continued. 'Is their nature, their culture. Yes? If I wanted them to be angry at Russia, make bomb appear to come from Russia. If wanted them to attack Arab lands, make the bomb appear to come from Arabs. As long as bomb appeared to come from country which US has demonised, their public opinion would let them attack. Are we agreed?'

I gave my grudging assent.

'So!' She was building to her climax. 'Come to suitcase bombs which look Russian. How hard would it be for criminal group to start American attack on Russia by bombing something American, with weapon clearly identified as Russian? Could even be American criminal group with some ideological dream or even crazies just looking for power.'

I gasped. 'This is all too fantastic to contemplate. It's spy thriller stuff.'

She shook her head. 'No, sadly, is not. They said that right up till 9/11. Now few people would doubt what analysts like me have been guarding against for decades.'

I was not sure that any comment I could make would be at the right level. I was well out of my depth with all these clandestine revelations and yet I didn't want to stop the conversation. My purpose was to jog Olga's memory not to chop at her myopic view of the Americans.

Her eyes were distant as she spoke again. 'Dilemma now is, even if I can recover memory, into whose care do I place information? Is not just simple exercise, is it? Can be nasty when one group is more powerful than all rest.'

'What a world!' I listened to my tone sounding so unusually resigned.

'Sadly,' agreed the Russian. 'Has been my world for much of my life. Although some pleasurable times too,' she added with her suggestive grin.

Laughing and splashing heralded the girls making their way back across the lagoon. The puritan in me made me rush to put my shirt and shorts back on.

'You didn't worry when was just me.' Olga laughed, and was making no effort to get dressed again.

I laughed cheekily back, 'No point in putting temptation in their way.'

We both dissolved in happy cackles but it also prompted Olga to dress in her blouse and skirt.

'Was starting to get cold,' she lied with a grin.

* * * *

The girls arrived back on shore and dried off.

'That was marvellous,' gushed Eva. 'What have you two been doing?' she asked of her Nana and me.

'Oh, just chatting,' said Olga. 'You were absolutely right. Water was super. Made me feel young again.'

She hugged her grandmother. I was pleased to see the happiness, especially at this time.

Melanie said, 'Now I have good news and bad news.'

'Give us the bad news,' I said.

'The boys have the vehicle so we will have to walk back to the house – or Eva and I can walk back and bring another vehicle over to pick you up.'

'And good news?' asked Olga.

'There will be a bush barbecue for a mid-morning feed, brunch, by the time we get back.'

'I think is all good news, Melanie.' She laughed. 'Has been brilliant morning. Thank you so much. Why don't you and Eva walk back and I will stroll along ... more sedately ... with Spencer. If you can't see us, you come back and pick us up. Okay?'

'Beautifully organised, Nana,' said Eva – and the two girls grabbed their gear and headed off.

'Beautifully organised, Olga,' I reprised as the girls disappeared into the distance. 'You are some lady. It's so good to see you chirpy. You deserve to be as happy as this, even if your perspectives on the world have a darkness about them. It is not until we hear the stories from someone who has lived them ... it is not until then that we can really start to understand.'

She took my arm and we walked slowly out onto the track. 'Am so glad to have met you, Spencer. You are intelligent sensitive man. Would be prize for any young lady. You make me wish I was young again.' She giggled like a schoolgirl.

'I am not used to such compliments.' I grinned. 'But I accept them from such a wise judge.'

She hooted again and then paused distractedly. 'Stop, Spencer. On log,' pointing at a whitened gum trunk, 'Am seeing suitcases again.'

The changing facial expressions reflected her thought processes as she struggled to capture the elusive thoughts. There was no sound – just the chirping of some birds in a nearby tree.

Several minutes passed before she opened her eyes blankly. 'Take notes, please, Spencer.'

'No paper. We've been swimming.'

'Then remember as I speak.'

'My partner was Captain Anatoly Sidorov,' she started and I scratched the name in the dirt with a stick. 'Was only other with me on that mission. Were two suitcases ... to take from Moscow out of country – fast.

'Difficult journey by vehicle, through Ukraine and onto fishing boat to cross Black Sea. We landed at Sinop on Turkish coast. By vehicle to Cappadocia. Suitcases are in Cappadocia. Can't remember exactly where ... but will come to me. I need to speak to Superintendent Fowler. Do you have mobile, Spencer?'

'That I do have, ma'am.' I tried to sound like a dutiful butler.

Olga dialed from the phone memory.

Chapter 47

'Superintendent Fowler?' she asked quietly. 'Olga speaking.'

'Go ahead.' I could hear him clearly on speaker mode. He sounded pleased to be listening again to his Russian Major.

Apart from a distant crow call, the empty landscape was silent.

'Had flashback from your information,' she said. 'Did move two suitcase bombs in early nineties. Can't remember precise timing. Do remember my partner on that mission was Captain Anatoly Sidorov. Saddened if he is no longer with us. Perhaps you will tell me what happened, at later time. Anyway, recall taking suitcases from Moscow on very secret orders. Smuggled them, on arduous trip, over Black Sea to Turkey.'

She stopped.

'Are they in Turkey now?'

'I expect. We hid them in region known as Cappadocia. Can't yet remember exact location but am sure it will come, now that thought process has started.'

'It shouldn't be too hard to narrow down surely.'

'You don't understand Cappadocia, Superintendent. Covers hundreds of square kilometres, cave systems going down many levels below ground. Millennia old. Many sealed. How you say? Honeycomb? Would literally be easier to find needle in haystack.'

'I see.'

'Have moral dilemma too, Superintendent, which you will appreciate. If I remember detail of cave site and pass it to you, to whom will you pass information?'

'Why do you ask?' he enquired, while Olga smiled at his pretence of naivety.

'In wrong hands, these bombs could alter balance of power, don't you think?' she said sweetly. 'Would hate to share information with any of current major powers. Have lived long enough not to trust imposters to honesty.

'Their game is only about control – and we are in very interesting times. Used wrongly, such weapons could be just as dangerous in their hands as with terrorist group, don't you think?' she repeated for emphasis.

'So who would you agree to share the information with?'

'Probably only you and Turkish government. Weapons are on their soil and I am on yours.'

I was amazed at the negotiating. Her brain may not be what it once was, but she was still one very astute lady.

'I'll have to think about that,' replied Fowler.

'No doubt,' she agreed, 'but am sure you appreciate dilemma. We both understand implications to wider picture of security information. Have moral responsibility, no?'

The policeman was quiet. Presumably he was thinking. 'Thank you for your information, Major. We know what we are dealing with now. I understand your concerns. I can't give guarantees. This is an era of international co-operation. Let's see what you can remember and then you and I will decide how we can use it.'

'My conditions won't change, Superintendent. You know that.'

'At the moment, I'm more concerned about protecting you. We assume that new agents have replaced the earlier people. When you return to Toowoomba, I will have Inspector Reid contact you again. The silence in our networks is interesting to say the least.'

'Superintendent, I'm sure you are excellent at your job.' Flattery. I supposed she hadn't been a GRU major by accident.

'Oh,' the policeman asked. 'You mentioned only you and Sidorov. What about the other three in the team? Where were they?'

'Can't recall. Were different tasks. Other projects to protect. But only Sidorov was with me and the suitcases. I'm sure of that.'

The phone call ended with both requesting to stay in touch.

*   *   *   *

Jeff Fowler was in deep thought as soon as the call to Major Davidenko ended. She had raised some interesting ethical points.

These were dangerous times. He was well aware of the unscrupulous nature of all governments in international operations. The world had moved into an era where the spy and the secret agent were often more important than the foot soldier in a conflict with enemies who didn't fight pitched battles. Deception and misinformation formed an intriguingly important arena for the military strategists.

Chapter 48

We were all enjoying the brunch barbeque on Melanie's property.

Steve, Warren and Melanie's father, Alan, had returned from the outer paddocks. They had chased roos and pigs, without firing any shots. They chattered away about a pair of jabiru they had seen at a distant billabong – Australia's only true stork apparently.

The girls and Olga were impressed. I looked at my Russian friend. She wore a perpetual smile. She seemed so happy. How she could have all that knowledge of international espionage and world dangers in her head and still look almost girlishly jolly? It must have come from a lifetime of living dangerously, acting out roles to glean military intelligence.

To me she looked more like a glamorous, if ageing, movie star than a spy. Maybe if her talents had been used in another way, she would have been up on advertising billboards rather than being hidden in the anonymity of foreign intelligence.

'Tooki and his friends would like it here,' she said.

Eva agreed. 'Remember Izzy's and Ellie's expressions as Uncle Herbie told his stories? They were fascinated – an empathy for his experiences and the quirky humour of drovers.'

'I bet Aunty Edna would like it here too,' said Steve. 'Her Dad was a drover out this way.'

Alan Bell looked surprised, so Melanie explained the Goomburra camp-out to her parents; the camp-site, the forests, the bush medicines, Uncle Herbie's stories of droving, killing a beast for meat ... and so on. We all tucked into our barbecued steaks and onions. 'Killing a beast' made sense when you lived out here. I was learning the vernacular.

Melanie's father was interested that youngsters like Izzy had been homeless and were getting their lives back on the rails. 'I remember the wandering swaggies on the stock routes when I was a boy.'

'Swaggie?' asked Olga.

'A swagman,' replied Alan Bell. 'You know, *Once a jolly swagman camped by a billabong ... Waltzing Matilda*, our national song? Your swag was your bed roll. Everything was carried on your back.'

She nodded understanding.

'These were often blokes who had returned from the wars,' he explained. 'Wanting to forget. Others couldn't stand city life. They became swaggies. Just walking from town to town. They had anonymity. No past. No real names. Doing odd jobs, singing songs or telling bush yarns. Full of humour.'

'You'd need a sense of humour to carry your swag over these distances,' I observed, 'And this is winter out here just now. It must be roasting in summer.'

'Oh yeh,' replied Alan. 'She can get a bit warm in summer,' with classic bush understatement. 'But the swaggies were welcome. It broke the monotony. They were generally pretty honest rogues, bringing news from other stations – in a world before mobiles and the Internet. They'd be offered a lift by passing vehicles on the road.' A glint came into his eye. I could see he was appreciating that his guests were interested. He continued, 'There's an old bush tale of a grazier stopping to offer a swaggie a lift out on *the long paddock* – the stock route – and the swaggie replies, *No bloody fear, mate. You can open and close your own bloody gates.*'

The country people all laughed while Olga, Eva and I tried hard to fathom why they were all laughing.

Alan explained, 'Out here, we have fences to keep stock in the right paddock. We can't afford too many cattle grids like you see on the little properties closer to the coast; so most gates are just three strands of barbed wire, stretched on a pole and strung out to form a gate of sorts. They are slow to untangle and slow to replace properly, to stop the stock escaping.

'If you're driving through a lot of paddocks and you have to get out regularly to open these gates, then it becomes a bloody nuisance. Having a passenger to do that task is a real bonus.'

The light came on for Olga. 'I see. More work opening and closing gates than if he just kept walking.'

'Aussie humour,' I noted.

'I can relate to that,' said Eva. 'I was the one having to open the gates on the way in to the Goomburra camp-out … and they were good gates, metal and on hinges.'

'But stock routes didn't have gates, did they?' said Olga. 'You couldn't be driving cattle and opening gates all time.'

'Never officially.' Alan grinned. 'The name of the game in droving is to make slow steady progress, ten or so kilometres at a time, or the beasts would lose their condition. That's why the teams needed all the cooks, and Aboriginal stockmen who knew the country, like your Aunty Edna's father, I suppose.'

'Oh, he wasn't an Aboriginal man,' said Steve. 'He was a whitefella. Aunty Edna said he claimed to be Russian, like you Nana Olga. It was a long time ago. He died somewhere out on the stock routes beyond Mungindi, she said.'

'There's a creek called Russian's Creek only ten clicks from here,' said Alan. 'It's on the old stock route. Maybe it was named after your Russian, eh?' He smiled at the unlikeliness of it all.

'How did they name creeks out here?' I asked.

'Most of the reasons are lost in history.' Alan's face was alive with enthusiasm. 'Explorers, farmers, drovers too. That's why you get names like Ten Mile Creek or Black Snake Creek … and some are named after people.'

'Could a creek be named after where a person was buried?' I asked.

'Sure.' A questioning surprise entered his voice. 'Are you really thinking Aunty Edna's father could be buried out at Russian's Creek?'

'Could be. This place would be *beyond Mungindi* if you were coming from up in west Queensland, wouldn't it?'

'Do you know his name?' asked Melanie. 'He wouldn't be called McGrady like Steve.'

'Aunty Edna said she was Edna Pope before she was married. Is that right, Steve?' I suggested.

'Yeh,' Steve agreed. 'Uncle Herbie said they called him Uncle Nick. So Nick Pope was his name, I suppose.'

'What year was this?' asked Olga. She spoke very slowly and carefully, while she rubbed the side of her forehead.

'They were talking about the 30s and 40s, I think. Aunty Edna was born just before the war,' said Steve.

Olga looked intently at me. Surely the coincidence taking startling shape was too bizarre to be real. I didn't want to speak and the others were starting to look at me.

She spoke. 'My father's uncle was called Nicholas. We know he came to Australia around 1919 and he would have been about twenty then. We know he went to outback and was sending letters back in 1920s and 30s. How many Russians called Nicholas would have been travelling bush back then?'

'Did he have a surname?' asked Alan.

'Would have been Popov,' she answered. 'Nicholas Popov.'

Eva gasped. 'Then my grandmother's uncle could be Steve's great-aunty's father. Do I have it right?'

'We are related, Eva.' Her Murri classmate had a huge laughing grin as he placed his dark hand beside her blonde hair. I knew Steve had a play going for her. I picked it long ago.

She gave him a confused but not unfriendly smile in return.

'Bizarre!' I said. 'Alan, do you suppose we could cover the ten kilometres to Russian's Creek and still be back in time to get to Toowoomba today.'

'It's only ten o'clock. Easy done. Hop in your bus. The road is dirt but it's good dirt.'

Alan drove. There was too much emotion and excitement in the rest of us.

* * * *

It was a picturesque creek, narrow, with just little pools, hardly flowing. Large trees overhung the water– Alan pointed out – coolabah, willow and gums with white trunks dripping with slashes of grey and orange bark. The bush was silent except for insects and the occasional duck in flight. A peaceful place; Russian's Creek.

'If Nick Pope or Nicholas Popov was buried here, would the site be marked?' I asked quietly.

'Not unless someone carved a stone gravestone,' said Alan. 'Not much rock round here.'

Steve recalled, 'Uncle said a couple of their people gave him a Murri burial.'

Alan shrugged. 'That could mean sealed in a cave, a river bank or a hollow tree, somewhere to protect him from animals... but not likely a gravestone. People on the stock route might have marked the spot with a wooden cross, but that wouldn't have lasted for fifty years or more.'

Olga had moved to the creek side, as the group followed to join her.

'Do you think,' she said, 'I could have five minutes just to sit and take in this place – maybe with Eva and Steve; just three of us ... to remember man none of us knew but could well link us together?'

* * * *

We watched from a distance. Nana Olga sat on the grassy creek bank, framed by the old gums as their teary leaves whispered their stories in the gentle breeze. The old Russian lady with her blonde-haired grand-daughter on her left and slim Murri relative on her right.

I thought if ever there was a spiritual scene to inspire, the one before me at that moment ranked high – a bonding of peoples across nations and across eras. Strangers linked by coincidence.

I cast my mind back to the old red-stone church in my Somerset village and singing hymns with my mother in the coloured lighting of the stained-glass windows; then to the hallowed chapels of Cambridge with their high vaulted roofs – all full of sacred presence, undoubtedly.

But here ... here on the bank of a Macintyre tributary, in the vast-ness of the Australian outback, was an equally moving setting.

Here, perhaps, lay the remains of an immigrant father and uncle; related to three of this visiting party.

I wished I could have painted to capture the essence of the occasion – an Australian artist; a Roberts or a Streeton or a Namatjira.

Here, in this pretty arm of a river system, with a tranquillity far greater than a peaceful cemetery, the ethereal feeling of a greater meaning enveloped us all.

Eventually, Olga rose and I watched her walk slowly back to us, clasping the shoulders of Eva and Steve. How many stages of separation? Maybe, we are all related if we go back far enough.

'Thank you for this time,' she said quietly. 'I feel we have given some closure to family mystery and may have forged new bonds of kin.' She hugged her two relatives. 'Am ready to go back.' Her face was peaceful. Eva dabbed her moist eyes. Steve had a faraway look. What sort of connection was he sensing with this place and his past? I could only guess.

The significance was shared by us all and the bus was heavy with silent thoughts as it returned to the property.

* * * *

An hour later, it was a happy smiling group of students and Olga who waved goodbye to the Bells amid expressions of appreciation, along with promises to catch up again. I drove the white mini-bus out onto the road, back towards Toowoomba.

We travelled along the Warwick road for a change of scene, taking the short-cut through Leyburn, on Melanie's directions, as a faster quieter route.

Two hours later, I let Melanie, Steve and Warren off at their houses in west Toowoomba before pointing the mini-bus south with just Olga and Eva on board.

Driving through the town, Eva pointed out the distinctive shapes of Izzy and a friend zooming along the side of the road on skateboards. They looked so odd to me – two black-clad, frizzy-haired, skinny people whizzing along on pieces of plywood with castors.

Izzy was almost adult and her male friend looked as if he could be in his early twenties – and here they were racing along on kids' toys. Even though I knew Izzy, this did not fit into my worldly concept of normal.

'Hi Izzy,' shouted Eva, out the bus window.

The surprised skateboarder looked up and recognised us. She waved back and said something to her male friend to explain the unexpected greeting from the blonde girl in the bus.

'They fairly zip along,' said Eva, impressed by the pace that two skateboarders could maintain.

'Will keep them fit,' observed her grandmother.

'Spencer, there's a flower shop,' said Eva suddenly. 'Can you pull over please and I'll get a bunch for Mum.'

I pulled the mini-bus into the side of the wide street, allowing Eva to jump out, and into the flower shop. She laughingly said something to Izzy and her friend as they caught up, passing the shop and mini-bus. I watched the two skateboarders slow to a stop and lean against a garden fence a little way ahead, for a rest.

The road was quiet. Sunday afternoon. I could only see a motorbike approaching from behind.

* * * *

Eva bought her bunch of winter blossoms and was just about to leave the shop when she heard the bang, followed by what sounded like firework crackers. At the door, her jaw dropped in stunned shock.

The mini-bus was whirling a U-turn in the road. Somebody dressed in black was driving. She could see Nana Olga's face. There was no Spencer. As the bus moved away at pace, a motorbike with a black-clad rider fell in behind.

It seemed that everything was happening in slow motion. The bus turning. The images of Nana's face. The motorbike.

Izzy was suddenly beside her, looking and asking something. The shop owner appeared behind.

'Was your Nana in that bus?' Izzy asked, her mobile phone already in her hand and thumbs moving at a bewildering speed.

Eva's mouth had not yet closed. No words came out. Her precious Nana was disappearing up the road and she was standing dumb-struck with a bunch of colourful flowers in her hand.

The shopkeeper had disappeared with, 'I'll call triple 0.'

Izzy said, 'Eva. Eva. Can you hear me, girl?'

Eva felt as if she was awakening from a dream – a very bad dream.

'Yes, Izzy,' she said, recognising her for the first time. 'Nana and Spencer. The bus!' was all she managed as Izzy's friend sat her down in the doorway before she passed out. The shop-keeper brought a bottle of

241

water which Eva sipped. She could hear the florist saying, 'The police are on their way.'

'Eva, listen to me,' said Izzy urgently. 'I have sent the rego and description to Tooki. The word will go on the network. There will be eyes watching. Do you know what happened?'

Eva shook her head. No words would form. Her brain wouldn't work.

'We won't hang around,' Izzy said urgently. 'We don't want to be questioned by police. We'll find her, Eva. She's a good lady, your Russian Nana. We'll find her.'

Chapter 49

As I waited for Eva to return from the florist shop, I thought what an inspiring daughter she was to be thinking of her mother after having such a happy time herself.

It had been a marvellous, and emotional, weekend.

With the bus engine in idle, I removed my seatbelt to stretch my back muscles, after two hours of continuous driving.

I scarcely noticed the motorbike with its pillion passenger moving up behind. I was parked well off the street so I gave it no more thought.

Bang!

I felt a huge push from my right which threw me onto the floor next to Olga in the front passenger seat. The creature on my right had a huge black ant-like head – an alien from outer space. Crackers banged. My head hit the passenger seat frame and it went dark.

* * * *

Olga had watched Eva almost skip into the flower shop. She marvelled at the freedom of Izzy and her friend as they skateboarded past.

The thump to the bus was stunning.

Spencer slumped on the floor as the stranger in a helmet and leathers wheeled the bus. Olga saw Izzy and her friend turn to look.

A motorbike skidded across the road to fall in behind. Banging, like fire-crackers going off – all very confusing.

She watched the gun, pointed in her direction, in the driver's right hand, as he straightened the steering wheel.

The bus moved fast, roughly north she thought. She reached down to help Spencer. Blood flowed freely from a cut on his forehead.

* * * *

Inspector Ian Reid took the call from the emergency room.

'Hi-jacking of a university mini-bus on the New England Highway, south of Long Street. Abduction of two people, believed to be Dr Spencer Avery and an Olga Davidenko.'

'Check the tracking device. Where is the lady now?' Reid asked his sergeant.

Lifting his head from the screen, the officer said, 'It's showing her being in northern New South Wales, not far from Goondiwindi on the south side of the river.'

An exasperated expression clouded the inspector's face. Damn! A question for a later time.

'*All points alert* out,' he commanded.

'As we speak. All cars are looking for the white mini-bus with a motorbike following.'

The systems moved smoothly and rapidly into their well-practised techniques. An officer was calling the emergency university contact for a registration number for the bus.

The police set up surveillance on all major roads out of Toowoomba. A chartered helicopter lifted into the air, with on-board eyes scanning the streets for targets.

A special emergency response team of armed police moved speedily into stand-by, ready to respond to any part of the city.

The trap was narrowing – but, as yet, no sighting of the vehicle.

* * * *

Jeff Fowler left his meeting, mobile to his ear, in response to the urgent call.

'Olga Davidenko has been abducted,' said Reid.

'The tracking device?' was Fowler's immediate response.

'Showing her in NSW,' replied Reid. 'Must have been left behind from her visit to Goondiwindi. She's definitely in Toowoomba.'

'Give me what we know.' He was the calm operator in charge of a crisis.

Reid relayed what had happened.

'Witnesses?' Fowler asked.

'Being interviewed now.'

'Media?'

'Being told it was probably a gang prank letting off detonator caps stolen from a quarry a while back.'

'Fine,' said Fowler. 'Keep it low-key. I want to be informed as soon as anything happens. Good work, Ian. I wish you well with the chase.'

As the superintendent ended the call, he was glad he'd had the chance to talk to Olga that morning.

At least, he now knew what he was dealing with. The investigation had moved to a new state of alert.

Jeff Fowler revelled in these high-pressure situations. It was when he worked at his best.

What did he know? Olga and Spencer allegedly abducted in a white university mini-bus, by perhaps only two people on a motorbike. Was it a planned operation or an opportunist attack? The granddaughter, Eva, had asked them to stop so that she could buy flowers. That had been unplanned, presumably.

Olga's tracking device was in New South Wales. Had she left it there deliberately or had that been an accident?

Ian Reid was a good man. He would have all the police systems mobilised.

Who were the people who had abducted the dying former GRU Major? Why had the AFP received no intelligence of criminal or new foreign operatives in the south Queensland area?

There was the question of Olga's moral dilemma. Supposing she did remember the location of the suitcases, could someone extract that information from an experienced operator who possibly had only weeks to live anyway?

If the Major were to give the information to the AFP, how should he handle it? His police training was being challenged by the ethics of international power plays.

Interesting, he thought, as he picked up the phone to his ASIO contact.

* * * *

Anna Grushko took the call from her distraught daughter, speaking of Nana being abducted, police, firecrackers ... on the streets of Toowoomba.

A policewoman's voice had come on Eva's phone. She explained that Eva was in shock and the ambulance personnel were now treating her at the scene.

Peter and Anna Grushko were heading for their vehicle before the mobile call had even ended.

They collected their daughter from the police car beside the florist's shop. No, having seen her, they didn't need the ambulance to take her to hospital. She would come home. Peter gave the police his contact numbers. He wanted to be told as soon as his mother was found.

Eva shivered quietly in her mother's arms as they headed home. She told her story – more relaxed for a moment until she saw a recurring image of her Nana's face, looking at her from the speeding bus. And what had happened to Spencer?

Anna settled her daughter into bed and held her hand until she dozed off.

Then she stood hugging her husband; so many thoughts going through their heads but for the moment they could only wait.

* * * *

To Olga, it seemed as if the speeding bus either had hit every green light or had avoided traffic lights altogether because it did not slow down.

She saw the tree-lined streets whizz by, comforted at least in knowing that she was still carrying her little tracking device in her underclothes. The police would not be far behind.

Spencer was regaining consciousness. His blood glistened wetly on the floor and the seat frame. She kept her red-soaked handkerchief pressed over the gash and egg-shaped bruise on his forehead, while stealing an occasional glance out of the window.

The buildings in the street now appeared to be run-down – paint-work faded, gardens overgrown.

The bus swung off the road. The open double-garage swallowed the bus and the motor-bike. A man in dark clothes pulled the doors down behind them.

The gun was still in the driver's hand. No expression was visible behind the visor of the helmet. Two others came onto the bus. They picked up Spencer and carried him into a downstairs room, with Olga being roughly pushed behind.

Her experienced eye took in a ten by four metre room, decorated in pastel tones of pale red, blue and cream – like a garish reminder of some sleazy club meeting places from her past. Thick maroon curtains obscured any windows or other doors, apart from their entrance point from the garage.

Their captors dumped Spencer onto one of two sturdy wooden chairs and secured his arms and legs with velcro straps. They placed Olga in the adjacent chair with similar velcro restraints. The people had scarcely spoken through the whole affair. Olga hadn't registered words, rather just grunted instructions.

There were three of them – all dressed in motorbike leathers with tinted visors on their helmets.

She waited, pain throbbing behind her eyes. No point in resistance. Experience had taught her to be patient. Every minute saved was a minute gained to the police rescue.

She felt responsible for Spencer. The university academic shouldn't have been drawn into this. He looked worse for wear with his bloodied forehead, no longer covered with a handkerchief. The flow had stopped. Even so, the egg-shaped bruise and the dried red-smeared streaks made Spencer look as unlike a university academic as it was possible to imagine. He needed ice and medical treatment.

The door closed.

'Who are you? Why are you doing this?' she asked with innocent annoyance.

'Major Olga Davidenko, I believe,' said an Australian voice. 'And Dr Spencer Avery. Yes?'

She had most of her answer in those words. This was no case of mistaken identity.

'Major, you have information that we want,' said the leader. 'I'm sure you know what I'm talking about. We can get it the hard way or the easy way. Which is it to be?'

Chapter 50

The gaunt face of Ellie looked over the window ledge at the neighbouring house; the weathered paintwork and unloved garden. She could see the double garage doors of the high-set house and the shape of the bricked-in rumpus room underneath. The upper building was wooden with open stairs accessing a verandah at the front door.

Everything was quiet. It looked as if no-one lived there.

Ellie had been called to this vacant house by a text message from Tooki. The place was being used as a squat by 'Aimless' – her real name was Amy – who had read the broadcast text from Tooki just a minute or so before she had heard the deep roar of a motorbike.

She had peered over the ledge of the uncurtained window in time to see a white mini-bus sweep up the driveway and into the right-hand garage next door. The motorbike, whose deep pulsating engine roar had alerted her, followed straight after, into the left garage door.

Aimless had only seconds to read the rego plate but the three letters had matched Tooki's text message. He had written 'Friend in trouble' and to text him if anyone saw the vehicle matching his description.

In response to Aimless's text, Ellie of the frizzy hair had now entered the unlocked back door of the texter's squat. She crouched under the window ledge in the debris of loose sleeping sheets, beside Amy and the striped carrier bag which held all of her possessions.

Having checked everything that Aimless had reported – it all fitted – she phoned Tooki, saying that it appeared like the right place.

Tooki phoned Aunty Edna who used her status as a long-term police liaison officer to call her old friend, Inspector Ian Reid.

* * * *

Reid was in the operations room taking no calls unless clearly related to the current emergency when his sergeant handed him the phone.

'Aunty Edna on the line. She said, *Tell Ian, Olga Davidenko.*'

'Hello Aunty Edna,' said Reid in a rushed but friendly voice. 'You have something for me?'

'Good to talk to you again, Ian,' she said. 'Tooki from our street network reports a white van and motorbike entering a double garage under a house in north Toowoomba.'

'Is it confirmed?' asked Reid.

'A squatter in the next house saw the vehicle enter,' replied Edna. 'The timing was right and the rego matched.'

'How did she know the rego?' asked the inspector. His men were still tracking down the university contact on a Sunday afternoon.

'One of our girls noted the number. She was at the scene,' said Edna, in a matter-of-fact way.

Reid chose not to ask why the girl hadn't stayed to give the police the information. He was just grateful he had such a good working relationship with Edna, Tooki and the street network. It was the product of years of building trust – what he called 'good community policing' even if it involved a leniency which the letter of the law didn't always prescribe. It was at times like this that kindness given was returned in spadefuls.

Edna gave the inspector the address; and the wheels of police action whirred into smooth action.

'Well done, Aunty! Tell the girls to stay put. A police officer will knock on the door in a few minutes. He won't look like police. He'll identify himself as *Derek.* We are sealing the area as I speak. Oh, and Edna … thanks, Sister. Deadly team work. Appreciated!'

* * * *

Ellie heard the knock and a male voice quietly saying, 'It's Derek.'

She opened the door to a long-haired, bearded man. He came upstairs to meet Amy; Ellie refused to use her put-down nickname.

Amy fidgeted, twisting her sheet in her hand as she told her story.

The policeman in Derek couldn't resist the question. 'You're squatting; how did you get a mobile?'

'Stuff you! I can still do odd jobs. Part-time.' She turned away, muttering and cursing quietly.

Derek scanned the house.

'No trash. The druggies haven't found it then.'

Amy turned back and humphed. 'No power. Water's still on. Cold shower. Toilet works.' She shrugged. 'Luxury.'

He nodded as he scanned the neighbouring house from the window. 'Good you had your wits about you; and a mobile phone.' He gave a faint grin to both of them. 'Thanks.'

They watched his eyes carefully.

'Now I need you out of here.' He spoke quietly. 'Out the back. The front street is sealed off. We're evacuating people. They're being told it is a suspected gas leak. Tell the uniformed men, *Derek*, and you'll be looked after. Stay around but say nothing to anyone but me, please. Give me your mobile numbers in case I need you.'

Ellie paused and glanced at the bearded man. *In case I need you.* That street-kids could be needed by this strange, strong man who had come to the rescue of the people in the next house.

They gave their numbers although Amy was not at all happy.

'Thanks again,' said Derek. 'You've done well.'

* * * *

'Don't know what you want and don't know who you are! Who are you? Why should I tell anything?'

Olga smiled a wry grin as the leader picked up a piece of rubber hose. 'Do you think you can beat information out of me?'

He swung the hose ferociously at Spencer's cheek and a large white stripe appeared on it.

'I don't intend to beat *you*. I intend to beat *him*,' said the man.

The pain had just registered with the already-drowsy Spencer and he let out an agonised yell. The white stripe on the cheek changed to red. His head was not a pretty sight.

Olga's face showed no emotion although her stomach was churning in sympathy with her friend. 'What you want to know?' she asked, in her most resigned tone.

'You know the whereabouts of some explosive devices,' said the leader in a satisfied voice. 'My employers want to know that location.'

'And then?'

'We will wait till the location is verified. Then you'll both be released out in the bush to enable our departure.'

She was back in the dangerous world of her working life. The optimistic window of her happy visit to family had hit an abrupt end.

The training of decades, the old hardness, reasserted itself in her mind with a coldness that disappointed her so much more that she had expected. There had been such a flicker of hopeful sunshine – a reward perhaps, though admittedly undeserved. Major Davidenko reassumed her military persona.

Her quick assessment of the chance of release in the bush was not positive. These thugs were torturers and most likely hit-men, who would dispose of her and Spencer in a most permanent way when they had their information.

She had to give the police time. They would be following her tracking bug.

'Explosives are overseas. How long will it take you to check location?' she asked.

'Just give me the information. Now is not too soon,' said the leader and he whipped the rubber hose across Spencer's other cheek, drawing an immediate loud scream this time.

Not patient men – and under stress. They were not going to get involved in conversation.

'Explosives are in Turkey, at place called Kayseri in Cappadocia.'

'Spell these names.' The leader wrote them down slowly as Olga spelled them and then he phoned a number to relay the information.

'Wait. They will check.'

Chapter 51

Ian Reid had absorbed Derek's briefing.

The long-haired man had silently planted two monitoring devices on the neighbouring house – one on the upstairs wooden wall near the back verandah and another on the glass of a small, curtained downstairs window. The devices sent signals to Derek's earpiece and to a sophisticated relay which transmitted by radio-wave to a mobile van in the next street and then onto police headquarters.

Reid's listeners had heard muffled movements in the downstairs room, then a clear scream. With electronic enhancement, the faint words of an on-going conversation were being recorded, enhanced and transcribed. There was no sound from upstairs. The inspector knew they had the right house.

* * * *

The special operations squad moved stealthily through the back door of the squat where Derek was waiting following his reconnaissance of the target house.

Their attack plan was formulated, to disarm probably three very capable criminal operatives; perhaps even ... overseas agents.

There was no time for delay. The tone of the scream flagged the urgency.

* * * *

Jeff Fowler listened to Ian Reid's briefing and the proposed attack strategy. They hadn't entertained the possible option of a peaceful negotiation – too many serious international implications surrounding the object of their interest.

The plan was a fast assault into the rumpus room, with stun grenades and heavily-armed special police.

Thick muffling curtains appeared to cover both a sliding-glass back entrance from the yard and two barred rumpus-room windows. A rear wooden door led through the laundry into the garage; where they expected to find a mini-bus and a motorbike. Two tilting garage doors might open from inside.

* * * *

The leader was listening to a voice on the phone.

He turned to Olga, 'Kayseri in Cappadocia. Where in Kayseri?'

'Not easy to explain. Can I speak to person who knows area, please?'

The rubber hose whipped across Spencer's right cheek again raising another high pitched yell. 'Where in Kayseri?' said the leader.

'Is in cave under ground,' said Olga. She would string out the instructions as long as she could. It could take hours of relaying instructions for people on the ground to get to Turkey and then to Cappadocia. Then she would lead them on a journey through the caves she had explored as a child – and they would still be a long way away from where she thought she and Anatoly might have hidden the suitcases.

This was the world she thought she had left.

* * * *

Baaa … doom! It was a numbing crash as grenades came through the side windows and back door. The thick curtains slowed their trajectory into the room but the noise and the flash were stunning.

The air continued to shake as the shock waves reverberated in the confined space. More loud bangs and the muffled crackle of automatic gunfire.

Olga felt a rubber-clad body lying over her as the noise subsided. The man said, 'Police. Lie still.' Not that she had an option.

She heard a loud call of, 'Over. Check vitals.'

Spencer also appeared to have a large body in a scuba suit lying over his unconscious form. The pain and the shock must have been just too much when the first bang had happened.

The man in black quickly righted Olga's chair and released her from the velcro straps.

'We are police. It's over. Are you hurt?'

'Fine. Look after Spencer. They have beaten him.'

Spencer seemed to be stirring as if trying to regain some sense through the mists of his mind. The black police shapes attended to him.

Olga watched as they removed his straps and released the very groggy lecturer gently onto the ground from his chair. The blood flowed steadily from his head gash again. One of the police performed a very fast and skilled medical assessment.

Olga could see the red welts across Spencer's cheeks. He moaned quietly. She thought how brave this poor Englishman was – university academic who preferred five-star accommodation to camping in tents. Not treatment his poor body and mind were prepared for.

The room appeared devastated. Remnants of thick drapes over the windows and back door smoked gently, in tatters.

The back glass doors were no longer there, except for a few shards still clinging forlornly to the frame.

The door linking through to the garage was gone, smashed from its hinges. Some mighty force had been applied. Olga was frankly surprised she and Spencer were still alive.

Their rescuers zipped two bodies of men in motorbike leathers and helmets into black plastic body-bags, with stretchers laid beside them. They lifted a groaning, trussed third person in leathers, with no helmet, out into the garage.

It was all happening very quickly – very efficient.

A scruffy bearded man with long hair came over and checked both Olga and Spencer as he talked on the phone.

* * * *

Inspector Reid took the call from Derek. He had been listening to the action from the microphone relay, following their progress by the bangs and shouts.

Derek advised that Olga and Spencer had been recovered alive. Spencer had head injuries from a beating and would need hospital help. No physical injuries obvious on Olga.

Two enemy killed, one wounded and on the way out in the secure vehicle. Three handguns and an automatic rifle recovered – two fired – along with three coshes and a length of heavy rubber hose.

No squad member injured, just bruises.

Ian Reid thanked his special undercover colleague; a polished operation from very well-trained officers – and he was already coordinating the next phase from headquarters as he was being briefed.

The cover story had been that a gas leak was suspected and so three large vans, the first showing an emergency services logo, had passed quickly through the police cordon and the enemy bodies were loaded into one. Spencer and Olga were loaded into another and the special police team left the area in the third, just as the uniformed police entered the street to secure the house from prying eyes.

The media liaison officer briefed the press about a nasty accident where a gas bottle or bottles had exploded in the rumpus room of the high-set house.

There had been no casualties. Thankfully, early warning of a gas smell had helped them isolate the street. Emergency services and gas specialists were rendering the area safe. Yes, it could take several hours. Yes, only one house was damaged. It was a rental property. No-one appears to have been at home at the time.

Yes, of course you will be able to take photographs of the house from the street – shortly.

* * * *

Jeff Fowler congratulated his Queensland colleague and his men on a job well done.

A transcript of the enhanced recording from the rumpus room interrogation was on its way to his computer. The abductors had been taken; one was still alive for questioning. No injuries to the special operations squad.

'I'm booked on a flight to Brisbane leaving in an hour,' Fowler told Reid. 'I need to listen to what this abductor has to say but I want the local police to do the questioning. I also want to speak to Olga Davidenko and this university lecturer, Spencer. I haven't met him but he seems to have the confidence of the Major.'

256

Ian Reid felt a glow of satisfaction that the Toowoomba police operation had worked out so well. It wasn't every day that the AFP in Canberra bestowed such praise on the local force.

Ian's next call would be to Aunty Edna.

* * * *

Superintendent Jeff Fowler viewed the transcript of the exchange between Major Davidenko and her kidnappers.

In a spirit of international policing co-operation, he passed those words to ASIO with permission to relay to Britain.

* * * *

In turn, that action caused a greying head to ponder, as his eyes surveyed the Thames below.

Then he issued directives to operatives in Ankara and Australia to be on alert for information indicating where, in Kayseri or wider Cappadocia, the objects of interest might be located.

Chapter 52

It was a discreet but powerful police presence as the anonymous van drove into the private hospital.

Dr Charles McBride had his two patients ushered quietly into the well-serviced double room. A non-uniformed policeman was seated beside the door in the corridor while others were outside the window and on mobile patrol through the grounds.

Only two nurses were vetted with the right security to enter the room. Reid was taking no chances.

Olga was placed in the bed near the door and McBride ran all his standard checks. He gave her some of his prescribed painkillers while she kept telling him to look after Spencer. She appeared very tired to the doctor's experienced eye – even more than this recent episode might have caused. She was a strong lady but time was not on her side.

The nurse had tidied the wound on Spencer's head and McBride moved across to the window bed to check the cut and bruise on his forehead. The egg shape was still prominent but didn't show signs of bruise colouring as yet. There were nasty whip marks across the right cheek and jaw, plus similar across the left cheek. Those marks were colouring into black and blue weals with amber and red tones near the edges.

* * * *

Dizzy and in pain, I couldn't get my mind to work properly. There were stark memories of an alien attack, ant-head monsters thumping me, tied up, bangs, flashes – Olga tied to a chair. Terrible nightmare.

A doctor was leaning over me. Hospital room. Was this real? But hospitals smell and sound the same the world over. Disinfectant and starch. Whirring machines. The scents were making my nose twitch. I could feel it. No dream.

'I'm just giving you a small injection,' the doctor said and a nurse gently applied ice-packs to my face. 'You have bruises on your cheeks,' he continued. 'The ice will give you some relief. Your cheeks will feel numb for a while.' He was smiling and confident.

I tried to return his smile; valiantly, in true British tradition. My mumbled 'Thank you' didn't sound like my voice or even like English words.

The doctor squeezed my hand. 'Your vital signs are fine. Just rest and you will recover.' I must have tried to say 'Olga', because he motioned to the bed on my right. I slowly turned my painful, frozen face and saw her worried eyes looking at me. The surge of relief was profound. She was safe. Had I crashed the bus? Was that what had happened?

'Just relax.' The doctor's quiet voice was soothing. 'You are in a hospital bed and everyone is fine.'

Another confident man entered the room and greeted us both cheerily.

'Well, you *have* been in the wars, haven't you?' he said. 'Inspector Ian Reid, Toowoomba Police,' he said to me specifically. Olga seemed to know him.

He could see my confusion. 'You and the Major were kidnapped, Dr Avery, but you are safe here,' he added with a smile, 'with guards outside the door and window. The only people who will be allowed entry are me, the doctor, two authorised nurses, Superintendent Fowler when he gets in from Canberra and the Grushko family when they arrive in an hour or so.'

Kidnapped? The images? My face? So confusing. Canberra? The Grushko family? Oh, what had happened?

Olga thanked the inspector for what I assumed was rescuing us.

'Knew you would come,' she said. 'Tracking device worked.'

'Without being too personal, Major,' said Reid. 'Can you just check that you have the tracking device?'

Olga felt under her sheets and gave a surprised, 'No. Has gone.' She looked quizzical.

'Your tracking device appears to be on a property in NSW.'

She paused while she thought and then suddenly laughed aloud. 'Must have dislodged – swimming at lagoon. Spencer, did you hear? Tracking monitor shows us in New South Wales.'

The lagoon. Swimming. She was laughing. I understood that at least. I gave my best chortle. It didn't work. A student of laughter would have assumed it was a dentist's-chair groan.

'So how did you find us so quickly then?' asked Olga.

'Do the names Aunty Edna, Ellie, Izzy and Tooki mean anything to you?' Ian Reid had a knowing grin. I was with it now. I knew who he was talking about. I wanted into the conversation.

'Indeed. Dey are good fwens fwom de camp-out,' I mumbled through my unresponsive numbed face. It hadn't been my intention to sound like a fool but my ears couldn't deceive me. To their credit, both Olga and the policeman controlled their impulse to mock my misfortune.

Olga said, 'We know them. But how did they help?'

'I'm told a girl called Izzy was skateboarding near you when the motorbikers lobbed a stun grenade at the bus; and some detonators on the other side of the road to distract attention.

'By the time the mini-bus had been turned in the street, Izzy had noted the registration number and was texting the information to Tooki at Fuzzy Electronics. Tooki has a distribution network of mobiles – apparently a lot of these street-kids have been given pre-paid mobiles. They were on the look-out for the vehicle before I had even heard of the incident.'

'The house, next to the one where you were held, was vacant. A homeless girl called Amy heard the motorbike arrive, got a quick glimpse of the rego plate and texted Tooki. He sent a girl called Ellie to check and she verified it was likely you were in the house.'

'Ellie,' repeated Olga, 'and Izzy.'

Reid continued, 'Ellie texted Tooki. Tooki spoke with Aunty Edna and she phoned me. We are old friends. She has worked in police liaison with young people on the street.'

The strange images were starting to make sense. So that was what happened. The visions of the room; the ant-heads were in motorcycle gear. Questioning. I remembered.

'The rest is history, as they say,' concluded a satisfied Inspector Reid.

Olga and I were silent as we listened and looked at each other meaningfully. Realisation dawned for both of us.

'We owe our rescue to communication network of homeless people?' she asked slowly and quietly.

The conversations at the camp out flooded back, where Tooki had explained how his homeless ones kept in touch – mobiles passing the news that was important to them. I remembered the grounds of the university where I had doubted how effective that might be. Well, it had proved its worth now – we may well owe our lives to it.

Reid continued, 'I spoke to Aunty Edna to thank her and she said to thank Tooki. He had made the system work by setting up the kids with mobiles. Apparently, Fuzzy Electronics provides pre-paids, where they are needed. Tooki gave them the confidence to look after each other, with a lot of help from Henry and the others.

'When I spoke to Tooki. He said to thank Izzy because it was she who understood the seriousness of the situation and acted fast.

'When I spoke to Izzy she said she did it because the Russian Nana is alright. She stuck up for us when she didn't need to. She said to tell you, *You're okay – and they're happy you both got out in one piece.*'

Perhaps it was the fragility of her health but this normally very controlled former GRU major had tears rolling down her cheeks.

When she looked across at me, my eyes were gushing too. I couldn't stop the flow.

Ian Reid politely said, 'You have both been through a great deal. I'll leave you now for some rest.'

Olga grabbed the policeman's hand. 'Please, Inspector. Please pass two messages from Spencer and me. First, to your men, for saving our lives. Was no easy task to storm room blind and kill desperate armed criminals.

'Second is to thank Tooki, Aunty Edna, Izzy and network – but especially Izzy. Tell Izzy from me that Russian Nana says, '*Spasibo*, that is *thank you,'* and sometime very soon, debt will be repaid in part to her and group.

'Please tell also that I love her for what she did for us. And tell her, Inspector, we had tears of gratitude in our eyes as we said it. And tell her maybe somebody's listening after all. She'll know what all that means. Thank you, Inspector,' as she squeezed his hand once more.

The tough policeman had a glisten in his eye as he bade us both goodbye for the moment and he promised he would pass on the messages.

Chapter 53

Inspector Reid met Peter, Anna and Eva Grushko at the hospital room door. He wanted to prepare them for Spencer's appearance. He advised them that the abductors had beaten the lecturer to force Olga to divulge a secret from her past.

The family nodded a vague understanding and entered the room.

They saw Olga first and Eva rushed over to kiss her Nana on the cheek. Peter and Anna followed.

* * * *

I watched them come into the room. Olga welcomed them and pointed to me quietly lying in the window bed. They hadn't noticed me in their rush. Eva ran over and then saw my bruised and battered face, swathed in ice packs.

'Oh, poor Spencer,' she said, looking at my cheeks and forehead. 'I was going to kiss you too but I don't want to hurt you.'

Olga chimed in, cheekily, 'They didn't hurt his lips.'

Eva immediately kissed me on the lips. We both looked at each other surprised while Olga cackled with laughter at the spontaneity of the gesture. Peter and Anna joined in.

'Oh, poor Spencer,' said Eva. 'It looks so sore.'

I mumbled, 'Malright', and tried to smile; probably still giving the frozen face look. Olga took advantage of my disability to wax poetically about what a hero I had been, taking the beating to spare her. That wasn't the way it had been at all. I willed her to stop all the hero stuff. I had done nothing except get hit. I felt embarrassed, like a hypocrite.

But I was only able to mumble and, in the end, it wasn't worth the effort. I lay back and pretended to be a fitting hero. It was easier. I was still recovering from the shock of being kissed so tenderly by this beautiful student – nice, even if absolutely inappropriate. The ethics committee surely couldn't complain. It had all happened in front of Eva's parents and grandmother – and I was incapacitated.

Olga appeared to enjoy telling her story. What hype! It bore only a scant semblance of the truth. Clearly her story had an effect because I could see it reflected in the adoring eyes of Eva. This was dangerous territory Olga was pushing me into – and I could see the grin on the grandmother's face. She was having a ball.

Gradually, she settled down and took the rest her medical condition required. I pretended I couldn't speak and just let Eva hold my hand in a comforting way as Anna thanked me for being so brave. I'd decided that I'd plead temporary loss of senses if anyone challenged my probity. I tried my smile back to her and squeezed her hand in thanks.

Later, I watched Peter getting some precious time with his mother. He didn't ask the obvious question. We could all see the tiredness. Olga was hiding her pain behind story-telling but the strain could be easily seen behind the eyes.

I listened as I rested.

* * * *

'Pyotr,' she said, almost in a whisper. 'Do you have good lawyer?' As he nodded, she added. 'One who can deal with international law? In Russia and Switzerland?'

'Yes,' he replied, as if it were a superfluous question.

'Would you arrange for lawyer and Dr McBride to visit me together?' she said. 'Soon,' she added for emphasis. 'Today or tomorrow?' with insistence in her voice.

She answered her son's questioning eyes with, 'I don't think is far away. Loose ends I need to tidy, for *your* sake … to save problems later.'

He nodded sadly as he gently squeezed her hand in understanding. 'They are both busy people. I'll see what I can do. Tomorrow morning?'

'Will be good, my son.' Her expression softened from business mode back to the mother.

Peter's head still bobbed slowly, like an involuntary reflex he didn't want to stop. They hadn't had a lot of time together, but the weeks before had allowed the questions to be asked, stories to be told, videos to be made; tears to be wept; open messages of love and understanding to be expressed in the privacy of a united family.

'Pyotr, time together has been too short. My fault. Entirely my fault. My choice so many years ago ... and over years since. Steeled myself to be cold, to stay away. Thought pain would be too great, for you ... but mainly was for me. Was wrong. Was so very wrong. Has been total joy being with you all.' Slowly and precisely, she said, 'I regret not being there for you, as you needed me over years. Please forgive me, my son.' She repeated in her native language, '*Pozhalsta prosti menya, syn moi.*'

Peter held his mother in a teary hug. His thoughts transmitted through the seconds of touch until finally he said, '*Konechno.* Of course, dearest.'

* * * *

Peter's expression showed that it had been a cathartic time. Behind the obvious anguish in his protective face, Peter pondered his long-held sense of unworthiness, stemming, he was sure, from having been sent away all those years ago – as the child that his family didn't want, that sense of being less than others, the boy who had grown into the man whose mother wouldn't see him and whom he could never meet. He had always masked his insecurities with his work ethic, his formality, his sense of order and his material success.

Now, brief though this visit from his mother had been, the reasons and doubts which had plagued his inner consciousness over so many years had been progressively dispelled – it had never been as he had believed over all that time. He *had* been loved – albeit from a distance – by a mother who had made the hardest of decisions which she had believed to be right for him, in her circumstances – in a different culture.

The tears at Kiev Airport all those years ago – he now understood what must have been rolling through her mind on that day. She had been alone, bravely sacrificing herself, so that her son could have a better life – after having lost her dearly-loved husband in battle. Oh, the darkness she must have felt. He was at last able to rationalise his mother's pain, at least on an intellectual level – and to see that world through her tortured dilemmas.

And his own need to struggle to belong, to be one of those successful people no longer seemed to be as important – those demons had been exorcised.

He was also strangely comfortable that, through his mother, he may well be distantly related to people who in the past he would have given scant regard – less through a sense of malice, more through the mere dismissiveness of his own self-doubt.

Cathartic indeed – through realisation and shame, to peace and a sense of purpose. He hugged his mother some more.

*   *   *   *

After the Grushkos left, I tried to tell Olga that she was making me out to be an unworthy hero. She grinned.

'Enjoy,' she said. I assumed she meant the kiss from Eva

Before I could respond, Inspector Reid arrived with Superintendent Jeff Fowler of the Australian Federal Police.

They made their welcomes and Fowler commiserated with us both over our ordeal.

'I'm pleased to meet you in person at last,' he said to me. 'Your mobile number has been quite a part of my recent life.' He looked closely at my wounds. His only comment was sympathetic. 'I'm sorry you have been through this pain.' He turned his attention back to Olga.

'Do we know more, Superintendent?' she asked, as the policemen drew up chairs between the beds.

'The initial interrogation of the surviving kidnapper has revealed all three are Australian criminals, hard men, up from Melbourne. They were being paid by people in the Russian Federation. He hasn't given much detail. He wasn't the leader. He may not know very much more. The leader's mobile contact tracks to Moscow. We'll see where that leads.'

Olga nodded.

'You asked about Anatoly Sidorov before. I followed that up. He had become a major by last year when he was working in northern

Pakistan, setting up networks out of Peshawar. You would know more about how all that works than I would.'

Her eyes were glued on the superintendent's face, silently encouraging him to explain further.

'It would appear,' Fowler continued, 'from our sources, that Sidorov may have compromised himself in the Kaghan valley of Kashmir in 2007.

'Perhaps, it might have been hubris at such a gathering of revolutionaries from several nations? Who really knows exactly what particular group Sidorov might have been meeting with? Certainly there were Pakistanis, Afghanis and Arabs from the Syria/Lebanon area at the larger gathering – although, there was possibly and probably only a very small number present, when he let his guard down. However – to our understanding of the facts – at least two people present received some damaging information from him.

'It seems he revealed that he'd been one of a select group charged with hiding special forces' weapons and, in particular, suitcase-sized nuclear weapons in the aftermath of the fall of the Soviet Union. He apparently gave no location but he must have mentioned some names and a Major Davidenko as the leader.'

Olga listened impassively. If she was shocked at the information she was receiving, it did not show. But the pieces were starting to fall into place for me. Now I was beginning to understand why she had become such an object of international interest after all this time.

'Go on,' she encouraged the superintendent.

'So last year, a couple of known terrorist groups made contact with the Russian underworld in Moscow – one was from Pakistan and another from Lebanon. They wanted to be put in touch with Sidorov and to share the potential of these weapons with the Russian gangs. This was to be a big money operation.

'Now, British Intelligence has many operatives in that area of Russia. They picked up the chatter, reporting back through their controller, someone who goes by the codename, Old Fruit. They became interested. Suddenly, a top-secret GRU project, which should have remained absolutely classified, was being discussed in criminal and espionage networks.

'Sidorov was approached by the Russian mafia. He may have been forced to give up more names. However it happened, the names of all the five appear to have become known. When Sidorov realised the magnitude of his mistake back in the Kaghan valley, he shot himself in his Moscow apartment – or, at least, that was how the scene appeared.

'Three others, who had been in the same special group, died shortly afterwards ... and not prettily. They were presumably easier to find than you, because they were all still in the service, in Russia. But they clearly didn't have the right information to find the weapons.'

I shuddered as I thought back to Olga and me, strapped in those chairs under the house. If the police hadn't arrived, there would have been a very permanent conclusion for us both. But Fowler was still speaking ...

'You, however, were the one they actually needed and were much more elusive. You had retired; you were inactive, and were travelling – walking in the wilds of Germany and France, for much of it, as I understand. And ... you had applied for a visa through the Australian embassy in Paris to visit your son in Queensland.'

Olga nodded with a faint smile as she acknowledged what must have been a very significant decision point in her later life.

The superintendent continued:

'The Australian authorities contacted London as a matter of course – there must have been something on your file which was flagged. Normally, that can be a lengthy process. Anyway, I suspect that senior British people may well have expedited your approval to travel here – keeping you in the Commonwealth as it were.

'By the time, the gangs had worked out where you were, you had left from Paris for Australia – and presumably they followed close behind.'

Olga rubbed her brow as she came to terms with what she had just heard. 'Sidorov was good young officer when I knew him,' she commented with a sorrowful tone. 'Hard to believe he was compromised in such way. Very foolish – but still sad.'

Ian Reid told Olga that he had passed on her messages to his people and to Aunty Edna, Tooki, Izzy and Amy.

'They understood your messages and thanked you, *Sister*. Their words. They would like to come to see you. They don't know about your medical condition – only that you and Spencer have been through the abduction. I'll leave it to you as to what you tell them. Are you okay with them visiting you? We have a secure sitting room just through that door.'

'Would love to meet them, Inspector.' She added with pointed look. 'Sooner than later. I'm sure my silent friend, Spencer, would like to see them too.'

I nodded enthusiastically.

* * * *

When the policemen had left, Olga sank back into her pillow.

I could see her exhaustion. The impact of our abduction had to be taking its toll and there had been a steady stream of visitors.

I lifted myself from my bed. It really was only my face that didn't work properly. I sat beside the tired lady on her bed, taking her relaxed hand in mine. She opened her eyes and smiled.

'Been busy,' I mumbled and she nodded without speaking.

I held her hand a little longer. Then I reached over and kissed her on the forehead. Her eyes opened again; she smiled as if to say, 'Thank you' and then she fell asleep.

* * * *

Some time later, Dr McBride came into the room. He looked at the sleeping Olga, felt her pulse and then moved over to me. He checked the facial injuries.

'The cut is knitting together well with just the tape. No need for stitches. The painkilling injection will wear off soon and you will have some feeling back in those whip marks. I'll give you some milder painkillers now while your face frees up a bit more.'

'It will be good to talk normally again,' I agreed, pleasantly surprised that my ability to form words was returning. The bruising and swelling were starting to reduce.

'Doctor, Olga? She's very tired. How much longer?'

'Not much longer. She must have a high pain threshold. She is quite amazing.'

'I agree,' but I wasn't just talking about her pain threshold. There would be some very difficult days ahead and I was not looking forward to saying farewell to this remarkable lady.

Tiredness was swamping me too so I lay back on the pillow and drifted off to sleep, dreaming happily of a delightful kiss. I could just see the family resemblance in the expression. She had some of her grandmother's gentle smile.

It was a happy odyssey in a fantastic kaleidoscope in the sky.

Chapter 54

I awoke from a beautiful dream and rolled over to check on Olga, hurting my cheek in the process. The worst of the pain was wearing off, if not the discomfort of the bruises. Probably about a fortnight, Dr McBride had said, before the marks would be gone.

She wasn't in her bed.

I could hear voices from the sitting room. The door was partly open. Dr McBride was in there, with a businessman and Olga. She was dictating instructions into a recorder and the businessman was clarifying points every so often.

I heard him saying he would return in the afternoon and she smiled her thanks.

* * * *

'Spencer, let's talk,' said Olga when she returned to the room. 'Was Peter's lawyer. Re-doing will. Need my affairs to be in order.'

I didn't trust my voice to speak just then.

'Spencer, you are lovely man. I want to thank you for being such good friend through these past months, weeks and days.'

I looked into the tired, smiling face and could see only a film-star charm behind the weary eyes.

She continued. 'You have given me so many laughs – in nicest sense. Have been so happy – even with shadow of my demise hanging over. Was terrible beating you took for me – and you never once complained. Do you realise that?'

I managed a weak grin. *'Tis a far better thing I do today than I have ever done. The English were always gallant.'*

'You see? Precisely what I mean. Such romantic, happy, reliable person; seeing fun and chivalry in every moment. Loved your shocked expression when Eva kissed you yesterday. Wish I had thought to have camera ready.'

'It wouldn't have been my best profile,' I joked.

'Yet,' she said. 'For all your expertise, you appear surprisingly unaware sometimes.'

She paused to check my reaction. My eyes asked the question.

'Spencer, dear friend.' She gripped my hand firmly. 'Is my time. I am at peace. Had we met forty years ago and been same ages, what fun we might have had. I don't want to see you hurt. You will be going back to Cambridge at end of year. Eva and Melanie finish degrees here then. Both of them have been intoxicated by you.

'Have told me they want to go to Cambridge for post-graduate study. I have money, if is what they choose. My concern is you, dear Spencer. You will have these two seeking attention. No doubt, there will be also many more Marys over there for whom you would be excellent catch. Romantic in me would like to think my granddaughter and you … Somehow, would be fitting for real affection I feel for you.'

She reached over and kissed me on the lips.

'Couldn't let young ones have all fun, eh!' She laughed, back to her old joking self … and she slowly, ever so slowly, released my hand.

I had a flurry of emotions whistling through me. Olga usually had that effect on me. 'We shall see what pans out.' I was not buying into her matchmaker role. 'Whatever happens in the future, I will always treasure these times we've had together. I could never have dreamed of meeting someone like you, let alone dancing the polka together at the Goomburra Dance.' I gave my best sentimental romantic smile. 'Not quite the Kirov, I know.'

She interrupted, 'Better than Kirov. Here people laugh as they dance. Is honesty in this land – so precious it should be bottled for posterity.' She grinned. 'Heard that term in England. Maybe, you won't stay long in Cambridge, eh? Maybe, other things are more important.'

The visits continued.

Olga was the same positive cheery strength as she spent time with Izzy, Aunty Edna, Ellie – and Amy, whom she met for the first time.

To Tooki, she said, 'Don't lose your noble spirit!' He gave her the handshake of the revolution, his worldly eyes dark and shiny.

Then, she had some quiet minutes with her possible distant cousin, Steve, and his Great-Uncle Herbie.

Warren and Melanie appeared shocked at my injuries. They had last seen me when I had dropped them off from the bus. But this time, I could speak to control Olga's attempts to exaggerate my bravery. My appearance would not have been pleasant and the students kept saying how impressed they were with my ability to have lived through the experience. Quite humbling really.

I confirmed I'd be back on deck within two weeks. I checked their progress with all their study assignments; pleased that they each had shown the initiative I would expect of good students.

Olga hugged them all as they left.

* * * *

The lawyer returned in the afternoon with Olga's wishes all typed up as a will, bound together by legal canvas tape. She read the pages and signed. Dr McBride witnessed the pages. She kept a copy and the lawyer had a copy.

The 't's were crossed and the 'i's were dotted – or so I thought until the policeman on guard asked me to come outside. When I went out, standing there were Tony from The Fair Dinkum Bush Band and Gary, the mandolinist, seeking permission to play a couple of tunes for Olga.

Apparently, Peter had told them how much his mother enjoyed their music and that she was now very ill. They had dropped what they were doing and hurried up to Toowoomba. That was the measure of such men. Not just comedic entertainers but good human beings.

Her expression was a picture of delight when the two walked into the room. She stretched over painfully to embrace them. Tony said they wanted to play a couple of tunes to cheer her day.

They gave a quick polished rendition of the *Irish Washerwoman* as Olga's eyes watched Gary's mesmerizing fingerwork. Peter came into the room just as Tony was saying, 'And now a special tune, Olga, just for you. Forgive us if we make the occasional mistake. We haven't played this to anyone before.'

The lager-phone started the slow, steady, complex rhythms of the Russian steppes and the mandolin sounded like a purring balalaika. The traditional powerful folk song, *Kalinka*, slowly filled the room, gently gathering in pace and passion to its scintillating conclusion – a highly emotional moment which only such fervent music can inspire.

Olga was in the arms of her son; tears rolling down her cheeks. The normally controlled Peter seemed to have found an ability to relax; taking pleasure from the moment, mother and son bonded in a long-awaited cloak of rapture.

'*Spasibo, Spasibo!* You have made old lady very, very happy. Don't know what I have done to deserve. Then,' she grinned with impish humour, 'have this illness and don't know what I did to deserve it either. Thank you for playing for me.'

I just shook my head in amazement. It must have been the bush band influence rubbing off on her.

'Is there anything I can do for you?' she asked of the band members. 'What about new instrument or equipment? Anything that would make your playing easier. A new lager-phone, perhaps?'

Tony took mock offence at the thought of replacing his prized instrument. 'I have had the *same* lager-phone for twenty years,' he answered in a miffed tone 'Changed the broomstick a few times; the bottle tops and cross stick too – but it is the *same* fine instrument.'

'Always humour, always quick wit.' The grinning lady bade them a graceful goodbye.

She was justifiably exhausted after all the visitors, but very happy. The family were coming back to be with her that evening as she rested.

Chapter 55

'Spencer, come and sit until Peter and family arrive. Has been so much happening. Need to tidy my mind; to relax and let cogs freewheel.'

I rose from my bed, taking in the starry evening sky through the open-curtained window as I moved.

She looked tranquil, lying back on her bed. 'Have to confess,' she said quietly, 'Can't remember exactly where we buried suitcases, Spencer. Turkish tunnels are very complicated. Wherever, would be deep and sealed. Was good at my job. Will be safer than having someone extract them – to create mischief or worse. Old Hittite ghosts can guard yet another secret in those ancient caverns. Can you tell Superintendent Fowler when you speak to him again please? Have been so lucky to have had this time in Australia. Super, as English say. Need to tell something particular.' Her voice was getting more croaky. Clearly, it was becoming an effort to speak.

I moved closer to listen.

'Am going to break vow of secrecy to my country for one only time.' She gulped to get moisture into her mouth and then continued. 'One of my jobs was to oversee recruitment of young people who would grow to be influential leaders of industry and politics. Have protected those names all my working life.

'One, however, in my view needs to be exposed. I do this out of love for you. Expect you will share knowledge. Have no problem with that. You use information wisely. You will know what needs to be done.'

I was quite bewildered. Perhaps the tumor was affecting her rational thinking.

'Spencer,' she continued, gasping out the words. 'Tobias Stanley-Smythe is Russian agent. One of my teams recruited him several years ago. Has been annoying me since feeling your pain when he took your Mary away. Don't trust him. Our people always had suspicion he was double-agent selling us out to British.'

I sat dumbfounded. Toby!!?

'What day is this, Spencer?' She looked suddenly aware.

'Thursday.'

'No, what date is this?'

I looked at the date on my watch. '28th August.'

She eased herself into a seated position on the bed. 'Help me to window, please. Need to see stars.' She leaned heavily on my arm, breathing with difficulty, as she shuffled past my bed and looked up out of the window at the night sky. 'Am not spiritual person, Spencer, but every year on this day I look up at stars and say *Ya lyoublyou tebya. Dosvedanya.* Have now done for forty years. Would like to believe Oleg was saying those words to me when he died, *I love you. Farewell.* If he is star up there, he will know I haven't forgotten him. Is anniversary of his death. Isn't that strange it should be today of all days?'

She knew.

I now realised the pain she had been carrying. What a loneliness! Is that what had driven her all these years? And now so close to rekindling the bond that she had chosen to break with her son all these years ago. Slipping away! No reprieve.

'Spencer.' She tilted her ear towards the corridor. 'Hear others coming. Make yourself comfortable in sitting room so we can say what we need to say.'

As she slowly walked me to the sitting-room door, wincing as she moved, she whispered carefully, 'Wonderful Spencer, thank you for past weeks. You made me so happy. Remember to listen to those with less power and distrust any demonisers. Wish you happiest of lives. Lucky girl who wins you. I will always love you, too.'

The poignancy of that remark, given without guile in such circumstances, was numbing; gratefully anaesthetising me from uncontrolled gibbering.

'Farewell, dear friend,' she gasped huskily.

She kissed my cheek and I hugged her close until Peter, Anna and Eva entered the room. Then, I politely and silently took my leave; salty wet beads coursing slowly down my bruised face, stinging the painful skin.

* * * *

Anna came to the sitting room door, tears rolling pathways down her cheeks.

It had been maybe twenty minutes that I had been sitting there, quietly thinking to myself.

'She is gone, Spencer. She is gone,' she said simply, taking my hand. 'We would like you to be with us at this time.'

As I entered the room, I could see Olga resting peacefully on the bed. Dr McBride was doing his checks and straightening the sheets. Peter and Eva hugged to the sound of their gentle sobs. They turned and embraced me as I arrived.

'Come,' said Peter. 'Hold her hand. She thought so highly of you.'

I took her lifeless hand in mine and looked at her face – so serene. The eyes were closed. The pain had gone. Even through the calm, there was a hint of a cheeky grin.

'May I kiss her one last time, please?'

Peter nodded. '*Konechno*. Of course.'

I leaned across and kissed the still warm forehead, mouthing the quiet words, '*Dosvedanya*, Olga.' The word that had meant so much to her. I felt an inner peace that I had closed the circle.

I turned, with tears flowing unabated and hugged Peter, Anna and Eva together.

'I am so grateful to have had this time with her.' I was trying to be strong but ... to hell with image and propriety. I needed to grieve and let the tears flow.

'And we thank you,' said her son. 'You helped make those last days so enjoyable for her, and for us.'

Eva touched my bruised face tenderly. 'Thank you from Nana Olga.' We gave each other a quiet kiss. Damn the restrictions of convention.

Chapter 56

The Toowoomba Crematorium was very full for the funeral of a lady who had only been in the country for a few months. Olga had left instructions to be cremated and her ashes to be sprinkled in her designated spots.

The family took up the front row. They had asked me to sit with them. Behind us were Uncle Herbie, Aunty Edna, Tooki, Izzy, Henry, Ellie, Amy and a dozen others in their distinctive dark clothes.

Steve sat with Melanie. Her parents had travelled in from over the NSW border. Others from the university were there because they knew how much this lady had meant to me. Barry was sitting quietly with them all. He gave me an encouraging wink.

Superintendent Fowler had flown up from Canberra. He sat in full dress uniform beside Inspector Reid and several members of his team including a long-haired bearded man whom Reid called Derek.

There were others too that I didn't recognise.

Some, seated in the front rows, were introduced as extended family from Brisbane, representing the late Uncle Ivan and Aunty Nina; there to support Peter, the adopted son, and his family – and there to pay respect to Olga, a lady they never knew beyond a name and photograph. What a strange world it could be sometimes.

Then there were Tony and Gary, from the bush band; with June, the jolly accordionist; and Dan, the quiet bass player. They were sitting with the Goomburra farmers; Graham, Jenny, Bill, Dot, Ron and Shelley – and Warren, looking after his younger brothers. Darren had especially asked if he could be there. 'For Lightning,' he had said with a conspiratorial grin to his big brother.

I looked around ... feeling the emotion of the occasion. This lady had made an impact. Four months was all she'd had in the end. What a disparate group of people she had brought together through her strong personality and that mysterious genealogical link. Quite remarkable.

The master of ceremonies mentioned Olga's service over many years in the Russian army, her son Peter and her sudden illness.

Then Izzy rose.

She had accepted Peter's offer to speak with a strength that amazed all who knew her. She seemed to have gained an inner strength since I had first met the shy formerly-homeless girl on the camp-out. This was the talented young woman that Tooki recognised, the ironic wit of the camp site, the rebel that Olga's inspiration was helping release from her self-imposed bondage.

Now, behind the lectern, she spoke of the Russian Nana who had stood up for them; who had said that it was alright to be different; and who had said that we shouldn't be branded as less good if we didn't fit the ruling group's mould.

She talked of the street-kids' pride that they'd been able to help her recently; and how she, Izzy, was pleased to have met Olga and heard her speak. 'Nana Olga had a special presence. She just did. I don't have a name for it. So cool, so wise; and so strong to speak up and have people actually listen to her views.'

Izzy, at that moment, had everyone's undivided attention, mirroring the graceful charm she so admired in her Russian role model.

I had the concluding comments, at Peter's request.

'It is hard to believe that less than five months ago, I had never heard of Olga Davidenko and now my life has been enriched forever, because of her.

'She was a happy, optimistic person who had lived in an often dangerous world of military intelligence – what she called *communications*. She had moved in social circles which most of us would never understand ... and she had learned that the simple things were the most important in life.

'She loved the experience of the bush dance – where it was alright to laugh, to make a mistake and to dance with every person in the hall. She found the Australian people to be so genuine – just *fair dinkum*.

'She encouraged us not to fall for anyone manipulating our thinking. She wanted us all to listen critically to other people, particularly those who didn't have a powerful voice behind them. She said the people that we don't value highly actually have the most important things to share with us – if only we can hear them.

'Yet, she was the most mischievous lady I have ever met – laughing, joking and teasing. I will cherish her elegant memory and her laughter till I die.

'May she rest in peace.'

* * * *

The ceremony was over and the diverse crowd mingled. Like all gatherings in country areas, people took the opportunity to catch up.

I made the effort to go round everyone in the room, thanking them for being there for the family and for Olga. When I caught up with the Canberra AFP superintendent, Fowler said, 'Your face is mending well, Spencer. Amazing what a few days can do in the healing process. You handled that whole business around the Major with a lot of courage and skill. Well done!'

I knew I was such an unlikely hero but I was flattered by the kind words. He didn't need to have said them. I told him that Olga had left a couple of messages to be passed on. His eyebrow raised in interest.

'She couldn't remember,' I said, 'right up to the end, exactly where the suitcases were buried. She was sure they'd been buried deep and sealed. She said to tell you the cases would be safe there. The Hittite ghosts would guard them along with their other secrets from millennia ago.'

The policeman nodded. 'She was probably right. I hope they will pass into the world of fiction now, though we do have strong evidence from a defector that they were very real. The world can do without such weapons in the wrong hands.'

I paused to let the thoughts be absorbed.

'I have one other piece of information for you,' I said. 'She told me the name of a Russian spy in Britain that she thought might also be a double agent. Are you interested in the name?'

'I am – very interested. I will pass it through ASIO to the right authorities.'

'Dr Tobias Stanley-Smythe of Cambridge. He is, was, a friend of mine.' My detachment surprised me. 'I would never ever have suspected him.'

'They move in strange ways, these espionage people,' said Fowler, 'hiding behind façades and they do it very cleverly.' He thought for a moment. 'Quite a lady was our Major Davidenko. Nice to have met you, Spencer. I wish you well for the rest of your time in Australia. I hope we don't have occasion to talk on your mobile again. Take care.' And he was gone with a smile. A busy man doing important work – but not too busy to fly to Toowoomba for this funeral.

The crowd was starting to disperse as I finally reached Ian Reid.

'It's over, Inspector.'

'Perhaps, Doctor. I would still like you to be careful, though.'

My look must have surprised him.

'There could be people,' he said quietly, 'who might think the Major passed information onto you. Can I have your mobile please?'

He was more adept than I was at keying. 'I have put two numbers in speed dial.' He handed it back. 'Top one. Just select it, if anything is suspicious. It'll go through to me and an emergency team. Just till we're sure it's all over.'

I gulped my thanks and changed the subject. Tooki and his entourage of dark-clad people were saying goodbye to Peter and Anna.

'You never see Tooki smile,' I observed. The realisation had just hit me. He had many expressions but not a single smile that I could recall.

'He's an odd one, our Took,' agreed the policeman. 'Known him for about ten years and I don't think I've ever seen him smile either, now that you mention it.'

'What's his background?'

'Tooki? A misfit. Left home in his mid-teens. Thrown out probably. He was wild back then. Hard for anyone to handle. Wanted to be a revolutionary hippy, if that combination is possible. Had a fair time on the streets, usually on his own – which can be a very dangerous way to be. Lots of minor charges; theft, vagrancy – until Edna and Herbie found him. They gave him some boundaries – a kind of security blanket and he started to flourish.'

'How did that work?'

'I think Tooki has some kind of disability that makes it hard for him to relate to people. He can be very intense at times, angry even.' Reid struggled to articulate the symptoms. 'He's really clever but I think a lot of general living was making him so wired up he rebelled. Does that make any sense?'

'I'm no medic but I get what you are saying.'

'Herbie and Edna don't see disadvantage or disability like we might do. They gave him a space, if you like, to be himself; and a cause, to help others. And Tooki gradually stopped his anti-social ways … or controlled them at least.

'You see, he's a problem solver. That's how he makes his living now – fixing lots of sophisticated software problems. Back then, he put his mind to solving problems for the homeless. That was how the network got started.

'Edna got him back to school and he ended up winning the prizes for maths and physics – some bloody good teachers worked with him. It couldn't have been easy having Tooki in school.

'He got his degree in computing at the university here and he's the technical brain behind Fuzzy Electronics now – others handle the public face of the company. Took wouldn't enjoy handling that. They even have the contract for the university computing system, but Took's heart is still in looking after the disadvantaged. He's been a big help to us over the years – usually working through Aunty Edna though.'

Intriguing. 'So he does computer work during the day, works with street-kids at night and never smiles. Is that what you are telling me?'

Ian Reid smiled patiently. 'You want everything simple, Spencer. Tooki is the brains behind the street network. It would fold in days without his maintenance work but it is Edna and Herbie that give the common-sense framework for that to operate; and Henry is the capable man on the ground who does the leg work, the relationships stuff. None of them could really operate without the others. If you left it to Tooki, everyone would be in arguments.' He laughed. 'Talk to him on his own he will tell you all his peculiar views on any topic, believe me. He doesn't need much prompting.'

'I believe you. I've heard some of his views.'

'Yeh. He has a good heart and lots of street cred. He's mellowed since the wild days – doesn't need to argue or be objectionable all the time; but he is still a closet revolutionary. Do you know he's even been dobbed in on that federal government terrorist hotline? Some frightened old dear scared by his looks and manner.'

I didn't speak. A shiver of *déjà vu* ran through me as my mind was back at the conversation on the camp-out. How close to reality that discussion must have been.

Reid spoke again. 'Tooki's alright. Look at how his systems have got all these fringe people working together. He has an important reason for living. Maybe, someday we'll see him smile, eh?'

'Thank you, Inspector,' I said. 'I think I understand a lot better now. You have good insights.'

'It's not all about pounding the beat.' He laughed. 'Each to his own. We all have a place in this world; all part of the bigger picture.'

* * * *

I saw more than the shadow this time as I glanced round.

The person had been at the funeral, in the background – merged with the crowd, watching, listening. But the shape had disappeared.

Who was that spectre?

Chapter 57

Olga had left instructions for Peter that she wanted her ashes sprinkled in important places on the Darling Downs, including a pair of fallen trees near the lagoon in NSW and one more solemn location – Russian's Creek.

I was back at work, catching up on missed time and concentrating on getting my students through their exams. It was busy. I gave the Grushkos space to grieve, but I did travel out with them to the lagoon. I understood the significance of the fallen trees. And on to Russian's Creek, where perhaps her Uncle Nicholas was at rest.

These were poignant moments, sprinkling the ashes; hearing again in my mind, the cheeky laughter; appreciating the courage of the lady, such an extraordinary life; and seeing that smile beneath the mischievous eyes.

Some things just needed to stay in the memories.

I had time to chat with Alan Bell while I was there. He mentioned Melanie's interest in studying at Cambridge. He was encouraged that I would be around if she was homesick – although, I didn't commit to being some uncle-like figure.

My advice was that Melanie should apply for post-grad and that she and Eva live apart, if they both ended up there. It would force them to get out and socialise. I used my own example on the Downs because I had learned so much being with local people.

Alan asked me to cheer for the Light Blues on my return. A rugby player in his early days, he had a dream to one day see the inter-varsity game between Oxford and Cambridge.

The NSW visit brought a sense of closure ... to move on.

* * * *

Mid-afternoon in Toowoomba; sunny, spring blossoms filling the air. Deep in thought, I was walking back through the university buildings to my campus flat.

Scarcely a soul about, except Barry, always busy – moving boxes with his trolley between buildings for someone.

He gave a casual salute. I suddenly realised that I'd left a box-file of expenses summaries in the office. I needed to work on them during the evening.

Hitting my forehead with the heel of my palm at my forgetfulness, I retraced my steps back into the Arts building, along the empty corridor to my office. There was the box-file, still sitting on the desk.

But my computer screen was active. I never leave it like that.

I stopped beside the desk – confused.

The movement behind me was just a sense in the air but an arm was round my neck before I could react. His head pushed mine forward – choking me.

I stomped back with my heel and jabbed with my elbow but my movement was blocked. I tried to pull, then scratch, the arm away but met only coarse cloth over hard muscles.

A red haze washed into my brain ... when the pressure loosened a fraction.

I could feel his mouth at my left ear. 'Easy. The suitcases. Where in Cappadocia did she say they were?'

I grunted what I hoped would indicate I had an answer.

The pressure eased a fraction more as I gulped air into my throat. Anger coursed through me as my right hand closed round a familiar object on the desk.

I grunted once more in an effort to speak and the arm loosened a fraction again.

My right arm swung from the in-tray, bashing the blunt end of the steel wedge into the side of his head, once, twice, proving the lightning analogy all wrong. I could feel a wetness splatter against me as the grip released, accompanied by a series of screams.

As he fell away, I hit him again on the shoulder with the metal lump, while blood spurted from his head wound.

A catalogue of screeched oaths preceded, 'You fucking idiot,' as he staggered through the door. My limbs were frozen. I shook my head to think.

The mobile. Top. Select.

A voice said, 'Dr Avery?'

'Attacked in my office,' I replied. 'He's running. Lots of blood on him.'

Barry was at the door. 'Heard the screaming ... What the f...' as he noticed me slumped against the desk. With a quick look to check that I was alright, he was off following the blood trail with, 'I'll get the bastard.'

Ian Reid was speaking to me on the mobile and, as I registered his words, I managed, 'I'm okay. Got a good shot on him with a steel paper-weight. He's bleeding a lot. The janitor's after him.'

'We're on our way as I am speaking. Tell me about him.'

'My height. Dark track suit top. Dark hair too – no cap. Didn't see much more as he ran. English, though. Midlands accent. Asked about the suitcases. Knew about Cappadocia. Tried to strangle me.'

* * * *

'The police have him,' said Barry proudly. 'Jeez, his head was a mess. You don't muck about, Spencer.'

I had scarcely moved, still leaning against the desk, shocked at the suddenness of it all, my breath now steadying into a normal routine, my hand clenching the bloodied steel wedge on the desk-top.

'They got him in a stairwell, collapsed. I followed the trail,' he added with pride.

'Well done, Bazza. Well done.'

* * * *

'We will deal with it,' Ian Reid said quietly. 'I've just spoken to the AFP. It's a national security matter. No publicity. He will be dealt with properly, trust me.'

It was hard to take in. 'He tried to kill me.' Olga's old world.

'Maybe. Maybe not. More likely he was after information and you caught him by surprise. Your janitor, Barry, has been told. I think a discreet acknowledgment could be coming his way. He will keep it quiet, as will you …' His intense look wasn't brooking any argument. 'And, when we are finished here, he will clean the room. Thankfully, there were few people around. The press won't print anything.'

'Who was he, Inspector?'

'I'll leave that to Superintendent Fowler when he can talk to you.'

'How much more?'

'I think this might be the end of it. The Super tells me the word is out that Olga didn't pass on where the suitcases are. Perhaps someone will turn up in Turkey some day, just looking around. If they do, they'll be noticed but they'll move on. These caves apparently cover a huge area.'

I nodded.

'You've done well, Spencer. You've cleaned this up.'

I listened but didn't feel at all convinced.

Chapter 58

A month had passed since the funeral.

Peter Grushko called and invited me to his lawyer's office. The international negotiations had been conducted with estates and banks. Now the intent of the will could be revealed.

Major Olga Davidenko had been a wealthy woman. Not only had she banked her salary over a long career; but she also had several million US dollars in a Swiss bank account. I remembered her telling me the story of the Venezuelan oil baron, Diego, and how she had come into a lot of money. Perhaps that was the story or there may have been other sources.

It was just the family, me and Dr McBride in the lawyer's office. The doctor had been the witness to the will.

Olga left one million Australian dollars to the street-people of Toowoomba in gratitude for their part in saving the lives of Spencer Avery and herself. I was startled to hear my name mentioned so formally in that context. The money was to be administered through a trust by Uncle Herbie and Aunty Edna with the specific request that half a million be used to buy and equip a house for people like Amy. The other half million was to support homeless people with a network, headed by Tooki, Izzy, Ellie and Henry. It would support hostel accommodation and a range of rehabilitation programs which the young people would endorse as the best way forward. *Listen to them*, Olga had written.

She left two million in a trust with the university to enable capable graduate students to be financially supported in post-graduate studies in any prestigious university overseas.

A contingency fund had been created in the care of her son to pay for matters which might come up after the signing of the will. The lawyer noted the only matter Olga had mentioned was money to make two high-quality banners for The Fair Dinkum Bush Band and a sum which was to pay for the production of a recording of *the laughter in their music*. Her words. I wondered whether that would include their humorous patter also.

She left smaller sums to the extended family; and *to Dr Spencer Avery for the joy he had brought to her final months*. I was touched. It was unnecessary but very moving nevertheless.

Some dresses, shoes and jewellery, currently housed in Russia, were specifically left to Eva, Melanie and Anna. The rest, still a very substantial amount, was left to her son, his wife Anna and their daughter, Eva.

For her granddaughter, there was the request that she use some of the money to broaden her education overseas – perhaps Cambridge, Olga had noted.

Still stirring the pot after she had gone. It brought a smile to my face as I remembered her cheeky chortle.

Chapter 59

London. October 2008

The nightscape had scarcely changed in six months but only two figures stared from the fifth-floor window, watching London's endless bustle traced in the subdued nocturnal lighting.

'Everything's been covered then?' the older asked, a bushy grey eyebrow raised in question.

'I believe so. Pity that bloody lecturer compromised things. But everything on our side has been sorted. Avery will return at the end of the year – still the naïve academic, I suspect – all dreamy theories and changing nothing. But he served a purpose for a time. With Davidenko gone, the link is broken, the chance has passed. The extremists have sent their checkers. They have found nothing and moved on. That particular threat is over … for the moment at least.'

'And the Cambridge connection?'

'A stuff-up, absolutely, but purged now from my perspective. Your high-level review should prevent a repeat.'

'Mmm. We've said that before. We can keep it under wraps here at our Vauxhall Cross base. The government has been briefed but I don't like that the bloody GRU got under our guard again there. And that Davidenko Major appears to have been a player in that – training the team, at least. That's not good enough. MI5 should have been all over that domestic espionage with so much history of the infiltration risks at so many of those top universities. But so should we have too, with the overseas stuff, especially with our own inside track to Moscow and controlling the approval of Davidenko's visa. All the sections should have been clicking together, like clockwork. That was the point of coordinating all our military intelligence units under the Secret Intelligence Service, here.'

'Your review will cover that. We won't have any more of anyone sitting on information, eh?'

The older man chortled, paused and gave a sly grin. 'Unless, of course, it's us. We are not playing team sport in *this* office. That's for the troops. We call the shots for our national interests. Someone has to master the strategy. It comes down to leadership. Us against them. *We* have to be on top of the issues. How else can we be sure there are no more moles sneaking under our guard?'

'Indeed. Indeed. You are very wise.' The younger man nodded, in deference.

Bushy eyebrows accepted the respect and paused thoughtfully, his chin cupped between thumb and forefinger. 'The Australians?'

The younger resumed his briefing mode and caught the other man's piercing eye. 'In the loop now. We have come to an arrangement over our man. A bit of grumbling, of course. Nothing serious. It was always a high-risk venture. The university, over there, has been quietly sweetened for being used. We've flushed out the vermin at least.'

The older man relaxed his thinking pose. 'Okay. I hope we have. It was one for the crazies, alright.' With a satisfied sigh, he patted his colleague on the shoulder. 'Time will tell. Time will tell. Nothing has really changed with this diversion. The challenge continues. The chess board is still the same – it's just the pieces that have moved their positions a little.'

'To moving on?' With an affirming grin, the younger passed a glass to the older.

'To moving on. Indeed.'

They chinked, sipped and slowly savoured the tender malt, while London and the Thames rolled by without care or interruption.

Chapter 60

Toowoomba. October 2008

Superintendent Jeff Fowler rang my mobile.

'I hadn't thought we would be speaking again,' he said, 'but the ramifications of your Major Davidenko haven't stopped yet. I have information for you.'

'Superintendent, it is actually good to hear your voice again. It reminds me it wasn't all a dream.'

'No dream, I assure you.' Fowler continued in business mode, 'First, based on your initial information, the British police have arrested Dr Tobias Stanley-Smythe. He has been tried quietly and sentenced to a significant jail term. So, thank you for the intelligence that led to that resolution.

'You were right – or Olga was, at least. He *was* acting as a double agent, selling British secrets to the Russians, while ostensibly being controlled by a senior British agent known as Old Fruit. As part of his plea-bargain, Smythe disclosed all of his contacts, including Old Fruit, who promptly committed suicide with an overdose of sleeping pills once the identity had been compromised. No doubt there would be considerable professional shame in supervising a double agent. No senior espionage controller should be able to be duped like that. It would be hard to live with the knowledge.' He paused to let the information sink in before, 'Old Fruit was a lady called Prunella Johnston.'

A numbing deadness settled over me. I couldn't feel my limbs. The cause of my pain – a spy master!

Fowler's voice was continuing.

'She managed a number of deep-cover agents in Moscow. She was the wife of a Faculty Dean at Cambridge and she used the association to mask her overseas trips. It's also quite possible – as British Intelligence has uncovered while investigating the matter – that she may have been acting in some form of double role herself with other nations or criminal groups. Though that appears to be unbeknown to Smythe. Either way, it is not proven – and unlikely ever to be. Are you still with me, Spencer?'

'Still with you, Superintendent … and working hard to take it all in. I know these people.'

'So I understand. It would appear you had been romantically involved with Old Fruit's daughter. Would that be correct?'

'Yes, for a few months.'

The policeman carried on with his explanation. 'That in itself has involved British Intelligence and ASIO running more checks on you. You may be interested to know that they have found that you are clean.'

'Pleased to hear it, Superintendent.' I gave a sigh of relief.

'In the interrogation of Smythe and the investigation into you' – he was building to something – 'it appears you may have been the unwitting victim of some cruel manipulation. It was Smythe who set up your time in Australia, was it not?'

'Yes. He suggested it anyway.'

'Apparently Smythe had been informed by Old Fruit that a Major Davidenko had applied in Paris for a visitor's visa to stay with her son in Toowoomba. Her research showed that Davidenko's granddaughter was a final-year geography student at the university. It appears that Old Fruit saw an opportunity to plant an innocent link – you – who could be used to track the movements of Major Davidenko, if as they suspected she was proving difficult to access. Did Prunella Johnston instigate the ending of your affair with her daughter?'

'Indeed she did.' I could hear the astonishment in my tone.

'According to the information pieced together from Smythe's confession and the circumstantial evidence, it is likely that the break-up of your affair and your move to Toowoomba were actually orchestrated by Old Fruit and Smythe; with some very high-powered clandestine approvals.

'Their agency quietly set up the additional position at the Australian university, along with the deception of flying you into Melbourne. They ensured that you would teach particular classes, moving the incumbent lecturer to an attractive sabbatical role. Johnston had information that the Major was the only person alive who knew the location of certain suitcase weapons. British Intelligence was very interested in those suitcases. It is elaborate, I know, but those are the sorts of complicated schemes these people deal in.'

I couldn't speak. My relationship with Mary had foundered when her mother vilified me for my ancestry and ability.

Was Mary also part of this charade?

Well, it had backfired on them anyway. But such pain to have caused.

I'd had the most wonderful of experiences in Australia; meeting Olga and a whole host of others. Indeed, I had even been considering whether or not I would go back to England.

'You have gone quiet, Spencer.' Fowler had a patient tone.

'It's been a lot to take in.' I gasped, my mind cartwheeling through a range of emotions. 'Is that all the information now? I don't know that I could handle too much more.'

'One more. The man who assaulted you in your office was British. He'd been on a watching brief for an agency, tracking you in the Toowoomba area for months, watching for action from other groups. But his role, after the Major died, was only to look out for extremist interest in the matter. He had no instruction nor permission to attack you. He must have panicked when you returned unexpectedly and caught him in the office. He has been extradited and will be dealt with appropriately for his crude over-stepping. I don't anticipate any others bothering you. The trail is cold now.

'So, Spencer. That's it. Sorry to be the bearer of such information but I thought you would rather know than not – especially if you are going to be walking back into Cambridge at the end of the year. Not far away now.'

I nodded – not too audibly over the phone. I was still thinking about Mary. Had she been dudded just like me? By her own mother? What an evil witch.

'All the best to you, Spencer. Thank you for helping us tidy up a potentially very messy business. It's been good knowing you,' said Fowler.

'Likewise,' I replied. 'I appreciate everything you have done for me ... and for the Major, through all of this matter.'

The phone call ended as my brain started to sift and sort through all the implications. What a mess these people had been prepared to create.

Chapter 61

I immersed myself in tying up my obligations to the university.

My final-year students had completed a very capable research prototype on Goomburra. The exams were finalised and Melanie Bell, Steve McGrady, Warren Davis and Eva Grushko had passed comfortably. They would be worthy graduate assets, in any company. For all practical purposes, the university year was over. I was no longer their supervisor. I liked that sense of freedom much more than I had thought.

Warren planned to head for a mining enterprise in Central Queensland where he would build on his degree skills in the specialist field of environmental rehabilitation negotiations. A whole new international world would potentially open for him, far beyond the dairy farm at Goomburra.

Steve was going to work within the planning community. He had a town-planning opportunity with a regional council but his specific interest was in ensuring equitable access to opportunity. Planning might well be his stepping stone to higher management and community decision-making.

Melanie had her heart set on going to Cambridge. She was interested in global agriculture, with a view to extrapolating models of possible farming strategies for the future. She saw an opportunity to inform international decision-making processes.

Eva was keen to follow her grandmother's dream that she would do post-graduate study at Cambridge. She was interested in international politics and the interface with trans-national corporations. It seemed to Eva that this was a progression of the work which had interested Olga.

From my viewpoint, these were admirable plans for my graduating students and the two girls would not be doing studies which would be supervised, in any way, by me.

The year was fast coming to a close. There were farewells and promises to meet up again.

My therapy, to keep my own inner peace, was to transcribe some cherished Queensland poetry in my best calligraphy onto my treasured writing paper. They were souvenirs, as valuable as photographs to me – and they would make personalised presents for some special people. Amongst the McKellar, Lawson and Paterson classics, I found the poetry of an Aboriginal poet, Cec Fisher – a Cherbourg man whose life story had been similar to Uncle Herbie's.

In particular, his *Empty Stock Routes* struck a chord with me. As I transcribed the five chapters of his flowing words, I thought of Melanie and the stock routes passing through her family property – once filled with lowing steaming mobs accompanied by Aboriginal drovers, like Herbie, playing an important role. And now, they were empty; long grass paddocks – just memories of the world that was, back then ... when Husk had been laid to rest at a creek, beside the route.

The poem resonated also because Uncle Herbie had put me on to it. It spoke to him, he said; and his life. The message was a quiet part of Queensland history.

I vowed that my framed calligraphy of *Empty Stock Routes* would be my present to Uncle Herbie and Aunty Edna when the time came for me to leave. How do you say a suitable 'Thank you' to those who had shared so generously with me, expecting nothing in return?

I also relaxed with Peter and Anna Grushko. I had, after all, spent many hours in conversation with Olga and we talked through the parts of her story which her son was keen to hear.

The former child migrant told me that the visit from his mother had been a defining experience. Just having been around her for these last months had helped him overcome the restrictive hang-ups from his youth. He had always been the intense self-made engineer. Now the adopted child had a new peace in his soul.

Understanding the role the street-people had played in our rescue had been a revelation for his emerging thinking. He acknowledged that, before the camp-out, he was contemptuous of those people, their views, their lifestyle and their worth.

At last, he had recognised his own tough façade for what it had been, an actor's mask to portray what he believed society wanted to see in a successful businessman and parent; a battlement behind which he could beat a humble retreat if he had picked his blustery foray wrongly, as he had with Tooki and his companions on the camp-out.

His thinking had tagged them all as losers. Now he had a whole new perspective – even to the extent of looking for part-time opportunities in his business for people with no permanent home, but who could be contacted on a mobile. Peter Grushko, formerly Davidenko, had rediscovered contentment in his real identity.

Eva was around a lot when I visited. She had an infectious urge to get on and do things now. Almost Olga-like.

Of course, she and I would meet at Cambridge, but no definite promises. I had learned from her wily grandmother.

Perhaps, I was every bit as manipulative in my own sweet way.

Chapter 62

Email: spenceravery@bigpond.com.au

From: maryj@googlenet.com

Dear Spencer

I hope this email finds you well. By my calculations, you will soon be getting packed for coming home.

I haven't heard from you since I told you about my friendship with Toby. I had hoped you would reply. I do sincerely hope the news did not cause too much grief.

My world has changed significantly since I last wrote. I scarcely know where to start. Toby and I did become good friends and mother seemed really happy about our relationship. But it wasn't the same as our time together. Not at all. You were the best fun to be with, Spence.

Then the bombshell came when Toby was arrested by the police special branch, charged with spying for Russia, would you believe?

And he admitted it.

I was beside myself. How could he have been so foolish and so unpatriotic?

Well, he has been tried and sentenced to ten years in jail. That's where he is now.

While the trial was going on, Mother took an accidental overdose of sleeping pills and died. Father just couldn't handle it, what with the police asking all sorts of questions and Mother being laid to rest. He has resigned his position at Cambridge. So that was a really traumatic time for us all.

Then the nasty rumours started. Do you know one rumour even suggested that Toby and Mother were in a relationship? It was all too surreal. I couldn't attend any functions. What with the snickering and having no suitable partner to accompany me, it all just seemed foreign to me. Do you remember how we used to punt on the Cam and then go to choral productions? It seems so far away now, dear Spence.

I am now living in London, enjoying the anonymity. I am doing copy for a London agency and part-time for a publishing company, some editing. I hope it will give me inspiration.

Anyway, Spencer, I would love to hear from you. It would be good to catch up on your return. I am deeply sorry if my actions have caused you suffering. We did have some beautiful times together. Maybe we will again? I would like to hope so. I have realised what I have lost. My fault; not yours.

The obstacle to our relationship, in Mother, has now gone. Father is working temporarily in an American university.

Hear from you soon.

Best regards

Mary

Stunning! Imagine suddenly hearing from Mary.

If I was to take the email at face value, then I might indeed have been the best love she had ever known. Well, well!

And she also seemed to think her mother had died from an innocent accidental overdose. That didn't sit right with Superintendent Fowler's information. One of Mary's endearing qualities had always been to avoid the deep meanings in everyday life.

Despite her undoubted academic ability, she could be remarkably innocent in other ways. At times, she had seemed not to notice there was a world beyond her sheltered exclusivity. From hunting to croquet, the Chancellor's Ball to the university boat race; to Mary that was the social barometer. Yet, she found it easy to be happy ... and I loved that about her – it had rubbed off onto me in those carefree days; even if it was all so superficial.

Yet, away from the posturing and pomp, she was a most affectionate and caring lady – one who could see beauty in a butterfly whirling by on an invisible flutter of air; a romantic with a pretty laugh. And passionate too.

I could feel a surge of longing as my mind recalled some of the scents, sounds and sensations of those many euphoric episodes.

Ah, did I want to be part of that scene again – one of those who saw the world through the lens of class, with all its interpretations?

Where would Herbie and Edna fit there?

What about Tooki and Izzy?

In their own ways, they had a respected impact on others, well beyond the status they would command in many perceptions of society.

What about an 'evil' Russian Major?

I had learned a lot of new perspectives over the past months.

I couldn't realistically stay in Queensland – it was an eight-month contract. And I had blown my bridges back to Somerset. How could I face my parents and the village again after taking off on this foolish carousel, shunning my roots?

So where else could I go but back to Cambridge?

Then again, if I had learned anything in the past few months, it was that facing up to the consequences of past decisions shouldn't be left too late. I could picture Olga's pensive realisation that an earlier reunion with her Pyotr might have been wiser for all.

I had been played like a fish on a line, a would-be important man locked into checkmate – every reflex reaction being anticipated by the masters.

But I was free now, wiser in the devious ways of mankind.

Chapter 63

I had organised to take Melanie and Eva to a classical music concert at the Empire Theatre in Toowoomba – a small high-quality affair and a gentle way to start building the repertoire of socialising skills which they would require in an English university town.

I sat between my two former students who looked fashionably lovely. Their separate perfumes gave me an olfactory delight akin to being transported on a magic carpet. Both were charming companions, engaged in the music and in anything Cambridge.

I was every bit the chivalrous gentleman and considerate companion, as my upbringing and social status would expect, enjoying their company.

Perhaps Olga had been entering more into wishful thinking than fact. Indeed, it was my Russian muse that I missed – the teasing comments and the name-dropping from another era; the long philosophical chats about the power struggles of the competing ideologies – even with her one-eyed views of all that was wrong in the world.

She had been a dangerous lady to be around. Life was never anything other than exciting where she was involved. And such a disarming composed charm. How many dying sixty-three-year-old ladies would suddenly strip to their underwear and swim out to the middle of a lagoon? It would take some time before anyone could fill the intellectual and exhilaration gap which Olga had left in my life. Twenty-year-old ladies could be lots of fun ... but I was interested in more than parties and being seen out.

The trip back to England promised to be bitter-sweet.

Cambridge had been my *raison d'être* – a pinnacle on the ridge climb from a humble Somerset background to potential professorial acclaim; the fulfillment of a cherished aspiration born in the nurture of a draper's family.

And I remembered vividly my dejected depression on arriving in Toowoomba.

Oh, what a jumbled set of priorities I had been using then to assess the value of my life; seduced by the trappings of wealth and the regalia of status. It had actually been a more defining healing moment than I had realised when Bazza had so intuitively decided that I needed the therapy of pies and footy. 'Poise'.

I had thought that arrant frippery and societal eminence were a purpose for living. And now? And now I had gained a whole new outlook on life through my time in Queensland.

Would I adjust? Be able to distinguish between the important and the banal? Move comfortably in all walks of life, respecting others while not falling prey to the imposters who would hi-jack my integrity?

Could I do all that while retaining the humanity I had so admired in such a range of people on the Downs?

Was I over Mary?

Maybe I'd find a bush dancing club at the university. Maybe there would be a Gary Tate clone playing the mandolin. Maybe I could teach them all *The Drongo*. A chess club might introduce me to interesting friends.

I needed to laugh raucously without inhibition again.

What lay ahead?

Chapter 64

Over Asia. Monday, December 15 2008

I looked out of the Boeing 747 window, down onto a wide snow-flecked land. The flight tracker on the screen in front showed the red line passing over a green landscape north of the Caspian Sea but, below, the real view was bleak, ice-clad winter.

I was en route to London Heathrow having left behind Brisbane International Airport, the vibrant colours of Queensland, the warm turquoise sparkle of Moreton Bay and its lush, green, sandy islands.

Beneath was the Ukraine, the land that Olga had called home. The blue haze around me was the same sky that young Pyotr flew into all these years ago, leaving behind a self-tortured mother to grieve. To the south would be Turkey and Cappadocia, where she had spent her early years – and the Black Sea over which she carried the suitcases to safety. Someday I must travel there, to understand the history of the tunnels and to visualise a secret hiding place.

I looked around the cabin. Could I tell anything about any person there from my superficial glancing?

Why did we even bother trying to fit people into categories? Were we all trying to be budding social detectives? What did it matter?

I glanced at my neighbour's video screen. A movie. The actor was playing a bearded professor-type. See, I had landed in the typecasting trap again – a *professor-type*; how easily we can fall for it.

It had taken me nearly thirty years for the lights to come on in my mind. I pledged to myself that, when the plane landed at Heathrow, my first destination would be Somerset, to smell the West Country air, to hear again that gentle accent.

I now knew that when I hugged my dear Mam and Dad, we wouldn't need words for them to understand that their prodigal son had returned, in spirit anyway. I must have been a terrible trial for their patience as I embarked on my charmed rise to another world, scarcely considering what hurts I might have left behind. But they had never once criticised, never once done other than encourage.

I doubted that I could have shown such unflinching love.

But I understood now how society's roles were choreographed. We were chess pieces being manipulated on so many levels, seduced by an illusion's lure.

I could act the parts, I knew I could; switching codes as necessary through cultural customs and social occasions without denigrating any particular group's needs, aspirations or beliefs – but still ensuring that I was true to me.

That had been the revelation of my eight-month working visit to Queensland.

I would return to Cambridge, successful from my overseas jaunt, ostensibly oblivious to the happenings around the Johnstons or Stanley-Smythes. The armadillo social defence of that particular closed circle would probably ensure that the matter was never even raised. The sniggers would all have passed and the discrete barriers would have descended – to protect not the individual miscreants as much as the social order which had existed scarcely trammelled since lineage had been important.

I felt a peace wash through me, coupled to a sense of shame at my arrogant dismissiveness of recent years, my hedonistic need to be a party to the norm. At last, I had realised my blessing to have parents who have such a profound unconditional love. I didn't need to be a parody of some misplaced notion of destiny. I would be worthy of them again.

The plane banked over the Russian steppes so far below, surprising me with a fleeting reflection in the angle of my window.

My wide disbelieving eyes drew the image into my stunned mind.

Familiar grey hair pulled back into a pony-tail. Mysterious pale-blue eyes. The serene face, looking at me. The corner of the lip curled into a cheeky smile. So clear that I could reach out to touch the window pane. The lips grinned into a pout. Old fingers touched her mouth. She blew the silent kiss to me before the image disappeared in a glint of sunlight, and the plane banked once more.

I discreetly dabbed the lovely tear from my window-side eye.

It all seemed to symbolise the omen of better days ahead.

Epilogue

Email: Grushkos@bigpond.com.au

From: Eva@btinternet.com

Hi Mum and Dad

Really enjoying it in Cambridge. Work is super interesting. The buildings and sense of history are mind-boggling. Hope everything is good 4 u back home.

Miss you both.

Spencer has been really kind showing me around all the sights. We've been having a wonderful time together. He's a very special friend. I'm sure you understand. I miss him when we are apart but he is such a busy man.

He's taking me to the Oxford-Cambridge boat race on the Thames. They row upstream from Putney Bridge to Chiswick; and delightful Spencer has charmed two VIP tickets near the finish line. I'm getting used to the posh way people speak over here. The secret is to adapt and follow their lead, I think.

Haven't seen much of Mel. She's in a different part of the university. Dare say she'll turn up at some function or other.

Bye for now. Lots of love.

Eva

* * * *

Email: bells@networx.com.au

From: MelB@google.com

G'day Mum and Dad

Hope you're well and the crop going OK. I'm doing fine here. There's a lot more to world agriculture than I had realised. Fascinating stuff.

People have been very friendly and Spencer has been super in showing me around. We've been to the theatre and listened to string quartets and even watched the light-blues play rugby union, Dad. They're good.

Don't know how Spencer finds the time to show me around because he leads such a busy life. He has such a brilliant sense of humour. We have so much fun. You understand, Mum!!

Haven't seen much of Eva. She must be in a different circle. She's on the other side of the uni. It's a huge place.

Take care. Love from Britain.

Mel

* * * *

Email: spenceravery@cam.ac.uk

From: took@fuzel.blackberry.net

Gday Spence

Hope U havent frozen or drowned in that Brit weather. Just a note 2 keep U in the loop. We have the new half-way house now. Can sleep a quite few. Izzy and Henry are making it work. It's called Nana Olgas. Gr8. They listened 2 us. Even Amy ripped into them when they tried to change our plan. Good 2 C.

Stay cool, mate

Took

PS Izzy asks if U want 2 B on her blackberry list. U have 2 keep up with the real news. R U on blackberry yet?

PPS We use Olga as our local link name. Shes still with us.

PPPS Izzy has just passed her software technology certificate. Next stop uni for the girl.

* * * *

Email: spenceravery@cam.ac.uk

From: TonyFDbushband @bigpond.com.au

G'day mate

Just thought I'd drop you a line or two to let you know that the band is still playing on most weekends. Olga's banners make us look as flash as a rat with a gold tooth.

Played out Dalby way last week. We've added a new tune to our repertoire. It goes over well. A drunk asked us if we would play that Clinker song again. Gary has been playing Kalinka to a new dance we have developed.

Always got to be ahead of the crowd. Thought you would like that. Reminds us of Olga. She was a champion lady!

Next thing is to make that recording she wanted. Trouble is that I don't think we ever play a tune the same way twice in a row. Could be a challenge.

Keep being a bushie, mate!

Tony

(The Fair Dinkum Bush Band)

* * * *

Email: spenceravery@cam.ac.uk

From: maryj@googlenet.com

Dear Spencer

Thank you for the most lovely time at the Jazz Club and Afterparty. It was a marvellous evening. Almost like old times again.

You are such a charmer. They all loved your Australian tales, especially about the Dinkum Music. Did I get that right?

I'm looking forward to welcoming you back down to London again, soon. I'm so much more comfortable being out of the Cambridge scene. How wise of you to understand and suggest I continue to stay in London, away from the past.

I appreciate how busy you are. I do understand you have lots of commitments and people to meet since your return. But I feel really good when we are together. I miss you so much, Spence.

Remember, there is always room here if you are coming down here, for any reason. No appointment required.

Looking forward to the next time

Love

Mary XXX

* * * *

Email: spenceravery@cam.ac.uk

From: goombmilk@bigpond.net.au

G'day Spencer

Jenny, Bill, Shelley, Dot, Ron and our herd of milkers all send their regards. Hope you have settled back into Pommieland alright. Trust you're getting a few laughs too.

We noticed there have been more terrorist attacks in the world news and more people not listening to each other. We need to be more tolerant, I think. Olga was spot on! Herbie and Edna had another group out here last week. It seems to work getting them out in the forest, getting a new view of the world.

Anyways, we are all okay here on the range.

There's a new teacher in the school and my young fella, Darren, has gotten offside with him already. He was reading a dairying magazine under his desk and the teacher said, 'Learning something by chance, are you?'

'Oh no sir,' he replied. 'I was listening to you.' And the teacher took it the wrong way.

Kids!

All the best from Graham and the Goomburra mob

* * * *

Email: spenceravery@cam.ac.uk

From: Ed&Herb@live.com.au

G'day Lightning

Herbie here. Henry is teaching me this E thing. Hope Ur well, brother.

Was in a fruit shop yesterday. I pointed to a tray of red Stanthorpe apples and said, I'll have one of those, please. The girl said, Which one? They're not all the same you know. I said, You don't know how pleased I am to hear you say that.

Like the man on the moon said, One small step for apples. Next, one giant leap for the rest of us.

You're always welcome here, my dear friend. Travel well.

Herbie

* * * *

Email: spenceravery@cam.ac.uk

From: Bazza70@bigpond.net.au

G'day Spence

Bazza here! Howyagoing, mate?

Everything is perfect here in the Sunshine State and the footy is going well too. What else could you ask for?

We toasted you at the last game with a pie and beer. I still remember your expression the first day you arrived. You thought you'd landed on Mars.

They miss you here at the uni. No smooth blokes in blue jackets around here now and no English accents. I still can't get over the way you say 'poi' instead of pie – or is it the other way round? I'm only a janitor.

I looked up 'poise' in the dictionary and it said it meant dignified, balanced.

Well, at the footy with me mates, I brought back four beers and four pies for the mob and they complimented me on my balancing act. Does that mean I have 'poise', then?

Cheers, mate.

Barry

About the Author

Jim Reay is a former high school principal and senior public servant; now a writer of short stories and mysteries. Born a Scot and educated to post-graduate level in Britain, he worked in London for several years before emigrating to continue his career development. He brings a range of perspectives to his stories; from the land of his youth as well as his love of history, learning, culture and Australia.

www.jimreaywriter.net

www.ingramcontent.com/pod-product-compliance
Lightning Source LLC
Chambersburg PA
CBHW062113170626
46813CB00002B/428